After
EFFECTS

L.J. GREENE

ISBN-13: 978-0-9982716-1-3 (print)
ISBN-13: 978-0-9982716-0-6 (ebook)

Titles by L.J. Greene

Effects Series:
Ripple Effects
Sound Effects
Aftereffects
Side Effects

Standalone:
A Fall of Light

Don't miss the *Aftereffects* bonus epilogue, as well as a preview of *Side Effects*, at the conclusion of this novel.

All of the *Effects* novels are standalones, but connected.
For more information on the series, visit my website at
https://www.ljgreenebooks.com

This book is dedicated to anyone who has lost a loved one to illness. Or anything else. I'm with you.

It also honors and was inspired by men for whom the call to parenthood is nothing less than sacred. Two of the most amazing ones I have ever known are reflected here in these pages.

Chapter 1

Selene

Maybe it should have been obvious by the way my bumper collided so decisively with his that the universe had something particular in mind for us. In hindsight it was. In fact, it was the perfect metaphor for the way our lives came together—jarring and serendipitous—and for the way our eventual untangling left its own sort of damage.

But in the moment, with my front bumper wedged under his rear one, and the crunch of plastic still echoing in my ears, I missed those finer points completely. All I could think about was the fact that I had *caused* this accident. Right smack in the middle of the Golden Gate Bridge.

And if that wasn't bad enough, I had exactly seventy-two minutes to get myself downtown, park, and triple-check that everything in my portfolio was flawless. Because today, of all days, was make-or-break for my career.

The graphic design firm I worked for was competing for an opportunity to refresh the image of a major consumer-facing brand. The client wanted a new logo mark, new color scheme, and a whole new visual language. It's a very big deal when a household name decides to change the look of its brand—these are multimillion-dollar decisions that twenty-four-year-old first-year designers usually don't get to come anywhere near. The fact that I was being allowed to submit my ideas for consideration was absolutely humbling.

The fact that my career was suddenly at the mercy of a food truck that advertised itself to be Blaze of Seattle was nearly comical. Or it would have been, if I didn't now have only . . . seventy-one minutes!

There just really weren't enough *shits* in the world for this one.

I began ransacking my glove box for an insurance card that hadn't expired when the other driver stepped out of his truck and shook his head at what he saw. His face was partially hidden behind a pair of black Oakley sunglasses, and through the windshield, it was hard to tell if his demeanor was signaling a cool self-possession or if he was just really super pissed. The best I could say was that he was young and didn't appear to be injured.

As for the truck . . . well . . . *shit.*

He crouched down to take a closer look, rubbing a hand over the dark stubble that shadowed his jawline. And I'm not saying I had any preconceived notion of what a food truck purveyor might look like, but if pressed, I would definitely lean more toward a Guy Fieri type than the one standing in front of my car. This one was tall and lean, with an elegantly muscular frame under a relaxed-fitting black T-shirt and jeans. He had a crown of shiny dark-brown hair that was ruffled by the wind coming off the bay. I won't lie—he was striking. Enough so that I was distracted from his off-putting demeanor for a couple of seconds, at least.

"I'm *so* sorry—" I said as I climbed out of my car. But with the roar of the wind and the rush of the traffic passing by in the two left lanes, I couldn't quite tell if he heard me. He didn't show it, if he did.

"I'm *really* sorry," I said again. "Are you hurt?"

Still no answer. I could plainly see, though, that he was now cursing fluidly under his breath as he stood with his hands on his hips, surveying the damage, which I thought was much worse to my BMW than to his truck. After what felt like an eternity, he exhaled deeply and acknowledged me for the first time.

But with his sunglasses on, I couldn't see his eyes, just my own reflection in his lenses—my white blouse and matching skirt in sharp contrast to the dark frames. So gradually, my focus fell to his mouth.

It was full and parted slightly, and seemed almost too soft to be nestled into the thistle of hair that surrounded it. It was so elegantly shaped that for several beats I was distracted from the fact that it had set into a very flat line. He seemed to be about to say something when he stopped and pulled off his glasses. And, wow! I actually needed a moment. He was—

"What's all over your face?" he suddenly asked me.

"What?"

"Your face. There's something black all over it."

Obviously, I couldn't see my face. But I looked down at my hands and, oh *god*, it was there too. And another huge black smudge was smeared across my skirt.

Shit.

The explanation seemed to sink in for both of us in the same perfectly clear moment. I wondered if it was even remotely possible for the bridge to magically open up and swallow me whole.

"You were putting on mascara while you were *driving*?" he demanded.

No, the bridge was apparently not going to save me. I felt a blush spread over my skin like a humiliating heat map.

"Are you *serious*?" he continued, even more slit eyed than before. Who would have guessed that eyes the color of melted dark chocolate could be anything but soft and warm? "Women actually do that?"

"We don't make a habit of it," I snapped, and pushed a cloud of blowing brunette hair off my face. "But—" Christ Almighty, I couldn't justify this, even to myself. "I have an important meeting I need to get to, and I'm running very late."

"And now I'm late."

His hard look stung—I'm not saying it wasn't deserved.

"I've already apologized." I heard my voice tightened to match his. That's when it struck me with absolute certainty that he *had* heard me before.

"An apology doesn't begin to cover it."

"Well, I don't know what you think you're entitled to, but that, plus an insurance check, is all you're going to get."

His dark brows rose slightly, and he blinked once. That beautiful mouth opened, but, fortunately, nothing came out. I definitely enjoyed him more when he was silent.

In the charged seconds that followed, I brushed furiously at the spot on my skirt, avoiding his stare with stubborn intent. Still, defensiveness and anxious energy were creating a strange brew in my veins, making me feel a little desperate.

To top it off, my *car* was crammed under his rear bumper—a realization that made my eyes swim with infuriating tears. The spot on my skirt was just icing on the cake. And now I had only sixty-four lousy minutes to get to the office.

I loathed this feeling of helplessness almost as much as I loathed the idea of letting him see me stress-cry, which was feeling like a real possibility. So I marched back to the trunk of my car and pulled out a jack that my dad had put there for emergencies. I guarantee he never pictured this.

"What are you doing with that?" Blaze demanded, standing there with his arms crossed over his chest, his eyes squinting against the cool wind.

"Don't tempt me by asking." There were several things I would have liked to do with the jack just then, but I knew I'd have to settle for its intended purpose.

"You are *not* touching my truck."

"Watch me."

It was pure gold the way his eyeballs seemed to pop out of his head. He let me push past him, but probably only because he thought I didn't know how to use a jack.

He had clearly never met my father.

Because here's the thing: My upbringing was the opposite of entitlement. My parents had plenty of money, yes, but my sister and I were raised to be self-sufficient. Thus, I had an eclectic collection of life skills under my belt: oil changing, lawn mowing, some basic plumbing; I could even replace the occasional bad light switch. Jacking up a car? Give me a break.

In a matter of minutes, I had blocks on both sides of the front passenger-side tire and had screwed the handle into the jack. Crouching to locate the jack point by the rear driver-side wheel, I could feel his eyes on me.

"That's not going to hold my truck," he said in his deep, smoky voice.

I rose to standing and turned around, pulling a chunk of hair out of my lipstick as I met his gaze directly.

After all, I was a goddamn picture of female empowerment, jacking up a car in *four-inch heels*. The fact that I was literally sweating anxious circles under the arms of my white blouse and my hair was blowing all over my face and into my mouth was beside the point. This guy was just standing there. *Critiquing.*

"How do you know that?"

"It has a lifting capacity of five thousand pounds. See the sticker right there?" he said pointing. "This truck weighs sixteen thousand."

I followed his line of sight, now very pissed. "And you didn't think to mention that *before* I did all this?"

"You weren't exactly asking me, remember?"

He was serious with that bullshit. "I told you I'm *late*. And I'm in a skirt," I said stomping one foot and gesturing sharply to my outfit in a glorious Greek manner.

He leaned in a little closer, making solid eye contact—his face, the picture of arrogance. "I wasn't the one who caused this."

"No, you're just the ass who would rather make a point than help me fix it."

I'd struck a nerve. I could see it in his face, though he made no apologies. But then he looked away, and without another word, strode to the back of his truck and came out with a much larger jack that made mine look like a toy. He went to work assembling it like he, too, knew how to use one.

I was seething, but begrudgingly had to acknowledge that it wasn't a bad view. I let my eyes travel again over his body, watching the way his T-shirt melted across his back as he worked. I would make every effort to scold myself for this later.

He straightened when the truck was lifted high enough to release my car, then wiped a bead of sweat from his brow with his forearm. "We should be able to get these apart now. Are you okay? To drive, I mean?"

I laughed, and with as much drawn-out sarcasm as I could muster, added, "Thanks for asking."

I felt like such a ridiculous fool standing in front of this man, a hair away from a tantrum-y explosion. *And!* apparently I had mascara all over my face! Plus, it looked like the wand had been doing doughnuts on my skirt.

I checked my watch. Sixty-one minutes to go . . .

"Look . . ." He paused, making a little breathy sound, and shifted his body uncomfortably. Out of the corner of my eye, I saw him rub a large hand across the back of his neck.

But I didn't care what he was going to say. Cars were backing up behind us, trying to get around. Drivers were honking, and it was obvious they were growing very annoyed by the delay. Needless to say, my stress level was quickly overcoming my composure. Hands trembling slightly, I pressed my fingertips to my eyes, then wiped my cheeks, sniffing hard.

What an absolute *mess* this morning had become.

"It's mostly all off now. The . . . mascara, I mean."

There was a different note in his voice that made me glance up, and when he met my eyes I noticed his expression had softened. Those hard edges seemed to have tempered a little with kindness, giving him more of a good-natured face than I had originally credited him with.

His body, too, had taken on a more relaxed posture. His hands were on his hips, and for the first time, I noticed he had a small collection of leather and woven bands on each wrist.

"Here, there's just a bit . . . "

He lifted one hand, and with deliberate slowness, started to reach out to touch my face. Then he seemed to think better of it. The hand wavered and fell back to his side. Instead, he made a small motion in the direction of my cheek, and I brushed the last fleck of mascara away.

"Thank you."

He shrugged, and one side of his mouth ratcheted up slightly higher than the other. What looked like a tiny dimple peeked out.

"So where'd you learn to use a jack, anyway?" he said.

"Why do you ask?"

"Easy, there. I'm just impressed, that's all."

I opened my mouth to reply, but he held up his hands to stop me. "It's not a chauvinistic comment. I'm just saying most *people* don't know how to properly jack up a car."

"Yeah, well, I have a great dad." Understatement. I had the best dad on the planet. I'd never met a better one.

He studied me for a moment, serious again, before nodding. "Obviously."

His hair was messy from the wind, and a bit of color still bloomed across his cheekbones and down his neck, making him seem younger and more approachable, somehow. For several beats, we just stood there as the traffic muddled around us in a profane opera of barking horns and shouting voices.

"Why don't you get in," he finally said, gesturing to my car. "Throw it in reverse when I say. We can get you to your meeting."

"You think?"

"Yeah. We can fix this." He seemed like one of those guys who could probably fix anything. Some of the stress drained from my system.

"I'm so sorry for all this. I really am. I was being reckless."

With just one heavy blink and a soft shake of his head, he shrugged off my apology. "This isn't the stuff to get upset about. I should know better."

It was one of those times when I knew I should say something, but I couldn't think of anything that wouldn't sound dismissive of my mistake. Maybe he wasn't looking for me to respond, anyway. So I just nodded gratefully and climbed back into my car, as he'd instructed. Through my front windshield, I watched him press down on the hood with the full weight of his body. I eased back on his signal, ignoring the angry sounds of scraping metal and buckling plastic.

At least I still had fifty-three minutes. My portfolio was ready, I told myself. I didn't actually *need* to check it again.

With my mangled car now free of its captor, I dug into my purse, found my wallet, and got out to hand him my information.

"I can let you know as soon as I have the estimate." He reached around to grab his own wallet from his back pocket and then handed me his insurance and ID. "It should be a pretty straightforward repair."

Keir Andrew Stevens, his license said. Thirty-one-year-old, six-foot-two-inch organ donor. One hundred eighty-five pounds. From Seattle.

"Did you just move here?"

"No." He looked up from where he was photographing my information. "I'm just down for a few months. With some luck, I'll be heading back soon."

"You don't like San Francisco?"

That was hard to imagine. Nowhere in the world is quite like San Francisco. In fact, the exact spot in which we were standing, nearly midspan on the bridge, was probably one of the most photographed, most visited, most romanticized places in the world. Just west of the southbound lanes that led into the city stretched the brown sands of Baker Beach and the majestic Marin Headlands. Turning to the east, one could see Angel Island and Alcatraz, surrounded by sapphire water sprinkled with whitecaps and sailboats.

And looking directly up from where we stood, the towers of the Golden Gate reached like a ladder to heaven. Heaven felt very close to San Francisco.

"It's not that." He handed me back my cards. "I grew up here—in Mill Valley, actually. But my life's in Seattle, my business—" He lifted his shoulders and let them drop. "San Francisco's just not home anymore."

"You're setting *Seattle* on fire now, is that it?"

For the first time, his brown eyes crinkled at the edges with humor. And it was like a light switched on behind them as the smile spread down to his mouth. Every bit of earlier antagonism evaporated. In its place was a pleasant expression that seemed much more at home on his face than the stern one from before.

"Something like that."

"And don't *mess* with the truck," I teased, straight-faced, as I photographed his information.

He outright laughed then, a deep and infectious sound that I had an instant positive reaction to. I knew right away that any woman could easily grow to adore the sound of that gravelly, masculine laugh. I was focused on the phone in my hand, but I could feel the way his eyes lingered on me—warm this time. It's amazing how you can feel something like that. I couldn't resist looking back at his face.

"It's my *truck*." There was a mixture of humor and fondness in his voice, as well as a new playfulness in his expression that made me smile. In unison we glanced over at the injured party. The whole center section of the metal bumper was bent inward, and paint from the hood of my car now peppered it with black smudges.

"I feel terrible. And I shouldn't have called you an ass."

"Forget it. I was an ass. And believe me, I've been called worse when I was much less deserving." He smiled lightly, and I found myself staring again at the elegant curve of his lip and his bright, straight teeth.

"Wait, are you going to be out of business while this is being fixed?"

"No. You can't make a living off just one truck. This is part of a fleet. The rest are in Seattle with my catering business."

"Oh." But that was even more confusing. "So how did you and one truck end up down here? Wrong turn?"

He coughed out a sound that fell somewhere between laughter and surprise. "That's *exactly* how it happened." He shot me a sidelong grin that was downright irresistible. The creases in his cheeks told me that he smiled that way often. "I was putting on mascara, and I somehow missed the exit for Seattle."

"Aren't you just *hilarious*," I said returning his sarcasm with pleasure.

There was more than a touch of mischief in those gorgeous brown eyes, and a little voice inside me whispered, *Uh oh. There's something highly likeable about this person.*

I could see he had a sense of humor and at heart was probably a good guy. It didn't escape me, though, that he hadn't actually answered my question. "I really do apologize for the inconvenience. And for making you late."

"I know. It's not—" He heaved a breath and looked at me more intensely as the grin shrank slightly. There was something more he wanted to say but didn't. His eyes were moving back and forth between mine, but then he shook his head and said simply, "I didn't mean to be such a dick about it. You just . . . caught me at a weird time."

Time.

The mention of it reminded me that I had only forty-seven minutes to go. And that would be just barely enough.

"Well, it was nice to run into you, Keir Stevens," I said, and was rewarded again by a flash of white teeth.

"Hope we bump into each other again, Selene Georgiou."

Chapter 2

Selene

The corner of Market and Montgomery Streets in San Francisco is a madhouse at lunchtime. It's located right on the edge of the financial district and just a few blocks off Union Square, and pedestrian traffic is always bedlam. For drivers in the area, it's a nightmare. For a food truck, it's a gold mine. And Blaze of Seattle was parked right in the middle of it.

This busy area was only a five-minute walk from my office, which is why, when Keir texted me that he had the repair estimate in hand, I so convincingly argued with myself that reviewing it in person was the responsible and prudent thing to do.

Granted, the uncomfortably logical side of my brain knew this was pure invention. Insurance companies can handle a situation like this just fine on their own without any oversight or involvement from me.

But curiosity ultimately won out. After all, why would the universe put an incredibly handsome man in my path, if not to give me one more opportunity to appreciate him?

I walked up to the front of the line at Blaze where a guy about my age in a dress shirt and gray slacks was waiting for his order. It was a warm August day, and the lunch crowd was already sizeable.

"What's good?"

"Are you kidding? Everything." He gave me the slow once-over. "How about if you let me buy you lunch?"

"I believe she's here to work." An unmistakable voice cut in on the conversation.

Keir Stevens stood in the service window, and the wry smile he gave me just hinted at a dare.

Today he had on a dark gray T-shirt that seemed to amplify the impact of that smile, and with his black baseball cap turned backward, he looked easily capable of more than a little mayhem if the occasion presented itself. Adding to this appearance was the scruff on his face that lent just the right amount of raw masculinity to balance his otherwise flawless features.

God help me, I'd never found the unshaven look so attractive.

"Work?" I asked him.

"I think you owe me," he said, arms crossed over his chest.

"Is that so?"

Another slow grin spread across his face like melting butter, oozing charisma everywhere, and he shrugged like the answer was obvious. Clearly, the realm of invention had made room enough for two.

"She doesn't really look like she's dressed for working here," his customer put in helpfully.

Keir's eyes made an unhurried sweep of my pink silk blouse and slim skirt, lingering for a moment on my bare legs and towering nude heels.

"No, she sure doesn't, does she?" His expression was innocent enough, but I thought there was a look of something else in his eyes. Yes, this man was entirely capable of mayhem. A warm flush crept up my neck and face.

"That's all right," he said. "I have something that'll work." He nodded toward the back door. "If you're up for it."

A gleam in his eye challenged me to say *no*. But who was I kidding? It was hard to refuse anything he asked in that low voice of his. I was well on my way to *yes* before I even considered the alternative.

Rounding the corner of the truck, I could see that the mangled back bumper—courtesy of me—was the only thing askew on this meticulously maintained vehicle.

Painted a pristine white, with the orange, gray, and black logo of Blaze of Seattle displayed on all sides, the vehicle didn't appear to have a speck of dust anywhere.

Inside, it was the same—wall-to-wall, gleaming stainless steel, a surprisingly high-tech and well-appointed gourmet kitchen on wheels.

As promised, just to the left of the door was a crate of crisply starched white aprons, complete with a bib. I slid the loop of one around my neck, pulled my ponytail out from underneath it, and tied a bow at my waist. I had absolutely no idea what Keir had in mind here, but he, too, seemed to be making it up as he went.

By the time I was settled, Keir was at the grill, and I noticed a young Asian guy taking orders and manning the register. He looked like he was probably college age, with a slight build and one of those faces that made you want to like him at a glance.

"Justin," Keir said with a brief tilt of his head toward his coworker. "And Selene," he added with a brief tilt in my direction. "She's the one who redecorated my bumper."

"Oh, I heard about you." Justin took his eyes off the waiting customer just long enough to acknowledge my presence with a quick nod. "Welcome to Blaze. Don't get your apron dirty."

Keir's answering look told me that last bit of advice wasn't meant for me.

Over the next few minutes or so, I was given the lay of the land.

His catering business in Seattle was apparently well known for its slow-roasted meats and vegetables, often prepared on location over an open fire in the Patagonian tradition in which Keir had been professionally trained.

But the requirements of a food truck operation differ from straight-up catering. So his food truck menu was a small subset of his much more extensive catering selection—rotating based on what were the choicest ingredients on any given day, and tailored for a gourmet lunch experience to go. Nothing frozen or prepackaged, he emphatically told me.

Today's selection included braised beef short ribs, chicken kabobs with fire-roasted vegetables, empanadas, and a spicy chorizo.

After washing up, I was put to work boxing his creations as he prepared them. I thought I was doing a pretty damn good job for a girl on her lunch break in stiletto heels. But at some point, as I was slicing up an order of chorizo as he'd instructed, I heard a clear, disappointed groan to my left.

"What?" I demanded, looking at Keir.

He shook his head. "You're killing me."

"Why? I'm doing a great job!"

He wasn't convinced. He turned and squared my hips up with his as I stood, knife in hand.

But I must admit, his close proximity dissolved a substantial portion of my righteous indignation. I was totally distracted by his facial hair, which so evenly covered his jawline that it looked like it was spread on with a butter knife. I had a strong urge to reach up and feel the prickle of it on my palm.

"Your apron," he said, commanding my attention.

"What about it?"

"It's filthy."

"It's an *apron*. It's supposed to be filthy."

I heard a chuckle and looked over in time to see Justin grinning as he handed change to a customer. Keir's eyes flickered in that direction too, and then back to me.

"If you ever walk into a kitchen and see dirty aprons or a dirty floor, turn around and walk right out. That tells you everything you need to know about how the place is run."

Then, he pointedly looked down at my apron, eyebrows raised. Sure enough, I had taken to wiping the blade of my knife across my midsection as a way of cleaning it between orders. Apparently, this was offensive to the chef. There were *towels* for that purpose, I was given to understand.

"You know, you're awfully fussy for someone who's getting free help."

Keir stepped back just slightly, dropping his hand from my hip. "You happen to be the most expensive free help I've ever had."

"Really?" I challenged. "You get a lot of volunteers around here, Justin?"

"You would be the first."

"I can see why. Is he always this way?"

"This morning he complained for a solid hour about farming practices in the U.S."

"I'm standing right here, you know," Keir interjected, but the small smirk on his face told me he took no actual offense to being discussed like an inanimate object.

"What is this issue you have with farming practices?"

"You really want to know?"

"You really *don't* want to know," Justin inserted, handing over another order ticket.

Glancing at it, Keir grabbed two portions of chorizo and tossed them onto the grill. Then he went to the refrigerator, where he pulled out what appeared to be a deformed tomato and placed it squarely in my palm. It was much smaller than the tomatoes you typically see in grocery stores and very obviously misshapen. And its coloring was in no way the consistent red most of us expect.

"So you're offended by ugly tomatoes?"

"No, see, that's exactly my point. *This* is what a tomato is supposed to look like."

Justin groaned but Keir ignored him and went on, undeterred. "It's been bred to prioritize flavor over appearance or size. But you almost never see this in the U.S. because here people want big red round tomatoes, even if they're mealy with no flavor. Most people don't even know how a tomato should actually taste."

He pulled a paring knife out of the block on the counter and, taking the tomato from my hand, deftly sliced off a piece and then offered it to me from the blade of the knife.

It *was* a very good tomato.

"So what you're telling me is that you *are* fussy."

A grin burst across his face. "No. I'm saying you can't make good food with flavorless ingredients. That doesn't make me *fussy*."

"Okay, sure. If you say so," I told him, returning to my work. And just for fun, I wiped my blade across my apron.

I could practically *feel* his posture tweak and he began shaking his head, but he was still smiling when he set down the tomato and picked up his tongs.

"What about you?" he asked with a sideways glance. "What's your thing?"

"I'm into fonts."

He paused from his grilling to look at me. "Like . . . baby deer?"

"No," I said laughing. "Not *fawns*. Fonts. With a *T*. Like letters and typography."

"Ah, got it." He was nodding now, but his eyes hadn't left my face. He didn't actually seem like he got it. "How is that better than baby deer?"

I laughed again. "I'm a graphic designer. Fonts are my thing."

"Okay," he said thoughtfully, drawing out the word as if he was now sizing me up in this new light. "Like logos and such?"

"Yeah. That's part of it."

"I designed my own logo," he told me proudly. "For Blaze, see?" He pointed to where the logo mark was repeated on the menu board.

"Great job." I patted him on the shoulder.

"What?" He squinted at me suspiciously.

"What? I said *great job*."

"Uh-huh." He eyed me a moment longer and then went back to the chorizo.

Honestly, watching him cook it was near torture. He had a sizeable flame going and placed the sausage right in the middle of it until the skin got nearly charred and crispy. But when he sliced it, the inside was still juicy and delicious. My stomach growled embarrassingly loud.

Thankfully, Keir gave no indication that he'd heard.

But then it happened again.

"You know you're in a food truck, right?"

"What do you mean?"

"Your stomach is practically screaming at me. When did you last eat?"

"I don't know, this morning. But everything here smells so good."

"Well, I would certainly hope so."

Without another word, Keir opened a warming drawer and plucked out three of the most gorgeous empanadas I'd ever seen in my life. The pastry was golden and flaky, and the rounded edges looked almost like they were braided. These were definitely not prepackaged.

Nestling them on a bed of arugula and drizzling them in a chimichurri sauce, he then handed me the plate.

"Really?"

"I'd be a little insulted if you left here hungry."

The artistry involved in this one dish made me wonder again about Keir as I sat on a counter, eating and watching him cook. Why would an obviously talented chef with a business in Seattle be operating a single food truck here in San Francisco? I couldn't make sense of that.

"I don't think you ever told me why you're here."

"Are you kidding? This is one of the choicest locations in San Francisco," he told me, misunderstanding my meaning. "My godfather has an old army buddy who was able to pull a few strings with the city for me. Otherwise, I'd probably be slinging hot dogs to five-year-olds outside the zoo in the Sunset District." He made a mock scary face and a smile played on his lips.

But the way he held my gaze just a bit too long—checking my expression—and the way his smile didn't quite reach his eyes made me think that the misunderstanding was deliberate.

"Seems like all of this is a lot of trouble for someone who's only here temporarily."

Of course, I had done a little internet stalking when I received his text and was somewhat surprised to find that Blaze was no run-of-the-mill catering business. It'd won numerous awards and been written up many times in the Seattle papers. Keir, himself, had trained in Argentina under some big-name chef, known for Patagonian–style cooking. He was clearly the heart of the business, which made his presence here seem that much more out of place. Maybe he was considering a business expansion to San Francisco? Or perhaps doing some market research? I considered those, but neither seemed like a logical explanation.

"I'm down here for family stuff," he admitted, as though answering these unspoken thoughts. "It's almost finished now."

19

"And you needed a truck down here for that?"

Keir handed several orders over to Justin and turned to face me directly. Once again the look in his eye made me feel like there was something more there, but he seemed to check the thought on his tongue.

"Originally, I thought I was going to be down here a lot longer. Mostly, I brought the truck because I enjoy it, and it gave me something to fill the time—we're now licensed and permitted in San Francisco."

Something flickered across his face, and I suspected it was the other half of his explanation that, once again, he didn't seem to want to voice. I gave it another couple of seconds, but no, that was all I was going to get.

"Did you like the empanadas?" he asked instead.

I glanced down at my near spotless plate. Honestly, if he weren't quite so good looking, or at least if he were gay, I would have set aside my pride and licked the plate clean right in front of him. I practically had anyway.

"Not that much." We both grinned. "What's in them, anyway? They were insanely good."

"Coincidentally, it's fawn."

I blinked—twice—and looked down at my empty plate, where the only thing remaining was a sprig of arugula and some crumbs.

"*Fawn?*" Visions of Bambi flashed in my head and my heart dropped into my stomach.

Keir burst out laughing. "No, they're just beef. But, god, your face!"

"You're awful!" He was still laughing, with actual tears now. "You know, you're lucky it's not fawn or I'd be protesting your sorry-ass food truck," I told my new friend. "I'd make some truly badass signs and use only the angry fonts."

"Angry fonts? Is that actually a thing?" Those creases I admired were now on full display. And his eyes looked almost backlit, with thick lashes that were shamelessly wasted on a man.

"Let's hope for your sake you never have occasion to find out."

§

The lunch crowd was served with astounding efficiency. Not by me. I'd been offered chorizo.

Still, I noticed a curious calm to being in Keir's presence. Maybe it was the way that he never seemed to be ruffled by the demands of his business, no matter how crazy it was. Or perhaps it was the relief of being far enough away from my own work to forget about the pressure I was under. Or maybe it was just the very simple pleasure of being around someone who felt familiar to me, even though we'd just met. He had a way about him that was hard to resist, especially when he gave me his full attention, which he did often. Another hour went by like it was nothing.

At close to two o'clock, Keir finished serving his last customer and closed the service window while Justin packed up his stuff and headed out.

"So how many people did we serve today?" I asked.

"About a hundred and fifty, I think."

"That's a good day, right?"

Keir had begun to wipe down the grill but paused for a moment. Then he turned to look at me over his shoulder. His smile was sweet, affectionate almost. But there was something underneath it, something I couldn't quite put my finger on. It gave me the strangest feeling, like maybe he could use a hug.

"Yeah," he said, turning back. The smile stayed on his face but altered somehow. "It was a very good day for me."

Had I better understood his tone or the soft look in his eye, I might have come up with a suitable response to match what I heard in his voice. Instead I just nodded, though he wouldn't have seen it, busy as he was with the grill.

"Well, I should probably get back to work myself."

I grabbed my purse from one of the bins by the back door and pulled out my wallet to pay him for lunch. Suddenly, that sweet smile turned itself into a very disapproving frown.

"Put that away," he insisted. "You're going to need it to cover your deductible."

I made a face at him, and he made one right back.

"Okay, then, I'll have to owe you."

But he ignored me and went to a small cabinet by the back door to remove several sheets of paper.

"This is a copy of the estimate in case you want it."

I reached over and took the papers without giving them a glance. We both knew today hadn't really been about that. Initially, I had come just for the curiosity of seeing him in his element, without any expectation of more than a quick *hi* and a little harmless flirting. But now that it was time to go, that didn't seem like quite enough.

"Well, I had fun," I said standing and brushing the wrinkles from my skirt. "If you want to hang out sometime before you leave, let me know."

He nodded, adding a polite smile. But it didn't exactly feel like a *yes*. It wasn't exactly a *no* either. It was sort of this weird in-between place that, honestly, was a little embarrassing.

I supposed I could have pressed him on it, but what was the point? After all, this was just a fun and frivolous infatuation with nowhere to go.

So I just smiled and let it pass. "Okay, then. See ya round, Blaze."

"See you around, Georgiou."

And before I gave it any thought, I pushed up on my toes and leaned in to place a quick kiss on that devastating jawline. And yes, for the record, his stubble *was* everything I imagined it would be: soft and prickly, and tantalizing to my lips.

Turning, I hopped down from the truck, taking with me the satisfying image of his surprised but genuine smile. It was like a tasty little to-go box for the road—a perfect ending to the short story of us.

Chapter 3

Selene

The contents of my refrigerator currently consisted of a few random, questionable vegetables, Lean Cuisines, and wine—a clear sign that my entire life, for the moment, revolved around work. I thought briefly about popping into the grocery store on the way home but knew myself well enough to know that shopping while hungry meant I'd most likely walk out with a cartful of cheese.

No, tonight called for Chinese delivery and a bath. Maybe together.

After leaving Keir's truck, I had gone back to the office to begin working on some changes my boss was suggesting for the design portfolio I was soon presenting to our potential client. I was always glad for the suggestions—Paula had a great eye—but it was hard not to feel like I was carrying the millennial flag for the group when the suggestions for my work were always *More! Edgier! Bigger!* Still, most people at my experience level would be lucky just to be in the room for the discussion—let alone be a contender for the final design, a design that could be seen by millions of people around the world. It was almost too mind-blowing to think about.

In the corporate world, *logos and such* was what most people thought brand was all about. But that was really just the beginning of it. At its best, my job was about inspiring an emotional bond between a brand and its customers. It sounds lofty and admittedly a little pretentious, I know, but think about Apple. People who love that brand *love* it. Enough to advocate for it with their friends. Enough to buy generation after generation of new products. Some, enough to wait in line for days in order to be among the first to purchase a new release. That's what brand loyalty is. And that's what everybody wants to create.

If a person can see their own identity within the identity of a brand, you've got them: *I* think different. *I* just do it. Apple, Nike, Starbucks—these are the rock stars of my world.

But great branding is more complex now than it ever was. With so many more places for people to interact with a brand, its visuals must be able to extend over a wide variety of channels. You may be talking to customers through a website or in print media or through a series of digital banners or on social media, and that brand must be recognizable in every single form. Sometimes audiences won't even see the logo. Successful design means they may just recognize a brand by its visual language.

So that's the job.

And if I was afforded the opportunity to put *my* stamp on a national brand, it could elevate my career in untold ways.

Plus, this was a particularly interesting case. The brand in question was Rival Athletic Wear. It had made a huge name for itself in the late '90s by securing key endorsements from several pro basketball players and boxers. So by default, it became largely a male-oriented brand. Its visual language still reflected that, with a graphical emphasis on heavy block typography, primary colors, and a lot of black-and-white photography of people sweating.

But in the last few years, Rival thought to grow its revenue by capitalizing on the frothy $78 billion athleisure market. The primary challenge, though, was that the athleisure market catered largely to women, not Rival's core demographic. Still, it had a respectable amount of success until consumers discovered that the stitching in the crotch of certain models of women's compression shorts and yoga pants was prone to popping open, often in less-than-opportune moments.

And one would have thought that, with women making up half the population, Rival would have responded to the issue swiftly and sensitively. But no. The company's first response was to deny all culpability, suggesting that perhaps women were squeezing themselves into the wrong size garments. And then, apparently not hearing the audible gasp from the Twittersphere, one rogue spokesman went further to suggest, in a tongue-in-cheek way, of course, that exercise, rather than a recall, was the solution to this problem.

What followed was an all-out media smackdown. Rival's CEO finally did declare a recall and issued a series of apologies, but they just sounded like sanitized, say-nothing, take-no-responsibility corporate BS-speak. Women weren't having it, and investors were losing confidence. By the end of the uproar, nearly $600 million had been knocked off Rival's market value.

Now, a year or so after Pantygate, as the episode came to be known, Rival was looking to build a new image. Or, at least new*ish*. It's hard to change your image if you don't change the leadership that was responsible for the old one. Nonetheless, that's where my firm came in. But we had serious competition from two other agencies, and as the youngest designer on the team, I knew I had zero margin of error. If my boss wanted *More! Edgier! Bigger!* that's exactly what she was going to get.

So by the time I walked back into my apartment at around seven o'clock, I was spent. A bath, a glass of wine, and Chinese takeout sounded pretty damn perfect. After digging my phone out of my purse, I called in the order.

I typically don't pay much attention to my phone over the course of the workday, especially if I'm deep into a design. Apparently, today I'd missed a lot. There were two messages from my sister, one from my best friend, Sarah, and one—surprisingly—from Keir.

I was about to begin listening to them when my sister, Mia, called again, and I answered.

That's when time stopped.

That was the moment when nothing made sense anymore, and I had to sit down because I could not find my center.

When I think back on that call, there are only a few things that remain clear. The rest is a complete blur—a fuzzy, shapeless mess of thoughts that I could not connect. I remember that she spoke of my dad using words like *tumor* and *treatment* and *time*. I remember that my mind went blank, hearing what she said but taking no meaning from the words. My heart had, though, and it froze in my chest. I remember she was crying.

And I remember that everything in my apartment seemed unnaturally vivid and detailed. There was a clear glass vase sitting on my kitchen table, filled with long stalks of white gladiolus that I had bought as a little present for myself. *Four stalks,* I remember thinking. Similarly, I had a family of four. Not three. *Four.*

My family had always been the center of my universe. For my whole life, it had been us against the world, tackling problems and cutting a protective swath for each other through the dirty and disordered jungle of life. That's who we were. Like Oprah says: that was the thing I knew for sure.

That, and the fact that three quarters of a family fell very far short of a whole one.

I didn't even realize how far my thoughts had drifted from our conversation when my buzzer rang. The food I had ordered arrived, and I didn't have the money ready to go.

"When can we see him?"

My voice sounded very clear but distant as I rose from the couch and picked up my purse. The clammy sensation on my face and palms had begun to disappear, but my hands still felt icy. It was all moving too fast and, oddly, not fast enough. I concentrated on unzipping my purse and then reached inside for my wallet. But my wallet wasn't in there.

"He's still in the ER. You can call him in the morning, and let's plan to go over this weekend."

"Yeah, of course," I said numbly, hitting the buzzer on the door. I noticed my hands were now trembling. And where was my wallet? I couldn't think. "Hang on a second, will you?"

"I'm in 3A," I told the delivery guy through the intercom. "You can come up if you want. I just . . . I need to get cash." But where the *hell* was my wallet? I glanced around the room, but I didn't see it.

"I can't find my wallet," I said to my sister.

"Did you try your briefcase?"

"No—"

The buzzer rang again. "What is *wrong* with this guy! I told him he could come up!"

I'm sure Mia could hear by the sound of my voice that I was losing control now, and trying hard not to. Of the two of us, my sister had always been the more contemplative and measured one. She was the organizer, the fixer, the source for all reliable information regarding restaurants, store hours, directions, and the cheapest parking garages. I was the more adventurous one, the more creative one, the one most like my dad.

I bit down hard on my lip as that last thought tore through my composure.

"Check your briefcase," she said calmly. "When was the last time you remember having it?"

"I don't know!" I said to her in a panic. I wasn't exactly in the frame of mind to be thinking very clearly.

I hit the intercom again, hard. "Dude, I'm coming! Can't you just wait a second?"

"The food's getting cold," he fired back. "And I have other orders to deliver!"

"Do you need to go?" Mia asked me.

"Maybe." I was too distracted by everything to do anything successfully. I found my briefcase next to the front door and literally dumped the entire thing out on the dining room table. Papers, pens, my headphones, my laptop, small notebook. All of it went everywhere, lipsticks and change rolling off the table and onto the floor in a disorganized racket. But my wallet wasn't in there either.

"I'll call you later, okay?"

I didn't actually listen to her response. I just hung up. I felt paralyzed, processing the magnitude of the news she had delivered, and knowing that I needed to function through it well enough to remember where the *fuck* my wallet had gone. But my brain simply could not do that; it was too busy conjuring defenses against the trauma. Defenses that took the form of false hopes I began to feed myself. And questions. So many damn questions.

So when my buzzer rang for the third time, I just broke down. My legs felt watery and gave way under my weight. I slid down to the floor with my back against the wall, buried my head in my hands, and cried.

I could not stop.

I was still sobbing when I heard a soft knock on my front door.

"Go away!" I swung my arm back and struck the wall with the pad of my fist. Frustrated by the impotent little thump of it, I removed a shoe, turned around, and hurled it against the door. "I can't find my wallet," I shouted through angry tears at that impatient son of a bitch. But my lips felt numb and stiff, rage giving way to cold despair. I was curled up on the floor and feeling more helpless than I had ever felt in my life.

Then came a different voice entirely. "I know."

§

Keir Stevens stood in my doorway, like a random act of kindness sent by the universe itself. He had arrived exactly when I needed him, for an appointment we didn't have. In one hand he held a bag of Chinese; in the other he held my wallet.

And it took him all of about two seconds to know that something was very wrong.

"Hey," he said with considerable concern as he took a full inventory of my features. "I left you a message."

"I'm sorry. I . . ." I drew a deep, shuddering breath and wiped my sleeve across my face. I didn't even know how to continue. I couldn't. "How did you know where I lived?"

"Your license. Tell me what's wrong." His voice was so full of sympathy that I lost control of my emotions entirely.

"My dad has brain cancer." I was shocked that the words came out as cleanly as they did, and even more shocked that such a phrase could ever cross my lips. Those were words that *other* people say about *other* people's families. Logically, of course, I knew that many people developed cancer every year—too many people—but you never think they'll be *your* people.

But when I looked up into Keir's face, I knew that everything I was saying was real. Because I watched as my words registered. I watched the way his expression changed. On his face was the gut punch I felt deep in my core. The very same one.

He pulled me firmly to him without speaking a word, and then his arms encircled me like a vise, so hard that the breath left my body.

He felt as big to me as I'd imagined, and his arms were as strong around me as I could have ever hoped. Those were the arms that I had said could probably fix anything. Anything, but not this.

But in those arms I broke, momentarily surrendering to my fear and heartbreak.

I don't know how long we stood there in the doorway. But I know how warm he felt to me as I shivered. And I know how his soft T-shirt grew damp under my cheek and smelled faintly of laundry detergent and barbecue. I know how the steady rhythm of his breath seemed to strengthen me.

This was where my broken heart found unexplainable comfort.

We were practically strangers, but he didn't hold me that way. He pressed my head against him, offering me the comfort of his warm, broad chest, and smoothing my disheveled ponytail with a gentle hand. He wasn't remotely tentative or awkward, not the least bit self-conscious. He didn't *feel* like a stranger. As we stood in that doorway, it felt as if something in our mutual chemical connection had said unequivocally, *I know you.*

"It's not good, Keir," I whispered, and leaned tiredly into the curve of his shoulder. I felt him nod against the top of my head, pressing his lips to my hair and squeezing me a little tighter still.

His voice came softly, a gentle consolation. "I know, baby," he answered. "I know."

Chapter 4

Selene

Keir arranged his tall frame on the couch in my living room. He was leaning back into the corner with his elbow propped on the cushions and his head resting lightly on his fist.

"How'd they find it?"

If I paused in answering, it wasn't under the pretense of any lack of understanding—it was simply because the answer seemed too impossible to believe. "He had a seizure."

"Motherfucker," Keir muttered under his breath. All in all, I thought that summed things up pretty well.

I had tried to convince him that I would be fine and he shouldn't feel the need to stick around. After all, this was too heavy, too much for people who hardly knew each other. But he wouldn't hear of it. He sent me off to change while he put Szechuan beef and spring rolls on plates from the kitchen. He had everything set up on the coffee table and was just pouring some wine when I came back out in a T-shirt and jeans—barefoot, with my hair loose around my shoulders—and, in fact, indescribably glad for the company. Because I knew the alternative was spending the rest of the night scouring the internet in a panic, reading every website I could possibly find on my dad's form of cancer, and mentally calculating his odds of beating it. Which I already knew from my sister were negligible.

"Do you want to tell me about him?" Keir asked.

I took a deep breath for courage and settled my plate on my lap. The truth is, I could tell Keir everything about my dad. He was my bedrock and my best friend. He was always the first person I wanted to call. I guess the only thing that had never occurred to me until today was that he was mortal.

"Well, for starters, he's very Greek."

"What does that mean?"

"He's the more emotional of my parents. He's extremely passionate and animated, and we've always said his hand gesturing could threaten dismemberment. And he's solely to blame for my sense of humor because he's laughed at every one of my jokes since the day I was born."

"He sounds great."

"Yeah. Everyone loves him."

As the image of my dad gathered in my head I smiled, and Keir smiled reflexively in return, looking at me in this bare, tender way. The degree to which he seemed genuinely interested threw me somewhat, but he was listening so carefully—head tilted toward me, eyes continually inspecting my expression—that I found myself going on.

"I guess he's kind of a man's man—he loves sports and tools and fixing stuff, but he prides himself on being surrounded by strong women." I pushed a piece of beef around my plate with a fork and, remembering I was hungry, ate it. "And he's a gentleman. A really old-school one.

"My mom is strong, but she's still madly in love with him after twenty-eight years of marriage, and I don't know what she's going to do without him." I wasn't ready to think about what I would do without him.

Keir studied me for several moments. Then he shifted on the couch, setting his wineglass on the coffee table.

"Here, put your feet up," he said, and patted his thighs with his palms. "I don't know how women wear heels like that all day."

Without so much as a question, I swung my feet up onto his lap and nearly groaned out loud as he took them in hand, rubbing his thumb in firm circles over the pads at the base of my toes.

"You don't like heels?"

"I didn't say *that*," he added pointedly with a quirk of one eyebrow. "I happen to like them very much. They just look incredibly uncomfortable."

He ran his knuckles squarely up the arch of my left foot, and I nearly melted into the deep-set cushions of my couch. And when he engulfed my foot with his palm and began kneading it from heel to toes, I let my head fall back and closed my eyes. We sat silently like this for several minutes while he gave the other foot a similar treatment.

I was still waiting for the weirdness of this whole situation with Keir to descend, but it never did, and for the first time since the phone call with my sister, the knots in my stomach began to loosen a little.

"Fashion does have its price," I told him lazily, now focusing on the warmth of his hand as he placed one over the top of my foot and massaged each toe pad with the other. "It's worth it."

"Well, you look nice in heels," he said softly, head bent over my bare feet. And not stopping his rubbing, he looked up at me. "But I think you look nice in jeans too."

If words were flowers, that little compliment was the equivalent of being presented with a single daisy—weighty enough that I knew it was honest, but not so extravagant that it was embarrassing to either of us. It just made me feel a little happier.

"So what took you to Seattle?"

He smiled wryly, still focused on my foot. "I guess you could say I followed a passion." Keir looked up and clarified. "*She* was my high school girlfriend and applying to be an English lit major at the University of Washington. I decided to apply there too."

I could not help my slack-jawed expression. "You moved to Seattle for a *girl*?" I can't say just why, but that seemed very out of character.

He laughed lightly and lifted his shoulders in a noncommittal way. "At eighteen, all I cared about was freedom and adventure—setting out for some place new. So looking back, I'm not sure it was her so much as it was me. But yes, at the time, my pop called it *full of enterprise and empty of caution*."

He shook his head and chuckled again. Meanwhile, he had both hands wrapped around my feet and was running his thumbs slowly over the curves of my heels, which made my brain momentarily incapable of a response.

"But you're not still together, you and Miss English Lit?"

"No," he said succinctly, though not bitterly, I noticed. Still, there had been a smile in his voice that disappeared as he continued. "After we finished our undergrad work, I went on to culinary school, and she went on to Boston." He shrugged. "That was it."

"Ouch."

"Yeah, maybe at the time. But things change, people change—you know." A tilt of his head seemed to put a period at the end of this topic. I raised a new one.

"So how did you get into catering?"

Keir took hold of one big toe and wiggled it gently. He may have understood that his willingness to talk about his life was providing me a welcome distraction from my own. He generously indulged me in another question.

"I've been cooking my entire life, actually," he said, catching my eye for just a beat. "I was an only child with a single, working father, so if I didn't learn to cook, I'd have been eating a lot of peanut butter and jelly." He laughed at the thought, a genuine sound that had a richness and a reassurance to it. "But I didn't plan on going into catering, per se. It's just that when I got back from Argentina, a door opened and I guess I walked through it."

"That's when you started Blaze?"

He let go of my feet and rearranged his long legs so that mine draped lightly across his thighs. Then he rested a forearm on my shins.

"More or less. A friend was getting married on the beach and asked me to do an open-fire grill like I'd been trained to do. I agreed, because, well, why not? Turns out, one of his guests was an executive at Microsoft, and the next thing I knew, I was getting requests to do all kinds of events. I wrote my entire business plan over the course of one weekend. And it just went on from there. Life is like that, I guess. You never really know what's coming."

"That's for sure," I said quietly, and sobered as I thought of my dad.

"God. I'm sorry. That was insensitive."

I waved it off. "So who runs Blaze when you're here?"

"Well," he said shifting on the couch, "so far, I've been able to handle the business end remotely. And, Kelly, my catering manager, runs all the day-to-day stuff. I've been flying back and forth a lot. But I'm wrapping things up here as fast as I can."

"What kind of things?"

His expression altered in the same way it had earlier in the day when the subject of his stay came up. But it wasn't obvious to me whether that meant he wanted to tell me, or whether it meant he didn't. In the end, he didn't.

"Just family things," was all he said.

"Doesn't it worry you, not being there to run your business?"

"It worries me every day." That was true; I could see it in his face.

"And yet you're here."

"Family."

Yes, I definitely understood that there were a handful of things in life for which you dropped everything. I didn't need any more explanation than that. "Family," I agreed.

He patted my shins lightly. "Speaking of my business, though, I need to go over some food orders with Kelly tonight. I should probably get going."

"Of course, yes," I said lifting my feet from his lap.

I didn't really want him to leave. But as he rose from the couch and carried our plates into the kitchen to rinse them carefully in the sink, I didn't know what else to say. I could hardly ask any more of him than he'd already given—and given to someone he barely knew.

"You're a good human, Keir," I said as we stood in the doorway of my apartment.

A small smile curled on his lips, and he held my gaze for a long, wordless pause. Then he reached out in a familiar way that made me kind of happy, and his fingers picked up a small lock of my hair, gliding down to the end and tugging gently. He held it there, for a moment—the soft expression lingering on his face—and then he let go.

"Promise me you'll take care of yourself."

I nodded. And just like that, he was gone.

Chapter 5

Selene

Two days later, I arrived at the office at nine o'clock and dialed Keir from my desk.

"What do you know about moussaka?"

"Pretty sure it's Greek," he said.

"It is Greek, wiseass. And, mysteriously, a pan of it was left on my doorstep yesterday with no card who it's from."

Moussaka is a semitraditional Greek casserole, and one of my favorites. But it's incredibly time-consuming to prepare, which is why I rarely made it myself.

Keir wasn't copping to it. A quick *hmm* was all he would say.

"What's curious is that only two people have keys to my apartment building. My friend Sarah and my sister."

"Well, it must be one of them."

"I thought about that, actually, and had it been a box of Lucky Charms and a carton of milk, I would have said *yes, this is absolutely from Sarah*. But it was a pan of *moussaka*, so it had to have been my sister."

"See, there you go."

"Yeah. The weird thing, though, is that I've tasted my sister's moussaka, and believe me, it's nowhere near this good."

"That *is* weird," he said in a disingenuous way that made me smile.

"So I asked myself who *else* do I know that would be arrogant enough to cook authentic Greek food for someone Greek and fussy enough to actually get it right? *And* be able to charm his way into my building without coming off like a psycho stalker. For some reason, I thought of you."

"So you're saying I'm both incredibly handsome *and* incredibly talented?"

"No, I think the words I used were *fussy* and *arrogant*."

"And a bit of a demigod."

I laughed. "So you *are* admitting to the moussaka?"

There was a long pause, and though I didn't know him well, I knew he was smiling too.

"For the record, Georgiou, I didn't cook you Greek food because you're Greek."

"No?"

"No." His voice softened just then, and it sounded as if he switched the phone to his other ear. "I cooked you comfort food because I thought that's what you might need."

See, *this right here* was the thing about Keir that made him so dangerous to me. Never in my life had I spent time with a man who always seemed to know *exactly* the right thing to say. Dammit if he wasn't the most perceptive bastard I had ever met.

So much so that my eyes welled up with tears, and I had to pull tight every muscle in my forehead just to hold them back. I did not want to appear as fragile as I sometimes felt in the wake of my father's diagnosis. Keir was so unexpectedly generous, but there was a limit, I thought, to how many times I could cry in his presence and not make him wish he'd been rear-ended by someone a little more solid.

"How are you today?" he asked. Despite my efforts, he was

reading precisely those thoughts I was trying to conceal.

"Terrible," I answered with complete honesty. What was the point of trying to pretend?

His breath came out in broken little bursts into the receiver, and I could tell he was nodding, understanding.

"You have to take care of yourself, Selene. It's not a selfish thing to do."

No, no, *no*. I would not cry. I took a deep breath to collect myself.

"Well, it'd take me a year to eat all that moussaka. You might as well come over and help me."

I could hear his hesitation—that odd not-quite-yes-and-not-quite-no thing from the other day.

"What? You don't eat your own cooking? That's really not a great endorsement of your skills, Keir."

He laughed, and I heard the sound of a metal bowl being set on a countertop. "You're a pain in the ass, you know that?"

"And you're a stubborn fool," I replied, knowing I had him.

"What time should I be there?"

Chapter 6

Keir

The honest truth was, I didn't think I should have been there. No, that's a lie. I knew I shouldn't have been there. But it was by far the best invitation I'd had in a really long time, and there wasn't a thing in the world I could do to stop myself from accepting.

Knocking on Selene's door, I checked my watch, and wanted to kick my own ass for being a few minutes late. But after I finished cleaning the truck and ran home for a quick shower, I made a stop to pick up a bouquet of mixed flowers, which I produced from behind my back as she opened the door.

She smiled when she saw them, and it nearly winded me.

"You're late," she said. "But since you brought me flowers, I'll forgive you."

She took the bouquet from my hand and pulled me inside by the arm. It was like a physical blow to the chest how much I liked to see her smile. Had I known the flowers could do that so easily, I probably would have bought seventeen dozen more, just to test the multiplier effect.

And *that* was exactly why I shouldn't have been there.

"Something smells *amazing*," I told her as she turned and headed for the kitchen with me right behind her. She glanced over her shoulder with a level stare that told me she knew that *I* knew it was my moussaka. I laughed at the look she gave.

But as soon as we reached the doorway to the kitchen, she stopped abruptly and turned to face me, effectively blocking the door. And there she stood, flowers in hand. Not moving.

"Are you going to put those in water?"

"Yes," she answered, still not moving.

I looked around behind her. A recipe card and a bunch of baking ingredients were set out on the counter, and she must have been starting a salad when I arrived. But in the doorway she stood with a little smirk on her face that led me to believe I was not welcome in the kitchen.

"Why aren't you letting me in the kitchen?"

"Why do you say that?"

"Because you're not letting me in the kitchen."

"I'm not letting you in the kitchen," she confirmed.

"*Why?*"

"Because you're too fussy and arrogant to leave well enough alone while I finish the cake. That's why."

"Handsome and talented?"

"No. I didn't say that. I think you only ever hear what you want to hear."

The truth of it is that as I stood nearly chest to chest with this stunning woman—my accidental friend—all I was really hearing was her lips. And her beautiful, long dark hair that fell loose and free across her shoulders. And those sage-green eyes. And the T-shirt that skimmed her breasts, just hinting at the shape beneath. Everything else was simply noise.

"I hear what you *mean*."

"I *mean* fussy and arrogant."

She wasn't budging. "What kind of cake is it?"

"Kahlúa chocolate. You'll like it."

"Sounds good." I craned my neck over the top of her head, which hit me at about chin level. "Let me see what you're putting in it."

"No. Get out!"

She put her free hand squarely on my chest, and I let her push me back a couple of steps, grinning at her feeble look of death. Holy god, I liked this girl. I liked her a lot.

"Go put some music on," she added, gesturing to the living room. "My phone is over by the stereo." Then she disappeared into the kitchen.

"You're a terrible hostess," I called to her. But she probably couldn't hear me over all her racket with the pots and pans.

"Whaaaat?" she called back right on cue. I laughed again. She was a riot.

Selene's apartment looked like something straight out of a catalog—no exaggeration. Go to any Pottery Barn and you'd be hard-pressed to find rooms that looked half as stylish. I wasn't surprised; she was probably the most stylish woman I knew.

The walls of the living room were a clean white, with a few interesting art pieces, including two black-and-white photographs of the San Francisco skyline at night, signed by someone named D. Moore. Centered in the room was a navy velour couch with an oversize wrought iron–and–glass coffee table. The rest of the furniture was distressed wood in sort of a blue-gray wash. It was nice.

On the far wall was a bookcase that housed a collection of art books and photos, as well as her stereo. I picked up her phone off one of the shelves and began to scroll through her music. She had a pretty eclectic mix.

"You like *Garth Brooks*?" I called to her.

"I can't hear you," she hollered back. And then she turned on the hand mixer.

Meanwhile, I was singing loudly along to the only Garth Brooks song I knew.

"Whaaaat?" Selene called out to me again.

And then something happened in there.

I can't even explain the noise, but over the sound of the music I could hear a sharp change in the mechanical whir of the mixer. Selene started shrieking.

I dropped the phone on the bookcase and ran for her.

Spending most of my adult life in a kitchen, I'd seen some pretty bad injuries—detached appendages, deep cuts, second- and third-degree burns. I was mentally preparing myself for something like that as I came skidding around the corner like a maniac.

But as I crashed into the doorframe, the sight I was met with was like *nothing* I'd ever seen. At first, I couldn't even make sense of it. The kitchen looked like something out of *The Exorcist*—that is, if you switched the vomit for cake batter and then shot it, literally, over every available surface.

"What the *fuck*?"

"Help me!" she pleaded.

The whirring sound was still going on, though I couldn't see the source of the trouble. But Selene was standing against the counter with both of her fists up at her forehead—squealing and struggling like she was trying to pull an alien off her face. Suddenly I realized with shock, it was the goddamned hand mixer! Its beaters were wound up like attack curlers into one side of her hair. And still attempting to rotate!

"Jesus!"

I lunged for the cord, yanking the plug from the wall, which brought an abrupt, quiet relief to the kitchen.

For several moments, Selene and I just gaped at each other.

She was standing there, hand mixer at her ear, blinking chocolate at me, and I'm sure waiting for me to somehow convey that this wasn't as bad as she thought it was.

But it really *was* that bad.

She was covered in chocolate from head to toe, like she'd been styled by a drunken baker. I'd be lying if I said it wasn't one of the funniest things I had ever seen in my life.

But then her cake-splattered face crumpled, and she started to cry.

"Honey, what happened? Were you doing your hair for me?"

"What?" she asked confused. "No, I was mixing up the ingredients, and I thought you said something. So I turned to hear you better, and I think my hair fell into the bowl because the next thing I knew, the mixer was on my head."

It took exactly three seconds for this image to form in my brain, and when it did, I knew I was screwed.

"Okay."

I could already hear the tremor in my voice as I laid my head on top of hers and tucked her in close, bringing my arms up around her shoulders. But she had hair like a rat's nest—full of batter—and a hand mixer now dangling from the side of her face. My whole body began to shake with subterranean laughter.

That's when she pulled back. "You're laughing at me!"

"I'm not," I insisted. But one more look at the carnage on her head and I doubled over helplessly. I was laughing so hard my stomach hurt.

All the while she stood there, hands on her hips. Finally, I pulled myself together again and wiped the tears from my eyes.

"You're a beast," she said, smacking me on the arm.

"I am. It's important that you know this about me early on."

Selene made a face that was some cocktail of wishing she could stay mad at me and knowing she couldn't. Because now we had a story together. And it was a pretty great one. As long as we knew each other, there would always be this.

"I don't know if I can get this out," she said, at least half grinning, and tugging at the mess.

Selene was the kind of person who always seemed to have her shit together, so there was something absolutely endearing about her when she was vulnerable; it was probably a side of her she didn't like many people to see. But she showed it often with me, and that made me feel humbled and protective and wanting to be whatever she needed.

Even knowing I shouldn't.

"Don't worry. I'll help you."

I handed her a paper towel to clean her face, and carefully disengaged the two blades from the base of the mixer. With the beaters still in her hair, I gathered her in my arms again, ignoring the slow seeping of cake batter into my shirt.

What was harder to ignore was the way she felt against my chest, her head pressed to my sternum like she fit perfectly there. She seemed to relax into my body, and her arms came around my back. For a moment we just stood there together, rocking gently back and forth.

I'd held her like this once before—the night I brought her wallet to her—but I didn't really remember it. We were both in shock that night.

This felt different. It would take a conscious effort to let her go. And in that absurd moment, I realized why: it had been quite a while since I had felt so happy.

Bending, I placed a small kiss on each of her tearful eyelids and, with a deep breath of resolve, stepped back.

"We can definitely fix this. Do you have peanut butter?"

"Peanut butter is for getting gum out of your hair, not small kitchen appliances."

I smiled. "Fair point, Julia Child. Come sit and let's see what we can do here."

§

I'd dealt with a lot of crazy stuff in the kitchen, though this was definitely a first. On a normal day, Selene's hair fell midway down her back, but at the moment, a good twelve inches of it on the right side was wrapped around two separate blades.

"Where are your scissors?"

"No!" she cried in horror. Then, seeing my expression, she softened. "You're just kidding."

I grinned. "I am. But do you have a toolbox? I need something to loosen up the hair. Like maybe a small screwdriver."

"I do. It's in the hall closet."

In the closet was a *fully equipped* toolbox. Selene had power tools. Good ones. And if the car jack were any indication, I'd bet a large sum of money she knew how to use them. Digging around in the drawers there, I found just the thing that would work—a grouting tool with a small hook on the end.

"How do you have a grouting tool?" I asked as I walked back into the dining room with my find.

"It's very useful for repairing broken grout."

"I know *that*. I'm just surprised you have one."

The look that followed would flatten a lesser man. "Really? Again with this?"

No, not really. She was just fun to rile, this one. The truth is, Selene Georgiou was nothing you'd expect. The Hollywood face and fashion sense notwithstanding, this woman was no princess. She always gave as good as she got, and she didn't accept bullshit from anyone. Least of all me. That's what I liked about her. She was my brand of crazy.

We sat for a solid thirty minutes at her dining room table—finally liberating a tangled mass of brown hair. And I'm sure I apologized repeatedly for hurting her in the process, though she didn't move or make a sound. But when we were finished, we both needed a drink.

"Wine or . . ." I surveyed the contents of a small bar cart she had set up in the corner. "A manhattan?"

"I think I need a manhattan." She nodded gratefully, causing a pouf of knotted and batter-infested hair to flop around on her head. Mocking me. I closed my eyes for a beat, fighting a laugh that threatened to break free again. "First, though, I should take off these clothes and get in the shower."

She rose from the table without looking at my face, which was a lucky thing, because the multitude of images that one sentence conjured was astounding and dangerous. I was unprepared. I opened my mouth to say something casual like *Yeah, go for it,* but if anything at all came out, it was most likely every thought-producing brain cell I had.

I blinked down at my hands and pretended to study the grouting tool intensely—like it was suddenly the *most* fascinating thing I'd ever seen. But I'm pretty sure that every nonplatonic feeling I had was now flashing neon across my face.

That had to stop immediately.

This *just friends* thing would work fine so long as everyone was in agreement. But if one person started having *thoughts,* the whole mess would come down like the house of cards that it was.

When Selene and I first met, I had the same reaction to her that any other warm-blooded male might have: she was *beautiful.* And a badass with a jack. And yes, I flirted a little; she flirted too. And if I were back home under normal circumstances, there's no question I would ask her out, and I'd take things as far as she'd let me. A night? Longer if she wanted?

But we didn't meet under normal circumstances, and I wasn't in any position to be starting something with her. A little flirting was fine, but I definitely couldn't let it go any further than that.

The problem was that finding out about her father changed something for me. It was a reflexive thing, an impulse that couldn't have felt more natural. My protectiveness cut through the very separation I was trying to maintain. I knew there were plenty of good reasons to be cautious, but I couldn't help but to want to be there for her. To hold her when she'd needed it, and to just listen, if that's the only thing I could do.

Still, sitting there at her table as I watched her turn and walk down the hallway to her bedroom, a familiar sense of wariness took hold in my gut. The more time we spent together, the more aware I became of how risky that impulse was, given the chemistry we shared. Our friendship sat like a lush oasis on the threshold of an abyss—a beautiful place for my mind to go when I needed it, when she needed it.

But pass beyond friendship, and there be dragons.

§

By the time she returned, wet hair pulled from harm's way in a ponytail, I had collected myself. But only by virtue of the fact that the kitchen needed a serious cleaning, and there was plenty of work to do on dinner.

"Cake is in the oven," I said, taking in this new version of Selene in gray yoga pants and a tight navy tank that I thought was every bit as good as the other versions I'd seen. "And I finished your salad. It's like I'm having myself over for dinner," I added with a grin.

She laughed and pouted at the same time, crinkling her nose into an adorable expression of embarrassment.

"You know I'm teasing you. It's a form of worship." I briefly touched her cheek at the spot where a faint blush had begun to rise. "Thank you for having me over for dinner. It's a nice change of pace."

I hadn't intended to say anything revealing, but I watched something new come over her expression. It was as if, for the first time, she began to consider where it was I went when I wasn't with her. Granted, we hadn't known each other long, and those things we didn't know about each other far outnumbered the things we did. But I felt a friendship had begun that ran a bit deeper than the length of our acquaintance might suggest, and that filled me with dread for the conversation now forming silently in my head, the one that I knew neither of us was ready for.

"You're staying with family while you're here?"

I nodded cautiously. "I'm staying at my pop's house." I pulled the dish towel from my shoulder, then set it on the kitchen sink beside me. "I need to do some work on it before I put it on the market."

She looked at me with a puzzled expression, but the pieces were coming together quickly.

"Your dad—"

I breathed in deeply, steeling myself. "He passed. Just recently."

I watched Selene's face change with a dawning realization, as though the sum of our previous conversations was finally adding up.

"When?" she asked with clear concern.

The timer went off on the moussaka, and though the kitchen was filled with the comforting smells of bubbling cheese and chocolate cake, no comfort would be found just yet. I turned off the oven, left the pan inside, and leaned back against the counter behind me, my hands grasping the edges on either side of my hips.

I met her gaze head on. "Three weeks ago." My insides hollowed out a little and I took another breath to fill the space. "I should also tell you he had brain cancer. Same as your dad."

My words seemed to freeze in the spot in which they were spoken, suspended tenuously between us. Then, slowly, they registered with obvious effect. I could see it happening in real time. The concern that had been etched on her features began to melt away as her expression evened out and her face went carefully blank, her jaw slack with shock.

She turned away, taking two steps toward the door, and then stopped with her back to me. Suddenly, she rounded.

"Why wouldn't you have told me that before?"

Her eyes burned into mine, and I heard in her voice some combination of hurt and anger. I shifted in my stance and crossed my arms over my chest.

"You didn't think I'd want to *know*?" she added.

"It didn't feel like the right time, Selene."

"When exactly is the right time, Keir?" She took a step toward me. "You sat in my house, listening to me talk about my dad, and you'd had exactly the same experience, and you didn't think it was a good time to tell me?"

I could see her fury growing with every syllable. I understood it: the lashing out, the misdirected anger. This was par for the course we walked. And, normally, I'd be absolutely fine taking the hits. But unfortunately, my own anger had been all too close at hand since my father's death. Hers called to mine in a way I struggled to control.

"We weren't talking about me," I said directly.

"Well, we're talking about you now," she snapped. "And I'd really appreciate if you were honest with me this time!"

"Honest?" The honest truth was too big and unfair a burden to lay on anyone in her situation, but in the heat of the moment, with control now tossed aside, neither of us was thinking about what was fair. "Fine. Here's your honesty: Four months ago today, I got a call from my pop that he'd had a stroke and would be in recovery for a year. I rented out my house and packed some stuff in my truck to

come down and help him. But the stroke turned out to be cancer. And the year we were expecting to have together turned out to be two and a half months. My job here went from helping a man get better to holding his hand while he died. And now I have the pleasure of dismantling his life. You tell me, Selene, how the *fuck* does that happen?"

I didn't realize how loud my voice had become until it stopped. Silence rang through the kitchen. Selene looked like she had been punched. She stood in front of me, but her eyes dropped away, unseeing, and the horror of a thousand thoughts played out openly across them. I was staring hard into her face, and I knew exactly what those thoughts were.

"I don't know how that happens," she finally whispered, her face crumpling. Tears spilled from her eyes and she sniffled hard, wiping her nose with the back of her hand. It nearly gutted me.

"I don't know either," I said, and had to look away. "But there's your honesty. And the last time I was here, you weren't ready to hear any of it."

Selene didn't respond. When I glanced over, she had turned away again and was pushing trembling fingers through her hair. I felt like absolute shit.

Her hands dropped to fists at her side, and I would have given anything to pry them open and hold them in mine.

"I need to go," she suddenly said.

She walked out of the kitchen, and pulled a coat off a chair in the living room.

"Selene—" I started, but she left the apartment anyway, and closed the door quietly behind her.

There I stood, hands on my hips, mad as fucking hell at myself, once again, for being so unnecessarily harsh. This had become commonplace since my dad passed, and I hated it in myself.

It was part of my grief that I could be so easily triggered, and I knew that, but I couldn't seem to stop it. Grief had not turned out to be what I expected. I expected the sadness, but this was something else. Every emotion I had, both good and bad, seemed to hit me in extremes. I was far more volatile than I'd ever been in my life, so much so that I was becoming wary of any emotion that felt significant. It was hard to know which ones were real and which ones were created or inflamed entirely as a vehicle for grief to work its way out. I had begun to distrust my emotions. In fact, I was learning to distrust *everything* I felt. I wanted to be numb to all of it.

And I hated seeing Selene upset by my anger. I hated that I had hurt her, and there was almost no limit to the lengths I would go to make that right—to erase the look I'd put on her face. I was determined to fix this.

§

I had no idea how long she'd be gone, but leaving her apartment wasn't something I ever considered. Instead, I did the one thing that came most naturally to me, the thing I had been doing since I was seven years old: I set a meal out on the dinner table, attending to every possible detail, and waited for my guest to come home.

After thirty minutes or maybe more, a key turned in the lock and Selene walked back in. I rose slowly from the dining room chair as she came to stand directly in front of me, her puffy coat still wrapped around her for protection. In the evening light, her expression was soft, though the corners of her mouth appeared tight with pain and her lashes were wet. She looked so young to me. She was young. Though she thought of herself as worldly, she was worldly only in the way you are when you grow up vacationing in exotic places, not worldly in the sense of having lived through real loss and hardship. Her emotional resiliency astounded me, but still, I knew how disorienting all this must have been for her, and it wrecked me.

"I'm so sorry," she murmured and pulled me into an embrace. What surprised me most was that that embrace offered far more comfort than it sought. The better part of me whispered that I should be the one doing the comforting, yet the devil in me accepted all the care she gave. I hadn't even realized how much I needed it.

§

Something as seemingly inconsequential as food does certain things very well. It's what I've always loved about cooking. In food, there's a coming together, a lifting of spirits, a fortifying of sorts, both physically and metaphorically. It's a beautiful thing. I realized after many years of cooking for my pop, and then, in turn, cooking for friends and clients, that feeding someone you care about is a matter of great intimacy. It's about nurturing. A little good food does no one any harm, and a fork clattering on an empty plate is a chef's ultimate reward.

"I'm sorry I got so upset with you," Selene said to me as we sat down together for our meal.

"You really don't have to apologize."

"No, I want you to understand that intellectually I get why you didn't tell me before, but I guess I was just kind of shaken and hurt by it too."

"You shouldn't be." I didn't really need to point out that only I could say when was the right time for me to feel ready to talk to her about my pop.

She shrugged, spearing a bite of salad but not lifting it from her plate. "Beyond the obvious shock, I guess it just felt weird to have shared so much with you, and to feel this . . . connection with you. Only to find out you had something just as big that you didn't share with me. It made me feel like you don't trust me the way I trust you."

I hadn't really thought about it that way, that she might view my withholding from her as a sign of distrust or a lack of investment in our new friendship. That wasn't the case at all, and it made me feel a little sad that it might make her less inclined to feel invested in me.

"I don't want you to think that. It's not true. I just didn't want to hurt you any more than you were already hurting. Especially because this disease doesn't affect any two people the same way. My experience may not be the same as yours."

She nodded thoughtfully and reached out to take my hand in hers.

"You can talk to me about this, you know. I want you to. I want to be there for you too."

I had no other family, and though my closest friends back home were every bit as supportive as they could be, none could truly relate to how shocking and devastating the last few months had been. Selene could, though her generosity was nearly more than I could handle. I couldn't even get a word out in response for fear I would lose it in front of her. So I just looked at her beautiful face as my eyes blurred. And I squeezed her hand back, probably way too hard, but she didn't say a thing, and she didn't pull away. She just continued to offer me the sort of human kindness that seemed to come as naturally to her as breathing.

For a long while, we sat at her table—talking and eating and even laughing together. It all felt so natural that, looking back, I think that's actually where our real friendship began.

We had met in such an accidental way, we'd flirted, and then we'd found ourselves side by side in the most random of fates. But there at her table, we took the best of our circumstances and made them our own. We didn't try to name what was happening between us. We didn't ask anything of each other. We just shared ourselves, giving and taking in equal measure.

I wouldn't have expected it, but I found that the simple act of caring for someone else and letting them care for me made me feel less victimized by the events that had brought me back to San Francisco. It wasn't weakness, I discovered; to seek the comfort of someone else is just humanity.

"Do you want to tell me about him?" Selene asked me at one point, generously offering my words back to me. I wondered if she understood yet how speaking of someone had the power to bring him back to life, if just for a moment. She would, I thought sadly, at some point.

"He was unbelievably cheap," I told her, unable to keep the smile from my voice at the image of my pop. "He was like two hundred pounds of nickels in a pair of Sears slacks. When I was a teenager, he used to march me back to my room just to make me turn off the light—even if he'd walked right by the switch. He told me that eventually I'd learn to value my own time over my laziness, and then he wouldn't have to remind me anymore."

Selene laughed, a loud abrupt snort, followed by a shake of her head. "Did it work?"

"It did," I admitted. "If you think I'm crazy about aprons, you should see me with light switches." I smiled at her smile.

"What else?" She took a sip of her wine and set the glass back on the table.

"He loved to fish," I said, picturing my pop in his waders. "It was about the only thing he ever did for himself. He didn't go very often, though, until I was much older. I think he felt guilty."

"Why?"

"Well, it was only he and I so, as a kid, most weekdays I came home after school to an empty house. It wasn't his fault—it's just the way it was. But he didn't like me to be home alone on the weekends too."

I thought that must have sounded foreign to someone like Selene.

Her upbringing was different from mine. Her family was traditional in the sense that her father had made a successful career as an orthopedic surgeon, while her mother was the primary caretaker of the home. She grew up with two parents, a sibling, and probably a ritual of after-school snacks and conversation.

"And you didn't want to go with him?"

"I did sometimes. But I got heavily into hockey, and then every weekend became about that. He traded his interests for mine, I guess—measured his contentment by mine. The funny thing is that for all his guilt about not being able to play both parental roles as well as he'd liked, I think he underestimated the value of just showing up to be a dad. Every day. He wasn't a man of many words, but hell if he didn't always show up."

Selene studied me for several measures, one arm in her lap and the other resting casually on the table in front of her. "You miss him."

"Every day," I said easily, and once again I felt my lower lids become heavy and wet. Every damn day I missed him.

"Keir," she began in earnest, and reached across the table to take my hand gently in hers. It was warm and soft, and I didn't pull away, just felt, as I took in her lovely face, how seamlessly her fingers fit between mine. "If there's anything I can do for you."

There was so much empathy in those light-green eyes. But how do you tell someone you hardly know that she may very well be the single reason you can finally feel like yourself again sometimes? That the laughter you share chases away the hollowness and the anger? That everything has been better since the day you met? You can't, of course. It's too much responsibility to lay on one person. Even just admitting it to myself made me feel a little foolish. So I spared her this confession and instead offered her a half smile, along with the simplest response I could adequately voice. It also happened to be the truth.

"You've already done it."

Chapter 7

Selene

If there was ever a day to stress-eat a package of Chips Ahoy! like Cookie Monster, Friday was it. Following weeks of preparation, we were set to present three design portfolios to Rival—all quite different and each with its own merits. Mine was definitely *More! Edgier! Bigger!* than those of my colleagues, Eric and Wade. It showcased the concept of the interlock between humans and technology in athletics, with modern hero graphics of faces that were half-human, half-mechanical. It used word combinations like *Protective + Instinct* to illustrate how high-performance athletic wear and human characteristics intersect. It also had a distinct typography; a bold, variegated color palette; and clean, modern iconography. It was a look that appealed to me as a consumer. And yes, maybe it would be too out-there for an established brand, but the team wanted to showcase our design range.

We were shown into a large conference room at Rival headquarters, where the air-conditioning seemed to be set to arctic tundra. The colossal space had a breathtaking view of the Transamerica building on Montgomery Street, with Alcatraz and Angel Island just beyond. Nowhere in San Francisco does it ever feel like you're drowning in an urban jungle. It's just not that kind of city. And September can be foggy, but today the visibility across the bay was perfect; only my nervous breath on the floor-to-ceiling window could obscure the majesty of that view.

Paula asked Eric and Wade to set up our laptop and test our presentation, and I was grateful because it gave me a moment to gather my thoughts and bring the butterflies to heel. Rival was a major corporation, employing more than fifty thousand people in 140 countries, producing hundreds of millions of products every year. This would be a very visible brand transformation. It was an opportunity I wanted so much, but in my head I was still struggling to feel like I had the chops to be here. Here in this massive conference room, alongside designers who were twice my age with twice the experience.

"Are you ready?" Paula asked me. Though I wasn't sure I would ever be *quite* ready, I wiped the condensation from the glass and answered with a smile.

"Absolutely."

§

I took the last few seconds to rally before the Rival team began filtering in. There were so many of them—and only one woman in the group, which is probably how they got themselves in this mess in the first place. At some point, I stopped bothering to try to learn their names and just greeted each one with a firm handshake.

As we went through our pitch, it was hard to get a read on Rival's mind-set. Considering the scope and cost of the project, they asked very few questions during Eric's and Wade's presentations, most often deferring to the chief marketing officer, a middle-aged man named Greg Cosgrove.

Cosgrove came across to me as arrogant and macho—a decently handsome guy who was well dressed, quick with the jokes, and loved the sound of his own booming voice.

So when Wade concluded and I stood to present, I was expecting much of the same.

I couldn't have been more wrong.

When I hit my fourth slide, Cosgrove, who had been so far mostly silent, leaned forward in his chair and turned to one of his junior people. "What is this?" he said in that big voice, waving a hand vaguely in my direction. I was so taken aback at first I wasn't sure how to react.

I stopped my pitch. My breath seemed to be lodged in my windpipe. "I'm sorry? What was your question?"

But he wasn't actually speaking to me. In fact, the question was more of a rhetorical one, apparently, because his underling didn't know how to answer either. His face took on this embarrassed, splotchy redness, and he just sort of gaped at both of us, looking horridly uncomfortable. The rest of the room went completely silent, apart from a lot of nervous fidgeting and a sudden fascination with hangnails and lint.

This, right here, was the challenge of being an artist in the corporate world. It's not like being an artist in any other capacity. Here, you have to recognize you're just a hired hand. You can't be emotional about your designs—they're considered a work product, plain and simple. Older, more experienced graphic artists like Eric and Wade understood this, but I was still coming to terms with it. So when Cosgrove glanced around the table and said to the group, "Is this a *serious* submission?" my heart plummeted to my knees, and the floor suddenly felt like Jell-O. Standing alone at the front of the room, I could only hope I was good enough at hiding it. The pinpricks in my eyes told me that perhaps I was not.

I swallowed hard and looked over to Paula for reinforcement.

It was in this exact humiliating moment that I began to get a sense of how extremely lucky I was—not only lucky to be working for probably the only firm on earth that would give someone so young a crack at a national campaign, but also lucky that I worked for a woman who would stand by that decision under fire without even blinking. No capitulation. Not even a twitch.

Paula Shaffer was a goddess in my book. When she hired me right out of Stanford, it was like winning the lottery. Her career portfolio read like a who's who of multinational brands, award-winning campaigns, and iconic designs. Her network of contacts was mind-blowing. She was five foot three, thin as a rail, flawlessly put together, and at sixty-two years old, a total powerhouse. She was my idol.

It would have been a very natural thing for her to jump in at this point and try to salvage the meeting. The firm I worked for had *her* name on the door, after all. She could have directed the conversation away from me, said something to the effect of how Rival didn't need to view my design in a literal sense but rather as a concept, just to get them to consider moving a bit more out of their comfort zone, blah, blah, blah. But had she done that, she would have forever undermined the credibility of my work. She would have weakened me in their eyes. She would have weakened me in my eyes.

Instead, she ignored all the whispers and the chuckles, all the *Well, we'd certainly get the millennial-girl vote* (hilarity ensuing), and made very solid eye contact with me. She didn't say a thing, just gave a single, decisive nod. *Go ahead,* that nod said, *defend your work.*

Defend my work. *Shit.*

They were all talking among themselves when I glanced over at the huge screen behind me. On it were a series of renderings I'd done to illustrate how the new branding would be applied to Rival's website. After all, women have powerful online purchasing habits and represent a huge financial opportunity. By being more inclusive, Rival could tap into that. They were horribly out of touch if they thought that including women in their branding would mean that men would no longer relate to the brand. Phrases like *protective instinct* don't just have a strong emotional resonance with women; they resonate strongly with men too. Rival's gender-specific thinking went out decades ago.

Holding Paula's gaze, I scraped together the tattered pieces of my conviction. As always, there was something in the way she looked at me that challenged me to be more than I knew myself to be. And that challenge was enough to make me stand a little taller and clear my throat loudly enough that everyone finally looked up.

"May I continue?"

There was a slight edge to my voice that probably shouldn't have been there, and I saw it register on Cosgrove's face. But why should any woman have to stand in front of a room and be condescended to? With Paula in my corner, the only thing I stood to lose was my own self-respect.

"How does this compare to the look and feel of your competitors' branding?" I asked Cosgrove specifically.

He looked at me as if I should know this.

I did know this.

"I guarantee you, no athletic wear company is doing *that*," he sneered.

"Exactly," I affirmed. And at the very same moment, Paula said, "That's the point."

The room went totally silent. Cosgrove met my direct gaze. If nothing else, I had his full attention.

§

Despite Paula's feverish support, the walk back to the office was excruciating. The four of us talked about the meeting, but honestly I had a hard time even pretending I could focus on the replay amid the mess in my head. I was devastated. I'd never had a professional embarrassment of that magnitude, and with Eric's and Wade's relative success, I felt *apart* from them. And criminally young. It made me want to crawl into a hole, or at least a cubicle, and stay there.

Which is where Paula finally found me again an hour or so later.

"You have no idea how good you are," she said with no preamble.

I looked up at her, my expression still a little wobbly. "Paula, my presentation fell completely flat. They hated it."

"You forget that I *approved* those designs. You did exactly what I wanted you to do, and I *love* the concept. And the execution. It was totally original."

A big part of me hung on every word she said. It was exactly what I needed to hear from someone like her, even if I hadn't realized *how much* I needed to hear it until just now. Still, the memory of Greg Cosgrove's condescending face rang like a gong through my head. It was hard to take much comfort with the memory so fresh in my mind.

"Selene," she said when I hadn't responded. "I put you on this because your work is unique. Your designs are exactly what they need, even if they don't recognize it. *I* recognize it and I'd put you up there again. But if you want to work with a national brand, you have to let the criticism roll off you. This is a tough business, and you can't be afraid of failing. At this point in your career, you should only be afraid of not maximizing your abilities, not having a broad enough view of what you're capable of, and not pushing yourself to take risks when it comes to your artistic vision. Do you understand?"

I wanted to. I really did. I had gone into this so hopeful and come out of it so shaken. I didn't want to feel that way. Work was my safe place right now, the only place in my life where normalcy existed.

I took a deep breath and searched her expression for the confidence I had lost. Finally, nodding, I let her know I was back in the game.

"Good. Now, you made several strong points today in your pitch," she told me. "Here's what they were . . ."

§

At some point during the afternoon, a text came through from Keir.

Thinking about getting a drink at The Arthouse in Mill Valley. The food is horrendous and the atmosphere is worse. Want to come?

His sales pitch was just terrible enough to make me consider it. I stared at my phone for a full minute, debating.

The truth is that my life had begun to assume a new shape, if not a routine. I was spending every Saturday and most Sundays at my parents' house. There was no question that I wanted to be there, to have as much time as I could with my dad and to help out as much as I could, but it was draining in more ways than one. Everything else in my life was on hold.

Friday nights were becoming a brief respite between the pressures of work and the intensity of family, when I simply opted for a quiet evening alone. I was fine with that; I didn't really have the energy to go out with friends or to be social. Most Fridays, the pull of my couch was strong, even if the prospect of it was, admittedly, a little lonely.

But today, after the day from hell, a stiff drink in a crappy bar sounded pretty damn near perfect. Further weighing in was the fact that of everyone I knew, Keir may have been the only person whose company I found easy. With him, there was no need to pretend or to explain. He made no comparisons between my old self and the person I was in this new circumstance. And he knew everything, so there wasn't anything I had to talk about or anything I had to hide.

Don't ever go into marketing. You stink, I replied. *Address, please.*

His response was quick. *How can you say that??? I designed my own logo!*

As I said . . .

WHAT??? That hurts me, Selene. I may cry.

You're a baby, I answered, smiling.

LOL. 103 Throckmorton. See you soon. I'll be the guy prostrate in the corner.

§

The Arthouse was a locals' bar. It was right downtown, but unless you were specifically looking for it, you might pass by it a hundred times before noticing. A faded blue awning over the door and a small neon Heineken sign in the window were about the only markers that would tell you you'd come to the right place.

Inside, it was a 1970s time warp. True to Keir's description, the decor was a questionable mix of brown paneling, and photos and posters that looked as though they hadn't been changed in decades. Colored Christmas lights were strung around and, given that it was September, probably stayed up all year long. The place was cozy and entirely unpretentious, despite the fact that Mill Valley—once a working-class suburb—was now very much gentrified. I could see why Keir liked this place. I liked it too. It was the sort of bar you could come to and hang out and just tell the world to shut its big mouth for a while.

The spring on the heavy wooden front door was tight, and before I was more than a couple steps inside, it slammed hard behind me. Keir looked up from where he sat on a stool at the bar.

It was always that first look of his that killed me. Unfiltered, it was like intensity and appetite combined in a way I'd never seen before on anyone. I couldn't say it was aimed at me specifically, but it definitely affected me. It felt like fire racing through my veins whenever he looked at me that way. Luckily, it only ever lasted a second before he blinked and something more benign replaced it.

Tonight that something was a broad, boyish grin that grew on his face as he rose from his stool, rocking that five-o'clock shadow and a pair of Levi's jeans like nobody's business. A forest-green sweater stretched across his chest.

It had been more than two weeks since he came to my house for dinner, and seeing him again caused a complicated ache to push through me. He had so quickly and unexpectedly become a friend in the most genuine sense. We talked on the phone often, and had forged a connection over our shared tragedy that I didn't have with anyone else.

But he was also like a warm chocolate brownie being waved under my nose.

I wanted to say I didn't notice how tempting he was. But the truth is, I did really, really love brownies . . .

"Straight from work?" He gave my lavender silk blouse and formfitting skirt an approving glance.

"I didn't feel like going home first."

"Well, lucky for me, then." A smile lingered in his expression.

"Why is that?" I asked, returning the look

He nodded to my outfit. "You just . . . look amazing."

My smile became a full-fledged blush. "So do you."

This was what most people would call flirting.

But the toughest thing about Keir was that he was flirtatious by nature so it was hard to tell when he was just being himself and when there was more behind it. And I wasn't unaware that misreading that difference could make things between us super awkward, superfast.

He rescued the moment by cracking a joke as I settled on the stool to his left.

"So I have no future in marketing, that's what you're telling me?" He was adorable when he was pretending to be offended.

"You know I love your logo."

I picked up his beer, taking a long sip from the bottle and allowing the contents to balloon my cheeks. He shook his head, smiling. He had turned his body to face me, with his feet on the rungs of the stool and his knees spread apart. He was giving me his full attention, as he so often did, and it warmed a little spot inside.

"How'd your presentation go today?"

"Eh," I said after a hefty swallow, "don't ask."

"Why? What happened?"

"Honestly, it's too depressing to relive."

Keir's teeth grazed his lower lip as he seemed to consider this. "Art!" he called to the bartender. "Can we get this girl a real drink?" Then he turned back to me with that easy calm I wished I could bottle and carry around with me all the time. "Nope. I'm going to need the whole story."

§

The bar's owner, Art Whittle, was an older man, heavyset and balding, with pink cheeks and kind, blue eyes. There was clearly some history between him and Keir, but neither offered it up right away.

"Welcome to The Arthouse," he said to me with a smile. Then turning to Keir, he added, "How do you two know each other?"

"Selene rear-ended my truck so she could meet me. True story."

"Not actually a true story," I interjected.

"*And*"—Keir said in a behind-the-hand remark—"she's the best graphic designer you'll ever meet. Crazy talented—but a *massive* ego."

"You're high," I laughed, batting his hand down. "But I'll still let you buy me a drink because I've had a really shitty day." It's funny that it didn't feel quite so shitty just then.

I turned to Art, feeling the warmth of Keir's attention on the side of my face. "It's nice to meet you, by the way."

Art smiled kindly, and his handshake was firm and meaty. "Likewise." Then his eyes flashed briefly to Keir, who, honest to God, did seem so happy to have me there. "What can I get you?" he asked me.

"Whatever he's having."

"Oh, I think we can do better than that for a woman who's had a really shitty day."

He stepped away, and when he returned, he had a beautiful crystal decanter in his hand. Someone needed to tell this man that shitty days meant *cheap* booze and lots of it.

That someone was not going to be me.

He removed three glasses from under the bar and poured a healthy round into each glass. Then he pushed one in front of each of us.

Keir was the first to pick his up, lifting it to his mouth to take a sip. When he swallowed, his upper lip curled as the liquid went down. "Scotch," he told me with a brief glance. But there was something about the movement of his throat that was so distracting I couldn't drag my eyes away. While he set his glass down, I studied the angles of his cheekbones, his Adam's apple, and the ropy contours of his neck. They were all so perfectly sculpted and beautiful that I had an urge to run my fingers over them, to record with my touch the way he looked in this exact moment.

"Not just scotch," Art said, pulling my attention away. "Macallan 25. The good stuff. I keep it for special occasions *and* shitty days."

He nodded to my glass with a questioning lift of the brow, but his small smile told me that he knew I hadn't been thinking about the scotch. I probably should have; my first sips went down all too easily and made my vocal chords feel mildly paralyzed.

Still, without a word, I let Art tip the decanter over my glass again, filling a little higher than he had the first. He did the same for Keir. Then he raised his own glass, turning it so the light illuminated the amber color to a warm caramel hue, and drained it in one swallow.

"I'll leave you two alone," he said to Keir with a wink. "Let me know if you need anything."

Art walked away, and I turned to Keir, clearing my throat. "How do you know him?"

"He's my godfather."

"*What?* When were you going to tell me that?"

"Just did. Why?" he added devilishly. "Nervous you didn't make a good first impression on my only remaining family?"

"I hate you."

He grinned. "You wish that were true."

The look he gave me just then was so *knowing*. Like in that exact moment, he could see I was admiring the way the colored Christmas lights were playing off his face and his dark, shiny hair.

Because, I mean, of course I liked him. I just rarely let myself think about how *much* I liked him. Or maybe, more accurately, *how* I liked him. He was gorgeous and funny and sweet, so duh, but it was weird between us too. Ever since he found out about my dad, he was careful with me in a way he hadn't been before. I loved his friendship, of course, and he was quickly becoming one of my very favorite people. But that didn't seem to stop me from wanting to run my hands up into his hair and make out with him until my lips were raw from the scrape of that stubble.

"Feeling good?"

"Why do you ask?"

Eyes glistening, he reached out to touch my cheek. "You're a little pink."

"Seriously?"

Did I actually look drunk?

"Yeah, but I like it." He held my gaze for what felt like the most loaded seconds in the history of time and then picked up the bottle of beer in front of him, tilting it toward his mouth. I could have sworn he was pointing to the exact body part I most wanted to lick.

For the good of our friendship, I had to look away. "I think I am a little buzzed," I said, making a quick mental calculation of my drunkenness. The alcohol was settling in my belly and triggering a quiet hum in my limbs.

"You think?" He grinned, before taking a pull from his beer. "But don't worry, you're in good hands."

"Okay, then," I said with a nod. I leaned back a little on my barstool and glanced around the place. "Because I think this is exactly what I needed tonight. I can't even explain my life right now."

Art came by and refilled us again as I recounted my horrific meeting, and Keir told me he was never, ever, ever going to buy another piece of Rival gear as long as he lived. And he said a few bad words and pushed his fingers through mine when I got to the part about the *serious submission*, and it was adorable the way his face scrunched up as he listened. He was a really good listener.

I think Art refilled us a couple of times more. I lost track.

Regardless, I was feeling much better than I had when I walked in. I loved this place. In here, it felt like the rest of the world had been put on mute.

"So I have some news," Keir announced after we'd finished with the topic of my meeting.

"What news?"

"I may get my restaurant soon."

I don't know what I was expecting, but my synapses had to quickly rearrange themselves for that one. "A restaurant? I didn't even know you wanted to have a restaurant."

He tilted his head back and forth like it wasn't a big deal, but the way his face lit up at the prospect said something else entirely. "Yeah, pretty much since forever. We'll still do the catering and food trucks," he added as a side note. "This would just be the next phase in our growth."

"You're kidding?" I was still processing this when he shook his head and went on.

"There's this location I've been watching for a while—this little brick building right near Pike Place Market. You can't believe how cool it is." He leaned in very close to show me a picture on his phone, close enough that our shoulders brushed lightly and I could study the long, dark lashes that framed his expressive eyes as he glanced down at the device in his hand. "It sits right on the corner of a walking street."

He blinked over to me to see if I was following, and I looked down at the screen. He was right—the place was cool. It had kind of a New Orleans–style look—wrought iron carriage lights and big picture windows on all sides. It seemed to be empty at the moment, but I could imagine a Blaze sign out front with a matching awning to add character.

"It's beautiful. Can you lease the space?"

"Actually, I want to buy the building," he said, sitting back a little now. "I can rent out the upper floors to offset the purchase price. The only problem is, it's not actually for sale.

"But," he continued with a giant smile on his face, "a realtor buddy of mine heard today that the owners might be willing to consider an offer. We're going to approach them and see what they say."

"Wow. I had no idea. I'm so excited for you."

"Yeah," he answered in his understated way. "It would be . . ." He paused, shaking his head, and I lost him for a moment in thought. "See the reason so many restaurants fail is that they're undercapitalized to begin with. And it takes a long time to build a name and a reputation. But I don't have either of those issues. I've *got* the name and the reputation. And the catering business has strong cash flow that we can leverage as we build up the restaurant's clientele. Meanwhile, the proceeds from my dad's house will offset a good portion of the cost of the new building."

This was a side of him I'd never seen. I suspected from things he'd said that Blaze was a successful business, but I'd never heard him talk about it in this way. And I'd never seen him quite so passionate about anything as he seemed to be about this restaurant. It was a big deal for him. He was practically glowing with excitement.

"So what kind of restaurant would it be?"

"Similar to what I'm doing now, and family oriented. Argentinian cooking is all about family and social gathering. That's why I fell in love with it in the first place." There was a deep reverence in his voice that struck me. "It's important to me that it feels comfortable and . . . nourishing, if that makes any sense."

"It does," I told him sincerely. Then something occurred to me. "You know Starbucks?"

"Yes, I think I've heard of it."

"You're a smart-ass."

"You're drunk." He laughed.

"If I am, it's your fault. You keep encouraging Art."

"I accept that."

"Anyway," I continued, with a little more difficulty than I would have cared to admit. "What I mean is, the Starbucks *brand* is built around this idea of a *third place.* It's basically that home is our first place, and work is our second place. But between these two, we need a third place—somewhere to recharge with conversation and community. What you're describing sounds kind of like that to me."

"Yeah," he said, and seemed genuinely moved that I understood his intention for the restaurant. "That's exactly the feeling I'm going for."

I smiled. "I think it will be amazing."

He continued to study me, his expression slipping just a little. Then he took my hand in his, running his thumb over the ridges of my knuckles.

"Would you come?"

It was a question that hung between us, for complex reasons. With it came the mutual acknowledgment that the bond we were forging was not quite disposable for either of us. Yet it was too premature to call it lasting. That very question held the realization that he was, in fact, leaving soon. And more than that—I'd miss him when he did. Perhaps that was the moment he realized he would miss me too. His searching eyes told me so.

"Of course I'll come."

A soft expression of joyful relief cascaded across his face. He smiled, just about to say something, when Art called from across the bar.

"Are you going to dance with that beautiful woman, or do you need an old man to show you how it's done?"

"By god, you're right," Keir declared, slapping his hand on the bar. He drained his glass and rose from his stool, holding his palm out to me. "Let's dance."

§

The Arthouse didn't exactly have a dance floor; it was more like a little spot in the back corner where a few tables had been pushed aside to make just enough room for this purpose. Keir led me by the hand to an old jukebox against the wall, pulling some coins from his pocket and making his selections. Almost immediately, the whistle of a harmonica rang through the speakers overhead, and Bruce Springsteen's "Thunder Road" began to play.

When Keir turned to face me, there was a soft, sweet smile on his face. He immediately pulled me in, flush against him, cupping one of my hands to his chest and sliding his other arm neatly around my waist.

"Is this okay?" he asked.

"Of course." Better than okay.

It seemed like the alcohol was driving all my nerve endings to converge in a single spot. I became acutely aware of his fingers at my spine, pressing as he leaned in to rest his cheek to mine. This was a new intimacy for us, being close enough to feel the rasp of his scruff on my face and to breathe in the masculine scent of his skin. He always smelled like fresh laundry.

"This is nice," he said at my ear as we moved together in small shifting steps. "I haven't danced like this in ages."

Outside, life was complicated and messy. But here, within the four walls of The Arthouse, with its Christmas lights and its Springsteen and its tiny dance floor, I was enjoying myself tremendously. I hadn't felt that way in weeks.

And Keir was humming. I didn't realize it at first—it was so quiet—but, slumping into him a little, I began to notice a low rumble, like a vibration, where my hand was clutched to his chest.

I didn't need to see his face to know he was feeling happy too.

§

Midway through the song, the tempo picked up, and his steps became more playful and harder to follow, only underscoring the fact that I am *not* a dancer.

Enough about that.

"How much do you *weigh*, Georgiou?"

"*What?*" Planting my feet, I glared up at him. "You don't ask a woman that! It's very rude." I smacked him on the arm, but he just grinned from ear to ear, not at all rebuked.

"It's a fair question when that woman is stomping around, crushing my feet." The grin widened substantially. "It's like dancing with Mr. Snuffleupagus."

I started to laugh—which was never a ladylike affair for me—and, horrifyingly, a very indelicate snort popped out. Keir's eyes widened in a greatly exaggerated look of shock that made me laugh even harder. He absolutely loved to play to an audience, and my reactions were only encouraging him.

"Or maybe Miss *Piggy*," he added with emphasis. "That's what I'm going to call you from now on. Piggy."

"You are *not* going to call me Piggy!" I could barely get the last word out. I was laughing so hard I snorted again.

"Oh, I am, Piggy," he said. "I am, for sure."

I loved/hated him in that moment. Mostly loved. And I was laughing too hard to argue with him effectively, so I answered his insult with a burp.

Keir, of course, thought this was *uproariously* funny. His laughter became so contagious that for a full minute, we were both bent over and unable to speak.

Finally, still smiling, he gathered me in his arms again.

"You're the worst," I told him, grinning. I couldn't remember the last time I had enjoyed myself like this.

"And *you*," he said with genuine fondness, "would be an upgrade to any man. Me, especially. Even with all your snorting."

He was looking down at me over those picture-perfect features: the impossibly long lashes that framed his intelligent, inquisitive brown eyes; the elegantly curved lips; the high cheekbones and the strong jawline. His face was drenched in warmth and affection. It was a look that said no matter what I did—no matter how he might tease me—Keir *actually* saw only the best in me. He only ever saw me in exactly the way I'd want him to.

I let my hand drift into the hair at the back of his neck and watched him blink slow and heavy with my touch. The softness in his face and the way his eyes moved around the room and then back to focus on me were his only tells that the scotch was affecting us both in similar ways.

I laid my head against his shoulder in a moment of unspoiled satisfaction and contentment. Like the whole world just breathed out a sigh. Keir began humming again. I could feel the vibration under my cheek.

"Where did you learn to dance?" I asked.

I felt his shoulders lift and then fall again. "Nowhere. You have to be light on your feet for hockey. Dancing's not that different."

"It's pretty different," I said, pulling back.

Conceding, he nodded side to side. "I guess at some point I figured out that girls love to dance. So if you had a few moves and a little bit of courage, you might score a kiss on the dance floor."

"Is that so, Casanova?"

"That is so." He laughed, a sound so low and rough it felt like a physical pleasure on every part of my body where we touched.

"Enough courage to score a kiss with me?"

It took about two horrifying seconds before my brain realized what my mouth had just done.

It took about two seconds longer for Keir, who suddenly went still in my arms. His eyes flashed to mine like he wasn't sure he'd heard me right. Or like his own brain was still catching up. Then his mouth opened a little, but no words came out, and his pulse seemed to take off in his neck. In the space of a single heartbeat, his face changed entirely. It was the first time I'd ever seen him without words.

After what felt like the world's most awkwardly pregnant pause, he cleared his throat.

"Well, I mean . . . if I hadn't already pledged myself to low-class, easy girls . . ."

It was an impressive attempt at deflection but it landed with a thud, and he knew it. One side of his mouth pulled up in a half-hearted smile that even he didn't seem to find convincing.

Because we both knew this train of ours was blowing right through Placating Humor Town and barreling straight toward Drunk Admission City. No way to turn back now.

The honest-to-god truth was, I hadn't actually intended to ambush him; it just sort of came out that way. Still, there was no doubt we'd been skirting this issue for weeks. He was playful and flirtatious, often openly admiring, yet he'd never actually crossed that line.

To me, it seemed like every male-female friendship reaches this crossroad at some point. For some, it happens right away and needs no discussion. For others, it takes a while longer and requires some sort of catalyst. But eventually, there comes a point when you have to declare yourself. Are you going to be just friends forever? Or is there the possibility of more?

Whether it was a good thing or a bad thing that we were both drunk for this conversation had yet to be seen.

Because, of course, admissions changed things. And yes, there was a little sober part of my brain that was setting off alarm bells—screaming *Abort! Abort!* But the larger part wasn't listening. That part wanted an answer.

Tellingly, Keir didn't say anything more but focused on the bar behind me with considerable absorption. All the while, thoughts seemed to be ping-ponging around in his brain.

Even more striking, there was a baldness in his expression when he finally did meet my gaze again that I'd never seen. Suddenly, it was obvious to me in a way it hadn't been before just how *much* he wanted to kiss me, and how very close to the surface that desire truly was. His jaw was a little slack, and his eyes dropped to my mouth, as if there was nothing in the world he wanted more in that exact moment than to taste it.

But there were boundaries there, too—firm ones I did not yet understand. Boundaries that kept him from acting on his impulse. In his face, the struggle between the two was obvious, even by the most casual observation.

"What kind of an asshole would hit on a girl who's grieving?" he said directly this time, all humor gone.

"You're grieving too."

"Yet another very good reason for me to behave." God, we were a pair.

We had stopped dancing entirely and now stood staring at each other in mutual bewilderment. My hammering pulse felt louder than the music around us. I looked away to where people were drinking and talking, and wondered if the striking shift in the air between us was as apparent to others as it felt to me.

Finally, I shook my head no in response to his reasoning and focused stubbornly on my hands at his chest. His heart thundered beneath them. We had long since passed the point that anything happening between us could accurately be considered a come-on.

"I don't believe that's the whole story."

He exhaled audibly, and his body went stiff. I didn't have to see his face to know he was not enjoying this conversation, and I'm sure he thought I lacked perception for forcing it like I was.

"Would you believe that I'm leaving soon and I don't want to start something I can't finish?"

I could feel the weight of his stare but dodged it until, finally, his hand touched my face. He lifted my chin upward so I could no longer avoid him. His eyes were intent on mine. Not angry, not mocking. Waiting.

I let several seconds go by, just absorbing that look and reluctantly considering his question.

I did, in fact, understand that Keir was at a point in his life where all he wanted to do was to look forward—to get back to his life and to heal. He was shedding his entanglements in San Francisco, one by one, as quickly as he could. Once his father's estate was settled and the house was on the market, he'd have no reason to return to the Bay Area or to take on the burden of a long-distance relationship, especially with someone he considered to be in a vulnerable place.

And yes, I did believe that in these circumstances Keir would defer to the better angels of his nature and let his conduct be guided by nobler principles than lust alone. But there was more to it than that. I knew it, even if he wasn't going to say it.

"If you're trying to protect me from some future hurt, I don't want that protection. I can't even think about the future right now. And I don't need to."

"Selene—"

"No," I insisted, cutting him off.

The future wasn't my friend. In the future, and probably a not-so-distant one, someone I loved most in the world—the bedrock of my family—would be conspicuously, brutally absent. I wasn't going there in my head. Today—*this* day—was all I could count on. Everything else was uninsured. And *this* day, I wanted Keir—no matter the consequences later. In fact, I don't think I'd ever wanted anything more than I wanted his kiss. It was nearly painful.

The scotch had taken its full effect, providing courage and, perhaps, poor counsel to push him like I was. Piece by piece, I knew I was wearing him down and testing his resolve. I could see the riotous effect our conversation was having. If I had ever questioned his desire for me, that question had been answered definitively. The searing look on his face made no attempt to conceal it.

"You want this, Keir. I know you do. I can see it."

"You're killing me," he said softly, his voice now fully baring his weakness. He seemed to allow himself three seconds to look again at my mouth before pulling his gaze up to mine. "Are you trying to?"

In those dark, soulful eyes was a current of vulnerability. I kissed my finger and pressed it gently to his lips. They were soft and firm, and I felt a little puff of air where his breath rushed over them. He closed his eyes, simultaneously relishing my touch and fighting his desire for it.

"Yes," I whispered honestly. I couldn't help it. The words were just falling out of my mouth now without any consideration for the consequences they held.

He exhaled sharply again, leaning his forehead to mine. I could feel his uncertainty in the stiff shape of his hand on my back. "Selene," he whispered, "I don't want to be the guy who disappoints you."

"Then kiss me for real and I won't be disappointed."

He hesitated for just a second more before there came a rumbling sound from his throat, a sound filled with defeat and the death of all good intentions. Pushing forward, he let his hands twist into my hair, and his mouth was on mine.

I could feel the strength of his broad shoulders, now under my palms, then felt them give way, their powerful resolve melting as his lips softened to me. In a release of breath, he crushed my body to his so tightly I felt my own breath leave. Then his mouth began to move over mine—sucking, pushing my lips apart as his fists tightened in my hair. His tongue slid inside, rolling against mine, deepening an already drowning kiss, and relentlessly taking what he needed. He was impatient. Ravenous. Fierce, like his starving body demanded it. Like mine did.

In his arms, I felt light-headed and reckless. The sharp stubble on his upper lip and chin, the velvet of his tongue stroking mine, the taste of alcohol on his lips—all of it filled me with a longing so enormous and disorienting that I could not tell if we were swaying together again, or even if my feet were on the ground. Head swirling, I took hold of fistfuls of his sweater, needing to steady myself against the intoxication of that kiss.

But I couldn't. My heart was pounding so hard it no longer felt like a safe rhythm.

If he let go, I knew I would be the one to crumble. There was the irony. And the justice, I suppose.

Safe or not, I would have kissed him like that all night, just like that, until we'd devoured each other's breath completely. But at some point, we both seemed to remember where we were. We separated, heads bent together, consuming oxygen in large, unsteady gulps. I had the most bizarre sense of returning to consciousness, returning to my body after a kiss that changed us in ways I didn't yet know.

I touched my tingling lips. I could still feel him on my mouth.

We'd always had this tension between us, and now we could be honest about that, but the feverish quality of our physical connection—that all-consuming, now-or-never type of impulse— felt both overwhelmingly tempting and frighteningly dangerous. Maybe he had known that all along.

"Keir," I whispered. I didn't know what I wanted to say, and he made no move at all, stood rocklike, rooted in his own emotions. But the hammering of his heart under my hands told me he was at as much of a loss as I. A small silence caught us—eyes closed, flushed, breath fast and entangled.

"Neither of us can drive," he said finally. "My place is closer— just come home with me and we'll figure this out." I nodded, intoxicated, yes, but far more so by him than the scotch. "But, Selene," he added with an intent I know he truly wanted to feel, "we've both had too much to drink. Nothing more happens tonight."

We had crossed many lines in the boundaries he'd drawn for himself, but he wouldn't cross that one. On that one point, he was primally unmovable. And suddenly unsure of what I had just unleashed into our little world of two, I was obliged to respect it.

Keir took my hand and led me off the dance floor. Nothing remained but a couple of hastily moved chairs to mark the puddle of stubborn conviction that had been left behind there.

Chapter 8

Keir

I made no claims on sainthood. On plenty of occasions, I've taken pleasure where I found it, at times with appalling carelessness. And I certainly can't deny that a large part of me wanted to take it to the limit of where all this was heading with Selene. Just go hard, satisfy one need, and not think about anything else.

Another side of me, though, could not stand the thought of parting with her on bad terms. I wasn't a long-distance-relationship kind of guy. I knew that about myself. In fact, with everything going on in my life and the way my head had gotten so messed up over my dad's death, I wasn't even sure I was a *relationship* kind of guy. Plus, she was in a tough place, and I would loathe any feeling of having taken advantage of her. It just felt inevitable that if anything more happened between Selene and me, it would only result in my losing esteem in her eyes. I never wanted to see what that looked like.

But unfortunately, as I'd so easily discovered, these two selves of mine, though polar opposites, were only a hair's width apart, and one was dangerously susceptible to her suggestion.

Though I wanted to punch myself in the face for it, I knew my reasoning for keeping things on a platonic level was entirely sound.

But it wasn't enough that I should decide in the sober light of day that what happened last night couldn't happen again. I realized I needed the reassurance of Selene's conviction too. Because although I'd spent the entire night on the couch telling myself otherwise, I suspected that the taste of her full, heavy lips, and the vivid memory it stirred in every part of my body, would stay with me for a very, very long time.

Chapter 9

Selene

I woke to the insult of a pounding headache and a dry mouth. It must have been about six thirty in the morning, but the shutters on Keir's bedroom window were closed tight, and the tiny bit of light that pushed through the cracks cast the room in a soft, gray hue. The house was still silent. I pulled the navy-blue comforter up tighter around me and readjusted the pillow beneath my cheek.

Nope. No more of that. That was more movement than my protesting head could tolerate.

What had I done to myself last night?

Last night.

Oh, god.

That kiss.

A flood of rapid-fire images washed over my fuzzy brain, bringing a surge of heart-pounding clarity: the way it seemed to happen so fast—one second he was staring at my face and the next second his mouth was on mine, warm and smooth and feeling so good. Better than anything. The way his lips parted, and I tasted the first tentative sweep of his tongue that had hints of scotch and beer. And how my brain melted into a messy pile when he wrapped his arms around me, pulling me tightly into every hard angle of his body.

I groaned into my pillow and glanced groggily around the room, taking care to open only one eye at a time. I hadn't actually been to Keir's house before and didn't have a chance to look around much when he shuffled me off to bed with a pair of sweatpants and a T-shirt. But awake now, I could take it in, to the extent a hangover would allow.

His childhood bedroom looked as though it hadn't changed much through the decades. The tan carpeting was worn, and he had a matching set of brown composite-wood furniture, complete with a couple of dressers, and a desk with a hutch. Some of the drawers no longer closed straight, and I could see the outlines of adhesive, where stickers had been haphazardly removed. Up high on the cream-colored walls, there were thumbtacks holding only the remaining corners of posters that once hung there, as if they'd been yanked down by an impatient teenager.

There was very little in terms of knickknacks on the shelves of the hutch—a dictionary and some books, a few hockey trophies, a scary-looking bobblehead, Keir's high school diploma, and a couple of photographs of him with friends. Still, I had a strong sense of the history in this room—that despite its now somewhat sparse feel, a lot of living had occurred here. You could almost hear the echoes of it through the thin veil of time. I closed my eyes and listened, until sleep silenced the effort with whatever dreams it would.

§

The room was bright with full morning light when I opened my eyes again. Like a magnet, my thoughts immediately returned to our kiss. I couldn't stop thinking about it. In fact, I was a little mad at myself that I hadn't been clearheaded enough to catalog every detail. But I remembered a lot of them: the little guttural noises he made that sounded like a combination of relief and pent-up frustration; the way his hands went to my face, restless and hungry to trace every line; the way his whiskers on my neck made my whole body feel like it was on fire, burning from the inside out.

Was it just me? Because the truth was, no one had ever kissed me like that before. I had no idea if there was some special chemistry between us or if he was just *that good* of a kisser.

I kind of wanted to know.

I kind of didn't.

If this was just a normal thing for him—

No, I definitely didn't want to know.

I could hear him now in the kitchen and could smell bacon cooking on the stove. My stomach wobbled. I knew for a fact I was not as good at schooling my emotions as he was, so a huge chickenshit part of me wanted to crawl out the bedroom window and escape the extremely awkward *we-need-to-talk* postdrunken make-out ritual that would no doubt accompany the amazing breakfast he was probably serving up. The one I would be too twisted up inside to actually enjoy. I could absolutely picture how this would go:

So about last night, he would start, like of course we would be on the same page with this.

Yeah, about last night, I would echo, laughing it off. *We were both pretty drunk.*

God, I know. Can you believe what we did?

Hilarious!

Soooo hilarious!

The problem with Keir was that I liked him, and—news flash— I also *liked* him. At the moment, those two things seemed very much at odds. I could still feel his mouth on mine, and his laughter reverberating in the space between us just before all the madness started. And I wasn't sure I could keep all that from my face as we went back to our *just friends* routine. We had kissed over and over for what felt like an eternity. It wasn't like *Oops, we accidentally sucked each other's face for a second. How'd that happen?*

There were fast ones and messy ones and slow, deep ones that felt like sex. Like really, really *great* sex. We kissed until we finally both realized how this might look to those around us. To his *godfather*. Ugh.

Still, I couldn't help replaying that kiss like a broken record in my head. All except for the end when he dropped my hand to call us an Uber and then didn't touch me again for the rest of the night—not in the car, not as we walked into his house, not as we said our goodnights.

Did I really need any more explanation of what was going on in his head than that?

I was drowning in these dueling reactions: on one hand, giddy from what we had done and the way he looked at me, and on the other, terrified that one moment of recklessness would make everything between us forever awkward and uncomfortable.

I couldn't let that happen. Yes, he was a warm brownie, for sure, but his friendship was too important to me. It was such an anchor in a life that didn't even feel like my own sometimes, with my dad and my job and the way I had drifted from my normal routines. Every day felt like more than I could handle—that is, until I saw him or heard his voice, and it grounded me. I didn't want anything to change that. Keir was my good place. My shelter.

Summoning my resolve, I found my big-girl pants, along with a comb, a toothbrush, and a little soap and water, and opened the door to face the music like a bona fide adult.

"Morning," I said, walking into the kitchen. I had that hollow, slightly shaky hangover thing going on, and I was pretty sure I still smelled like a bar.

Keir, on the other hand, looked freshly showered and not at all like the mess I felt like in my head. I wondered what was going through his mind. Was *he* replaying last night, or was he just thinking about his hangover? I could never tell with him.

He was standing next to the cooktop, keeping an eye on a frying pan while he sliced fresh strawberries and bananas on a cutting board to the right.

"Hey, how are you feeling? Did you see the aspirin I left for you?"

"I did, thanks," I told him. "Don't ever let me do that again, by the way."

Keir smiled sympathetically. "You and me both. Have a seat. You can just move those papers out of the way."

So about last night.

Yeah, about last night. We were both pretty drunk.

God, I know. Can you believe what we did?

Hilarious!

Soooo hilarious!

I took a place at the table and pushed a stack of pages aside. On the top of the pile was a real estate contract for the sale of the house. Beside it was a shiny black folder holding the business card of an agent, Rona Dennis.

"You found someone you like?"

"I think so," he said with his back turned. He had removed the bacon from the pan and set it on paper towels alongside the cooktop. In a metal mixing bowl, he was stirring batter vigorously with a whisk. "The market is pretty good right now. Rona thinks she can sell the place quickly, but I need to do a bunch of work on it first."

I nodded and glanced around. The house was in a very desirable location, but he was right, it needed a lot of work. The kitchen, in particular, looked as though it probably hadn't been updated in years—from the Formica table and vinyl padded chairs, to the mustard-colored appliances and linoleum flooring. It was all very functional and practical, without any extravagance or hint of a female influence. Very much a home of men. But a home, nonetheless. Keir's growth through the years had been penciled on the doorframe, and there were magnets on the refrigerator commemorating some of the places he and his father had been. There was a calendar on the wall that struck me as a little eerie—maybe because, for its owner, there were no future dates to mark.

In some ways, Keir's father was still so unmistakably present in this house. It felt as though he might walk through the door at any time—as though the house had absorbed the memories made here and kept them like an unspent aura.

But in other ways, it felt like something great and beautiful and timeless and confounding had just disappeared, leaving a void that time would not fill. Nothing would fill.

So the house just waited.

As I sat at the table on a creaky chair, it nearly killed me to think of Keir coming home here, alone each night, living among the ghosts and the shadows. The silence. No wonder he was anxious to get back to his life in Seattle.

I watched him cook and my heart broke for him. Utterly. All thoughts of my own self-indulgent obsession with our silly, drunken kiss seemed incredibly juvenile.

"When will you list it?"

"Within a month, probably. Once it's on the market, I'll be able to go home." He turned to face me, leaning back against the counter with a spatula in his hand. "Selene, that's why I can't . . ."

He let the thought trail off.

Oh god, here we go.

In the space of his delay, I begged myself to go back in time to last night and never have started this.

"I know . . ." I said, filling in the silence but not completing the thought either. The truth was that most of what we might've wanted to say—the important things that could've touched some of the rawness inside both of us—was better off left in the silence between words. Our kiss was a curiosity, nothing more.

"It's not a question of attraction," he continued after a long, awkward pause.

"I know."

"Do you?" He stared at me so intently, eyes roaming over my face, that I had to look away.

"Yes, of course. You don't have to—"

"What happened last night wasn't just because of the alcohol. And it wasn't just because . . ." His eyes dropped away and he let out a little frustrated sound like he wasn't sure he should say what he wanted to. "It wasn't just because you're—stunning."

I didn't miss the way he blushed, and under any other circumstances, that might have made my entire week. But just now, it was hard to take any pleasure in it.

I found myself nodding like Keir's scary bobblehead, honestly hoping we could just drop this whole subject. I wasn't embarrassed by what he was saying; I was ashamed because I had pushed him into a situation he obviously didn't want. Now sober, sitting in this lonely kitchen, I realized how selfish it was. My recklessness had only compounded the painful things he was already dealing with and made him feel—wrongly—like he had something to apologize for.

"I wanted you to know—"

"Keir, honestly, you don't have to explain."

"No, I do," he insisted. "What I'm trying to say to you is that I think you're—god, you're so amazing, Selene. And I don't want to lose you on account of my own limitations—because *I'm* not well suited for a long-distance relationship. And I just think—I think there's a better chance of being able to stay in each other's lives if we try it just as friends."

His explanation came out so quickly that I realized he'd probably had these words in his head, practiced them over and over, all night long. Or maybe longer. And I came to understand as I watched him struggle with this whole discussion that I sincerely just wanted Keir to be happy. He was a really good person, and he truly deserved it.

"I'm sure you're right," I said in as assuring a manner as I could manage. I was staring at his chin and finally forced my eyes to his so he could see in my face that I meant it.

I did mean it. Keir's friendship wasn't some consolation prize; it was an incredible gift. He was thoughtful and funny and sweet. He understood me in a way no guy friend or boyfriend ever had before. He never minded when I talked his ear off about a new font I'd discovered, or when a quiet mood struck me and we just hung out together without talking at all. And though he insisted on demonstrating the difference between a vine-ripened vegetable and a store-ripened one in hopes that I might someday become more discerning, he never judged me when I failed the taste test and picked the store-ripened one. He never judged me for anything. And he was incredibly generous with his time and attention.

His friendship meant everything to me.

But a heavy weight settled on the room, and I looked away. I could feel him watching me, until finally he turned around to face the stove. I hated this so much. This wasn't us.

"So what are you doing this weekend?" I asked him with false brightness. I was desperate to clear the air between us.

"Nothing exciting." He picked up a bowl and poured batter into a waffle iron. "I have to take apart a rusty shed in the backyard and haul it away. And then if I have time, I should get to work on fixing the back fence. It needs all new posts, and most of the slats are rotted. How about you?"

I took a deep breath, thinking if we could just stay on neutral ground like this, maybe we could put the awkwardness behind us.

"Going over to see my dad. That's pretty much it these days."

Keir was about to throw some fresh fruit into a pan with butter and cinnamon sugar when he stopped. He had become pretty good at reading the nuances of my voice and now turned back over his shoulder.

"How is he?"

The tears welled up in my eyes but didn't fall. I shook my head.

"Not good. Worse every week."

There was always a part of me inclined to hold back the details of my dad's illness because Keir's own experience was so fresh; he didn't need a further reminder. But he wouldn't have it. He set down the spoon he was holding and came to the table, picking up my hand. His instincts with me were always so tender.

"Tell me."

"He fell a couple of times this week. He's pretty much wheelchair-bound now. And frailer every time I see him."

"It happens fast," Keir said squeezing my hand. "Do you want me to tell you that? Maybe you'd rather I didn't."

"No, I do," I insisted tearfully. "No one ever tells us the truth. No one ever just says, *He probably has a month left.* They always give us these ranges and tell us about this person or that person who lived two years or whatever. I just wish someone would be honest."

That was one of the things I appreciated most about Keir. From the very beginning, he never gave me the old *if anyone can beat it, he can* routine. Because we both knew that he wasn't going to beat it; Keir never tried to pretend otherwise.

As if hearing my thoughts, his brow furrowed. "In my experience," he began carefully, "right now . . . if you ever feel like you just want to talk to your dad—to hear his voice—you should pick up the phone and call him. Because there will come a time when you can't. And don't worry that it may not be a good time for him, or that he may not be feeling well. Just do it. He won't answer if he doesn't feel up to talking."

I nodded, fighting for composure. Keir was sympathetic to the effect his words were having, and the implications they held, but he continued anyway.

"And do something for me. When you see your dad today, make sure you really make eye contact, that you really look at him when you talk to him. And don't forget to touch him. Hold his hand or touch his arm. It'll be comforting to both of you."

It's hard to describe what it felt like to hear those words. For all my life, I may never be more indebted to anyone for providing that simple guidance—guidance that would allow me to make the very most of a time in which there were no do-overs. I didn't know what providence it was that had brought this man into my life, but I was more grateful than I could ever say for his compassion and understanding.

"Sometimes—" I stopped. Words rose in my throat but I couldn't push them past my lips. There were things you felt but maybe you should never say out loud. Or perhaps, if you're lucky, you have one person you can say them to who wouldn't think worse of you for it. "Sometimes I dread going," I admitted in a rush. "I honestly do, Keir. I know that's terrible."

I had dropped my gaze, ashamed to give voice to my failings. But when I looked back up, Keir's eyes were soft on mine. He never judged. He just observed in his own thoughtful way and breathed a sigh.

"I hate seeing him like this. And I'm scared that I can't be what he needs me to be."

"Selene, all you need to be is *there*."

A small smile came gratefully as I looked at his face—that

beautiful face with the unquiet but infinitely compassionate eyes.

"Somehow when you say that, I believe you. But I never feel that way when I'm driving over."

"Then take me with you. I can be your courage."

"You'd come?" I was sure I'd misunderstood his offer. Maybe he meant like . . . in spirit.

"Why wouldn't I? As long as your dad is okay with it."

No, he meant for real.

And as I studied him, I wanted to say, *Why wouldn't you?* Because you just lost your own dad to cancer. Because being around sick people is hard. Because it takes someone incredibly special to willingly put himself in the middle of a heartbreaking and traumatic situation.

"But you don't even know my dad."

"I'd come for you."

Did he even know how much I wanted that? But Keir's heart was just too big sometimes; he always felt first and thought second. I couldn't take him up on it; it was too much to ask. Sitting in his kitchen I had a strong sense for what had happened here. What he'd been through here. In this room, the telltale signs of prolonged illness were no longer present—the medicine bottles and the sticky notes and the unending the stacks of paper—Keir had cleared all that away. But the reverberations of what had transpired in this kitchen were very much present. I could almost hear the hard conversations and the harder realities that had been faced. The suffering and the loneliness. The agony for a fixer who was powerless to fix what he cared about most in the world. It was all so close at hand.

Keir had come into my life exactly when I had needed him and had given generously and unselfishly of himself. I couldn't ask any more. It was my turn to give.

As I sat there at the table, I realized the best thing I could do for him now was to let him go, with no strings attached and no hurt feelings. If we could just have this time together until it ended, keep it precious, we could both look back on our friendship as a bright spot in a dark day. And that would be enough. Or it would have to be enough.

"Maybe sometime," I said with far more steadiness than I felt. And then I changed the subject before the thought of letting him go had a chance to weave its way into my expression. "So what's for breakfast?"

"Sit tight," he said jumping up to put the finishing touches on our meal. "Waffles with a warm fruit compote. And bacon."

"Jesus," I gasped as he set a heaping plate down in front of me. "You know, it's a very good thing you're leaving in a few weeks. Otherwise, I'd weigh four hundred pounds in no time. How do you not weigh four hundred pounds, by the way? I don't know if I can trust a skinny chef."

Keir laughed and sat down opposite me at the table with an equally full plate. "I'm not *skinny*."

"Um," I said taking a large bite and waving my fork at him. "You definitely don't have the physique of a guy who's around food all day. Just saying."

"So good chefs have to be overweight?" he asked with playful indignation.

"They don't *have* to be, but aren't they usually?"

"No. That's a complete fallacy."

"But don't you have to taste everything you make?"

"Yes, you taste a little of everything, but not a lot of anything. A busy kitchen is a very active place. You're constantly moving."

"I'd be constantly eating."

He laughed. "Actually, the more cooking I do, the pickier I think I've become. Now I only eat what I love. Like with chocolate. I'm not even tempted by the crap you see in the grocery store."

"No Snickers?" He shook his head. "Milky Way?" Another blank stare. *"Heath bar?"*

He laughed at my expression. "Not even Heath bar."

I watched him for a minute as he shrugged casually and dug into his breakfast.

"You are a freak of nature. You know that, right?"

Keir grinned. It was something I could always count on with him. Something I loved. Plus, he listened, and he was funny and kind. He was entirely his own self, and that easy confidence made him irresistible. The fact that he was gorgeous didn't hurt either.

"So I had an idea," he said. "What are you doing Tuesday night?"

"I'm not making a lot of plans these days."

"Good. Come with me to a Sharks game. Pre-season opener."

"Hockey?" I said, and did not bother to hide my lack of enthusiasm for the idea.

"Hockey?" he said mimicking my tone. "Yes, hockey. It's the best."

I made a face. "I don't know."

"Why not?"

"Why would you want to take someone who doesn't actually *like* hockey?"

"Have you ever been to a game?"

"No."

Keir's sigh was long-suffering. "Then how do you know you don't like it?"

I had no response.

"Anyway, you don't have to like it. You like me, don't you?"

"Sometimes."

He grinned. "Well, I like you *all* the time. So how could it not be fun?"

"Your logic doesn't follow."

"How so, Piggy?"

I almost choked on my breakfast when he called me that—the nickname he gave me just before the *thing* happened, the one that would forever be associated in my head with our crossing from friends to more, even if it was just for one kiss.

His expression straightened with awareness, too—his jaw set tight, eyes comically wide. "I'm sorry," he rushed out with. "I shouldn't have—I'm sorry."

"Seriously, that horrible nickname is why I only *sometimes* like you," I told him. And thankfully, he laughed like I hoped he would. He actually looked a little relieved. "All I'm saying is, What if I asked you to go shopping with me?"

"Shopping?" Keir was genuinely unimpressed with my counterargument.

"Yeah."

"For what?" he asked suspiciously.

"Clothes."

He took another bite and shook his head vehemently. "That's not the same thing at all," he said around a forkful of waffle. "Shopping is boring."

"No, it's exactly the same thing. You claim to like me, so why wouldn't it be fun? And I would *love* to shop for you. You have a ridiculous body, Keir. I'm dying to pick out some things for you."

"Not happening."

"See, then. Your argument doesn't follow," I said, and shoved a piece of bacon in my mouth.

Silence fell upon us. Keir eyed me narrowly as I pointedly ignored him.

"So you're saying if I agree to go shopping with you—"

"*For* you," I interrupted.

"If I agree to go shopping with you *for me*," he said, "you'll go to the game with me on Tuesday?"

I put my fork down and eyed him right back. "I didn't realize we were negotiating."

"Let's negotiate." He leaned back and crossed his arms over his chest, highlighting again those very nice biceps. Damn, damn, damn.

"Okay, fine. If you go shopping with me, then I'll agree to go to your game, but no face paint or body paint. And no foam fingers."

I leaned back and mirrored his stance.

"Agreed," he said with a trace of humor. "And I'm not trying on anything pink. Or plaid. And I won't go to more than two stores, so choose carefully."

I took in the darkly handsome man across from me who looked uncannily like the cat that just ate the canary. Myriad hockey images flashed through my brain—from fistfights to spilled beer to male bravado. I shuddered.

Then I pictured Keir in a fitted black sweater and slacks.

Damn.

"You have yourself a deal."

Chapter 10

Keir

Selene answered the door of her apartment and did a little double take when she saw my face. Yes, I hate shaving. And no, I don't know why I felt compelled to do it tonight, but I did, so there it was. Christ, I was a stupid asshole.

But it turned out she wasn't the only one surprised by what she saw.

"Nice shirt," I said, instantly recognizing my black hockey jersey. I hoped I was digesting the sight of her in it like a friend would.

It was always tempting to look at her a little too long, a little too closely. And she never shrank from my inspection; she gave it right back. But it was a slippery slope for me. What started as a lingering glance could easily lead to my secretly staring in an *un*friendly way at her flawless olive skin, and beautiful hair, and her perfect curves. If I wasn't careful, I'd start thinking about our kiss and find myself wanting to hold her and touch her and wrap myself around her when she slept. I was pretty sure that's not what friends are supposed to want to do.

"You like it?" There was no doubt that I liked very much the way it draped on her body, teasing out the slopes and hollows of her breasts. And it would have been really good for our friendship if I could have looked away, but somehow I couldn't.

Thankfully, she turned away from me, and I was proud of myself for only passingly looking at her ass.

My last name was printed across her back, and I took another small pleasure in that, which I should have paused to consider but, again, deliberately didn't.

"Where'd you find it?"

"I *stole* it," she answered over one slender shoulder in an exaggerated stage whisper.

I shook my head, smiling. That seemed to be my perpetual state with her. Smiling.

It's true the black jersey was one of my favorites, but I'd give it up in a heartbeat if it meant the chance to see her in it with those tight-fitting jeans and her high-heeled black boots.

Fuuuuck. Those boots.

Only Selene could make a fashion statement out of a shirt that had seen more than its share of bone-crushing hits. And only she would think to wear it with a solitaire necklace. I doubt very much that a hockey jersey and a diamond necklace are two things often paired together. But then, maybe the same could be said for her and me, and just look at us.

"I like it," I told her, nodding with approval.

She smiled again, that radiant smile that made me feel like a king to have inspired it. That's when I realized how utterly screwed I was if I thought I could play it cool with her tonight. Like I hadn't been killing myself for the last four days, trying to stay busy enough that I didn't replay what it was like to feel her mouth on mine and hold her body in my hands.

Every time I saw her, her beauty hit me again. But tonight—

standing here in a hockey jersey with a flash of mischief in her eye—
she was a goddamned *vision*.

It was my very worst nightmare.

§

The SAP Center in San Jose, dubbed the Shark Tank, was packed.
You'd be hard-pressed to find crazier fans anywhere—and I say that
in the fondest possible way. They were all dressed in black and teal,
and hungry to wreak a little havoc with the Anaheim Ducks.

I loved everything about this place—the cold arena air, and the
slightly sticky floor, and the thunder of feet that rumbled in your
bones as you climbed the risers. We had great seats, just seven rows
back behind the penalty box.

Coming here felt like coming home. This was my happy place.
While the goal of hockey is simple—put the biscuit in the basket—
the practice of it is something else altogether. It's a complicated mix
of speed, grace, strategy, and skill that I could never quite get enough
of.

And yes, it's violent. The fluidity of the sport ensures that most
contact is body to body.

But for all the focus on hockey's violence, it's really the beauty of
the sport that made me fall in love with it as a child. The athleticism
is almost poetic. It is first, last, and always a team sport. Maybe more
than any other. It's a well-orchestrated dance with partners who
always have each other's back. When a team is in harmony, there is a
rhythm and an order that are simply stunning to witness.

It's the Greatest Game on the Planet.

§

It was during the first period of the Greatest Game on the Planet that
the Greatest Girl on the Planet received a text from work.

"What is it?" I asked her.

She wrinkled her brow as she read the message. "Well, it's official. We didn't get the Rival contract."

"I'm sorry."

"I know," she said still reading. "My boss says they sent her an email saying they've decided to go in a different direction but that they *value our continued patronage of their brand.*" She stuck out her tongue in a vomit face.

"*What?* You've got to be kidding me. How can someone even write that without knowing what complete bullshit it is? *Patronage of their brand.* Screw that."

Selene glanced over at me side-eyed with a touch of humor in her face but it didn't stay there long.

"It's fine," she said, though her expression said otherwise. "It's probably better right now, anyway. It might be fun, but I'd have had no life outside of work, even if it wasn't my design they picked. You know how these things go."

I nodded, though I didn't know. Not really. But studying her, and seeing her disappointment, I felt sad on her behalf.

I took her hand in mine and gave it a squeeze. "I'm really sorry."

"Like I said, it's fine. It's just . . ." She breathed out a little sigh and squeezed my hand back. "It was fun to think about, that's all."

"I know. I get it. My restaurant's only a business plan on paper, but in my head, I've already bought the perfect building and created my ideal menu. It's hard to rein in your head when your heart's involved. But listen to me," I said, ducking to hook her gaze directly, "you're going to have so many more opportunities."

I had seen her work, and it was clear to me that her success was just a matter of time. She was absolutely brilliant with typography, at illustrating through type style. I'd never really considered how important typography could be until she mentioned *Star Wars* and the *New York Times* and *Disney*—all iconic typography in which the letters could be scrambled and you'd still recognize the brand.

In fact, we had this conversation at The Arthouse that began with my insistence that my logo for Blaze was pretty good. I was proud of it because I'd managed to incorporate a flame into the design. A flame . . . in Blaze . . . genius (!), I thought. And just like that, she flipped over her cocktail napkin and sketched out something by hand I *never* could have conceived—this awesome partial decomposition of the letters of Blaze inside a much more modern and sparse rendering of a flame. And this was just chicken scratch on a napkin—so cool that I kept it—but nothing compared with what she could do when she was pulling out all the stops. She was brilliant. And, side note, she also happened to be one of the smartest, sexiest people I knew. She could do it all.

Still, in the midst of a setback, no amount of reassurance can change the way you feel. For her, this was a tough break.

"I know," she said with nonchalance that fell a little short. Our hands slid apart, though I noticed it was a little more slowly this time. Then she looked away.

"Hey," I said, getting her attention again. I picked up my beer and tilted it in her direction. "I'm *never* patronizing their brand. So fuck 'em. They're idiots if they don't see the brilliance in your work."

"You always say that."

"And I mean it."

She gave me a half smile, which meant she probably only half believed me. But I was satisfied to think she might take to heart even a fraction of the confidence I had in her.

§

Throughout the second period, Selene seemed a little distracted, but to her credit, she followed the game pretty well. All things considered, she seemed to be enjoying herself.

Then in the third period, there was a fight on the ice. It initially began over a hit in which Getzlaf nailed Karlsson cleanly. But Karlsson hit the dasher pretty hard and had to leave the ice. Dillon picked up the beef on Karlsson's behalf, and what followed was a fairly standard fistfight between Dillon and Getzlef.

"I can't believe they allow this," Selene said turning to me in horror.

This wasn't even a bad one. No blood was spilled, and there were only two guys involved. Most of the time, fighting is just a strategic move in hockey to alter the momentum of the game.

"No one's going to get hurt here, I promise."

Selene watched the two players throw a flurry of punches and then separate, skating off unharmed in opposite directions. Meanwhile, the crowd was cheering wildly.

"Have you ever been hurt?"

"In a fight or in general?"

"Well, I mean, you've been playing since you were, what, eight?"

"About, yeah."

"Is it always like this? Or is it just professional hockey?"

"It's always like this. Sometimes it's worse. See this?" I opened my mouth and pointed to my eyetooth on the right side. "That's a cap from when I took a stick to the face. The tooth was smashed."

"Jesus! That's allowed?"

"No. You can get a match penalty for anything intentional involving a stick. This was an accident—friendly fire by a teammate. But this one was a fight." I pulled my jersey to the side to show her a small lump on my right collarbone from a break that had healed unevenly when I was nineteen because I was impatient with the process. And then I lifted the leg of my jeans so she could see a scar from a gash to my left shin. "That one was just bad luck."

We were leaning in together on the same armrest, and when I

finished adjusting my pant leg, I looked up to find her staring at me.

"What? You don't like this?" I asked her, referring to the game. I thought this might be my only shot at selling her on hockey and at the moment, it seemed like a no-go.

"It's not that. I like watching you like it. That's the part I like the most. And it's exciting," she offered. "I'd come to another game with you."

"But?"

She hesitated. "But I don't think I'd ever be able to watch you play."

She seemed so vulnerable just then that I didn't know quite what to make of her concern. It caught me off guard and honestly left me feeling like kind of a dick for apparently overplaying my injuries. I didn't realize she would translate them into any danger to my current well-being. Or, frankly, that any of it would rise to the level of concern I saw on her face. But then, fear isn't always a rational thing, and it tends to heighten when you're already losing someone you care about. My heart hurt for her.

"The league I play in now is really tame. It's just a bunch of professionals who are definitely not interested in losing their teeth or breaking any bones, believe me. There's very little risk to this pretty face."

My smile was an unconscious thing, instinctual as a result of her proximity. She smiled, too, in a way that always ruined me.

And then for some reason—*hell*—neither of us looked away.

In her expression, the depth of her affection was plain. On one hand, it scared the shit out of me—it was exactly what I thought I didn't want to see. On the other hand, that look took my breath away. I felt warmed by it. I carried such a hollowness since my dad passed that nothing seemed to be able to reach. Except her, sometimes. And when that happened, as it did the other night, it was hard not to mistake the feeling for happiness.

Very selfishly, I didn't discourage it.

Selene lifted her left hand and touched my face with her palm. It was definitely a new kind of closeness for us, at least sober—one to which I gave no resistance. Her skin felt warm and smooth as she stroked my cheek gently. And I couldn't take my eyes off her face. My god, she was stunning. This close, I absorbed the perfection of her features, of her delicate earlobes. A tiny piece of dark hair curled around the back of one.

The air between us seemed to crackle quietly, and I sat frozen in my seat in case any movement might cause her to draw away.

"I don't think I've ever seen you clean-shaven," she said softly.

I could feel her breath, too, warm against my face. My fingers itched to reach up and touch her mouth, to feel whether it was as soft as I remembered. My heartbeat picked up not only faster but harder, like it was punching me from the inside.

Had a goal been scored just then I wouldn't have noticed. Nothing could have pulled me from that trance. I didn't hear anything going on around us. Not the crowd, not the announcer, not the buzzer.

Only her.

Only her voice and her eyes and her breath. The memory of her mouth.

"Do you have a preference?" I asked roughly. I had no idea what possessed me to ask her that.

No, that's a lie. That *other* side of me wanted to be everything she wanted and would have shaved every single day if that's what she asked of me.

"No." Her beautiful lips curved slightly upward. "How could I choose between James Bond and Indiana Jones?"

Her palm came to rest on my jawline, and I took a deep breath.

When had the gnaw of wanting her turned into this painful ache?

Under the sanctity of her touch, I had a sudden and startling thought that maybe we could write a different ending for the two of us. One I hadn't yet considered. Maybe there was a different story we could tell in which the things we had to offer would be enough.

There was obviously more to our relationship than just friendship, and perhaps we could figure out how to have something beyond what we'd allowed ourselves. After all, there was care and respect at the heart of everything we did together. That had to mean something.

Looking into her soft green eyes and with her fingertips still on my skin, I suddenly felt hopeful. I felt great. I didn't know when the feeling had started, but I knew that *this* woman, who challenged me and made me laugh and made me proud, was somehow the source of it.

And that's when I realized I was staring. My focus had again fallen to her lips. And I swear I could feel every tick of the clock. My breath sounded loud in my ears, even over the cheers of the crowd.

One more fraction of a second would have seen me lean forward and place a kiss to those lips. One more fraction of a second and that kiss might have promised any number of things she needed. There was a moment in my head in which all this felt possible and right, in which the sincerity of our intentions could overcome our less-than-optimal circumstances.

But what one moment gave, another took away.

Selene's attention was drawn to something behind me. Looking up, her face changed from the quiet, conspiratorial warmth of our conversation to something outwardly focused and animated. Suddenly, she rose from her seat.

"Kevin!" No, that was not at all what I wanted to hear her say. "Hey! What a surprise!"

Standing next to my chair on the aisle was a nice-looking guy, about my age, with a slightly heavier build. He could have been dressed for the library in his collared shirt and slacks, and he was smiling at her like she was a long-lost, favored toy he'd found under his bed.

"I know! I have to say, Selene, this is probably the last place I'd expect to see you."

Then he glanced down at me. His smile faded slightly as we exchanged far cooler and more assessing looks than the one he shared with her. I tried to tamp down the curl of possessive heat in my stomach.

"Let me introduce you," Selene said. I got up from my seat, and it gave me no small pleasure that he had to tilt his head to look up at me. "This is my friend, Keir Stevens. And Keir, this is Kevin Laughlin."

That's what she said.

This is my friend, Keir Stevens.

My friend.

My friend, Keir Stevens.

The words turned over and over again in my head. *And this is Kevin Laughlin. This is Kevin Laughlin.*

As he shook my hand, he looked at me like he'd heard the difference too. And he was elated about it.

"Good to meet you, Keith," he said to me, but he was solely focused on Selene.

Selene stepped past me, and while they stood in the aisle talking, I took my seat like an asshole, feeling like I'd just taken a syringe of adrenaline straight to my quietly hopeful heart.

My friend.

What the *hell* was wrong with me? This is what we had agreed to. This is what I had truly wanted. What I wanted still. How had I gotten so fucked-up about it?

I'd let myself come far too close to the edge of an abyss that I *knew* I needed to avoid. And worse, I had almost gone over.

I knew I wasn't fit for her right now; I wasn't fit to be anybody's *anything* right now.

I looked up at nonfriend Kevin Laughlin again. He was showing Selene something on his phone, and they were laughing in a very familiar way. Was she into this guy? He was definitely into her.

I tried to concentrate on the game. I tried to concentrate on my phone. I tried to concentrate on anything but their voices, and the voice in my head that was telling me I was a mess.

I had a plan that was unquestionably the right one. I had a home and a successful business and friends and a life in Seattle. I had women I casually saw, which suited me just fine.

Selene and I were like a summer camp friendship, where you get to know each other in this intense way and everything is wild and goes by in a blur. And yes, in a few short weeks, we'd shared a lot of meaningful experiences, but it was coming to an end, and it was better for both of us not to try to make more of this than there was. Warm affection was good. Even adoration in check. But not more.

"Is your cell number still the same?" Kevin was asking her.

I watched the Ducks' defenseman hit a beautiful slap shot, and it reminded me of how much I wanted to be back on the ice. Back with my own league.

In Seattle, I knew exactly who I was and what I wanted for myself. It was only when I was here in the Bay Area, with grief clouding all rational thought, that I was falling easy prey to these tricks of the mind.

I didn't need a different ending; what I needed was to get back home.

When Kevin moved on—and the bastard called me *Keith* again—Selene sat down beside me. She put her hand on my arm, but this time I didn't make a move.

"What'd I miss?" she asked.

"Nothing," I told her, eyes on the game. "Nothing at all."

Chapter 11

Keir

The next day I took a flight to Seattle. I just needed to be back on familiar ground and get my head together. I felt shitty that I didn't tell Selene I'd gone until she texted me.

How did I not know this? read her response.

Last minute decision. I need to check on some things. That was true, but it wasn't the whole truth.

There was a long pause, as she appeared to be typing. Then her reply was short.

When are you coming back?

Not sure.

Ok. Another long pause. *Call me when you can.*

I didn't call her. I didn't text either. And I let her subsequent messages go unanswered. I was disappointed in myself for it, but I just couldn't talk to her. I didn't know what to say. I dug around in my head, but the only words that bubbled to the surface were words about *us*, or last night, or her, or my own messed-up head. I kept thinking about the way she'd looked at me and how it felt—how it changed something inside me—and, although I knew I shouldn't want that, I couldn't quite get myself back to the whole *just friends* veneer. If she could so easily, it just might wreck me a little.

Over the next five days, I threw myself into my business. I was never one to believe you could drink yourself out of a funk, but I tried very hard to prove the theory that you could work yourself out of one.

To an extent, I was right. Coming home allowed me to find an anchor point in my head and distracted me from the torrent of emotions taking their toll on my sanity. After all, my business was not only my livelihood; it was great medicine for my grief. It was a source of enormous pride, of creativity, of usefulness, of responsibility for twenty-seven employees who trusted and relied on me for their rents and car payments and everything else. This was where I was needed, where I thrived.

Getting back to old friends and old routines provided a respite from the disorientation I'd experienced since my pop's death—a disorientation I wasn't prepared for but shouldn't have been surprised by. After all, the whole situation had started only five months ago, like most of these things do, with a phone call. A stroke, he'd told me with some difficulty, that would require a year of recovery.

It was such a bizarre thing that someone could be perfectly healthy one day, and the next, he's facing twelve months of speech therapy, occupational therapy, and physical therapy—just to get back to where he was the day before. And of course my natural response was to try to find some sort of purpose in this shitty, fucking senseless thing that was happening to him.

At the time, I found that purpose in the idea that spending a year helping my pop recover would give us the chance to get to know each other again as men. I hadn't lived at home for thirteen years and was, then, too young to recognize him as a man or to honor his story and his sacrifices. But after years of tackling my own big questions—Who am I? What constitutes manhood and adulthood? What are my freedoms and my responsibilities?—I thought at least now I'd have the opportunity to better understand *his* journey. And maybe he, mine. After all, he and I were different people, and there'd been some hard reckonings between us in my earlier years—no more so than any other teenager and his father, but certainly no less. That's the thing with fathers and sons: You grow up together, in a way. And through the process, it's entirely possible to know each other both too well and, at the same time, not nearly well enough.

Then overnight everything changed—with flat, unpoetic immediacy. His diagnosis, his prognosis, the purpose of my stay. What they thought was a stroke turned out to be cancer, and that cancer turned its cold, predatory eyes on him—hungry, and indifferent to the things we'd planned, and to the time we expected to have together.

There's a lot in this world that can be altered: Things that can be remade or rebuilt. Things you can find, and lose, and find again. But not time. Time is spent—well or not—and when it's lost, it's just lost.

Even now, a month after his death, I wanted to follow his stoic example and be more serene about it. I wanted to be of the mind that everyone's moment comes at some point. But the way it happened was still unimaginable. Like a lightning strike that leaves a hideous scar and is gone.

For the first time in my life, my internal compass was spinning. For the first time in my life, I felt lost.

§

Being home helped. Here in Seattle I found my footing within my normal life. I could summon my resilience and feel better again. Even more, here in Seattle stood the place where the future I dreamed of was physically within reach. It gave me something to look forward to. And that's exactly where I went on Sunday morning.

The historic brick building that might soon house my restaurant stood right on the edge of one of my favorite places on planet Earth—Pike Place Market. At about nine square acres, the marketplace district overlooks Elliott Bay to the west and is graced on all sides by views of the majestic, snow-tipped Olympic Mountains. The district itself is almost a city within a city.

With hundreds of stalls housing a rotating cast of farmers and artisans throughout the market, you could easily spend entire days appraising fish, listening to buskers, tasting produce, and appreciating the long and storied history of the market itself.

For me, it had always been a cornerstone for my business—a place to source the freshest food products, from fish to produce to seasonings. But honestly, that was just the start of it. The market offered so many outstanding restaurants and strange-in-a-good-way concessionaires that on many occasions I debated with myself whether it would be wrong to follow my morning croissant and coffee from Le Panier with another pastry and coffee from DeLaurenti. Or whether I should buy a CD from that guy with the rolling piano. Or whether my friends would think I was completely high if I came home with a cigar-box guitar made by that guy in the arcade.

I absolutely loved the market. The energy was like nowhere else I've seen. And returning to it on Sunday morning was rejuvenating. It felt more like home to me than almost any place in Seattle.

But the main purpose of my visit was a chance to see the little brick building that, for better or worse, I already considered to be mine.

In the time away from home, I had forgotten just how much I loved it—the elaborate brickwork just below the roofline and around every window, the beautiful millwork painted beige, and the bright-blue door. I loved its charm and character. I loved the location and the fact that the area was bursting with activity. I loved the smell of the sea and the constant cry of gulls.

I seemed to live my life on wheels these days, but this place had roots. It had existed on this site for over a hundred years, enduring two world wars, the Great Depression, and the rise and fall of generations. It had seen a city grow up around it and thrive. It was a fixed point in a sea of change. Not flesh and blood, but brick and mortar, and less susceptible to the vagaries of fate.

I walked around the corner to the west side of the building near the bay and laid my palms on the cool, rough surface of the brick. My fingers traced the mortar between. I could almost hear each block whispering secrets and promises. Leaning forward, I let my chest brush against it as I tilted my head back and looked straight up its solid face to the tin roof several stories above. It was good to feel small standing here. It was good to feel like the weight of my life was insignificant, a mere flash in time by comparison to the life of this building.

I felt reassured by its relentless permanence—its strength. Its promise for me in my life.

I was just closing my eyes to let the sunshine warm my face when I heard a woman clearing her throat behind me.

I turned around so fast my cell phone flew out of my hip pocket and I had to scoop it up before straightening. Jesus, what could she possibly think I was doing?

"This looks weird," I said, preempting her agreement on the matter.

There was honestly no way to explain my behavior without hours of time and plenty of alcohol, so I was relieved when she just laughed. Not that she was disagreeing, of course.

"I've seen *weirder*," she said with a thick Southern accent that sort of softened the fact that she'd just confirmed I looked like a freak.

"I don't think I want to know where."

"No, you don't. It was something I accidentally googled." She smiled. "I'm Janelle Davis, the building manager."

Ja-*nail* was sort of the way it came out.

She was attractive by any standard. Petite, though a little thin for my preference, with a lively face and a rather surprising irreverence that I found appealing. She shook my hand firmly, and her fingers felt small and bony in my grasp.

"Keir Stevens. I don't actually make a habit of hugging buildings. But I do have an offer in to buy this place."

Yeah, sure, that explains everything . . .

"Oh, you're the one who wants to open the restaurant."

"That's right." I could have kissed her for so generously moving on. "You haven't heard anything from the owners, have you?"

"No, but they're definitely considering it."

"Really?"

"Yeah. They've had other offers, and they usually just turn them down straightaway. But they're really thinking about it this time." *Time.* I played with the sound of her accent in my head. Kind of like *tahm.*

"That's great to hear. Thank you."

"I think they like the idea of a restaurant breathing new life into this place." She looked up at the facade that was clearly the work of a craftsman, and touched it briefly with her fingertips. "Their great-grandfather built it himself around the time the market opened in the early 1900s."

"You're kidding?"

"No," she said, shifting her purple leather bag on her shoulder. "It has a lot of sentimental value. That's why they haven't sold."

Off in the distance, we could hear the bells chiming from the

Plymouth Congregational Church on Sixth Avenue, the same toll that had probably sounded at high noon for a hundred years or more.

"So what kind of a restaurant would it be?"

"My specialty is open-fire grilling. I actually have a catering business here in town called Blaze that's kind of its predecessor."

"Oh, I've seen those trucks around."

"Well, you should stop by one sometime. Tell them I sent you. They'll fix you up."

"Maybe I'll come to the grand opening of your restaurant," she offered, smiling.

"Absolutely," I said returning the look.

"Or," she added with a heavy drawl, "you could call me sooner."

I wasn't unaccustomed to women being forward, and I didn't mind it. I just hadn't been expecting it here, and it took a moment to process what she was suggesting. Even more, how I felt about it. Was I interested in this woman? She *was* pretty; she seemed like she might be fun to hang out with. Plus, *she* lived in Seattle.

"True," I answered in a noncommittal way that made me feel like kind of a dick.

She took the phone from my hand, letting her fingers brush mine, and put in her information. While I stood there watching, she dialed herself. "Now we have each other's numbers."

I nodded, still measuring my interest. "Well, it was nice to meet you, Janelle."

"Nice to meet you too."

"I'm sure we'll be talking soon."

"I hope so," she said with a smile.

The seconds that followed felt so loaded, like maybe she was waiting for me to ask her out. I didn't. Instead we fumbled through a handshake that was sort of a hug and went so awry we ended up laughing about it. And rather than continuing with the awkwardness,

I just leaned in to give her a small kiss on her cheek. She turned instead, though, and her lips sought mine.

They were nice. Sweet tasting, and offered up in a straightforward, carefree way that I found appealing. She was appealing.

But that kiss brought to mind another set of lips: soft, supple ones that belonged to a woman who, quite frankly, made the whole comparison more than a little unfair. Maybe I just *wanted* to want Janelle because things with her could be simple. Maybe I just wanted to finally give a rest to the memory of a kiss that had been endlessly looping in my head for more than a week.

You want this. I know you do.

Then kiss me for real and I won't be disappointed.

With just those words, Selene had blown through whatever strength lay behind my convictions—made me lose all sense of restraint until I couldn't remember why I resisted in the first place.

I had hoped that coming back home might help me regain some perspective on whatever this thing was between us—that maybe time and distance would work their magic. As I watched Janelle turn to walk away with a flirtatious glimmer in her eye and a little wave of her hand, I realized that they had—just not in the way I expected.

Standing there, alongside my future restaurant with my hand resting reassuringly on the cool brick, I began to make room for an uncomfortable thought: my life was in Seattle, but my heart, or at least a meaningful piece of it, was back in San Francisco with Selene.

How the fuck did that happen?

Ours had been nothing more than a chance encounter, a brush between two people that might never have happened but for one split-second distraction. And yet somehow that random meeting had turned into a true friendship that had then evolved into . . . I honestly didn't even know what to call it—but it was more than friendship and it mattered to me. A lot. And because it did, the whole situation had given rise to a confusing twist of emotions that were constantly at odds in my head.

I was mad as hell at myself for doing the exact *opposite* of everything I professed to want when it came to Selene. And I was mad at Selene for highlighting my inconsistency. And whether or not it was justified, Kevin had now assumed the face of everything I despised about our situation. Don't even get me started on how I felt about him.

Yes, of course I knew that as a matter of principle, I could hardly object to the idea of Selene dating anyone she chose, especially since it was *my* idea, for fuck's sake, that we keep things as friends. And yet! And yet, as a matter of practice, it turned out that I *profoundly* disliked it. Imagination is all well and fine, but it wasn't equal to actually seeing her with someone else. Someone who, by stated *fact*, was *not* her friend.

I could feel the anger boiling up once again, but to what end? Everything I was was in Seattle. And yet, in San Francisco, expecting a call from me that hadn't come, was someone who'd given my joy back to me, my laughter, that part of me that felt like me. And I missed it. I missed her.

Under all of this was a truth I needed to acknowledge but didn't want to: I wasn't going to be able to just step back into my old life and pretend nothing had changed. Two big things *had* changed: I'd lost someone of great importance to me, and in the process I'd gained someone too. And I couldn't restart my life until I fully faced up to both.

I couldn't presume to know what Selene wanted of us—I hadn't exactly encouraged that conversation—but I had to start by being honest with myself about what *I* wanted, no matter how messy that could be. And I needed to be very intentional about this because there was risk to our relationship either way; I could definitely see that now.

The way Selene and I had connected over our eerily similar fates was evidence that sometimes your blessings and your curses come in the very same package. I couldn't say in that moment what the endgame for us might be. From here forward, it was going to get complicated. But I knew this: Selene deserved far better from me than silence and indecision.

And when it came right down to it, my pop did too. After all, he had raised me to live better in the world than the way I was currently behaving, and it would've been an insult to his memory not to put this right.

So Monday morning, I boarded a plane back to San Francisco.

Chapter 12

Selene

Hey.

Out of the blue on Monday afternoon came a text from Keir. I was in the middle of designing social media banners for a client's charitable event, so I picked up my phone, gave him the same *Hey* back, and set the phone down again on my desk.

There was a telling pause as though he was waiting for me to say more. I didn't.

Are you hungry?

For what? I asked. *It's 3:00.*

Have dinner with me tonight.

So I guess you're back.

I am.

I stared at his messages for a moment, debating. The truth was, I was pissed at him. I get that he was busy, but it was mildly fucked-up that he couldn't be bothered to answer a text. It seemed uncharacteristically inconsiderate. Or maybe it wasn't uncharacteristic—hell if I knew. And that was exactly the problem: we had a lot to learn about each other. It made situations like this really hard.

The best I could judge was that I had overestimated the

importance of our friendship in his life, and that stung a bit, if I were being honest. But it also underscored what I suppose he'd been trying to say to me all along: don't get too attached. Maybe I *had* gotten too attached; I only had myself to blame for that.

I want to cook for you, he texted again when I didn't answer. *At your place.* Even over text, it felt like there was a canyon between us.

Yes, I was being a baby; I knew that. And probably making things even more awkward. I was pissed at myself because I was letting him turn me into the kind of person I didn't want to be. *This* kind. Fragile and overly sensitive and petty.

I had made a promise to myself to let him go when the time came with no hard feelings and no strings attached. If he was beginning to break away, I might as well get over myself and start that now.

Ok. How about 6:00? Make sure there's chocolate.

☺ *Yes, Ma'am.*

§

I opened the door, and my heart stumbled. It was so unfair that the sight of Keir Stevens never failed to have that effect. Standing on my doorstep, handsomely put together in a black sport coat with a dark gray T-shirt and jeans, he was a breathtaking sight.

"Hi there," I said with a casualness I didn't feel, and stepped aside to let him pass.

"Hi." He was smiling.

At first, it seemed like he wanted to lean in and give me a kiss on the cheek, but mid-gesture he decided against it and pulled back, blushing. I was trying to follow his lead, stiff and awkwardly, but the whole thing felt like one big fumble. It exactly illustrated the weirdness between us at the moment, which must have traced back to something, though damn if I knew what.

"What's all that?" I asked, shutting the door behind him.

"Dinner." He looked at me oddly and adjusted the two large bags of groceries in his arms.

"Looks like you're going to a lot of trouble."

He shrugged in a way that made me think I'd embarrassed him by mentioning it. "Not that much."

"Okay, well . . . what do you need from me?"

After setting the bags on the dining room table, he removed his sport coat and draped it over one of the chairs.

"Nothing, really. Why don't you go get changed. I'll get started on dinner."

"I will, in a bit. I kind of like watching you cook."

That was the truth. He was so competent and precise in the kitchen. I'd never seen anyone chop vegetables with that kind of skill, except maybe on TV. He was manically particular about his ingredients like he was about his aprons. He inspected and tasted everything. If a carrot was a little sour, he'd set it aside. If a strawberry was white in the middle, he'd choose another one. He got more excited than anyone I knew about the taste of a good tomato or the marbling in a piece of meat.

I stood to the side as he unpacked his bags and laid the items out on the counter. True to earlier impressions, it was quite a spread— some sort of meat wrapped in pink butcher paper, mushrooms, onions, garlic, brussels sprouts, and white potatoes. And lots of fresh herbs: tarragon, rosemary, and thyme. It looked as though he'd brought half the farmers market here.

"It's good to see you," he said in a way that felt exceedingly tender. It made me ache to bury my cheek in that cozy spot at his sternum and feel his arms pull me close again, erasing the awkward distance that seemed to have crept between us in the last week.

"It's good to see you too," I admitted, hoping my face didn't admit much more. "Plus, you promised chocolate, so . . ."

Keir grinned for the first time since stepping through my door, an expression of relief that filled me with such relief for this tiny splinter of familiarity. Maybe we could find ourselves again if we just released any expectation of what this thing between us actually meant.

With that bit of hope, I watched him pull a large gourmet chocolate bar from one of the bags, waving it temptingly in front of me.

"I would never cross a woman in need of chocolate."

"You're a smart man," I told him, and was rewarded once again as his grin widened.

"Okay, sit here, then." He patted the countertop next to the oven. "Let me at least pour you a glass of wine."

I hopped up on the counter, legs crossed and dangling, while Keir pulled the cork on a red blend he'd brought.

"Try this."

He handed me a glass, and as I took my first sip, he casually rested his hand on my bare knee. Just that simple touch, and the lingering look that accompanied it, was undermining hours of mental jujitsu I'd performed on myself.

"You look really pretty, by the way." He gestured to my Audrey Hepburn/*Breakfast at Tiffany's* homage. "I like your hair up like that."

His compliments weren't helping matters either.

This was where the whole friendship thing got messy. Sometimes I wished I could split Keir in two. That way, I could chase the chemistry between us that was more compelling than anything I'd ever experienced without jeopardizing the friendship I was coming to rely on. Because I realized that part of what I missed most over the last week was that feeling of comfort I took from him. He grounded me, and I was truly surprised by how quickly everything in my life had come to operate against the backdrop of his ever-reassuring presence. And yes, it was brutally hard setting aside the memory of that kiss, but compromising our friendship would be so much worse. I just had to force myself to move on.

I blinked away from his steady gaze, not wanting him to see the thoughts that simmered steadily in the back of my mind. The important thing was getting *us* back, whatever that meant.

"I've got a porterhouse steak to share in a red wine peppercorn sauce," he said unwrapping a beautiful piece of meat. "With tarragon mushrooms, roasted brussels sprouts, and garlic mashed potatoes. Sound okay?"

"God, yes."

Keir always said that cooking for someone else was a privilege. I suspected in this case it may have also been an apology. But it was a good one. And sincerely meant, I thought.

While he peeled and sliced the potatoes, we talked about my dad, about work, about a lot of things.

"What do you think of the wine?" he asked me at one point, dropping a spoonful of butter into a sauté pan.

"It's good. It would be great with this."

I was leaning sideways to reach for the chocolate when my hand was batted away with a wooden spoon.

"Hey!" I said glaring at him.

"Hey yourself! That's for the soufflé."

"You're making me soufflé?"

"Did you think I was going to serve you a chocolate bar for dessert?"

"I didn't know what you were going to serve me. I haven't talked to you in a week."

Oops.

Dammit.

Keir's open expression sobered at once, and guilt, of all things, drained the color from his cheeks. A short silence fell between us.

"I'm truly sorry about that. It was . . . inexcusable."

I shrugged, though I didn't drop his gaze. And I didn't say more. Or perhaps I did; he always seemed to be able to read the things I didn't care to speak.

"I owe you an explanation."

"You don't," I said brushing it off, though this acknowledgment somehow buoyed me. "How's business?"

Keir's brows pulled together, and his normally smiling mouth became a thin, pale line. I could see him working through my deflection. He took a deep breath and dropped rosemary, thyme, and garlic into the pan. The fragrance filled the kitchen almost immediately.

"Pretty good, actually. We're having a strong month, and we've got some really high-profile events coming up. But I still worry that I've put more responsibility on Kelly's shoulders than she's ready for, and that isn't fair to her. I just needed to take some things off her plate—make sure everything was okay."

"Yeah, of course." I knew it couldn't have been easy running a business like that from a distance. *No strings,* I told myself again, glancing down at the glass in my hand. *And no hard feelings.* When I looked up again, Keir was watching me.

"I also needed to look for a place to live," he continued. "The renters who leased my house have it until June, so I found a couple of good options that I can rent month to month until then."

"Are you still thinking mid-October?"

"Yeah. That's the plan." That was only a few weeks away.

Every day that went by, this was becoming a more difficult topic for increasingly complex reasons. Neither of us wanted to dwell on it. I watched as he gave the garlic and herbs a half-hearted stir, and then his face cleared of some heavy thought.

"I went by the new building," he said, changing the subject.

"Really? Any word yet from the owners on your offer?"

"No, but we've given them some time to respond."

Keir poured a handful of peppercorns into a mortar he'd brought and began crushing them with a pestle. Each firm, precise stroke brought about a flex of elegant muscles in his forearms and chest.

"I don't know why, Selene," he said pausing, "but I have a good feeling about this. I think they're going to say *yes*."

"You still love the place?"

He sighed heavily and resumed the process, and the scent of fresh pepper wafted over from where he stood and mingled nicely with the sautéing garlic. "I do. More than ever. I was there yesterday and really looked again at the foot traffic and the available parking. It's just perfectly situated. I can't believe it was never a restaurant before."

"See, then, it's meant to be," I said, taking another sip of my wine. "You'll be a restaurateur in no time."

Keir's eyes shone gratefully. He was never one to seek out encouragement, but he glowed with it, particularly about the restaurant. It was his One Big Dream.

"I met the property manager."

"Oh yeah? What did he say about all this?"

"She, actually." He dug into one of the bags while I ignored the pinprick to my heart. Eventually, somebody back home was going to grab his attention in a serious way, and she'd be lucky for it. If we managed to stay in each other's lives like we said we wanted to, I had to prepare myself for that. "She didn't know anything specific," he said, finding the kosher salt and adding some to the crushed peppercorns. "But she said they're strongly considering it."

"Well, it sounds like you had a productive trip. I'm glad."

He looked up, and his mind seemed to return to the earlier topic. He set the mortar down and washed and dried his hands. After shutting off the burner under the pan of garlic and herbs, he turned to me. An uneasy expression came across his face. "Like I said, though, I owe you an explanation."

I honestly wasn't sure I wanted it. I was beginning to see just how easily this thing between us could hurt me. It wasn't his fault; it was just *him*. And maybe his explanation would reveal how unevenly distributed the feelings were between us. At the moment, I had enough hard truths to face.

But before he could go on, my cell phone blared on the counter, with the ringtone "I'm Too Sexy" by Right Said Fred. It was so loud it startled us both.

Kevin's name came up on the screen, along with an old selfie he'd taken with my phone when we were still together. It was a close-up of him making a loopy Dr. Evil face.

He was my last serious relationship, and it ended when he graduated from law school at Stanford and moved up to San Francisco for a job. I was still finishing my undergrad work, a mere forty-minute drive that might as well have been forty days. With the way our lives diverged, even that small distance was too much for our two-year relationship.

He hadn't called me in a very long time, and not until the phone rang did I remember the ringtone and photo were still set that way.

"Are you going to answer that?" Keir said flatly, but with an unmistakable edge that drew my attention instantly back to him. Gone was the uneasiness, but in its place was a testy look that surprised me with its intensity.

"No. I don't need to talk to him right now." I hit *Ignore* and tossed the phone aside.

If Keir was irritated by Kevin's call, so, too, was I. While I wasn't sure I wanted to hear his explanation, a morbid part of me couldn't resist.

"You were saying?"

My question seemed to draw his attention away from where he

was glowering at my phone. He looked unhappy, but collecting himself, he began again.

"I wanted to say that—"

To *both* of our great frustration and disbelief, my phone rang again. Kevin. That idiotic lyric came ringing out from my speaker. It sounded even worse the second time.

"For Christ's sake, is he just going to keep calling until you pick up?"

"Hell if I know. I don't even know why he's calling."

I fumbled for the device, trying to silence it, but the longer it rang, the more impatient Keir became. "Just answer it then."

"I don't want to talk to him right now." *Why did I have to explain this?*

But the hard look was back. I imagined, perhaps, that his dark eyes also held a hint of suspicion.

"He obviously thinks you do."

"I don't care what he thinks," I insisted. My voice took on the sharpness of his.

Keir turned away, but as he did, I saw a faint, bitter smile flash across his face. It was a smile that lacked all warmth, just a twist of the mouth and then gone.

"What?" I demanded. "What was that look?"

"There was no look," he said, his back turned, arms braced on the counter. I could make out the definition of every muscle in his back, all tense and unyielding.

"Bullshit. And what do you have to mad about anyway?"

For the longest time, he didn't answer. He took a deep, audible breath, and it was then that I realized his apparent calmness was taking some effort to maintain.

"I didn't want to do this with you tonight."

"Do what? Talk about Kevin? He's my ex, Keir. We're not friends."

"I know you're not friends," he responded, and sharp eyes swung back to mine.

"What is that supposed to mean?"

He shook his head. "Just that you made it pretty clear at the game where we both stand. That's why he's calling you, by the way."

Ah, so this was *my* doing, his face clearly said.

"You think I introduced you as my friend because I wanted to let him know that I wasn't on a date?"

"Am I wrong?"

I felt a shiver move down my spine with the realization that he wasn't entirely okay with that, despite his whole *just friends* bullshit.

"Yes, dammit, you are! And don't you dare try to put this on me, Keir. You're the one who set these ground rules, remember?"

He was fully staring at me as he digested this fact in stony silence. I could see he regretted the entire tone of the conversation, but it was too late. The tension was there, and thick enough to cut with a knife. Finally, his hands went to his hips and his head dropped. For several seconds, nothing else was said between us.

Honestly, I was dumbfounded. I felt like I was being bested at a game for which I didn't know the rules. And the stakes were apparently high, because things that meant something were suddenly at risk.

"You don't have to tell me I'm being the world's biggest hypocrite," he muttered. "I know I have no right to feel so indignant about any of this. I sound like a giant dick." There was a note of self-recrimination that I despised, despite however well deserved it may have been.

"Okay—so why don't you tell me what this is really about. Because it's not about Kevin, is it?"

He rubbed a hand over his jawline. "No, it's not about Kevin."

Keir picked up the netted bag of brussels sprouts and a knife like he was going to do something with them, but then he set them both down and stared out the kitchen window. Of all the conversations I imagined us having tonight, this wasn't one of them.

After what felt like an eternity, he said pointedly, "You *matter*—to me, Selene. It *matters* how this goes. That's why I told you I thought it was better for us to be friends.

"But when I heard you actually refer to me that way, and saw how your *ex* reacted to it"—Keir's body tensed again, as though finally processing this new information before he seemed to catch himself and let it go—"it just felt . . . wrong. Like it was too trivial a way to describe us. There should be a different word for this, but I don't know what it is."

He glanced sideways at me in the most bewildered way, as though he thought *I* could supply the answer. But I was at a loss too. My thoughts were a cyclone. He was right. The category of *friend* ranged from someone you'd connect with on Instagram to someone like Sarah, who'd been my unwavering supporter and confidante since we first met as freshmen at Stanford. And Keir was something else entirely. I didn't know what the right word was either.

Still, had things been different between us, I would have gone to him just then—maybe laid my cheek to his back and wrapped him in understanding arms. But we were too separated by our own thoughts and questions at that moment to make a gesture like that feel possible.

"I wasn't telling him something *about* you," I said, as he stood head down, listening. "What I said, I said *for* you. *For* you, Keir, because that's what you said you wanted. And because you felt that way about us, as your friend, I wanted it for *you*."

God, it was all so confusing.

"I know. I understand that. It *is* what I said I wanted." He turned. "Sometimes it's still what I want because it's much less complicated than how I feel right now. The problem is, when it's a good match, like it is with you and me, your heart ends up thrown in too."

The cautious part of my brain snapped to attention, and my breath caught in my throat.

"Meaning what?"

I was trying so hard to keep up with this conversation, but his mention of the word *heart* made everything feel scrambled and nonsensical. Like he'd put everything I knew to be true about us in a can, shaken it up, and let it explode. He had the chance to change things after The Arthouse, but he didn't take it. I couldn't imagine he was saying he wanted to complicate our friendship *now*—now that we were finally putting the whole kissing incident behind us.

But something *was* shifting between us. I could feel it, and I couldn't quite keep up with how quickly it was happening. I was staring, struggling to adjust to what he was saying, what it sounded like he was implying. I wanted to be absolutely clear because it would be a disaster for our friendship to make assumptions that weren't right and to admit to things he didn't want to hear.

But he didn't rush to answer, just cleared his throat of some obstruction.

"Meaning," he said finally, "that the rest of the time—pretty much all the time, it turns out—I just want you."

Our eyes locked, and neither of us broke away. My heart and stomach felt like they'd taken off in a tandem sky dive.

Outside the window, my neighborhood in the SoMa district of San Francisco was coming alive. You could hear Giants fans cheering from AT&T Park, and the sounds of people on their way to any one of the trendy restaurants nearby.

But here in my kitchen, between Keir and me, it felt like a vacuum of sound and breath.

I wasn't able to form a response to his admission—I just kept waiting for the *but* that had always followed these kinds of conversations between us.

It didn't come this time.

And when that understanding finally arrived, it hit me hard.

As he continued to gauge my reaction, his intensity softened, and those beloved, tiny creases formed on his cheeks. He stepped closer, close enough that his clothing brushed against my knees and I felt that semidrunk sensation I always got when I was this close to him.

"I want you," he said again with a rush of conviction in his voice that told me he'd had enough of arguing his case with his own conscience. "I want you in your sexy heels. Or with cake batter in your hair."

His head tilted, and chocolate eyes were warm on mine. Then he lifted his wrist, adorned with braided and leather bands, and pushed a stray strand behind my ear, resting his hands again on my knees. I touched one with my fingertips, maybe to know that he wouldn't pull away. That what he was saying was real.

He didn't pull away. Instead, he entwined his hand in mine, squeezing firmly as if to emphasize the certainty of his intent.

"And I want you when you're laughing at me. And when you're feeling broken inside. I want you naked in my bed," he added with a hint of confession that caused something to swell in my body and make my knees go weak. "Every side of you in every light of day, for as long as we have. That's what I want."

I felt like I'd been pulled from my body, like I was watching this exchange from across the room. Keir's tall frame was pressing firmly against my bare legs. And he looked at me with such a complicated mix of emotions; I hardly knew where to begin in dissecting them. But I couldn't take my eyes off his impassioned face and I knew I'd never forget it.

He always had this startling quality of maleness that commanded absolute attention and made other men seem anemic by comparison. But not since The Arthouse had I experienced it at such close range. My chest squeezed tight, and I felt overcome. Even more so because that first small taste of him had been nearly all consuming. It was hard to imagine what the second might be.

"I want that too," I whispered, my lungs feeling suddenly very thick. Until this moment, I didn't realize just how much I wanted this friendship barrier to dissolve and how much I wanted whatever it was that came next.

"Tell me we're not going to fuck things up between us," he said softly.

He had dropped all his masks. The hope, the doubt, the fear were all there as plain as day in his expression, and so intense and earnest that it gave me pause.

Still, I willfully silenced that part of me that similarly recognized the potential jeopardy to our friendship.

"We won't," I stupidly replied. Like I could have known such a thing. Like I wasn't the *worst* person to ask because I was pointedly avoiding all thoughts of the future. For my own reasons, I was turning a blind eye to everything beyond today.

But Keir accepted my assurance because he wanted to. His searching gaze moved over my face, taking inventory of any possible hesitation. Finding none at all, he took my cheek in hand and kissed me soundly. And this time, it didn't feel like a battle being lost.

Chapter 13

Selene

It wasn't a sweet kiss.

And it wasn't returned that way.

Leaning forward, he pressed his lips against mine, digging his fingers into my hair and pinning me against the upper cabinets behind me. My own hands mirrored his, pushing up into his thick hair and closing my fists roughly around handfuls of silky strands. My heart was rioting inside my chest, and every blood cell was rattling the bars.

Teeth clashing and breath tasting faintly of wine, it was as if we were two lovers long kept apart—two lovers for whom the clock was relentlessly ticking, eroding that precious time we had to get closer, to feel more, to leave nothing on the table. We quickly grew messy, ardent, melting together as if this long-delayed and mutually understood brief love affair had always been meant to be.

As long as we have. That was the time frame we were working with. We were making an uneasy bargain with the future, and we both knew it.

Keir bent, sucking my neck, my jaw, releasing his fingers from my hair so he could run his hands under the skirt of my dress to touch the skin on my upper thighs.

We both looked down, almost in awe, our foreheads together, breathing heavy and fast.

"I can't believe we're doing this," I whispered, holding on to his shoulders while my knees gripped his hips. "I've imagined it so many times."

"I know," he nodded quickly. "Me too." There was an urgency in his voice that was rough, and naked with need. "But let's go somewhere more comfortable. I'm not leaving tonight."

"No. Here," I insisted. The fever beneath my skin was making me impatient; I didn't want to waste a single second. Maybe this was just one night, and if it was, I was going to have to condense everything I wanted from it into a few hours. After all, I wanted him enough for a *hundred* nights. This night, or the uncertain number of those that might follow, was not enough—would never be enough.

Keir pulled back, just for a moment, and in his ardent face was a question. But the answer came easily, and dark eyes flashed with understanding. He had said it himself—*you never really know what's coming.* And he was right: grab happiness when you can; live fully in every single moment.

Still, a tiny suspicion in the back of my mind told me that this urgency wasn't about any of that. It was more about *him.*

Keir nodded, then reached across his shoulder and tugged his shirt over his head, dropping it carelessly to the floor.

The sight of him was absolutely stunning—like everything I imagined it would be, and still a little bit more: clean lines of perfectly toned muscle that tightened under my hungry touch; a dusting of fine, dark hair that curled across the top of his chest, diminishing to a point at his navel; deep cuts down his abdomen and across his hips that disappeared behind the waistband of his jeans.

His nipples were knotted tight, and he inhaled sharply when I set my mouth to one. Then, exhaling forcefully, he gave himself over to the pleasure of my tongue. His hands found their way into the twist of my hair, releasing it to tumble around my shoulders.

That was the moment the reality of what we were about to do fully set in. We weren't just going to break the friendship barrier; we were going to obliterate it. And once we did, there was no going back. *Tell me we're not going to fuck things up between us.*

No, we could do this. *Oh, dear god, I hoped we could do this.*

"Tell me what you need tonight. I want to give you everything." His voice was husky and rough, and my chest twisted to see how anxious he was to please me. Like it meant everything to him.

"I don't know," I whispered, suddenly painfully aware that I had no plan for this. How could I? Making love to Keir had never felt like a real possibility. "I think I just want to see you come apart like you do in my mind every time I close my eyes."

He laughed softly and reached up to touch my face. "I think we both know I've been coming apart for weeks."

He lifted me and set me down on bare feet in front of him, then stepped back only far enough for me to turn, allowing him to unzip my dress and push it to the floor. With a flick of his fingers my bra came undone and I shrugged out of it. Following quickly behind was my underwear, which he tugged down my legs and off.

"Fuck, you are so beautiful." He took a step back and leaned against the counter for support. His eyes were like hot coals, dragging over my body from head to toe, setting my skin on fire. "It's staggering what that does to me."

And, god, I believed him. I blinked down to the button fly of his jeans, now distorted with the shape of him, hard as stone beneath.

With every passing moment, I was experiencing Keir less and less as this amazing friend and more as this gorgeous man who I was growing increasingly desperate to get closer to. Yet it was exactly because of who he was, and who he was to me, that I was so lost in him.

I couldn't hold on to the inclination to be self-conscious. I felt nothing but powerful and beautiful and strong. That's the effect he had on me.

That's why the two of us together, side by side, could have easily felt like the future being written. But I wasn't that naive. In life, there are things you can have but you just can't keep. Keir was one of those things for me. He had a great big, beautiful life ahead of him—ready for the taking. And I had, literally, a once-in-a-lifetime opportunity to focus on my father and to ensure that there were no words unspoken, no future regrets to be shouldered.

So *this* moment between Keir and me—no matter what else followed—became everything.

We stumbled blindly together to a dining room chair, four hands waging war on his jeans and pushing them impatiently down his hips until his cock strained up, thick and heavy between us. It was as magnificent as the rest of him. My palms slid down the expanse of his torso, the ridges of his abdomen, the sharp curve of his hips, to the silkiness of his erection. It was one thing to see all this—it was another thing entirely to touch it. I wrapped my hand around him, gliding down and then back up, causing him to groan a long, drawn-out sound.

He wasted no time pulling me astride, and tugging his length from my hand, he aligned it to me. With a guttural growl that honestly could have come from either of us—or both together—he thrust deeply inside.

His cheeks were flushed with desire as he looked up at me from under a fan of long, dark lashes. Then we began to move, rocking forward and back. His heavy lids fluttered closed with a groan of helpless relief that I recognized, and mirrored, entirely.

The last of the daylight was giving way to evening, causing the sky outside my window to offer up ribbons of clouds in pinks and purples and golds. It bathed the room in the most splendid tones that lit our skin in a soft glow.

I stretched into him, pressing my bare chest to his, and he let out a shaking breath, sliding his hand down my side, where he pulled my hip against his abdomen, working himself into me, deeper still. His lips were distracted and hungry over my jawline, licking the taste from my skin.

"Selene, my god. It feels so—"

He cut himself off when his mouth found mine again, already open and searching for his, and I knew the second I tasted him that we were skipping the slow exploration. Instead, our movements quickly turned into a frenzy, the dining room chair slamming against the table behind.

We made love feverishly, passionately, the rasp of his beard dragging over the delicate skin between my breasts, and his deft hands knowing instinctively how to touch me.

Somewhere deep down I always knew it would be like this between us.

I opened my eyes to the sight of his, hungry with need, pushing me—pushing me further, guiding me when I faltered. His mouth curved into a knowing smile as he watched me take what I needed from his body, growling words of praise and encouragement.

"I thought you were pulling away from me this week," I whispered.

"I tried to, but I couldn't."

It was such a bare and straightforward admission that it felt *big*— like I should be paying more attention to both why he wanted to distance himself and why he wasn't able to. But I wasn't sure my heart was ready for big. It felt too fragile.

Plus, he was grating across the most sensitive part of my body again and again, each time with more intent, knowing exactly how close I was. So that was as far recognizable as my thoughts could go.

Beyond that was all feeling. My head fell forward, and I was pulled deep inside myself, captured by the searing sense of being alive in a moment that only an orgasm of this magnitude can command.

Pleasure clawed its way up every limb and tore through me in a rain of wild bliss.

And I wasn't fully back into my thinking brain when I felt him lift me, hard as steel inside, and lay me on the table behind. It was then that he finally gave in to what his body truly needed. His guttural sounds became unrefined as he gripped my thighs with his fingertips, hammering. I loved how the closer he came to his own release, the less nuanced he was. And I didn't know how sex with Keir could ever be slow again, now that we both knew how it felt when he completely let go.

He came with a loud groan, a choking, rasping approximation of my name, and his movements suddenly became jerky and uncoordinated.

Then, every fiber of muscle seemed to dissolve with fatigue, and he collapsed around me, heavy and spent; his breath was soft and warm on my neck. His hand slid softly, tenderly, over my breast and down my waist, along the curve of my hip, and then up again. I wrapped my arms around his broad back, and there we stayed, frozen in a state of satisfaction and relief.

Chapter 14

Keir

I could barely move.

Every limb felt like it weighed a hundred pounds. Even on my feet and bent over the table, I could easily have passed out with my chest draped heavily over Selene's and the vanilla scent of her hair filling my senses. I was still deep inside her, half-hard, but nowhere near ready to let her go.

When her hands drifted across my shoulders, and she shifted a little beneath me, I realized I was probably crushing her under the weight of my torso. I forced myself to lift off just enough to press a soft kiss into her neck, just below her ear.

"Hey, you."

"Hey," she breathed, her fingertips drifting down my arms.

She looked so perfect under me, so languid and content, I could still hardly believe it. This was the girl I had wanted from that very first day, and the one I had fallen a little harder for every day since.

I kissed her again, this time on the corner of her mouth, and then straightened reluctantly and finally pulled out.

I'd fantasized about Selene naked more times than I would probably want to admit, but the reality of her here, spread out in front of me, was much better. It was so much better. She looked sweaty and ravished, and certainly the most beautiful thing I'd ever seen. It absolutely rocked me. I couldn't stop looking at her—eyes still closed, dark hair and long legs spilling over the edges of the table, her hands drifting over the soft curves of her stomach.

"Did I break you?"

A smile teased out from her strawberry lips. She stretched her arms up over her head, and her breasts lifted into these perfect round swells.

"No," she said, finally opening her eyes languorously and meeting my gaze with a softness that struck me somewhere deep in my chest. "But I think you may have just set an impossibly high bar for all my partners going forward, and probably put to shame anyone I've been with up to this point."

I'll admit the caveman inside me fell a little in love with that idea—that I could override her sexual history in one night together and reshape the way she thought about past lovers. But another part of me—a part that felt like it had been dormant for a long time—stirred and twisted at the thought of some other man someday having the opportunity to see her the way I did at this moment: so open and trusting and satisfied. Just the idea of it made me feel surly and rebellious. And that part of me wanted to leave fingerprints so indelible in every corner of her mind that no one else could ever whitewash the way it felt to lose ourselves in each other like we did tonight.

"Did you just call me godlike in bed?"

She laughed so naturally and so unguardedly that it lit her whole face from inside and made her eyes glow in warmth. The sound was much louder than you'd expect from someone as elegant as she, but that's what I loved about it. It was surprising. She tilted her head back, exposing her long slender neck and unblemished skin, and I was instantly addicted to the way she looked and to the sounds she made that felt happy in a soul-deep way.

"I don't remember that."

I would. Probably forever.

"That's because I just blew your mind, and now you're babbling and incoherent. How about we take a shower and then I'll make you dinner? If you think you can walk."

"Always so cocky, Stevens."

"Apparently, not for nothing."

She shook her head, licking her lips to a delicious shine, and held out her hand to me. I took it, threading my fingers between hers and tugging her up and off the table so I could gather her close to my chest, just to feel the way she pressed against me. Her body was still a little damp from the mixture of our sweat, and I kind of loved that too.

With both hands, I pushed her hair away from her face. My thumbs caressed the sculpted lines of her cheekbones, holding her still as I delivered a kiss to her lips, capturing her breath. The moment I felt her open to me, I pushed deeper inside, struggling to balance my desire to be gentle with my tendency to be impatient.

There were a million things I knew I should say about how happy I was when I was with her and how right it felt to make love and how I wanted to stay in this thing with her for as long as she would have me. But the language for what I felt just then wasn't forming fast enough. I couldn't quite articulate any of it. Because as she pulled me tighter against her body, the thought of touching her again, slowly, when I could savor it and enjoy every one of her sounds and the way she tasted on my tongue, erased everything else in my head.

§

Selene climbed into the shower, then turned on the water and watched through the glass door as I stepped out of my jeans. I took my time, liking the way she made no attempt to hide her appreciation of my body, and liking even more the way the water rolled over the lines of her breasts and her backside. I followed her in, and in only seconds I was rigid and felt a fever slide over my skin and dig down deep into my muscles. My cock poked at her hip when she turned to kiss my neck.

"I can't really figure you out, Keir," she told me, dragging her teeth along my jaw. "Tell me, why were you trying to pull away from me this week?"

Big eyes met mine, and a knot took hold in my gut. I'd been a prick. The fact that it was unintentionally cruel didn't make me feel any better about it. Resting my hands on her hips, squeezing, I leaned my forehead into hers. How could I explain what months of grief and turmoil had done to my head? What were the right words to explain how being with her both calmed and fueled that chaos inside me?

"Honestly . . . I feel a little out of my depth with you. Maybe it's partly due to what's been happening in my life, but I think mostly it's just you. I don't know what to do about how I feel or how to stop feeling this way about you. And I don't think I've ever been filled with so much longing for someone and had no idea how it would play out. I know that's not a worthy explanation for disappearing on you, though. I'm truly sorry."

I could see how my answer winded her. Like maybe she was expecting me to make a joke or play this off like it was just about sex. Attracted to her as I was, this had never just been about sex.

"So what changed? Why did you text me again?"

Something in her voice, some vulnerability or dip in its strength, told me these were questions whose answers would decide her level of trust in me. Though as she asked them, her fingers were drifting over my chest, and down my abdomen. I could barely think when she did that.

"I missed you. So damn much. And I realized I needed to be honest with you—and, frankly, with myself—about what I'm feeling because it isn't something I can just go home and try to forget about. I couldn't stop thinking about us and what having you in my life means to me, even if you didn't feel the same way. I just needed to tell you . . . Selene, I . . ."

I was stumbling closer and closer to the truth, the *whole* truth that is, but when she wrapped her hand around me and her mouth began sucking at my nipple, anything else I might have admitted dissolved into the physical sensation of her touch. I was so consumed by the feel of it I had to reach out to the tile behind her to steady myself as the water ran warm down my back. Selene let out a little moan, and her hand slid over the head of my cock and lower, incinerating any coherent thought. She had me literally and figuratively by the balls. I gave in, a full surrender. Whatever resistance I may have been able to muster up to this point in our relationship was gone.

I belonged to her. It was that simple.

"If it's any consolation," she said, pulling me out of my head, "I couldn't stop thinking about you either."

I had to admit, after nearly a week of torturing, mental madness, it sort of was. But even as I was thinking that, a part of my brain registered a change in the tone of her voice. It wasn't vulnerable or hesitant like it had been before. It was . . . I had to see her face to understand it. I opened my eyes to a sexy little smirk that lit my bloodstream like a match to kerosene, causing my entire body to stiffen.

"Did you ever think of me when you were in here? In the shower?" I asked her.

"I may have."

My thoughts were spinning. This was *new*. I began to guide her hand down and up, over the tip, just the way I liked it. "What was I doing?"

"You were very good with soap."

Fuck. This girl.

I took a step back, pulling from her grasp, and a grin threatened to split my face. If only I could have climbed into her head just then I would've wildly ransacked her brain like I was robbing the place. I suddenly wanted to know everything about what turned her on and what she liked. Everything.

Just to see her reaction, I picked up a bottle of bath gel and lathered up my hands. Cupping my balls with one, I stroked up and down my shaft with the other while Selene watched me caress my own body with naked interest.

"Did I say anything when I was being particularly good with soap?"

Her eyes were transfixed on my fist. "No. Mostly you kept your arrogant mouth shut, which was refreshing."

There was no containing my grin now. I added more soap to my palms and stepped close enough to her that her breasts touched my chest. I ran my hands, lathered and warm, under her arms, over her breasts, and down between her legs, where I could feel her heat on my fingers. I leaned in to kiss a line up her neck.

For some reason, I decided to test her a little. I had no idea where the urge came from but I was finding myself in this wayward, eccentric mood, half–rebellious, half–pleasure seeking.

"That's no fun," I murmured. "I wasn't whispering filthy things in your ear like how phenomenal your tits are and how I love to feel the weight of them in my hands when I suck your nipples? And how my cock would look against your skin and what it would feel like to take you between your breasts?"

She exhaled a gust of breath against my neck, and victory surged sharply in my gut.

"You might have said something like that."

I had *never* said anything like that to her. And the fact that she might want me to gave me a serious rush of adrenaline. Modern and liberated as she was, I would never have guessed a little dirty talk would make her blush. But I loved the way her breathing accelerated and her eyes grew big like saucers—like pools of ink in a sea of green. The way her pulse quickened in her neck. My girl liked dirty talk. *Amazing.*

I suddenly realized that there was a whole new side to us that we could explore now that we'd torn past the restraints of being strictly friends. There were layers and layers of Selene to discover, and I wanted to know them all—to peel back each piece and lay them out carefully so that I could solve every little mystery of her. I wanted to make her body give up all its secrets. And even more than that, I wanted to know how her mind worked. I wanted her to tell me things she wouldn't tell a guy friend but things she might tell a lover. I wanted a level of intimacy with her that I hadn't wanted to have with anyone in a lot of years.

"Maybe I said how beautiful you are here between your legs and how I'm dying to cover you with my mouth and with my tongue until you come on my lips?"

"Jesus, Keir," she whispered in a trembling voice.

"Tell me what you want me to do to you. What do you like, Selene?" When I kissed her neck, I could feel her swallow against my lips.

"That. What you just said."

Oh, thank god.

I dropped to my knees in front of her, looking up to meet her eyes. The heat and the excitement I saw there almost made me lose my mind. Her hands went to my hair, fingers running through the messy wet strands, as I lifted one leg over my shoulder. I couldn't wait to taste her. Couldn't wait to hear the sounds she made when she was lost.

My palms down drifted along the silky skin of her calf, and I planted biting kisses along her thighs. The closer I got to the space between her legs, the more I could feel her muscles tense, her breath hitch.

She was swollen and slick, and she gasped when I blew a soft stream of air across her heated flesh. I met her gaze again and gave her one more wicked smile before opening my mouth over her. My eyes closed at the taste of her, and I groaned, sucking gently.

She tugged at my hair. "Oh god, Keir," she whimpered, her voice pleading and her hips rocking farther off the tile in search of me.

The taste of her filled my mouth, making me feel wild. Every pass of my tongue elicited a moan that made me even more desperate for her pleasure.

"Don't stop," she whispered. Like I could? I needed this as much as she did. I felt like everything inside me was coming unraveled at such an alarming rate, and the only thing grounding me was this physical connection to her.

I added my fingers, finding where she was the neediest. The heavy drag of my touch made her a little unsteady on her standing leg. As I watched, tiny sounds of pleading misery and pleasure slipped from her lips, and I did everything I could to keep up the intensity.

She was right there, hovering at the edge. Her thighs started to shake, and I wrapped my free arm around her to keep her from falling. I pushed deep, sucking until my cheeks hollowed. I was staring up the length of her body, at her perfect breasts and long neck; I didn't want to miss the moment she let go.

Finally, she arched deeply, letting out a ragged cry, wild and wide open, as I roughly devoured her. I couldn't for one second look away from the sight above me as the water pulsed around us.

I was completely lost in her.

Even after her breathing slowed, even after her head lolled back to the wall and her jaw fell slack, I couldn't stop looking at her. I wanted to memorize everything. I wanted to make sure I would be able to remember every detail when our time together was through. I never wanted to forget what she looked like *right now*. These were the moments I knew I was plummeting deeper and deeper into my feelings for her.

"Come to me," she breathed. I could barely hear her over the pounding of the water on my back, but I watched her lips form the words I wanted her to say more than almost any others.

I was harder than I think I'd ever been in my life. I released her leg from my shoulder, then rose, dragging the weight of my cock along her thigh as I tasted every inch of her skin, licking the dip of her belly button, the rise of her breasts, the tight pull of her nipples. Being with her in this way was like being able to take a full breath for the first time in weeks.

The beast in me wanted to have every part of her. I wasn't kidding when I said I wanted to see what my cock looked like in the valley of her breasts. But right now, more than anything, I was aching to be inside her. I couldn't imagine anything better than that.

I wanted to savor the feeling of her—the perfection of her and me together, all the things she made me feel when she touched me. Being inside her was like all of life itself and a small flash of eternity pulsing through me. I felt remade.

In every way except one, we were so right together. But that one— that last fact that I lived in Seattle and she lived here—was a big one. Our lives weren't tidy little bundles of activity we could just fit together like a puzzle. They were messy and irregularly shaped, and they felt dauntingly incompatible. Owning a catering business meant long hours every day, but nights and weekends were especially insane. Throw a restaurant into the mix, and I was going to be married to my work. I didn't know how to fit a relationship into that, let alone a long-distance one. And Selene's life was just as crazy. Launching a career and making a name for herself meant there was no way she could be running off to spend time with me. And perhaps a bigger hurdle was the needs of her family. Her dad was everything to her; she certainly couldn't be away from him now. Even after he was gone, her mom and her sister would need her close by. And she would need them too. No one understood that better than I. I wanted more than anything for her to fare better than I had these last months after losing my pop. I wouldn't wish that on anyone.

The unanswered questions were piling up in my head, and she sensed it. "Where are you right now?" she breathed. "Come back to me."

I stilled over her, resting my forehead to her shoulder.

Thinking about all this made me feel a little desperate to make this moment last as long as I could, to prolong the feeling of *us* in this tiny, protected place where none of that could come between us. Just to have her now and figure everything else out later.

"I never left, Selene," I told her honestly. "You're all I can think about."

Very slowly, I began moving in and out of her with my face buried in her neck. The chaos turned to peace. Her arms came around me so tightly, not like she was holding on to me, but like she was holding me, my heart in her hand. Like she could hear it beating, and she knew what it meant.

And I almost said it. Right then, I almost said *I love you.* The words were so close that I literally had to turn my head away because I knew I couldn't look at her without projecting those feelings across my face.

"It's never felt like this for me," she whispered.

Her words were like a dim echo of my thoughts. This felt like nothing I'd ever experienced, that was so true, but it was more than just a physical thing. I'd had plenty of girls in my life that I considered friends, and I'd had plenty of lovers whom I cared for. I'd had a serious relationship that over time became more of a friendship than a romance.

But I'd never had a woman who meant so much to me as a friend, and who *also* happened to be my passionate lover and the person I most wanted to spend time with.

No, it had never been like this for me either. Nothing had ever felt so much like what I imagined real love would be. For the first time, I was in way over my head. And I knew right then, making love to Selene under the warmth of the shower with my teeth on her skin and her body pressed tightly to mine, that when our time was up and this thing was over, it was going to fucking hurt.

Chapter 15

Selene

Stealing Keir's T-shirt after our shower together had two amazing benefits: First, it smelled like him. It was some combination of his soap and his deodorant and a hard-to-define maleness that I savored as I pulled the collar up to my nose, leaning against the kitchen counter with wet hair and not much more.

The second benefit was the more obvious one: a shirtless Keir. For more than a month, I'd admired his shoulders, his throat, and the curve of his bottom lip. But until tonight, I'd only seen glimpses of the way these parts transitioned through elegant arches and sharp angles to the broad slopes of his chest and the tight lacing of the muscles down his abdomen.

As if he could feel me staring, Keir grabbed a teaspoon out of the drawer and scooped a small bite of the potatoes he'd been whipping from the pot.

"Here, taste." He moved closer, holding it to my lips. "Good?"

"Yes, definitely."

"Are they smooth enough?"

"Yes, perfect. It's all perfect."

A small grin tugged at the corners of his mouth, and no wonder.

Even to my own ears, I sounded like a lovesick teenager. With anyone else, I might have felt self-conscious about that, but he leaned forward and touched his lips to mine in a way that wiped those thoughts from my head completely. This wasn't a ravenous and hungry kiss like before, but it was real.

We were in this, both of us.

If we had meant to somehow spare each other's emotions by maintaining a certain distance, it seemed we were very much too late.

And yes, a little voice in the back of my head urged me to take a closer look at the wisdom of that, but the voice evaporated almost immediately. In my mind, the feel of him was still too fresh, too overwhelming.

"All perfect, huh?" he asked, pulling back a bit.

"The *potatoes* are perfect," I clarified. "The sex, if I'm being honest here, was a little disappointing."

A grin burst across his face like I knew it would. He was fun like that.

"You know, when I was sixteen, my friend Sean told me that girls don't actually like the sex part of sex. He said they only like the kissing and touching and stuff like that. So I should just get in, do my thing, and get out."

"Your thing?"

"Oh, yeah."

"And did you listen to this lover-genius?"

"I think I did," he said laughing. "I mean, he'd probably only slept with, like, one girl, but it was still one girl more than I'd slept with, so, I mean, *expert*."

"Well, of course!"

We were both smiling as he glanced down to take the spoon from my hand and set it on the sink. Then he gathered me against his warm, naked chest, my hands settling there, where he seemed to like them. He had that sensual smell that made me want him all over again. Suddenly I was seeing us three hours ago in this very spot with nothing but awkwardness and uncertainty between us, and in the contrast, there was this moment when

everything
felt
so
surreal.

He was standing in front of me, with his hips against my stomach, half-bare, blatantly happy, and it was like the universe had somehow bent itself backward and was now spinning in the opposite direction—like Cinderella and the Wizard of Oz got together and had a cosmic baby that was *this* moment.

I looked at my hands on his chest, where lean muscle and soft hair were tantalizing to touch. My fingers spread apart and lifted slightly so they were just barely making contact with his smooth skin.

I had woken up this very day, not sure if I would ever hear from him again, let alone this. But here he was. Not just here, but here and mine.

And sex. And kissing. And everything.

For one night, at least.

My hands moved fractionally in unison, absorbing the feel of him, warm and present. I looked up again into eyes that had so many more colors in them than I'd ever realized before.

"What?" he asked, and his brows twitched in question.

I shook my head.

Because how do you actually talk to someone about happiness?

He continued to watch me for just a fraction of a second, and I knew he was reading the moment correctly. Bending, he touched his lips to mine and held there for one, two, three achingly beautiful heartbeats.

Then he went on as if there had been no interruption in our conversation at all.

"You'll be glad to know I was more discerning with advice after that."

"I am glad to know that. So what's the best sex advice you ever got?"

"Have it as often as possible."

I laughed. "I'm serious."

Keir released me as he thought about this and moved to the sink where he sliced the netting on a bag of brussels sprouts he'd abandoned earlier. Then his eyes swung to mine. "Probably from my pop."

"Really?"

He nodded. "He wasn't big on giving advice, and this was probably the one and only time we ever talked about sex. But I remember he told me once that when I take a woman to my bed, I should always be gentle with her and treat her with respect, even if I don't love her."

"That's what he told you?"

"I always remembered it," he answered nodding, and poured the contents of the bag into a colander to wash.

"And have you followed his advice?"

"I think so. Well, maybe not *always* the gentle part." He looked at me with a pointedly cringy face.

I laughed. "I'll let you slide." Keir came back and took my face in his hands, planting a small kiss on my mouth. With my fingertips, I traced the outline of his face, the sharp lines, the angles and slopes— the smooth skin along his cheeks and the rough part along his jaw.

"And what if you *do* love her?" I added, letting my eyes adjust to the closeness of us.

It didn't occur to me that I had asked such a loaded question until I noticed he was studying me. By then, it was too late to take it back.

He didn't answer right away, his hands finding their way to my hips. But then he tilted his head to the side, and what I saw spoke more of contemplation than discomfort.

"That bar was set pretty high for him," he said in reflection. "But judging by his life, by the fact that he never wanted anyone after my mom, I think he would have said that loving someone means you're given the stars, and that's only given once."

Outside my kitchen window, the clouds were lit at their edges by a nearly full moon that gave them the appearance of cotton balls dipped in silver.

Keir returned to his work, shaking the sprouts in the colander and then pouring them out onto a cutting board. In the absence of conversation, his answer floated between us like a delicate bubble: something beautiful to be considered and appreciated but not to be touched—not at all—or it would burst and disappear.

It was just a small glimpse into him, and into the man who'd raised him single-handedly, but it made me want to know everything—to assemble a more complete picture of the person I was falling for, even if I shouldn't have been.

"Keir, what about your mom?"

"My mom?"

"Yes, I've never heard you mention her before."

"Oh," he said glancing up. "She died when I was very young."

"I didn't know that."

Seeing my reaction, he quickly went on. "I never knew her. Not really. She was diabetic all her life, and by the time she and my pop got married, they already knew her health was fragile. But they wanted each other, and they wanted me, so . . ."

He let the thought go like it had exhausted itself, and stood watching as I processed the full implication of this.

For me, it was a huge revelation. Absent another explanation, I assumed Keir's mother had left them early on—perhaps not ready to be a parent. I'd always been a little afraid to bring it up. But this . . . this was a massive act of love on the part of both his parents and it left me a little breathless.

"She must have loved you."

"Yeah, she did."

His conviction told me this fact had been so lovingly reinforced throughout his life that it just became part of his DNA. Something elemental to who he was. And I had the sudden hope that there was a very special place in heaven for single parents.

"Was it hard for you?"

"Not having a mom?" He paused thoughtfully, and chose a different knife from the block. "You don't know what you don't know. I mean, I had a happy childhood. I always felt safe and well cared for."

He began slicing the sprouts, all the while considering the question further.

"I probably could have used a little more supervision as a teenager. And, of course, I would have liked having a mom, though I never felt like my pop wasn't enough. If anything, he probably felt her absence more than I did, trying to raise me by himself."

"Why?"

Light from the window caught his eyes as he glanced over. "Well, looking back, I'm sure he felt ill equipped for me. I was a small human hurricane. A chronic spiller. And I broke a lot of stuff, myself included. I'm sure there were times he would've liked to sell me to the nearest traveling circus, but instead he got me into hockey. I think that's what you resort to when you have a tiny Tasmanian devil on your hands." Keir smiled broadly. "*Spirited* is the word we used."

"Spirited," I echoed with a grin.

"When I was a teenager, I wrecked both his cars in a single weekend."

"Seriously?"

"Seriously. He was out of town, and my friend Sean and I had this idea to take his old restored Chevy off-roading."

"Sean, the lover-genius?"

"Right." He laughed, catching my eye. "Anyway, we cracked the main cylinder. And then the next day on some similar dumb-ass idea, I wrapped his Buick around a tree. It's a wonder we didn't kill ourselves."

"Holy shit, Keir."

"I know. My pop called me at Sean's house and actually told me not to come home for a few days. I'll never forget—it was a Wednesday night when I finally walked back into our kitchen, and he was sitting at the table with his hands folded in front of him like he'd been just sitting there for hours. I don't think I've ever been so scared in my life. I think it would have been easier if he'd have kicked my ass like I deserved, but he wasn't that way. He was mad as hell, but he was also disappointed in me, and that was so much worse."

"I can't even imagine what my dad would have said. I think he would have grounded me for *years*. That is, after he exhausted himself with some wild gesticulating."

I smiled with that thought, but then the expression froze on my face as I tried to remember the last time I'd seen my dad do that. Growing up, I would have sworn he couldn't take a breath without waving his arms around. But that all seemed so distant. He was weak now. So diminished.

Keir seemed to understand the change that moved across my expression or had some awareness of my drop into melancholy.

"I think I'm actually *still* grounded from that episode," he said. "Releasing myself has been a real moral dilemma for me since he passed."

I sniffed out a breath, and he winked at me, coming over to cup my face and place a kiss to my forehead. I set my hands on his forearms.

"So how does a guy go from total destruction to being meticulous about his truck and his aprons?"

"He starts paying for shit himself, that's how."

On Keir's cheeks sat deep lines—nearly dimples—that bracketed a widely curved mouth and perfect white teeth. His eyes sparkled with a vibrancy I thought was probably very characteristic of him—like something inside him that screamed life was *on*! In fact, if all of us have a look that most defines us, this was probably his.

He and I had met at a difficult moment in his life—a moment that understandably clouded who he naturally was. In fact, when I thought back to that angry, impatient man I first met on the Golden Gate Bridge, I would hardly recognize him to be the same one standing in my kitchen now—shirtless, relaxed and, between conversation, humming.

It was a gorgeous thing to see his joy returning, and a hopeful reassurance that it was possible to get to the other side of what was still in front of me. I nestled close, absorbing the happiness he exuded, and pressed my mouth lightly to his.

"So does this mean you like me again?" he asked.

"What do you mean?"

"You were mad at me when I got here, and now you're smiling."

"Oh, that. Well, I'm trying very hard not to like you again, but it's not going very well."

Keir chuckled. "I'm glad to hear it." He bent slowly to place a featherlight kiss on the soft part of my neck just below my earlobe. "Because after I feed you, I plan to get *spirited* all over again."

That low, sexy voice and the rasp of his beard on my neck made my stomach clench. I closed my eyes and ran my hands over the sleek, powerful muscles of his bare arms. The warmth and closeness of his body erased all awareness of time, of hunger, of everything.

We were two people living in the moment and feasting on pleasure and distraction. Both of us in flight—me from the future, Keir from the past. So the touch of a fingertip over the curve of a shoulder became exploration, and then an invitation, and further satisfaction. But there was no satiety.

We placed little value on sleep, simply made love until exhaustion took us.

And that's how, in the hours together, neither of us heard our cell phones ring. And even if we had, chances are we would have been too far-gone to care, and definitely too far-gone to check that those phone calls had produced urgent voicemails, and those urgent voicemails would mark the beginning of our disentanglement— messy and painful like the angry sounds of scraping metal and buckling plastic that had foretold this moment from the very first day we met.

Chapter 16

Keir

I always wanted to learn to draw but never had the temperament for it. Growing up, I was a bottomless well of energy that, when channeled properly, was a mighty force. When channeled poorly, I tended toward destruction. Drawing was simply too restrained an activity for me.

But had I had a pencil and the talent, a scene like this might have been my inspiration. Selene lay in bed sleeping, her body just an outline—a dark, tousled ridge of covers. Thick, shiny mahogany hair spread across her pillow, and a look of dreaminess graced her expression. In the early-morning light, her absolute beauty hit me squarely, all over again.

I'd risen before dawn, needing to get to the produce mart early before all the good stuff was gone. But showered and dressed, keys in hand, I couldn't quite pull myself away.

It was not yet six o'clock, mostly dark in the room still, and the day was just beginning to come up in streaks. I sat down heavily on the edge of the bed and stroked the curves of her face at her hairline, where soft wisps framed the transition to her flawless olive skin. She looked so perfect.

"Hey there," I said softly. "You awake?"

We'd made a complete mess of her bed. The sheets were pulled from the mattress at all corners, pillows were shoved between the mattress and the headboard, and the comforter had been pushed to the floor. Selene lay on her side, one arm under her pillow and the other bent in front of her. Her hand was softly curled at her breast, which was partly exposed by the sheet, and on her shoulder was a small hickey I didn't remember giving her. At the sound of my voice, she nodded sleepily but didn't open her eyes.

"Are you sure?"

Her full lips parted slightly as though she might speak, but then closed again, wordless. They were a little red and swollen from the drag of my day-old beard, and I had to kiss them.

"I have to go to work," I told her in a hushed tone, touching my forehead to hers.

She nodded again vaguely.

Reaching over, I checked that the alarm clock on the nightstand was set to wake her by seven o'clock. I wasn't surprised she was exhausted—I knew I would be feeling the lack of sleep, myself, in a few hours, but at the moment I was filled with an energy that felt almost limitless. The images I held were ones I knew I would still be thinking about for days to come, months even: the taste of her lips that I now knew so well, the feel of her breasts in my hands, being achingly hard inside her, watching her come apart in my arms, coming apart in hers. It was as if we'd made love with twice the intensity in case our time together was half as long. And with this one night, we had fixed our relationship so that there was no going back to what we had before. Only forward.

Throughout the very early hours of the morning, I'd lain in bed feeling almost foreign to myself, but in a good way. With this beautiful woman in my arms, sleeping quietly beside me, I felt happy. Whole.

And, strangely enough, in no particular hurry to get back home. For the next few weeks, we could just enjoy this thing between us. *For as long as we have.* After that . . . well, we had time to decide what came after that. No way was I going to give her up unless she made me.

"I'm going to wear your underwear on my head today," I whispered, just to see if she was really awake. And sure enough, very slowly, a sleepy grin developed on her face, her eyes still closed.

"There she is." I smiled, too. "Do you have plans tonight?"

"With you," she said yawning.

I couldn't believe how happy that made me. I'd kick my own ass for an eternity if I ever messed this up. I bent down and kissed her soft lips again. "Minty."

A tiny frown crept its way onto her face, and then her free hand groped for a pillow, and she lobbed it half-heartedly at my head. I laughed, blocking it with my arm.

"Did last night actually happen?" she mumbled.

"You mean did I fuck you senseless and then admit that you basically own me? Yes, that definitely happened."

"Good." She yawned. "I thought I was dreaming."

It still felt like a dream to me. Probably always would.

"I'll see you tonight."

"Leave the shirt," she said yawning again.

"Hmm?"

"When you go. Leave that shirt."

"You want my shirt?"

"Um-hmm. And the leftover soufflé. And also you."

I smiled down on her sleepy, perfect face and stroked the soft strands of hair that framed it. She would probably never know how much I wanted to honor all those requests—especially that last one—for the rest of forever. Or at least for the rest of today.

I kissed her again, for real this time, running my hand down the column of her neck to cup her shapely, exposed breast. Lingering a moment, I held her lips with mine before finally mustering the discipline to let her go.

"I'll see you tonight, beautiful one."

§

"James, I got your message. What's up?"

Walking out of Selene's building, I'd scrolled through a handful of texts and missed calls from friends. No voicemails except one—a key seafood supplier in Seattle, who didn't normally call me in the evenings. In fact, I don't think he'd called me on my cell since I came down to San Francisco.

"Yeah. Listen, Keir. I'm sorry about calling last night. And I'm really sorry to hear about your dad."

I must have caught him on the docks because I could hear the sounds of boat engines in the background and guys shouting to one another. A bell was ringing somewhere in the distance.

"Thank you. What's going on?"

He exhaled a deep breath into the receiver, and that feeling of contentment I had when I left the apartment faltered.

"Look, man—we've been doing business together a long time, right?"

"Yeah. Seven years, maybe."

"And I really appreciate that. Not just the partnership but, you know, I think of you as a friend."

I couldn't imagine where this was going, and, quite frankly, my head was still back in the shower with Selene's naked body pressed against me. Plus, I was without coffee. "Likewise."

"But, Keir, man, I got a business to run too. And I understand if things are tight—"

"Nothing's tight," I said, confused, and unlocked the door of my pop's Chevy Impala. "Why would you think that?"

"Have you talked to Kelly?"

I climbed into the driver's seat and shut the door but didn't turn on the engine right way.

"About what?"

There was another long sigh, and a pit of unease opened up in my gut. "About the fact that I got five grand in crab sitting in my warehouse going bad as we speak. Kelly ordered it—rush ordered it, in fact—and then yesterday when we delivered, she said she'd ordered too much, and she wasn't taking half of it."

"What?" I looked out the window and, in my head, began running through the conversations I'd had with Kelly yesterday. None of them mentioned this.

"Refused it," he continued. "Or had one of your guys refuse it. And seriously, man, if it were anyone else but you—"

"Wait, *what?*"

This whole conversation was feeling like a spiral into madness. It just didn't compute. We had very specific guidelines in place for estimating our requirements for each job because at the quality level we catered to, food products were our single biggest expense. I was a *fanatic* about managing waste. With the systems and processes we had, I couldn't even conceive of how this might happen. And if somehow it had, Kelly would have told me. *Wouldn't she?*

I pulled the phone from my ear and glanced again quickly at my list of texts and calls. Nothing from her.

"I don't know if I can even sell it at this point," he was saying. "I'm trying. But even if I can, it's going to be at a loss. I just can't keep doing this kind of thing for you."

"Hold on—let me get this straight. We ordered crab from you for the Henderson event last night."

"And for the Barkley event."

"No, the Barkley event is on Wednesday. We wouldn't have ordered it that early."

"I don't know, man. All I know is Kelly ordered enough for both, and now she won't take delivery, and I'm sitting on two hundred pounds of colossal crab I can't sell."

"That makes no sense." I mindlessly watched the progress of a street sweeper heading toward me in the opposite direction. "Why would she order product for the Barkley event so far in advance?"

"I can't answer that—I'm just telling you how it is."

"Okay. Let me call her right now."

There was a thoughtful pause in the conversation. James had been reasonably pleasant throughout the call, but I sensed a steely reserve at the back of it.

"James, if we fucked up, I'll pay you for the crab, whether you can sell it or not. I'm certainly not going to stick you with it."

"Ok," he said, clearly relieved. "I appreciate that. I really do."

I was expecting that concession to bring our conversation to a close, and frankly, in my head I'd already moved on to what in the *fuck* was going through Kelly's head when she placed that order. I just lost five thousand dollars, and it wasn't even six thirty in the goddamned morning.

"Is there something else?"

"Keir, look. I don't know quite how to say this." That gnawing feeling came back with a vengeance. There was a shuffling sound like maybe he was moving the phone to his other ear. "But for the time being, I just need to prioritize my business differently. When you get back—"

"What does that mean? You're not going to supply us anymore? Is *that* what this call is about, James?"

"I hate this, man. I really do. You and I started our companies at the same time—we've practically grown up together. And I'm really sorry about your dad."

"You said that."

"And I mean it. But I just can't run my business this way."

"What way? Look, James, whatever happened here, I'm going to make it right. I think you know that about me by now. But I don't know what more I can do than to pay you for the order. We've been doing business together for a long time—are you honestly telling me that the first time something happens, you're going to *walk*?"

"Dude"—he blew out a breath into the receiver—"it's not the first time."

Anything that might've been moving inside me froze in place.

"What are you talking about?"

"You need to ask Kelly."

"I'm asking you."

"Fine. There's probably been half a dozen incidents in the last four months. Or more. Payments bouncing—"

"That's impossible. I handle the payments."

"Who does the deposits?"

The question winded me. In most cases, payments from our clients were sent electronically. But occasionally, we got checks in the mail that had to be deposited. And I obviously couldn't handle that remotely. If Kelly was late in depositing something significant without letting me know, it's possible the timing of an automatic payment could be off.

I honestly didn't know what to say. This was my business—my absolute pride and joy. My goddamned livelihood. My name, my reputation, everything. I thought I'd been so careful—put in place systems and processes to make sure shit like this *never* happened.

But as my head was spinning through the unimaginable *how*, James went on.

". . . urgent orders, wrong orders—she's a nice kid, Keir, but . . ."

"Jesus," I said, rubbing my forehead.

When I made the decision to care for my father myself, I worried day and night about how this would go. But he and I were it. We were all we had.

Still, running a business long-distance carried substantial risk. I knew that—that no amount of preparation could fully mitigate it. As I listened to James go on about one problem or another, it became clear that my absence had placed a strain on my company and my employees that went beyond what I'd been able to prevent.

Clearly, I'd been distracted.

I had an outstanding staff at Blaze—Kelly, chief among them. Still, the fact remained that Blaze was growing. Our events were getting bigger and more elaborate. And in a business of this nature, there is just no equal substitute for the owner's daily, invested presence.

I was ultimately responsible for all of this, and I had to put it right; there were just too many fortunes at stake.

But as I leaned back against the headrest, eyes closed, a sickness began to spread in the pit of my stomach. And it wasn't about business or money or reputation.

It was about Selene.

It was about the implications of what this would mean for *as long as we have*. Spending an unforgettable night with her certainly didn't make the endgame for us any clearer. But it did show me one thing: Though I hadn't been looking for anything with her, now that I had it, I wanted it. I *wanted* it.

That's what made the necessity of doing what I knew I had to do feel so unbelievably shitty.

"I'm really sorry, man," James told me. "I know this is the last thing you want to be dealing with right now."

He had no idea. I let my chin drop to my chest and, *Christ*, my shirt smelled like her. My brain was suddenly flooded with images, and each one felt like a paper cut to my skin.

"It's not your fault. But I'm asking you as a friend not to do this. I'll fly up in the morning and get everything straightened out. And let's just plan on you dealing directly with me from now on. I'll be back in Seattle for good next week."

There was a heavy silence through the phone.

"James?"

"Yeah, okay. We can give that a try."

Chapter 17

Selene

Strong hands slid around my hips and to my stomach, pulling me back against a broad, solid body.

"Your ass is *magical* in that skirt," Keir murmured. He put his face against my cheek and inhaled a deep breath.

All day long I'd obsessed over the memory of that voice, the way it vibrated through my skin when he whispered his praises and curses, his lips pressed to my naked breasts.

Now standing in my kitchen, his closeness filled my veins with steam, thick and warm, and I could not help the smile that tugged at the corners of my mouth. It had been only twelve hours since he'd left my apartment, but his return was the best thing that had happened all day. And it had been a pretty interesting day.

"You're quite the sweet talker, Stevens." I reached up to stroke his jawline and found it unexpectedly silky and smooth. My James Bond was back. "And you *shaved.*"

"I do that sometimes," he said, still at my cheek and rubbing it intentionally with his. Once again, he squeezed me tight and inhaled the scent of my neck and hair like he could live on that alone. "I thought your face could use a break tonight."

"How long do you think I have with this?" I continued to stoke his smooth skin with my fingertips and melted into the warmth of him. It was well understood that Keir grew facial hair like a Chia Pet.

"A few hours at best."

"Then we should make it a quick dinner."

"Forget dinner."

I turned in his arms, abandoning the salmon steaks I was preparing.

He had on a crisp white dress shirt that set off his dark features and gleaming, straight teeth. His shirt was untucked over jeans and unbuttoned at the neck, and his thick hair, exactly the color of black coffee, seemed to *beg* for my hands to run through it.

And believe me, I could *easily* forget dinner. But there was something in his voice or demeanor that was off. Something that gave me pause.

"You're beginning to sound like me."

"Because now I see your point." He leaned in to press his mouth to my neck while my hands found their way to his biceps. The firm feel of him was so distracting that it took a second for that to register, but when it did, I pulled back enough that I could once again see his face. Something was definitely off. Normally, I was the one punching the gas in our relationship, while he was the one more thoughtfully hovering over the break.

"What's with you?"

"Nothing." His expression evened out, and his tone was far too practiced to be genuine. There were gold flecks in his eyes that I hadn't noticed before, and they gave unexpected dimension to the lie I knew he was telling me.

"Something," I insisted, calling his bullshit.

Releasing his hold, he stepped away, and it was as if a block of ice dropped between us. Every ounce of his sexy playfulness was gone.

He shrugged, offering nothing more. His long, dark lashes were motionless as he looked straight at me. No, it wasn't *nothing*, but the larger question was, Did I want to pursue it? Several more seconds ticked by. Keir and I weren't strangers to silence, but this one felt pretty heavy.

He was the one to put the moment out of its misery. "How was work?"

I could hear the subtext in his voice, his asking for space.

And hey, I understood it. The last twenty-four hours had been a lot to digest for both of us. It was a big change to our relationship, but it didn't necessarily entitle either of us to a full-access pass into the contents of the other's head.

"Honestly," I said, respecting his unspoken wish, "you wouldn't believe it if I told you."

§

Truth, they say, is always stranger than fiction. And the story Paula heard from an insider at Rival Athletic Wear illustrated that point beyond anything I could have dreamed up.

Apparently, ever since the whole Pantygate episode, the board of directors of Rival had become increasingly disenchanted with its embattled CEO, Mike Bannon. It had insisted that Bannon bring on a chief operating officer to ensure that the company didn't see a repeat of the public embarrassment (and probably, more to the point, the decrease in financial valuation) it had suffered over the past year. Wisely, key members of the board recommended a highly capable woman by the name of Cheryl Gagnier, and Bannon, recognizing his own precarious position with the board, had hired her.

After all, Bannon had more pressing human resource issues to deal with.

Greg Cosgrove had long harbored his own CEO ambitions and apparently not made much of a secret of it. He had been part of the old regime at Rival, predating Bannon's tenure as CEO. When Bannon joined Rival, he swept in with his own team of executives— sales, HR, product, and merchandising—and the balance of the executive team, including Cosgrove, never quite felt on equal footing with *Bannon's people.* Those resentments smoldered for three years, until Pantygate finally brought them all to a head.

So last week, sensing Bannon's vulnerability, Cosgrove decided it was time to play his aces: he was popular with the old regime, meaning he'd have their support with the board when he threw his hat in the ring for the CEO job. And, after nearly ten years with the company, he had friends on the board. He didn't do Bannon any favors with the things he was whispering in their ears.

But Bannon was no political sheep either; he held a couple of aces of his own. The first was that he knew Cosgrove was having an affair with his public relations director—a fact that had come to light by way of a whistle-blower who felt Cosgrove's relationship undermined the integrity of the marketing organization—and that put the company at legal risk, particularly in light of its recent PR disasters.

The second of Bannon's aces was that he was, in fact, CEO. He may have been on shaky ground himself, but he was fully within his power to fire Greg Cosgrove.

So late Friday afternoon, flanked by the executive vice president of human resources, Mike Bannon walked into the glass-walled office of Greg Cosgrove and canned him on the spot. And not even the thick glass of the thirty-eighth-floor executive suite could contain the shouting and name-calling that ensued. Nor, of course, did it provide any privacy for the fistfight that came next. The same fistfight that was videotaped by one of the executive admins and bounced around the company until finally finding its way to social media.

By the time the video hit Motley Fool's website on Friday evening, Cosgrove was out. And within three hours, so was Bannon.

And when the dust finally settled, Cheryl Gagnier was at the helm.

As had been the board's plan all along.

Corporate America in a nutshell.

Had I checked my voicemail last night, that's exactly the urgent news I would have received.

"So long story short," I told Keir, "apparently karma is a bitch."

"Clearly. What does this mean for the rebranding?"

"Nothing. It's already moving forward."

"Still," he said. "That's crazy."

"Yeah, it's crazy, all right. Tell me about your day."

"It was okay." He cleared his throat, and for the barest second, he hesitated. But I think he knew he'd already exhausted my patience with his evasiveness. "I need to go home for a few days. Tomorrow, actually."

"Oh. Again?"

Keir didn't speak; he just nodded slightly, watching me. It was the intensity in his face that made everything inside me drop low in my belly. Something unsettling crawled up my spine.

"Keir, what's wrong? And don't say *nothing*."

He sighed, reaching back to take hold of the countertop behind him with both hands. His head dropped briefly, and then he met my gaze again. "I've got some trouble with a key supplier. I think it's manageable, but I need to be there to get things straightened out. And it's possible there are other issues I need to deal with."

"Wouldn't Kelly tell you?"

"I think she's been afraid to. Some of the mistakes have been costly."

"Maybe you need to hire someone to help her out."

He shook his head, dropping his gaze from my eyes to the floor as his jaw worked over something unreadable. "What I need to do, Selene, is get home. Permanently. My being away isn't working for the business."

"So, permanently like . . . when?" I was going for causal but failed epically.

"I hired painters to come in while I'm gone this week. And Rona knows someone who can do the landscaping. I'll be back this weekend to finish clearing out the house . . . And then . . ."

His last words were delivered slowly and almost as a whisper, but they rang through my head like a cymbal crash.

And then?

Oh.

Oh.

The sensation inside me felt like sinking. My chest went tight. The reality of what he was *actually* telling me was this: our expiration date had arrived.

The thought pushed a sharp spike of pain between my ribs, stealing my breath. Suddenly I understood why he had been so hesitant to tell me. Now that the words were out there, our reality was a *reality.*

Keir was watching me carefully again, and neither of us knew quite what to say. You can't really immunize yourself from a moment like this. I thought I was prepared, but I think I was just in denial.

"So I guess maybe we *should* forget dinner."

"Selene." I watched as he searched for the right words. He was pointedly ignoring my lame attempt to put a little levity around our loudly ticking clock. "I feel . . . Fuck. I've been feeling all day like we need to talk."

"Okay." Something sharp wiggled in my stomach. That was never a good way to start a conversation. I leaned back against the counter and felt awkwardness push its way into my posture.

No strings attached, and no hard feelings.

It wasn't actually the hard feelings I was thinking about just then. It was the soft ones. The ones that made my heart feel like sock-covered feet in fuzzy slippers whenever he smiled at me. The ones that recalled every sweet thing he'd ever said, which was a lot, and could practically recite them in alphabetical order. The ones that recognized in him a friend *and* a lover, and counted them with equal importance. Now that our time together was actually up, the thought of him leaving for good was shockingly painful. Whatever this was between us, it wasn't just curiosity, and it wasn't going to be fleeting.

"No," he said, stepping closer and tracing my frown line with his fingertip. "Don't do that. That isn't what I mean. Selene, last night was one of the best nights of my life. I'm not ready to let this go. Are you?"

"Do you mean am I ready for you to leave? *No.* I . . ."

I wish you never had to go.

I miss you and you haven't even left.

I'm

afraid

I

might

love

you.

Keir picked up my hand, and I felt the sweep of his thumb over my knuckles. He looked at me with such adoration that everything inside my body pulled to the middle in a bundle of warm tightness. But there was an edge there too. Like he was inching closer to something he found a little scary.

"There have only been two times in my life when I've even considered trying to do the long-distance thing but ultimately—"

"Ultimately—" I interrupted him. It wasn't a calculated thing— it was more because a part of me probably believed that by speaking the words myself, I could somehow lessen the pain of hearing them spoken by him. It wasn't a good plan, but I had no plan for this. "Ultimately, the first time you followed her up to Seattle, and the second time you let her go. I know you're not a long-distance guy, Keir. And between your business and everything I have going on here, I get it. You don't have to explain."

The sharp stab inside nearly winded me but I tried smiling and hoped the expression looked more convincing than it felt. It felt like crap. Both instances in his past were with the same girl—a six-year relationship that had started for them in high school and had lasted through their undergrad years. He didn't seem bitter about the way things had ended, but to my knowledge, he hadn't wanted to have a serious relationship since.

"No, you don't understand. When I think about those same options with you . . . well, they both feel. . . pretty inconceivable. So I guess what I'm asking is, Would you be up for giving the long-distance thing a try? It's not ideal but it's better than the alternative."

"You'd want to do that?" My heart swerved to the edge of my chest and something inside me loosened—something I hadn't even realized was clenched.

"I don't have a choice but to want to do it. I want you."

Keir waited to see how I would react to this, and his expression was warm but carefully neutral. For several moments we just stood there silently in my kitchen, staring at each other with equal parts hope and doubt that we could somehow keep a piece of what we had, once our everyday lives took their share. For the first time I noticed that he looked tired—not just sleep deprived but tired. His chest rose and fell with every breath as though his heart were beating as hard as mine.

"You can stop looking at me like I'm an alien inhabitant," he told me. "I'm just being honest here. I have feelings for you I haven't had before, and I don't know what that all means, but . . ." He exhaled, and it was a massive trembling gust. Clasping his hand around the back of his neck: "I want a thousand nights like we just had. I know it isn't going to be simple, and I've never done this before so, truthfully, I don't have it all figured out. But I just want to try. I mean, if—"

He froze midsentence, and his composure broke. "Come on, Selene, can you just tell me what you're thinking?"

He wanted me to condense a million thoughts into a single sentence? Impossible. My brain felt like a can of alphabet soup, and my heart seemed to be pounding in every single corner of my body—like it was trying desperately to get out. I took a deep breath and it shook heavily the whole way through my lungs.

It had been easy to march along for weeks with blinders on, burying my uncertainties in the pleasures of Keir's company and deliberately suppressing all thoughts of the day when he went back to the life he'd put on hold. This was a wake-up call that that day was coming. What he was proposing was a way to postpone it—and I wanted that more than I could ever say. Still, somewhere in the back of my brain, I knew: there would be *consequences* to bringing him deeper into my life, to allowing myself to love him, and maybe even to need him. Keir's hopeful yet mildly panicked expression only reinforced this. It also underscored that what we were talking about here was doubling down on the bargain we'd made with the future and, in the process, raising the stakes.

Tell me we won't fuck this up.

The more invested we became, the possibility that we *could* fuck this up seemed increasingly real. For starters, I wasn't even sure what he meant by *giving the long-distance thing a try.*

So I should have asked him to define what he wanted more clearly.

And I should have admitted that I didn't honestly *know* if we might fuck things up.

And I should have told him that he was quickly becoming so important to me that the idea of fucking things up actually scared the hell out of me, if I let myself think about it.

I should have taken the chance to have an honest discussion about our feelings and our future. Because if I thought for a second that crossing a line in our friendship hadn't also meant crossing a threshold into the territory of likely heartbreak for one or both of us, well, I was a damn fool. But then, that was pretty well established already.

In the end, I didn't do any of the things I should have. Maybe I didn't want to know just how precarious all of this was. Maybe I didn't want to ask how two people who had never actually been successful at *the long-distance thing* could be successful this time around. Maybe I just wasn't ready to tell Keir that it might not work between us, for fear he would believe me.

Or maybe I just wanted to have this moment to let the two of us be happy for just one damned second without worrying about what *could* happen or what *might* be. I felt like that's all I ever did. In fact, if I could've somehow managed to stop time, I would have. Because that would mean I would forever have in my life every single thing in the world that actually mattered to me. In this moment, it was all still here. Still safe from the ravages of time and illness and mistakes. So maybe I just found it better to be grateful for what we had and let tomorrow's cards fall where they would.

Because the truth was, I simply cared more about having Keir in my life for as long as we had than I did about the risk of anything that might come after.

So there it was.

I looked down at my shoe and poked the tile floor with my toe. "I guess I'm thinking *yes*."

Chocolate eyes flamed with relief, giving way to a shy smile I wish I could adequately describe. It was a soft, vulnerable show of happiness that flashed in the tilt of his mouth and the narrowing of his eyes. But it said everything I needed it to, and I knew no matter what happened, that smile would be burned into the pages of my storybook from now until the end of time.

Chapter 18

Keir

Selene made no noise in the bed where she slept, but I felt her presence the moment I stepped into the room—a warmth, a thickening of the cool air all around me, and the soft scent of her perfume. It was nearly one o'clock on Saturday morning by the time I finally reached her apartment, and the relief of being close to her again was all I'd been able to think about for days. As quietly as I could, I got out of my clothes that still smelled like bonfire and salty air, and slipped into bed behind her, pressing my lips to her smooth, naked shoulder. The warmth of her body next to mine melted away any tension that remained from a long day and an even longer week. *This* moment made every other spent apart worth the hardship of our separation—none of it mattered to me as long as I knew we would eventually end up back here, together.

I wrapped one arm around her and pulled her closer. It was like her body was made for me, like two puzzle pieces snapping into place. It was an instinctive thing, the way my hand always found her soft breast in the dark and held it gently. Even her breast in my palm was exactly the right size, not more than I could hold and not a bit less.

"Hey, stranger," she whispered groggily. "How'd it go tonight?"

I had been in Seattle since Tuesday, and it had been a hellish and frustrating week. Lots of problems, hard conversations, finger-pointing, and staffing issues. Our communication during the days I was gone was limited to some texting and late-night conversations that involved a lot of vigorous yawning. Running a business was no picnic to begin with, and I was definitely paying a price for my extended absence from it.

To cap it off, tonight we catered a celebrity rehearsal dinner at Alki Beach, and I wanted to be there until the food service was done, which meant I had to catch the very last flight out of Seattle if I wanted to maximize my time in San Francisco over the weekend before having to be back in Seattle for an event on Sunday evening.

"Good," I told her on a long exhale. "But I'm exhausted."

That was a massive understatement. Every limb felt heavy, as though they weighed three times as much as they normally did. I could barely keep my eyes open. With every passing moment, I felt myself sinking farther and farther into the mattress, the warmth of Selene's body and the vanilla scent of her hair lulling me into that fuzzy place on the edge of consciousness.

Still, something deep in my core—something as primal as breathing—ached to be closer to her. I flexed forward with the only part of me that didn't know I was wrecked.

"Is it bad if I just want to shove up inside you right now and take a nap there for a week?" I mumbled.

There was a little burst of silent laughter before she raised my hand to her mouth and I felt the warm drag of her lips against my thumb.

"Pay no mind to the naked chef hanging from my vagina."

"Just go about your business. Nothing to see here."

I settled my hand again on her breast, squeezing it with slightly more intent. Despite the fatigue, my brain was beginning to compile a list of potential activities to fill the next couple of hours that had nothing to do with sleep. Being around her was always like that for me. The craving was relentless. But I loved the feeling of desperately wanting something that was already mine.

"How do you think we did this week?" I asked her. "Our first week as a long-distance couple."

It was sort of a rhetorical question because I thought we did pretty well, all things considered. I missed her like crazy, but I was better than I thought I would be about managing my near-constant string of thoughts about her while focusing on the demands of my business.

So it surprised me that she hesitated. It surprised me even more that she turned in my arms to face me in the dark, as if the question weren't rhetorical at all.

"*Are* we a couple?" she asked quietly.

Though she was right in front of me, I couldn't actually see her face; I could make out only the silvery outlines of her features, dimly lit from behind by the moonlight coming in from the window. I could feel her breath on my face, her soft exhale forming the only sound I could hear—that is, besides the black tires laying screeching tracks across the asphalt surfaces of my brain.

Was that even in question?

As my eyes struggled to adjust to the darkness, I began flipping through everything I could remember about our conversation in her kitchen. I thought I'd been pretty clear about what I wanted; I just couldn't remember if we'd actually used the word *couple*.

But yes, a *couple* was how I thought of us. And to me that implied commitment and exclusivity and some sort of investment in time. It was certainly more than just *Hey, I'm going to be down in San Francisco again in a few weeks. Wanna grab a bite and hook up?*

And it's not like I didn't know the difference.

To me, nothing we'd ever done had felt like hooking up.

Suddenly, I was very much awake and very much aware of the limitations imposed by the darkness around us.

"Are we *not* a couple?" I asked her.

Selene reached up to stroke my face with her fingertips, touching where the stubble cut across my jaw. "I don't know. We never really talked about it."

But didn't we?

Searching her face as hard as I could in the dark, I couldn't see what was behind this. Did she not *want* to be a couple? Or was she just not certain about what I wanted. Since we'd met, we seemed to vacillate in this space between wanting clarity and seeking the shelter of ignorance. But more and more, it was clarity I sought. I wondered whether our relationship would always be this constant process of feeling along walls in the dark, never quite sure of where we were, and never quite confident in where we were going.

I hated that this was how we seemed to reveal ourselves, in these tiny pieces of vulnerability. Inches, rather than feet. I wanted to crush that pattern with a rock.

"Let's talk about it now, then."

She yawned, continuing to touch me—to smooth her warm hand over my shoulder, my collarbone, running her fingers across the scar and knot of misaligned bone that testified to how impatient I could be, even against my own self-interest. I wasn't great at waiting for things.

"We don't have to tonight," she offered. "It's really late."

She was right, of course. It *was* late. I mean, how many quality conversations happen at one o'clock in the morning? Only a lunatic would seriously consider sitting up in bed, turning on the light so he could see her face, and settling this question—absurd as it was—at one o'clock.

I was such a lunatic.

But Selene pressed forward and put her mouth to mine. And that first kiss, lingering and sweet, was like a little promise to my impatient self that I could just give in to sleep, and we'd talk about anything we needed to in the morning.

But the second one she gave me, wrapping a long, sleek, naked leg around my hip, was like a little promise that I wouldn't be sleeping at all. And *that* was the kiss I really leaned into.

Chapter 19

Selene

It was almost shocking how different everything looked. Keir stood next to me, in the entryway of his father's house, and I could see by the way his face registered the changes that he was having the same reaction. For a long moment, he was silent, his eyes moving about the open, mostly empty space that was so full of memories for him. He lifted one hand to his jawline and rubbed thoughtlessly over the stubble he found there.

The house looked great, don't get me wrong. Painters had erased the dark rectangles on the living room walls that marked the places where pictures had once hung. Now the walls boasted a fresh coat of creamy tan paint without so much as a scuff. And the little pencil lines that had tracked Keir's growth on the doorframe of the kitchen were well concealed under the new, gleaming white trim. Even the old beige carpet, whose wear and tear testified to decades of foot traffic, had been removed, and in its place something pristine had been installed that seemed to be waiting expectantly for life's imprint.

"They did a good job," he finally said, his throat tight as he continued to survey the kitchen and living room.

"They did." In some ways, it made what we had to do here a little easier because it was already beginning to feel like someone else's house. I placed a hand on Keir's arm, feeling it tense, and then he looked over at me and gave me a forced smile.

"You're sure you want to do this?" he asked. He wanted me there, but his concern for me in situations like this always overrode everything else.

"What else do I have to do today?" I said casually.

He didn't bother answering; he knew that wasn't really the question.

Whether he admitted it or not, this was going to be a tough day for him. There were hard goodbyes that needed to be said, and a lot of hollowness I could never fill. I wasn't much of a consolation, but we both knew there was no way in hell I would ever let him do this alone.

§

The final rooms to clean out before the house was put on the market were Keir's bedroom, the kitchen, and the garage. Most of the furniture had already been junked or donated, and the last load was being picked up by a charity in the morning.

We decided to divide and conquer the chore, with Keir taking on the garage and his bedroom, and me tackling the kitchen. No matter who you are, it's a very strange job to clear out someone else's house. Cupboard after cupboard held artifacts of a life that no longer existed.

Above the refrigerator, I found a bunch of old photo albums and pulled one out. The binding was falling apart, but the photos inside of Keir's fourteenth birthday were in perfect condition. Tellingly, his smile beamed openly and expectantly from the pictures. He was tall and gangly; his hair looked like he'd cut it himself with a pair of orange-handled scissors, and his mouth was full of braces. The expression on his face made me laugh out loud because it was one he still made. I ran my finger over the dimple on one of his cheeks and then sat down on the floor to look through the rest of the pages.

"What is that?"

"Jesus, ninja. You scared me."

An older version of the birthday boy strode back into the kitchen. He pulled a beer out of the fridge, twisted off the cap, and flicked it into the sink.

"It's a photo album I found. Here, look." I offered it up from the floor where I sat.

Keir took it from my hands and dropped down beside me, cross-legged and bent forward at the waist. He set his beer on the floor by his foot.

"Ah, puberty," he said, flipping through the pictures. "Good times."

"No, look how cute you were. Fourteen-year-old me would have been all over that."

He shook his head, smiling, then leaned to the side to press his lips to mine. It was just a slow, lingering touch, and I moved toward him, chasing the kiss. I still couldn't get over the fact that we could just do that. Whenever we wanted.

"I grew like a weed," he said glancing back at the book. "There was like a three-year period when my pants never reached my shoes."

We looked through the pictures, laughing at some, and then his smile lingered as his eyes drifted to mine. He reached for my hand, squeezed it, and ran his thumb across my knuckles.

"Thanks for being here today," he murmured. "I know how much this sucks. I'd rather be doing anything else."

"I know." I leaned my head into his shoulder and he let go of my hand to wrap his arm around me, pulling me into the side of his chest so that the top of my head rested below his chin. He smelled of mild sweat and laundry detergent and dust, and I loved it.

"Somehow, even more than the funeral and everything else, doing *this* makes his passing seem so final. I think that's why I've been dreading it so much." With the hand that wasn't holding me, he picked up his beer, lifting it to his lips, and then paused for a moment before taking a pull and swallowing. "I actually had a dream the other night that he walked back into the house like all of this had been one big misunderstanding—like he'd just been away for a while. And he was so angry at me for giving his stuff away."

"Oh, Keir." I put my arms around his waist and hugged him tightly, my head pressed into the crease where his shoulder met his chest. I felt the pressure of tears in my head, that heating behind my eyes, the tightening in my throat that made it feel like it was full of sand. When I looked up into his pained expression, I didn't even know what to say. "That's so awful. I'm sorry."

"No, I mean . . . it's fine." He shrugged off the concern, not one for pity. "I'm not saying I think it was actually my dad trying to talk to me or anything . . . it was more just my brain rebelling against the finality of it, I guess. It's just strange that someone could be here one day and then completely gone from the earth the next."

I lifted my chin so I could see his face in profile. The strong line of his jaw seemed to be working over some significant thought. His gaze was locked on the bottle in his hand.

"So you don't believe a person's soul can . . . I don't know . . . stay with us? Or at least look after us for a while?"

He knew why I was asking. It wasn't an entirely academic question on my part. For us, this whole subject was more than philosophy; it was more than religion. It was our reality—he on one side of an experience, and I on the other.

Keir turned his eyes to me briefly, and in that quick three-second glance, I could see the ongoing battle he seemed to fight: his desire to be honest with me and his inclination to protect.

"I don't know," he said, gently closing the photobook and setting it aside. "I mean, nobody can know for sure, I guess. But I haven't felt like that with my pop. I haven't felt him . . . around. Not once since he passed."

"Well . . ." I thought about that. I thought about a dozen articles I'd read about people seeing signs like a bird coming to the window, or a song playing, or something put in their path—all supposed to show that the deceased person was okay or close by or expressing their love. I wasn't raised in a particularly religious household, and I honestly didn't know if I believed it either. But I definitely wanted to.

I always imagined that when I got to where Keir was, sometime after my dad had passed, that I'd be able to say I'd had some dream where my dad would speak to me and I'd know he was okay. And there would be some relief or closure in that. But in my more atheistic moments I wondered, too, if we weren't all merely the stuff of dirt and stars. I understood what Keir was saying about a person being here and gone; it was a hard thought to process.

"Maybe your dad just didn't think you needed it. Maybe he knows you're okay."

Keir sniffed out a laugh, though there wasn't any humor in it. Sometimes, I knew, he was still angry at the world for what had happened. And his reaction told me there were still times when he was not okay. But he also knew I wasn't trying to poke at something vulnerable, and he squeezed me tighter and kissed my head to soften the fact that my words were clearly not having the hoped-for effect.

"All I'm saying," he continued, "is that if it were really possible, you'd think there would be at least one irrefutable case in two hundred thousand years."

"Maybe. But maybe it happens all the time, and we're just not conditioned to it. Maybe we lack the perception or the openness or the sensitivity to know when it's happening. Maybe alongside scientific proof, there's still room for instinct and intuition and . . . I don't know, mystery. Don't you ever feel like you just know something, even if you don't know why?"

He took a deep breath and nodded in his slow and thoughtful way that let me know he was listening, considering. His eyes had been trained on the floor in front of his feet, but then he looked at me, and the corners of his mouth lifted.

He set his bottle down carefully to his left and rolled to his right so that I found myself flat on my back, my head cradled in one large palm while he settled between my legs, bracing himself on his forearms. Dark hair fell over his forehead. He was taller and broader than I, and his narrow hips were sharp on my thighs. His hands went to my face, and then his mouth was firm on mine, opening, sucking on my lower lip, my tongue.

He was so warm in contrast to the cold linoleum floor beneath me, and his expression when he pulled back looked as serene as I had ever seen it, not a line or a furrow anywhere. Those beautiful brown eyes were soft and earnest as they absorbed every feature of my face. His fingertips stroked my hairline.

And he let just enough time go by for me to realize that his answer to my question might not be casual or teasing.

"I love you," he said simply. "That's something I just know."

It was like a physical force the way those words pushed the breath from my lungs. They were laid out so bare and so straightforward that they were immediately met with a flood of equally strong reflexes within me. Shock? Ecstasy? Terror? It felt like something wrapped itself around my heart, growing warmer and tighter the longer I looked at him. He seemed to like the way he had stolen the air from my body, because a curl tugged at the corners of his mouth, causing those tiny creases to reappear. Sunshine began to fill his expression and overflow from his eyes. He lowered down to swallow my surprise with a deep kiss, pressing his lips to mine.

"Keir," I said stopping him with a palm to his chest. I was hyperaware of this feeling pulling my ribs tight but I needed to be able to process, to give this moment the space it deserved. I was speechless. And quite frankly, there was a part of me, looking up into his face, that wasn't even sure I had actually heard what I thought I just heard. And that's when he shifted his weight and placed his right hand over my left, settling it to the spot just over his heart. While mine was a wild pounding, pounding, pounding, his was a slow and steady beat I could feel through the soft fabric of his Good Charlotte T-shirt. Not panicked or tentative. Not nervous he'd just said something unintended in the heat of the moment. But a physical confirmation, as if I needed one, that he was absolutely certain about us.

"I love you," he repeated, probably because I looked like a deer in headlights. A smile found its way to every muscle in his face, almost as though he was unburdening himself a little more each time he said the words out loud.

And he wasn't looking for me to say it back. Or maybe he was, but it was probably all right there in front of him where he could see it plainly. Because when someone works his miracles on you day after day—when he cares for you and is there for you and laughs with you and gives so much of himself—what you have together doesn't feel like just friendship anymore. And it doesn't feel like just sex either. It starts to feel unmistakably like love. And that's pretty hard to hide, even from yourself.

The longer he looked at me, the more I knew he was thinking the very same thing.

"Keir, I love you too."

He nodded, and his mouth formed the words *I know.*

The little puff of breath that accompanied his broad smile had the homey scent of beer. I savored it as he covered my mouth with a soft, generous kiss, his lips clinging with obvious affection. *I love you,* that kiss said, both gentle and masterful. And when his arms bracketed me, creating a small space just for us where nothing else existed, that was *I love you*, too.

We lay on the floor, just kissing, and he told me he'd never felt this way, and I told him truthfully that I never had either, and he laughed into my mouth because, duh, that was obvious by the way I was doing everything I could to get closer and feel more and capture every one of his little sounds and swallow them so they were mine forever. Forever. No matter what happened.

He was resting nearly the full weight of his body over me, and my hands went around his shoulders and drifted across the solid strength of muscle in his back, coming to rest at his waist, where my fingertips could touch the skin just above his jeans, up under the hemline of his shirt. *I love you.* And in the next second his shirt was off, *I love you,* and then mine was, *I love you,* and we were skin to skin, and I'd never felt closer to another human being in my entire life.

I'd never had this connection with anyone, never wrapped myself around someone like both our lives depended on it, never felt like getting naked on a kitchen floor could be considered a spiritual experience.

The hard shape of him was pressing against my hip from beneath his jeans. I began unbuttoning them, my hands working the soft denim, pulling the fly open one tiny pop at a time. But he stilled my progress with his fingertips.

"Tell me why you asked me last night if we were a couple," he murmured against my lips.

"I mean . . . I knew we were *seeing* each other—"

His brows pulled together. "And not using condoms."

"And not using condoms, yes. I guess I just wasn't sure what to call this."

That bothered him.

His eyes fell away, internally focused for a moment, before they came back with intent. His mouth found mine again, his tongue touching my lips for soft strokes before leaning his forehead into mine.

"Even if we *were* using condoms, it wouldn't have changed anything for me," he whispered. "I love you, Selene. I wouldn't be okay with some casual thing. Would you?"

"I don't think I've ever felt casually about you, Keir."

"Okay then. It's not that complicated."

Wasn't it, though? Keir thought we had done well this last week, and I supposed that was true. But for me, the reality of the *long-distance thing* was a little depressing. I realized how much I had come to look forward to seeing him after work, how my heart would leap when I got a call or text from him unexpectedly at odd moments during the day, and how much I depended on his company and his reassuring presence amid the disorientation of my current life. And to be perfectly honest, how much I liked the smooth, warm strength of him in my bed at night, and waking to his tousled, smiling kisses in the morning.

Still, my brain always seemed to repel any thoughts of our future together because it didn't feel real. Or possible. The incompatibility of our lives made the idea of being together as an actual *couple* feel like we were overreaching our reality. To me, it felt very complicated.

"I wish I could fill in all the blanks here," he said with a sigh. "But I know this is right. And I want it more than anything."

What he didn't seem to understand was that I wasn't necessarily looking for him to try to fill in the blanks. I couldn't see that there were any good answers to put there. Only dead ends for us. And I had too much pending loss in my life to face up to the possibility of another. Honestly, I didn't want to think about any of it, not the risks of what we were doing, or the consequences of falling in love or the likelihood of this all going up in flames. I just wanted to focus on him and on us and on the sunlight taste of his skin.

So I found myself nodding.

"Then what else is there?" I could hear a twinge of exasperation laced through his words. "Why do I feel . . . ?"

His voice trailed off and I know it was because he sensed some resistance in me to declare an unqualified win for Keir + Selene. He was frustrated by it.

Lifting my lips to his, I kissed him softly. *I love you.*

Wasn't that enough for now?

With his warm breath mixing with mine, I felt him set his frustration aside. It wasn't easy for him, I know. But he wanted me, more than he wanted to press for answers. And when I pushed my hand below the waistband of his boxer briefs, finding and squeezing the warm, wet, silky tip of him, he groaned deeply in relief, soft pleading curses woven into his exhale. His body seemed to fall into mine.

He began working my yoga pants down, pushing them low on my thighs while his stubbled chin grazed the delicate skin at my throat.

And for just a moment—for one beautiful moment in time—I couldn't hear the sound of the clock.

We had the gift of a full night stretched out before us with no schedule to keep and nothing more to do than to nurture this thing between us.

Just this day.

And this feeling.

And something so big between us we finally had a word to describe it. After all this time.

My hands found his hips, and I helped him push his jeans and boxer briefs down so he could kick them off somewhere to the side.

He was gentle and unhurried, pausing now and then to kiss me deeply, moving again only at my silent urging. I ran my hands softly down the slope of his back, where the long muscles trembled under my touch.

"I want you to know something," he whispered. His cheek was pressed to my cheek, and his lips were just below my ear, the warm humidity of his softly spoken words floating in the small space there.

"What is it?"

He hesitated for just a moment while his eyes absorbed each of my features in slow sequence. "Whatever flaws I have, whatever mistakes I made in how I handled things between us early on, there are no flaws in what I feel for you. There never have been . . ."

His voice was tight, and then his breath fell away with mine, because in the next heartbeat, he was deep inside me.

§

Feeling seeped back into my body one limb at a time. I felt heavy and limp, suddenly so exhausted I could hardly keep my eyes open. Keir rolled to his back, taking me with him, his skin damp with sweat.

With my ear to his chest and his fingers drifting lazily up and down my spine, I could hear his heart returning to a slow and steady cadence.

"I want to take you to dinner tonight. Somewhere good. What do you think?"

"Um—" Honestly, I was happy right where I was, but okay. "Maybe Black Sea Cafe?"

"Yeah, let's go there. Do you think I need to dress up?"

I shrugged. "I don't know. It's kind of nice, I think."

Keir glanced over at his jeans on the floor. "I packed so fast, that's about all I brought. I'm trying to think if I have anything down here I can wear."

But it took only about three seconds before his face lit up with an idea, and then six feet two inches of awesome nakedness were gone in a streak.

§

He came back looking like a giraffe, sewn into an old gray suit.

The decades had moved on, but apparently in Keir's childhood closet, it was prom 2003 all over again, and fashion mayhem still reigned.

"What do you think?" he said nodding, eyes wide and smiling. Then he turned around so I could appreciate the full effect of his achievement. When he came full circle again, he grinned down at me, waiting to be congratulated.

"It's . . ." Honestly, I was at a loss for words. I almost felt guilty pinning an innocent adjective to this display. "Wow."

That's literally the best I could come up with. *Wow.*

True to his word, the pants hit him above the ankles, sleeves somewhere north of the wrists. The fabric was straining across his shoulders and looked like it was ready to spontaneously combust under the burden of postpubescent musculature. Every button and seam was working overtime.

"Wow," I repeated.

"Can you see it?" He busted out a little dance move that literally split his pants, which, in turn, left me helpless with laugher. I was doubled over, naked on the floor, while Keir's fancy footwork came in and out of view.

"You know what this means, right?" I asked once I'd finally caught my breath.

"That you want another piece of this?" He made a show of gesturing to the whole of himself with no lack of male smugness.

"Oh no, my friend," I said, practically exultant. "It means the time has finally come for you to pay up."

Chapter 20

Keir

"This would look great with your coloring," Selene told me.

She pulled a shirt off the rack in the men's department at Bloomingdale's and held it up to my chin.

There wasn't a guy on the planet who wouldn't call it pink.

"No way."

"It's not pink, if that's what you're thinking. It's salmon. It's actually more orange."

"That's not helping."

Ten minutes into shopping and I'd already hit my max. I would have been fine grabbing something off the table as we came in and calling it a day. But that's not how this went; at least I was smart enough to know it.

After a failed attempt to herd Selene toward the Lucky Brand Jeans store using my subliminal powers of suggestion, I had to admit that, apparently, I had no subliminal powers of suggestion. Which is why we sailed right past that storefront filled with perfectly good denim and leather and ended up here. Looking at a pink shirt.

"Just go with black," I told her and pushed the thing away.

"You already have a lot of black, Keir."

"So? Why change what works?"

"How about something like this?" She turned to face me and held up a shirt with a giant turtleneck collar that was too hideous to even acknowledge. I don't care that it was probably high fashion; it was ridiculous.

There was nothing at all subliminal about the look I gave her. She hung it back up.

"Listen," I said leaning against the silver metal bar and watching her flip through more shirts with superhuman speed. "I was thinking I want to do a cookout for you and your friends. Out at the beach in Half Moon Bay. I'll pull the permits, and we could do something cool."

"Okay," she answered distractedly. She started to show me some sort of button-down but then changed her mind. "Nah, you hate brown." I did hate brown, but I couldn't remember ever telling her that. "So *why* do you want to do a cookout?"

"What do you mean *why*?" I was in love with this girl, and it all happened so fast I hadn't even met her friends or her family. Or she mine. It kind of made everything feel like a bubble. Not quite real. "Because you talk about your friends all the time, and I'd like to know them. And because it would be fun."

Selene looked up at me, more focused this time, and shifted the small pile on her arm. "No, you're right, it would be fun. It would. I want you to meet them."

"*But . . .*"

"There's no *but*." She hesitated, and I tilted my head at her encouragingly, although in truth, I knew exactly what she was going to say.

"It's just that right now I see so little of you as it is. I don't know how I feel about sharing what small amount of time we have together."

Yeah, this was a hard one, made harder by the fact that we didn't seem to be all that good at discussing our plans, or maybe we were just avoiding it. I don't know.

Selene picked up a shirt that apparently made the cut and draped it over her arm with the rest. At least it was black, but it looked like it had some sort of paisley print woven into it. Christ, how did I not think to add paisley to the list of stuff I would not try on? Any subliminal powers of suggestion I hoped to have were apparently also powerless against paisley.

"I think that's exactly why we need to do this. I'm not around much. And when I'm in Seattle, you spend all your time working. I haven't heard you talk about going out at all lately, and that's not like you."

"I see my dad a lot."

"You see your dad," I said pushing off the rack to stand directly in front of her. I ran a finger over the hairline at her temple, which had become my favorite spot, and brushed back a stray lock. "Which is good. But you also need to keep up your relationships, Selene. You need the support of your friends right now, and you need to keep your life full."

The truth is, sometimes I worried that when we were together we were too much of a pair, complete within ourselves, too self-contained. In the short time we'd known each other, we'd walked some tough roads together, under terrible circumstances that only we understood completely, and we'd come to need each other, to trust each other. It was a beautiful thing, a really triumphant thing that something so amazing could come out of something so difficult. But if we were going to make this work over the long haul, if we were going to be able to withstand the physical separation and the emptiness of longing that was inevitable, she had to have a life here that was fulfilling, and she had to be well supported and cared for, especially when I couldn't be there to do those things myself. Since her dad got sick, I knew she wasn't giving her relationships the attention they needed. I knew I was partially responsible for that.

"I know. It's all just . . . a lot right now," she sighed.

The way she leaned her forehead into my chest ignited every protective instinct I had. I wrapped my arms around her, squeezing tightly, and placed a kiss on the top of her head. I knew what she meant—what it was like to have so many things coming at you that you can't find your center. With an illness like her dad had, and mine had had, every day introduces a new challenge, and just when you think you've got a routine that works, cancer says no. And it's not like the rest of your life is on standby while you figure it all out.

"I get that. But this'll be fun. And you don't need to do anything except invite your crew. I'll take care of the rest."

"Okay, I'm in." She smiled, though it wasn't one of the ones I liked best. This one took effort. There was a long pause, and then she added, "So when are you talking about?"

That was actually the harder question. The one we seemed to actively avoid.

"It may be a couple of weeks before I can get back down. We've got a ton of events going on, and I don't think I can leave them to Kelly."

"Two *weeks* . . . ?" I could hear the way that reality hit her and how she had to work to straighten out her initial reaction. She blinked several times, and her eyes fell away. The truth is, I didn't really know how to have this conversation. We were at the point where the rubber met the road on the whole long-distance thing. My pop's house was being listed this week, which officially put me back as a resident of Seattle and officially made Selene and me a long-distance couple. I'd never done this before; I felt completely out of my depth.

"Hey," I said touching her cheek so she had to look at me again. "It's a long time, I know. I don't want to be away from you either. Maybe I can come down for a day, here or there. I just don't know yet."

She nodded against my hand, eyes holding mine. "Maybe I can come up."

"I'd love that," I said, but my tone said I knew it wasn't really feasible. She was too junior to get much time off work, and I definitely didn't want to take her away from her dad on the weekends.

She seemed to come to a similar realization at almost the same time, and the look she gave me broke my heart. It felt like surrender, and that didn't sit well with me.

"We're going to figure this out," I insisted, nodding, willing her to join me in that assumption. "People do this all the time."

"I know," she said, and smiled as best she could. But we didn't have any real strategy for it, so I understood the half belief I saw in her face. Still, I knew what I felt for her—what we felt for each other—and I knew my belief was big enough for both of us.

In heavy silence, we spent the next minutes side by side, silently flipping through pants. I wasn't really looking at them, and I think we both knew that. When it came down to it, she could dress me up any way she liked; I didn't really give a shit. I was just happy to be with her. I loved her; I was lucky she loved me. And we were together. I couldn't think of anything else that mattered beyond that.

"I like these. These are nice," she said.

I could tell she wanted to set all the heavy stuff aside and just focus on shopping and our time together. It was fine. Like I said, we'd figure this out at some point. I definitely understood her need to just do ordinary things and feel normal. No matter how hard these next months would be for me, they would be much, much harder for her as her dad's illness progressed.

We had plenty of time to make our plans.

"Yeah," I agreed, looking at the black slacks in her hand. "Those'll work."

"The only thing is, if you want to wear them tonight, we don't have time to get them altered."

I took the pants from her hand and held them to my waist. "They won't need altering. They'll fit."

"How do you know?"

I shrugged. "They're my size. They always fit."

"Oh my god, that is so unfair! You're like the fit model size, aren't you?"

"Look who's talking," I laughed.

She made a face and shook her head in quick movements. "I have to try everything on. I have an ass like a *pumpkin*."

With a hand on her shoulder, I turned her enough to be able to check out the ass in question, and not at all subtly. Wrapped in tight yoga pants, it was nothing short of miraculous. I ran a hand over it reverently. "A pumpkin, you think?"

She tried to pull away, but I wrapped my arms around her from behind, closing any available space between us, and leaned in so close that my stubble grazed her neck. I could feel her surprised, uneven breaths in the rise and fall of her chest.

"Let me tell you something about your magnificent ass, Selene," I murmured. "I live to see it naked in my hands while I devour your honey sweetness."

A small sound escaped her lips, and in profile, I could see her swallow hard, eyes wide.

It was the best reaction.

"*Keir,*" she whispered, quickly glancing around us to see if anyone was watching. I didn't give a damn if they were, but even so, what they would've seen was a girl in a ponytail, flushed, breathless, a little discomposed, and so very beautiful. And the guy she was with was looking at her like he wanted her. Like he loved her.

She turned in my arms and hooked a finger through my belt loop, tugging me forward at the waist so she could whisper in my ear. "I have no idea why I like that so much."

A grin nearly broke my face, pressed to the delicate skin of her neck. "But you *do*."

"Is it that obvious that I do?"

I pulled back and glanced down to meet her eyes, nodding. "To me it is. Because when I get really filthy, you flush and start fidgeting, and I can tell you want to kiss me, either to silence or encourage me—you haven't decided yet."

She stood staring at me for what felt like forever. It actually seemed like she *was* trying to decide that. We hadn't talked a lot about her sexual history other than the requisite *how many people have you been with* kinds of conversations, but I got the impression that Selene had never been with anyone who really helped her to explore what *she* liked, beyond just the basics. I'd met Kevin, and believe me, he didn't strike me as someone who would be particularly creative in bed. But maybe that was my own possessiveness speaking. Maybe below the legal brief–loving exterior, he was a dynamo. I didn't know. But I did know that I loved the way her pulse was racing and her chest was rising and falling in quick breaths. I loved the idea that this was all new ground for her. For us. She was looking at me like she was thinking about letting me do some or all the things I mentioned, and god, I wanted to. I wasn't kidding about that.

She bit her lip and then let it slide wet from her teeth. It was one of the sexiest things I'd ever seen.

"Let's go try these on."

§

I'll admit—I was really hoping *go try these on* was code for *have sex in the dressing room*, but apparently it wasn't. She actually wanted me to try the shit on. And I have to say, that was a little disappointing.

Some guy named John let me into a room while Selene went out to canvas the floor for anything we might have missed. I think she knew this was her one shot to get me here. The fact that I was not a willing shopper came as a surprise to no one.

When she came back to the dressing room, I was in a black cashmere V-neck sweater and a pair of flat-front, slim-cut black slacks.

"Wow." She blew out a small breath as her eyes ran all over my body, slowly looking me up and down. It was definitely a good *wow* this time. And right then and there, I vowed to buy this exact set of clothes in ten different colors and wear one every day I was with her. "You look amazing."

"I don't know," I said critically in a mock-serious way, glancing at myself in the mirror. "Do these pants make my cock look big?"

She coughed out one of her hearty laughs, and I decided I loved that laugh every bit as much as the look that went with it. Making her laugh was honestly my greatest joy on the planet. It was a little crazy how much I lived for it.

Glancing over her shoulder and then back to me, she stepped into the dressing room and closed the door quietly behind her.

Her head was bent as she came toward me, close enough that I could feel the rise and fall of her chest as she breathed faster. Her hands stroked the cashmere from my shoulders down the sides of my abdomen, making my breath catch the lower she went. I was watching her face, the way her eyes followed her hands but didn't really see them. She was thinking, deciding something.

"What are you up to, Ms. Georgiou?"

I swept loose strands of her dark hair behind her shoulder with the back of my hand and realized I was shaking. What this girl could do to me, with just her proximity . . .

"Let me tell you something about your cock . . ." she whispered, and I saw that familiar hunger darken her eyes.

But it was so unexpected in here that I lost my words for a beat, though she had 100 percent of my attention.

With one hand, she plucked opened the three buttons of her Henley T-shirt so the upper curves of her breasts were visible to me. It was by far one of the hottest things I'd ever seen, and I had to shift my stance to accommodate what was happening in these slim-cut slacks. I could not tear my eyes away from the way her fingers drifted over the cleavage she exposed. It took every ounce of self-control to be still and let her play this out how she saw it in her head.

She was feeding my words back to me for a reason, and when green eyes lifted to mine, it was with a look that made my entire world spin free of its axis.

My heart took off in a rough, feet-kicking-in-all-directions kind of gallop. Every ounce of blood I had ignited and rushed straight to my dick. She was trying something on in here that was mischievous and bold, and it most definitely fit.

She moved a hand to the top button of my pants and, tugging, slipped it free while holding my eyes in silent question. *Um, yes to everything* was the answer. I think we both knew that I was *completely* on board. My zipper burst open with only a gentle coaxing, and she slipped a hand past my clothing. It was the most exquisite torture. Her palm skimmed over my tip, pressing, her fingers gripping me on all sides.

I wanted more—of her hands, her mouth, anything.

My head fell forward, and I exhaled sharply as I felt my body give up a drop of arousal onto her hand.

"You like this," she whispered. But it wasn't a question. *Fuck yes, I liked it.*

Without a word, she freed me, taking me firmly in both hands. Her breath came out warm and fast on my neck, and she tilted her face to mine, requesting a kiss.

Fuck yes, I'll kiss you. And, yes, I want your hands on me.

Yes, yes, yes!

My mouth opened against hers, tongue sweeping over her lips for gentle strokes, tasting her as I felt myself lengthen in her palms. I was trying to go slow and fighting a raging desire to rush. I didn't know what her goal was, but I didn't care. It was all good. Anything she wanted to do to me was good.

"I'm obsessed with your cock."

"That may be the best thing anyone's ever said to me," I choked out.

There were the times I still couldn't believe this was allowed between us. Not just the sex, but everything—the kissing, the knowing looks, just putting my arms around her when we were waiting in line somewhere. There was a part of me that wanted to throw open the door of the dressing room and point at Selene, calling to anyone who could hear, *Look! Look what I got!*

The fact that my pants were open made that not, immediately, a great idea.

Still, that's the way my heart felt about it. Like with every beat, it was shouting that very thing. *Look! Look what I got.* Somehow I got *her*.

I'd fallen in love. How often does anyone see that coming?

"I've never wanted anyone the way I *always* want you," I told her. Then my mouth found hers again, and she swallowed my sounds of need, stroking me in this slow, nearly lazy way until I was shifting against her, shaking, until my kisses had to stop because I was too focused on the pleasure of her hands wrapped around me, working me. My lips went slack, simply pressed against hers, and I felt greedy for the little sounds of encouragement that began when she realized I was so close. I was nearly swollen to bursting in her hands and struggling hard to contain the noises that would betray what was happening in here.

I felt her lick her lips, and then she purred into my ear, "I'm obsessed with the idea of your climax on my breasts. Sometimes I need to touch myself when I think about that."

"Oh, fuck, I'm coming," I gasped. Those words falling from her lips were the cracks that shattered the last vestige of my control.

There was victory in her eyes as an inferno barreled down my spine and up my legs like a cannonball. I leaned heavily into her, coming hard with a low groan, wet and slick in her hands.

In the small confines of the dressing room, I had no idea how loud I was, or if the music playing through the speakers was enough to camouflage our ragged breaths. I found her mouth again and kissed it thoroughly, begging her with a tiny tilt of my hips not to move her hands anymore. But I didn't want her to let go of me. I liked this secret space, and the warmth between our bodies. I liked the way I lay satisfied and heavy in her hand. I liked this feeling of connection so deep I couldn't breathe.

Chapter 21

Keir

Fire.

I've been fascinated with it for so long I can't even remember *becoming* fascinated with it. There's just something about its sheer, awesome power that captivated me from a very young age. You have to respect fire, and its most basic ability to preserve life and to take it. It's always exciting, always unpredictable. Both terrifying and beautiful.

So if you had asked me at ten years old what superpower I most wanted? Fire hands, of course. Favorite comic hero? No question: Human Torch. Flame on!

I shared every kids' impulse to play with it whenever possible—in fact, my father's worst nightmare was probably me sitting in front of a campfire with a stick in my hand and nothing to do. That would yield about a 97 percent chance of melted sneakers, assorted burns, or someone—likely him—taking an accidental stick to the face.

I distinctly remember one summer when we were camping up in Henley Woods near San Francisco, and I want to say I was maybe twelve years old. Rather than quizzing me on state capitals or American presidents like he usually did to pass the time when we camped, he handed me my own Jiffy Pop, the kind with the long wire handle.

What he wisely understood about me and the whole process of making Jiffy Pop over a campfire was that if I got too close to the open flame, the foil would burn, and the popcorn inside would be ruined. And if I was impatient and tried to rush it, I'd end up with almost nothing popped that was edible. But if I took my time, was careful, and focused on the end reward—all things that went directly against my nature, by the way—I could make something I wanted, and keep myself out of trouble in the process.

He saw it as leveraging my innate competitiveness to teach me to overcome a tendency toward hyperactivity. At twelve, I saw it as me battling a great force of nature, and bending its power to my will.

I saw it as my own kick-ass superpower.

Over the years, Jiffy Pop became our tradition, and he and I would have contests to see which of us could yield the most perfectly shaped dome, which of us could produce no burned pieces, which of us could end up with the fewest unpopped kernels. I held the record at six. He was neck and neck at seven.

It's no wonder those quiet nights with him remain some of the best memories of my life.

In time, that fascination with fire evolved into my multimillion-dollar partnership with it, a catering business inspired by Francis Mallmann–style cooking. Preparing a meal over an open flame has never lost its thrill for me.

It has never stopped feeling like my superpower.

§

My fire had been burning all day on the beach at Half Moon Bay under a gorgeous blue fall sky, and the ancient, intoxicating smell of slow-roasted meat was attracting a crowd. It always did. Regardless of your particular food preferences, there is something so fundamental about the smell and flavor of smoke that people have very visceral reactions to it—universally, across every culture.

Add to that the fact that most people have never seen, let alone eaten, food prepared in the Patagonian tradition—whole, trussed chickens and a big, beautiful rib eye hanging by cooking wire from six-foot irons over a flame for seven or eight hours—and it became quite a spectacle.

That's why I left Selene and Justin on the beach to keep an eye on the pit while I ran back up to the parking lot to pull a few more ingredients from the back of my truck.

In addition to the meat, I was serving grilled vegetables and a fresh salad with amber-colored dates, Bartlett pears, mint, and creamy blue cheese. And for dessert, I'd planned peaches and figs, roasted quickly in caramel, deglazed with amaretto, and topped with lemon zest and freshly picked mint leaves. It was one of my favorites.

"Keir?"

I turned at the sound of a female voice behind me.

Standing there with an armful of blankets and a folding chair was a girl who, to me, looked just like a dressed-down version of Sleeping Beauty. She had the sweetest face I'd ever seen—really pretty, with big light-blue eyes. There wasn't a sharp edge on her. And for just a moment, I knew she was looking me over, too, making a mental assessment, as best friends should. But, even then, she was smiling as if she were as happy to see me as I was to see her.

"Sarah." I set the bag of groceries down on my bumper and wrapped my arms around her in a bear hug, rocking her back and forth. "I'm so glad you could make it."

"Oh my gosh, I can't believe it took so long. It feels like we've all been hearing about the mysterious Hot Chef Boyardee for months."

"Hot . . . *what*?"

"You might as well know that's what we all call you."

I laughed. "Okay. Well, I've definitely been called worse."

Just then, a guy walked up behind Sarah, carrying a large cooler. "For the record, I've *never* called you that," he told me emphatically, and then he set the cooler down and extended his hand with a grin. "Dan Moore."

"My fiancé," Sarah added turning toward him. He smiled proudly back at her.

"Wow! Congratulations to both of you," I said as we shook hands.

The truth was, I had real admiration for the institution of marriage—aspired to it someday and believed that's what manhood was about. I'd just never been ready for it, myself. I wasn't unnaturally opposed to that kind of commitment, but until I met Selene, I saw relationships as requiring a lot of work and energy and time that I didn't have while getting my business up and running. But standing here talking to a guy who seemed genuinely thrilled at the prospect of marriage made me wonder if it wasn't time to reconsider where my priorities lay.

And seeing the two of them together, I also understood the whole Barbie and Ken reference that Selene joked about. Dan Moore was about as good looking as a human person could be, with strawberry-blond hair and green eyes and a wide grin that instantly told you he didn't take himself too seriously. I liked him right away. Together, they did kind of remind me of Barbie and Ken, if Barbie had more human proportions and Ken had a G.I. Joe death grip for a handshake.

"It's great to meet you, man," he said. "Thanks so much for doing all this for us."

"No, no, I'm glad to."

I really was. A big part of the evening for me was that I wanted to do something special for my girl. And I wanted to show her that she could blend the various parts of her life without subtracting from any of them. She didn't have to divide herself between her friends and me; she never needed to feel guilty about the time spent with her family or building her career. I didn't need to be her everything. I just wanted to be among the most important things in her life and I wanted to have a piece of her that no one else got. Standing there with two of her best friends in the world, I suddenly felt closer to her, connected to her life in a way I hadn't before. It made me wonder why I hadn't pushed for this night sooner.

"So . . . *Keir,*" Dan said, studying me in a very academic way. Defying all stereotypes and clichés, he was a nationally recognized middle school science teacher, who'd recently finished his PhD in education at Stanford and now taught evening classes on education reform there. Academics were apparently *his* superpower. "That's . . . what? Scottish? . . . Irish?"

"Scottish," confirmed a very Irish voice behind me.

"Yeah, that's right," I said turning.

Coming to a stop by the truck was Dan's best friend from childhood—a guy I recognized instantly from the internet and TV.

Jamie Callahan.

In my line of work, I met a lot of famous and powerful people—most of whom were shy and many of whom were very standoffish. That's sort of what I was expecting from Jamie, given the fact that his band, Cadence, was a big name in alternative rock. But when he pulled off his Ray-Bans and extended his hand, shaking mine with genuine exuberance, there was none of that famous-guy shit.

"Jamie," he said with a nod.

On TV, he seemed taller; in actuality he was maybe an inch or two shorter than I. With the auburn hair and a smile that seemed permanently fixed in his eyes, he looked like he was always just seconds away from bursting with the best goddamned secret on the planet. How do you not like someone like that?

And Mel, his wife, was just as warm and approachable. Tucked under his arm, she looked tiny by his side, almost doll-like.

"It's about time we met you," she said. Leaning in to me for a kiss on the cheek, her shoulder-length medium-brown hair brushed against my face.

"So, *Hot Chef Boyardee?*" I asked her. Something about Mel told me I didn't need to hold back. I could tell she was cool. She managed a *band*, for Christ's sake.

"How do you know about that?" she said, and turned a wilting gaze on Sarah.

I laughed, taking the beach bag from her hand and throwing it over my shoulder. "Don't worry, I get that a lot."

"Really?" she grinned, and I shrugged like it was an everyday thing.

"I can't wait to see the setup down there," Dan told me, nodding a chin in the direction of the beach. "I was just reading an article on Patagonian–style cooking—"

"Ohhhh, no you don't." Sarah swung around to him with wide, emphatic eyes.

"What?" he asked her, grinning broadly.

"*What.* I know exactly what you're thinking, Danny, and, *no.* You need to leave the barbecuing to the *professional.*"

I bit back a laugh but kept my mouth shut. It didn't take a genius to know this was a thing between them. Covertly, though, I gave Dan the thumbs-up. We both knew how this worked.

"Do you have relatives in Scotland?" Jamie asked me as we started for the beach.

"No. Well . . . I don't know. Maybe. But I never knew them. My mother grew up there, though. *Keir* was actually her surname."

"Ah, that's brilliant. D' ye have any Gaelic then?"

I laughed, lifting my baseball cap and replacing it. "I could probably order a drink or start a fight. But that's about as long as my teenage interest in learning Gaelic lasted."

"About as long as my recent interest in the *no-red-meat* diet that Mel put me on, then," he said, grinning.

"Well, I certainly hope that's over, my friend. Because this right here," I told him gesturing to the fires below, "is *meatopia*."

§

Conversation looped around the campfire throughout the evening, breaking into smaller groups and then returning to include everyone. The best part for me was that every time I looked over, my girl was laughing. I studied her as she told this crazy story about Sarah and Dan in a bar with a tampon. Her arms waved around wildly as she spoke—so much her father's daughter—and I felt the weight of my love for her settle into a heavy warmth in my stomach. I finally understood what it meant to measure your own happiness by someone else's. I was desperately in love for the first time in my life.

As if feeling my gaze upon her, Selene's eyes met mine, and they seemed to bend upward with the corners of her mouth into a look that reflected something intimate and knowing between us. I loved that we had that—that we didn't always need words to say things to each other that were meaningful.

I watched her rise out of her chair, wineglass in hand, and come around to where I was crouched by the fire, adding fresh logs to the embers. Her fingertips on the back of my neck were warm and drifted softly into my hair, sending a contented chill down my spine.

"Join me," I asked her, and collapsed back onto the sand, patting the spot next to me. She dropped down and leaned into my shoulder, and I pulled her in close.

It had been a long time since I'd cuddled on the beach with a woman, and I forgot how nice it was. But with Selene, it was borderline blissful to enjoy a beer and the fire and this perfect night, and to listen to the goofy stories of four other people who were just beautiful to be around. I felt an unfamiliar ache to be part of their group somehow.

While the others continued their conversation about Dan and Sarah's upcoming wedding, Selene leaned in, her face turned to me with her nose just a centimeter from mine. "Thank you for this," she whispered so only I could hear.

"You're having a good time?"

"The best."

"Good," I told her in the same hushed tone. "You can thank me later by putting my dick in your mouth."

A smile burst across her face, just like I knew it would, and even in the dim light of the fire, I could tell she was blushing.

I think if she ever stopped having that perfect reaction, I would stop saying these coarse things to her. But I was quickly growing addicted to the way her whole face lit up when I teased her, and even more by the way we were developing this secret little place that only we knew.

Selene was absolutely stunning in this light, the glow of it clinging to the tips of her lashes and making her olive-toned skin appear luminous. I closed the distance between our foreheads, placing a tiny kiss on her lips.

"I missed you." Her words were barely audible, even up close like this, but there was no mistaking the sadness in them. My heart melted into my gut.

She lifted her hand to my chest, and I could feel the warmth of it through my sweatshirt. I covered her fingers with my palm, squeezing gently.

"I despise every single night I spend without you," I whispered.

How could she possibly know how true that was? But I felt her nod against my forehead before she pushed forward just enough to touch her lips again to mine. It was as if the entire world went silent, and there was nothing else but her and me, and an endless starry sky.

I took a small breath and realized there was truly nowhere else I'd rather be. And I felt this great sense of calm, which was unusual for me because for as long as I could remember, I had always been pulled in every direction, simultaneously. Seeking adventure, seeking business success, seeking myself. Standing still had never really been an option. Though I knew this quiet was only temporary, for the first time in my life, I could see the attraction of it. To be contented well beyond the reach of your anxieties, and to be finally, blessedly, present.

I leaned deeper into her kiss, swallowing her protest that we weren't alone, as I tried to shape every one of these new and unfamiliar feelings into it. It was hard to explain, but in that moment, I had every single thing in the world that counted.

Mel's voice broke into our universe of two. "I think that may have been the best meal I've ever had."

There was a chorus of agreement around the fire that felt very gratifying, and Jamie stretched, muscles shaking, fists clenched, head thrown back in the relief of it. After an enormous happy groan, he said, "I feel like I'm in a food coma."

"It's the fire," I told him. It was also the fresh air and the alcohol and the sound of the waves and the way you could dig your bare feet into the cool, dry sand. It's what I always loved about doing this.

Beside me, Selene snuggled deeper into my side and laid her head on my shoulder again.

"Did you know that fire *fundamentally* changed human biology?" Dan asked, pausing with his wineglass halfway to his mouth. He glanced around at the group as if this should be a hot topic of conversation. Instead his question was met with various forms of complaining that made me laugh.

"You are the biggest nerd I've ever known," Sarah told him. But she was smiling when she said it, like it was a good thing. Like it was a great thing, actually.

"It's a fact," he insisted, now grinning, as well.

"Of course it is," she teased.

There was a really beautiful silent communication between the two of them—much like what Selene and I had, but more developed, perhaps, because they'd been together longer. Mel and Jamie had it too. Maybe that's what happens when you find your person, and you come to realize you're not alone anymore in the world. You're understood.

"No, he's right," I put in. "Fire was the first human technology. Once we started cooking, we could eat a wider variety of things and get more nutrition. Our brains actually grew. Plus, we got physically bigger and stronger."

"See?" Dan said, and he looked over at me like he had just met his twin.

Jamie laughed. "I just like how you think Keir's agreeing with you makes you less of a nerd."

"I just like how you keep stretching so your wife can check out your abs," Dan shot back.

"Were you checking out my abs, love?" Jamie asked her.

"No, don't drag me into this. You are *both* giant nerds in my opinion." And then turning to me she added, "If you wondered why they've both been looking at you all night like heart-eyed emojis, for this one," she said pointing to Dan, "it's because of your barbecue, and for this one," she said pointing to her husband, "it's because of the meat."

"The meat *was* outstanding," Jamie agreed.

His accent had grown broader over the course of the evening, making his words come out sounding like *'twas*. And for the first time in a while, I thought about my mother. I wondered how she would have said those words. Scottish and Irish accents were different, of course, but related.

As a kid, when my mom spoke to me in my imagination—to sing me a lullaby or remind me to tie my shoes—she always sounded American, like me. But, then, she wasn't. In reality, she would have sounded more like Jamie. I had this strange impulse to make him say something else. To hear her voice through his.

"Glad you enjoyed it, man," I answered, and leaned over to touch my beer bottle to his.

"Keir, my mate," he answered as if, instinctually, he knew my private wish and let his full Irish burr roll roundly off his tongue. "Y'er just brilliant. Everything about tonight was *grand.*" *Grand.* I smiled to myself.

"Speaking of which," Mel cut in, "did I hear you're planning on opening a restaurant?"

"Yeah. In fact, I should know soon if I got the building I put an offer in on."

"That's so exciting!" she said, looking back and forth between Selene and me. "Where is it? Which part of the city?"

"Pike Place Market," I answered. And maybe on instinct, I hesitated for a beat. "In Seattle."

"Seattle?" Mel's face changed from genuinely elated to something decidedly less than that, and she shot a confused glance over at Selene. That look, which was the physical manifestation of every single one of my worries about Selene and me, made me pull my arm up around my girl a little tighter. Beyond Selene, I noticed Sarah shifting in her seat.

"Seattle," she repeated. "Sorry, I don't know why I assumed . . ." Mel looked at Sarah and then back to us. She cleared her throat and said, "Well, that's really great, Keir." But it wasn't the same unqualified enthusiasm. "Sounds like . . . very exciting."

She specifically didn't look at Selene, who was now focused on her feet.

"It's exciting," I agreed, "and a lot to take on, but not unmanageable." I hugged Selene firmly to my side. "My catering business is maturing, and now that I'm back full-time, it's running smoothly again. And I'm planning on bringing in some extra help."

Mel nodded and pushed a smile out—with some effort, I could tell.

"Well, count me in when you open it, mate. We're in Seattle quite often, actually," Jamie said. That was a generous thing. Where Jamie went, so did cameras and reporters. I'm sure that's why he offered.

"Me too, man," Dan agreed.

"So will you bring someone in to run it?" Mel asked.

"No, not for a while. I'll need to be there every day for the first year, at least."

It didn't take a genius to know how that sounded in relation to the long-distance commitment I'd made to Selene.

Crazy. That's how.

And I couldn't exactly disagree. A restaurant was a major undertaking.

Mel looked again at Selene, who just shrugged and said something like, "We'll figure it out," and everyone else nodded and focused on the fire, quieter now.

I watched as Mel sat back, expression softening somewhat, but I had the feeling it was a conscious effort on her part. This was a crowd of straight-shooting women and when it came to Selene, their mama-bear instincts were on high. I was glad for it but, honestly, also a little uneasy.

"So how would that work, exactly?" Mel asked us, as if she just couldn't help herself. "For you two, I mean?"

She loved Selene. I knew that. So her question sort of landed between Selene and me like a lead balloon. An awkward silence grew, and I felt inspected—not in an unkind way, just very concerned. I'd worked so hard to get to this point in my career, and I was really excited about the restaurant, but suddenly I found myself desperately wanting to change the subject.

Jamie reached over and squeezed Mel's hand. "Love," he said, quietly using her pet name, and then shook his head in a gentle admonishment.

That's when my confidence faltered and I felt less sure that we could do this. *Were* we crazy? Until this very minute I hadn't had a single doubt. True, I didn't know just what the path would be in the short term, but the end result was very clear to me. Like starting my catering business had been. Like the restaurant. The end result was what I always focused on.

That was the Jiffy Pop.

But Jesus Christ, it was glaringly obvious that we should have talked about our plans before now. Selene always seemed to want to be together without any discussion of our future—without any promises. And there was a simple beauty in that. I was okay with it because in my mind, the hard part was finding each other, and letting each other in. In our past, there were times when I'd tried to set limits on how deep I would allow my feelings to go, and she blew right through them. I'm sure the same was true for her. But we were beyond all that now, so it was just a matter of getting through some period of time apart. We could totally do that.

Still, I realized there could be no more waiting on this discussion. We needed to have it. If not for her, then for me. I mean, we didn't have to have it all figured out. But shouldn't we at least have some of it figured out?

"We haven't nailed down all the details yet," I told Mel, glancing at the girl in my arms and trying to sound reassuring. "But for starters, I want Selene to design the restaurant. So that should give her plenty of reasons to come up and see me."

"Wait. You want . . . *what*?" Selene pulled back from my side and stared at me. And I'll admit that I was a little shaken by the intensity in her expression. "Are you *nuts*?"

"Not that I know of." At least, I didn't think so. Until now.

"I don't know anything about designing a restaurant."

"Yes," I began carefully, unsure of what I was hearing in her voice. "But you know a lot about design."

"Graphic design."

"That's a big part of it."

"Keir, come on. That's a small part of it."

"The rest is interior decorating. We're not talking about moving walls here. Just the cosmetic stuff. And I know you can do it. Look at your apartment. You have great instincts."

Selene stared at me like I had two heads, her posture rigid beneath my arm. When she looked back at the fire in silence, a cold lump settled in my gut, and a sudden distance crept between us.

"She's the most stylish person I know," Sarah put in, trying to be supportive. This seemed to steer the conversation into slightly less awkward territory about Selene and her impeccable design sense, and I let go of the little extra breath I'd been holding. It was possible that the only thing more nerve-racking than meeting Selene's friends for the first time was explaining my intentions to her under their scrutiny. I guess it wasn't such a good idea to bring this up in front of them. So I held back on what I *really* wanted to ask her, which was not just to design the restaurant but to move up to Seattle with me and build it together.

I wanted to bring our relationship out from under this cloud of uncertainty. I wanted to spend all our nights together and make a life together. For real. No more of this long-distance bullshit.

And I wasn't unrealistic; I knew it couldn't happen right away. She needed to be in San Francisco for the time being, and I was fine waiting as long as necessary. For her, I'd wait forever.

But maybe the disappointment with Rival was a blessing in disguise. Maybe it opened up a different door for us. There were plenty of graphic design agencies in Seattle, and with the references she had, she could easily continue to advance her career. She was brilliant, and I wanted her to have all the success in the world. If she chose to, she could live with me, and take as long as she needed to find just the right opportunity.

Ultimately, I just wanted more time with her. I wanted a lifetime. I wanted the luxury of taking her for granted for days at a time, then realizing my mistake and falling in love with her all over again. And more deeply, because every single day I found new reasons to be in awe of her.

Still, it was great for me to admit that but it 100 percent didn't matter as long as Selene and I were on different pages about it. What I saw in her face made me worry for the first time that maybe we were.

The conversation had moved on without us, which I'm sure was intentional on the part of the group. I leaned into Selene, who still sat stiffly beside me, and spoke quietly by her ear.

"What's wrong? Why are you upset?"

"I just feel like we should talk about this before you start thinking in those terms. I mean . . . I want to help, Keir, but I don't know how often I'll be able to come up, and I really don't think I'm qualified."

"I think you're the most qualified. Who knows me better than you?"

"I just think you should give this some thought," she said in the same quiet voice.

Some thought? What did she think I'd been doing all this time?

Did she honestly think I was making something *other* than a thoughtful decision about this? I ran a business, for Christ's sake. I wasn't asking her to do this out of charity; I was asking her because I honestly thought she was the best person to help me achieve what I wanted to achieve with the restaurant. And it was such a personal thing for me that I wanted her to be a part of it. She understood my vision, my passion for it. She understood me—at least I thought she did. This reaction was really troubling, but I couldn't figure out what about it felt the most unsettling: that she couldn't see how intentional I was about this proposal or that she didn't think she had the talent for it.

"You think I haven't thought about this?"

She let out a quiet, frustrated sigh. "I just think it feels right to you right now. In this moment around the fire. And that's not a good enough reason for us to do this."

§

Selene

What I saw in Keir's eyes was hurt. Plain and simple. And, my god, the last thing I wanted to do was to hurt him. But this was crazy! This was his *restaurant*. His Big Dream. What if I screwed something up, and he didn't have the heart to tell me? What if our relationship fell apart when we were neck deep in this project together? He was so confident that I knew him best, but was that really true? What if the project revealed that I didn't really know him well at all? What if we didn't work well together and it broke us?

I honestly wasn't sure I could handle it if I didn't have him in my life.

Everything felt like it was spinning out of control: my dad's illness, pulling myself out of a major failure at work, and the new pressure of designing Keir's restaurant—it was too much. It was way, way too much.

Keir turned away, and I could see the flickering of the fire reflected in his eyes, but I knew he wasn't actually seeing it. His head was somewhere back in the tone of my voice, which had been really unfair to him. I felt like such a jerk, and I knew it was deserved by the way Sarah and Mel were now looking at me. Meanwhile, Jamie tactfully glanced away, and Danny got up to throw another log on the fire.

"I'm sorry," I whispered to Keir; the press of my feelings were almost too much to bear.

"It's all right." He shrugged. "We can talk about it later."

His arm came around me again. But in spite of his assurance, I could sense the things unsaid, the little reserve. His hold was looser this time, and the energy between us had definitely changed. As I sat taking in the way his face looked in this light—the angles growing tighter and sharper with all the things piling up between us—something turned over inside me, exposing a vulnerable underbelly.

Honestly, I wanted to cry.

That impulse was so close at hand, as it seemed to be all the time now. Sometimes I looked in the mirror and I barely recognized myself. My reactions to things weren't necessarily proportional. I was quick to anger, quick to tears, quick to despair.

But Mel's questions really struck a tender spot, like a thumb pressing on a bruise. Because, of everyone I knew, Mel truly understood the implications of prolonged separations. She understood the loneliness and the danger of two lives growing apart. She had lived it for years. Plus, she was the most contemplative person I knew, and if she was concerned, I knew it was with good reason.

"I didn't mean to be a jerk about it, Keir. I just wasn't prepared."

He nodded a few times, swallowing a sip of beer before answering. But he still didn't look at me. "I should have talked to you first."

"Can we talk about it when we get home?"

"Yeah, of course."

But we didn't. We came home quietly and got into bed. Clinging to his skin was a brine of sand and fire and salty air, that perfect alchemy that would always remind me of him. I'd missed him so much in the time we were apart that all I wanted to do was to close the distance between us, not do *anything* that might widen it.

His hand was at my breast, and I lifted it and kissed his palm. Turning in his arms, I kissed his mouth. He let out a small, tortured sound and kissed me back, deeply, stroking my face in the dark, sharing the same breath. Here, we closed the door on an intrusive world, and once again retreated deeper into that sacred place in which only we existed.

Chapter 22

Selene

Monday morning came hard. The only good thing about it was that Keir was staying over an extra night to sign some papers with the trust attorney handling his father's estate. That meant that our goodbyes could wait one more day.

But it had been a rough weekend. Between Keir and me, things were okay, I guess, but still a little strained after our conversation on Saturday night. I hoped he understood why I didn't feel I could lead the design work on his restaurant. He hadn't brought it up since, which told me that either he did understand or that he wasn't all that serious about it to begin with.

Or maybe he didn't bring it up again because another part of my life had unexpectedly taken a left turn in the early hours of Sunday morning. My dad had a setback, which put him in the emergency room overnight and reinforced what I was trying very hard not to acknowledge: his decline was accelerating.

It was a horrible occasion for him and Keir to meet for the first time, but that's how it happened. And both men, seemingly understanding the enormity of the circumstance, embraced each other in the most heartfelt and dignified way possible. It was abundantly clear that they shared a strong love for me and a sincere desire to assure the other of their primary interest in my happiness and well-being.

I don't think I've ever loved anyone more than I loved Keir in the moment when he said something to make my dad laugh and then placed a hand on his shoulder and told him that it was his mission in life to make sure I would always be well fed. The subtext of that didn't need to be spoken: *I'll take care of your girl for you.* It nearly broke me to pieces.

Twenty-four hours later, it was still hard to think about it without crying. But for god's sake, there could be no tears. Not at work. And that was hard enough on my best days.

I suppose as a defense mechanism, I had developed the capability of walling off my dad's illness in my head so I could go to work and not fall apart every minute of the day. I could even talk about his illness selectively without crying—could discuss it as if it were happening to someone else. I might flatter myself and call it strength, but it wasn't strength. It was survival, pure and simple. I simply could not coexist with it when I was working. I had to create almost a separate identity for myself—and that *other* person was the one dealing with a hideous, brutal, and untimely death. *She* was the one who was gutted every minute of every day. And she had the luxury of shattering. She did shatter, often actually. Usually at night in the dark, alone. And then in the morning she left me with the indignity of puffy, tired eyes that I struggled to conceal with makeup and glasses. I resented her deeply for it.

I often wished that life could stop for a time and just allow me to deal with all these things individually. But, of course, it wouldn't. As my dad's illness worsened, there were still bills to pay and meetings to attend and deadlines to meet. Life was cruel that way. Or . . . maybe it was kind that way; I really didn't know. I just knew I was bone-tired, always feeling a step behind, and terrified of falling short like I had so many times lately.

Paula's door had been closed for most of the morning, and when she finally came out, she headed straight for my desk.

"I need you to grab your notebook and come with me," she told me in her usual no-nonsense way. That was one of the many things I liked about her. You always knew exactly where you stood, although you never got the details until she was good and ready to give them.

"Pete," she called to her assistant. "Can you order us lunch, please? We're going to be in here awhile."

Notebook and pen in hand, I followed Paula into her office. It was a huge room with big windows, clean white walls, and the quirkiest, most eclectic, and most colorful collection of artwork you've ever seen. Some of the pieces were based on things she had designed throughout her career that she was particularly proud of, most of which would be instantly recognizable to several generations of Americans. She had done everything from the rock-and-roll album covers of major bands in the 1970s, to the branding of multinational corporations, to environmental graphic designs for some of the highest-profile performing arts centers in the world. Her talent was limitless.

So it shouldn't have been a surprise to me that, as I closed the door behind us, a woman rose from the couch to shake my hand. She was stylish, obviously successful, and she looked me in the eye with the very same directness I appreciated most in Paula.

In a flash of realization, I knew I had met her once before.

"It's a pleasure to see you again, Selene," she said. "I'm Cheryl Gagnier."

My jaw fell open, and my heart felt like a ball of fire in my chest. If I had anything intelligent to say, it had already taken off down the hallway, followed closely by my abilities to blink and close my mouth.

"I remember you," I stupidly said.

"Good!" she laughed. "I'm glad to hear it. And I hope you can clear your calendar for the next many months because the three of us have an entire company to reimagine."

Chapter 23

Selene

My footfalls on the pavement felt heavy under the late evening sky. Along Throckmorton Avenue, the last of the light seemed to choose only its favorite buildings to illuminate, throwing shadows on the rest. It had been such a long, bizarre day of strategizing and messaging and overhauling my design ideas for Rival that I hadn't really had a chance to process the magnitude of it.

I was leading the rebranding of a multinational corporation. This was the graphic design equivalent of making it to the Big Leagues—easily the most exciting thing in my short career.

And for that exact reason, I knew I should have been feeling over the moon—calling everyone I knew to share the news. But all day, I couldn't quite bring myself to do it. I kind of just wanted to hide away. Any conversation I had with friends or family was likely to lead to questions I didn't feel like answering about my dad or about Keir or why on *earth* I didn't sound as *excited* about this project as I should. The truth is, all I really felt was numb. Numb, and so damned tired.

And as irrational as it was, it also felt wrong to have a win like this in the midst of such an extraordinary loss with my dad. I couldn't reconcile the two. I felt guilty for being happy about anything, knowing what he was going through.

Of everyone I knew, Keir would understand this. He wouldn't judge me or try to reason with me or talk me out my emotions. He'd just take my hands and surround me with love until I didn't hurt anymore. He'd been through it, after all; he understood what survivor's guilt was all about. The thing he *wouldn't* understand was why I didn't tell him. And I didn't have an adequate answer for that.

As it always did, the front door of The Arthouse slammed behind me, and Keir looked up from the bar. He smiled in a way that normally made me feel calm, like he had the secret solution to everything in my life that felt out of control and overwhelming, including us. That was always the magic of Keir. From the very first day we met, he took my crazy and made it sane. He was my anchor, my go-to person. In fact, it was hard to imagine what my life would have been like these last few months without our friendship to keep me whole. Or how it would be in the next few, as we saw each other less and less.

I drank in the sight of him, rising from his stool in a crisp navy dress shirt and jeans, looking at me like he had no idea things between us were about to get so much more complicated.

Because, of course, he didn't.

And even now, faced with the immediate prospect of the coming conversation, I couldn't think of the right words to say that wouldn't make the enormity of the project sound like the death knell for our relationship.

Sometimes the fantasy of getting everything you want is so much better than the reality of it.

"Hey, beautiful one," he said in that smoky voice I loved. He leaned in to place a lingering kiss just under my earlobe, and the barest scrape of his stubble on my neck sent a chill straight down my spine.

"Hi." Despite the swirling trepidation in my heart, the smile that grew on my face was entirely real.

"Hi, Selene," Art called from behind the bar. "Glad to see you again."

"Hey, Art."

"What can I get for you, darlin'?" he asked, stepping closer and gently rapping his knuckles on the bar.

"Maybe just a . . . I don't know." I paused, turning to Keir. "What are you having?"

"Bring out the Macallan," he said to Art. "We're *celebrating* tonight."

Art smiled. "Now, that's more like it."

As he stepped away to pull out the crystal decanter from behind the bar, I looked over at Keir and my breath sliced in half. I felt the lump in my throat grow larger.

"How did you know?"

Keir gestured to two seats at the bar and helped me with my coat, gently dragging it down my back by the collar, before draping it over the bar and sitting down beside me. All the while, I was mentally flipping through every possible person with whom he might have spoken who could've told him about Rival. I couldn't think of a single one.

"How did I know what?" he asked, meeting my eyes.

"About my news."

"You have news?" He looked as confused as I was, his brows rising on his forehead as he leaned forward, one arm on the bar. I realized that he always did that; it was his instinct with me to lean in as he listened, as if every single thing I said mattered to him.

"I don't understand. You said we're celebrating. What are we celebrating?"

"I got some news today. But wait, what's yours?"

"No, tell me yours first."

"Selene," he said, and stopped there, holding my gaze and gently exposing his impatience with this circular conversation.

For a moment we just stared at each other—thinking the other might speak. Then, in exasperation, we both spoke in unison.

"*I got it.*"

It was weird the way our words lined up almost perfectly together. It was like the way our lives had lined up, as mirror images of the other—at times pushing, at times pulling, but almost always in this odd, synchronous motion.

And as we sat looking at each other, an awareness grew between us.

"The restaurant?" I asked in a rush of breath. He nodded, and for some reason I felt like the wind had been kicked out of me.

I knew this was coming, of course. We'd spent many hours talking about his ideas for the restaurant and his offer on it. But I guess in my head it was always this future thing, a hypothetical. Now it was suddenly real. It was actually happening. All Mel's questions and the look on her face came flooding back in a rush. I could not breathe.

But I also could not let him see anything less than complete joy for his joy. This was his dream, and I would not be so unforgivably selfish. So rather than risk my own poor poker face, I practically launched myself at him, throwing my arms around his neck and hugging him as tightly as I could. Tears burned like acid in my eyes. I looked up, fighting to pull them back inside.

I didn't let go for what felt like forever. Instead, I breathed in the scent of him that I never wanted to forget—soap and fresh laundry and warm skin and raw masculinity. There was no one who smelled like he did.

"Oh my god, I'm so happy for you, Keir."

I was; truly I was, even if in that exact moment it felt far more like heartbreak than happy. You can't love a man without loving his dreams—without wanting to protect them fiercely like they were your own.

"Your restaurant is going to be so amazing. I can't wait to see it."

Slowly, I felt his arms come around me, too, and they were as strong and as desperate as mine. He hadn't said a word, just continued to hold me tightly, his warm breath coming in bursts at my cheek. After what felt like hours, he pulled back from my grasp.

"You got the Rival contract."

In his eyes flashed the question I knew he would be thinking but would never ask directly: Why had I not called him? He who had been with me for every step of this journey; he who would be most affected by it. In my head, I reasoned it was because I'd been so busy all day and hadn't found the right moment to make the call. But in my heart, I knew that was a cop-out. Sending a quick, *holy shit, you won't believe this* text takes no time at all.

The real reason I hadn't called him was the *other* thing I saw in his face, the thing I dreaded seeing more than anything else: our friendship doing battle with our relationship.

For the first time since we met, I wasn't sure we truly *could* be both friends and lovers. Because just then, as his friend, I wanted to pop champagne and throw fistfuls of glitter everywhere to celebrate his getting the restaurant. But as his lover, as the woman who loved and needed this man beyond anything she'd ever experienced, his news was devastating. And as much as he tried to hide it, my news was devastating too.

"Yeah," I managed. I put my elbows on the bar and leaned my head into my hands. It seemed much too heavy to hold up anymore. Tears threatened again in my eyes, and I waited until I was finally able to meet his gaze. "Can you believe it? I still don't . . . I don't even . . . I mean, it's so . . . ."

I had no idea what I was trying to say—it was all just nonsense. An attempt to fill the uncomfortable silence with noise that might distract us from the need to finally have a real conversation about this. He'd wanted to, of course; I'd been the one playing ostrich all along, just taking every day with him as a gift and trying not to play the chessboard too many moves ahead.

Keir's expression was as serious as I had ever seen it—eyes searching for something behind mine, and at the same time hiding so much more.

But slowly, the sweetest, most genuine smile I'd ever seen began to develop on his face. It was an access of pure pride and joy and love. It took my breath away. And it also broke my heart.

The battle, it seemed, had produced a winner.

"*Of course* I can believe it. And I'm really proud of you right now."

He took my hands in his, smiling broadly. When I looked into his soft brown eyes, there was nothing there but absolute sincerity. He and I didn't really know how to be anything *other* than best friends. It was the basis of everything between us. The starting point. In a contest between our love and our friendship, I should have guessed that friendship would emerge as the bloodied winner. That's why I knew beyond a shadow of a doubt that he *was* proud of me, and he was happy for me in a completely genuine and selfless way.

A laugh burst from my chest, and then, inexplicably, it was immediately followed by a flood of tears I could no longer hold back. It was like the gates just busted open, and everything bottling up behind them came tumbling out all over the floor.

"Hey," Keir murmured with concern, and handed me a bar napkin. "Talk to me."

"Ugh," I said, inhaling a huge breath and blowing it out slowly as it trembled. "I'm sorry. I'm such a mess right now."

"No, you're not. You just have a lot on your plate. And this opportunity with Rival is mind-blowing to me—I can't imagine how it must feel for you."

"I don't know if I feel anything yet."

Keir squeezed my hand understandingly and then gave a quick nod to Art, who was apparently waiting for the right moment to interrupt. After setting two highballs in front of us, Art moved away without a word, tactfully avoiding my teary face.

"Why don't we start with a drink?" Keir let go of my hand and picked up one of the glasses, offering it to me. "So how did all this come about? I thought they decided to go with someone else."

"They did. But Cheryl Gagnier considers the rebrand a top priority for the company, and she wasn't happy with the direction it was taking. She's overseeing it herself now. And they want to use all my ideas. It's so insane, Keir," I said, holding the glass between my palms. "This is multinational brand."

"A multinational brand," he repeated, watching me with his intelligent, warm brown eyes. "I'm telling you—this is going to be a case study for the *Harvard Business Review*."

"Don't even—"

"I'm just saying, this is going to get attention."

"It's going to be *a lot* of work, Keir."

Keir looked at me silently, understanding exactly the implications of that. Then he lifted his own tumbler and took a sip, setting it down carefully on the bar and nodding a few times before answering.

"I know."

His focus was on his glass, and I studied his face, the near-perfect symmetry of it, the way his lashes fanned out across slightly ruddy cheeks. The conflict in his expression was obvious, and I hated to see it.

"So what's the timing on the building? When do you sign the paperwork?"

"It's going to take about a month, and then it's mine and I can start the plans."

A month. *Jesus.* That was nothing. Without any warning, the tears were back.

"Hey, don't cry." Keir offered me another napkin and watched as I blotted big, fat tears from my cheeks. "We're going to figure this out. This is a short-term challenge. But a good one, right?"

"*Short-term*, meaning what? My dad?"

Keir's face sobered immediately. "No, baby. I don't mean that."

"Keir, do you have any idea how *much* work this project is going to be?"

"Honestly, no."

"It's not just picking a design and applying it everywhere. It's brand research and A/B testing and studies to understand how the core concepts would be received internationally."

The calmness I was trying to maintain began to unravel, and I could sense the impending explosion. I just had no idea what shape it would take.

"It's developing messaging and brand guidelines, making decisions about whether or not to keep the logo mark, or come up with a new one or get rid of it altogether, which, in itself is a multimillion-dollar decision. This isn't a short-term problem, Keir. This is my *life* for the next year or more."

He was quiet for too long, and when I looked again, I found him watching me, considering.

"Okay. I understand."

"And the restaurant—that's *massive*. You're never going to be able to take a weekend off."

"I know, Selene. I'm not being unrealistic. But people do this. Hell, Mel and Jamie have been doing it for fifteen years. And they have a family."

"It's not the same. Jamie and Mel are both working towards a common thing—towards the success of the band. And yes, Jamie is gone a lot, but the band is what keeps their lives connected. Keir, we're both going to be buried in our own things—both going in different directions. I'm so scared about what that will do to us."

It was the first time I'd ever said that out loud—the first time I had ever admitted how terrified I was that we wouldn't be able to hold on to what we had together once our lives again diverged. The tears were really flowing now, and there was no stopping them. It was like a river raging inside me—a release of emotion so powerful that it caught other things up in its path: my father's decline, my own secret fear of not living up to the expectations of the project I was entrusted with, and the overwhelming fatigue that was both physical and emotional.

And, of course, Keir was right there. To comfort and reassure me, to say just the perfect things about how time apart could never diminish what we feel for each other, about how strongly he believed in me, about how proud my father will be, and how when I look back on this time, as hard as it is now, I'll know that I put my very best into every aspect of my life that matters and I'll have no regrets.

But, god, was that true? As always, Keir knew exactly how to comfort me, how to give me just what I needed in words or deeds so I could be better and do better than I thought possible in these weak moments. He was my strength, and he had become the salve for all hurts in my life—this all-consuming force of nature.

But what if he was wrong? What if this new relationship we had *couldn't* withstand the pressure of our separation? And what if the casualty of that was not just our love affair but also the friendship I had come to rely upon so deeply? What if when I looked back on this time, *Keir* was my regret?

Suddenly I was filled with the instinctive fear of losing *everything* we had, the inevitable changes to us, the possibility of a life without him altogether.

I tried to imagine that, and my heart faltered. He was my best friend, my support system, the love of my life. He had become so necessary in my life that even the idea of losing him sent me careening headlong into the kind of panic I could equate only with losing my dad.

Like another death.

My thoughts and fears became this writhing, seething mass. I thought I might be sick.

He was right here with me, leaning in close with his warm hands around mine, but still mine felt icy. The laughter around the bar was so incongruous with what was happening inside me that it seemed to amplify my panic.

And Keir was talking, but I realized I wasn't registering any of it—I was just watching his lips move as they formed the words I could barely hear over the pounding of my heart.

"That's exactly why I want you to help design the restaurant," he was saying. "It'll keep us connected and give us something to work on together while we're apart. It'll be *ours*."

The seriousness was gone from his face, and in its place was that magnificent optimism and headstrong belief in the future that so defined him. As he spoke, I tried to memorize it. I tried to see details of his face that I hadn't seen before, like the curve of his chin, the tiny crease in the middle of his bottom lip.

Maybe he knew I wasn't following carefully; maybe he was just talking me down from a ledge, giving me a chance to collect myself, but he went on without any response from me, the words falling from his mouth in this easy, mesmerizing cadence.

"This will be so much fun. You'll have free rein to pick any color scheme you like, any fabrics you like for the furniture, any artwork.

You can choose the dishes, the silverware, the linens, everything. I want to walk into the place and have it feel like you've made it yours. *Ours.* What do you think?" he asked encouragingly. "That'll be great, right?"

I wanted to tell him that, yes, that it would all be great. But I couldn't quite see it. I couldn't make that leap forward in my head from where we were, past all the bad stuff that would inevitably come before we arrived at this magical Emerald City.

The more we talked this through out loud, the more I wondered if he was right to worry from the very beginning that we'd screw everything up—that we'd lose both our love and our friendship and have nothing at all.

And yet, if I had to choose between them I couldn't. It would be like choosing between my heart and my lungs—neither felt survivable.

I felt something break inside me, unleashing fears that threatened everything.

"Keir—"

"I know what you're thinking, but it's going to take a while to get the restaurant launched, and in that time, you'll focus on Rival, and I'll come down here as often as possible. It won't be much different from what we're doing now. We'll make this work. The hard part is just temporary."

"What do you mean?" I asked him again in frustration. "Why do you keep saying this is just temporary?"

He took a deep breath and said, "I want you to consider moving up to Seattle with me."

I stared at him in complete bewilderment, my mouth open but soundless with shock.

I *literally* had no response. I could barely breathe. Let alone process *that*. Let alone think about anything I might do beyond this very moment. Even lifting my glass felt monumental, and my hand shook the entire way.

It was like everything around me was spinning, and I couldn't get a handle on anything. Keir and I had never discussed the possibility of my moving; I couldn't even wrap my brain around that.

And he was waiting for an answer.

I felt the panic inside me begin to spread. It was like this toxic ooze that started in my chest and crept outward, incinerating everything in its path. Desperation took over my pulse.

"Not right away," he added quickly, seeing something more than ordinary reluctance in my face. "I'm just saying that after the Rival project is finished, you'll have your pick of opportunities. There are lots of great agencies in Seattle, and you know Paula would give you a stellar recommendation."

I couldn't even think how to navigate this conversation. I was trying to find words to explain myself, but with no success.

"Keir . . . I don't—"

"I'll wait as long as you need me to. I'm not in a hurry, Selene. It's not that I'm trying to rush you into a decision or a timeline. It just feels so good to finally be able to talk about this. About us and our future together. And I want you to know what's in my head. I want forever."

"Oh my god, Keir."

"I know it feels overwhelming, and you have a lot to deal with at the moment. I get it. And at first when you said you got the Rival contract, I'll be honest with you, I felt a little freaked out myself. But the more we discuss this, the more I know we can do it. And it's all good. It's what we wanted—"

"Keir," I said in a rush with a voice I barely recognized as my own. "I can't commit to that."

As soon as the words left my mouth, I could see their impact. Keir fell silent.

I watched him process this for a breath. All that hopefulness that

I loved left his expression as he searched my face. He looked . . . devastated. A tiny line formed between his brows, marring the smooth landscape of his forehead.

"To what, exactly?" he finally asked.

To what, exactly? My god, a world of unknowns in that one question. I truly believed myself to be the least capable or qualified person to answer it.

The quiet that followed was terrifying. It was almost more than I could manage just to swallow past the heavy swell in my throat. I felt like an emotional land mine, wishing more than anything that I could take refuge in the thick-walled chambers of his heart, which had become my safe place, but fearing I was about to say something that might close that place off forever.

"I . . . I just need time to think."

"Okay," he said carefully, his eyes never leaving my face. I realized I was desperately afraid of what he might see there, and looked down to where my hands were clenched in my lap.

"Keir, can we just go home?"

He turned that over for a long, slow moment, then nodded briefly. "Yeah, of course," he said, absently rubbing his sternum with his fist.

There was an adoring part of him that always made me feel like I could do no wrong in his eyes, and that part was trying to be understanding, trying not to react to my obvious panic. But another part seemed to sense the very real danger that his own heart was in. Lightly, he put a hand to my lower back as we rose from our stools, but he didn't look at me as he led me out of the bar. And I knew with all certainty that *that* part of him was instinctively beginning to protect itself.

From me.

Chapter 24

Keir

The silent drive back to Selene's apartment felt like a crash happening in slow motion. This was a metaphorical crash, but the sensation was exactly the same as I remember from my teenage years, joyriding recklessly in my pop's cars: There's a certain point when you realize you've lost all control of your own trajectory. Everything is swirling around you, blurry and misshapen, and the only thing you can actually hear is your own heart pounding. You can't pull out of this. You can't go back and make a better decision. There's nothing more to do but brace yourself, while you careen helplessly toward the inevitable.

We walked through the front door and into Selene's living room, and a strange sense of wrongness seeped into my gut. I'd spent a lot of time in this room—watching movies, sharing a meal, talking and laughing and kissing and other things until late into the night. But tonight the room felt foreign to me. Like I was the foreign body in it and I had no place here.

I'd meant for this evening to be a celebration—a new beginning for us, a chance to finally choose our path forward and take our first step toward a life together of our own design. That's how I saw it in my head, anyway. But as I watched Selene carefully set her purse down on the table, her back still toward me, gathering her thoughts, all of that felt hideously naive.

When did I start assuming our story would have a happy ending?

I stood silently, keys in hand, not moving to approach her, and not settling in to finish our conversation. I felt like I needed to be on my feet for this. And I didn't think it was going to take long.

"You told me you loved me," I said quietly, though my voice belied every bit of the emotional hurricane underneath.

I'd had more than enough of the bullshit and beating around the bush. I thought I knew what was coming, but I needed to hear her say it. Out loud. And it was strange; maybe a part of me had been waiting for this for so long that more than anything—more than the anger, more than the frustration or confusion, even more than the hurt that would inevitably come once the shock wore off—I just felt this insane relief. Like there was *finally* something concrete to push against and something within her that was finally pushing back. I'd sensed it for a while, but it was like taking on the wide-open sky; I could never quite put my finger on what it was that was coming between us, and I couldn't get around it.

"I do love you," she said. "More than life itself, Keir. That's the point."

"I don't get it, Selene."

She turned to face me and the rims of her eyes were red and watery. With one heavy blink, the tears started to fall. "I already want to be with you every second. I hate being apart. I miss you constantly—more than is good to, I think. And, god, this is *nothing* compared to how hard it's going to be a month from now when our careers obliterate everything else in our lives. I've never really done this successfully before, and I don't even know how to balance the two. I mean, do you? You haven't done this either."

"I also haven't been in love before, and I don't think I'm sucking too badly at it."

"No, you're not. You're amazing. And sometimes it scares me how much I've come to need you."

"For fuck's sake, Selene, that's what you're supposed to do."

"Yes, but I don't just need you as my lover. I also need you as my friend."

"I *am* your friend. There was never a single second when I wasn't."

"I know that, but if we have to choose—"

"Why would we ever have to choose?" I didn't understand any of this. Why the fuck would we have to choose?

"I just mean . . ." She looked away. "God, this is so hard."

She broke down crying, covering her face with her hands, but I couldn't take so much as a step toward her. There was only a fraction of me that could hold back from wanting to comfort her or make this easier. The rest of me would give her anything she asked. I'd chew my own arm off to do it. But I needed to hear her say whatever it was that she was going to say, even if it killed us both.

"I just mean," she continued, chest heaving as she gulped for breath, "maybe being together in a relationship is too much right now for us to manage. Maybe it's better to cool things down."

The moment she stopped speaking, her words seemed to wrap around my throat, choking off my next breath.

Cool things down?

What kind of a solution was that?

She looked up, begging for some sign of understanding from me, but there was none. Absolutely none. In fact it took several tries before I could even form a response.

"Maybe you're forgetting the part where we're in love."

She swallowed hard, shaking her head. "I'm not forgetting. I'm just wondering if that's the best thing for us right now."

"Are you kidding me with that?"

Ice slid into my veins, chilling every part of my body, and I felt like my gut was made of lead.

"Keir, we're talking about major life changes here—" she said, swallowing back tears. "For both of us. I don't want us to be one of those couples who just falls into a big decision about our relationship without a lot of thought and then winds up resenting each other after the fact."

I looked away, rubbing my face. I didn't even know where to begin with that one. First of all, did she have any idea that that was *all* I'd been thinking about? That I'd thought of almost nothing else for weeks?

I mean, yes, her news about Rival was a surprise, and, yes, it would require us to have more patience with our plan. But we would do what we had to. There's so much shit in this world you can't control. But the things you *choose*—your life, your lover, your place to make a stand— *those* are the things that define you. Those are the things you fight for.

"Resent each other for what, Selene?"

"I don't know, specifically. For not having enough time for each other; for not being able to juggle all these priorities well enough; for being distracted, even when we're together; for being jealous of the other people in both our lives who will spend more time with us than we'll spend with each other; for holding each other back from giving a hundred and ten percent in our work, even if it's unintentional. It could be anything, Keir.

"I feel like in a friendship, you can navigate all of that because the expectations are different," she went on, gesturing broadly with a trembling hand. "But in a relationship, there are so many things that can go wrong. I don't want that for us. I never want that for us. Maybe it's like you said before. Maybe we would have a better chance of keeping each other in our lives if we do it just as friends."

Well.

Fuck me.

I finally understood how harsh those words sounded from the other side of the conversation. There was definitely a joke in here somewhere, and believe me when I say I knew it was on me.

"So when you said you can't commit, you weren't talking about moving up to Seattle or even designing the restaurant. You were talking about us. You can't commit to *us*."

She didn't utter a word. She just stood there, staring at me while the tears gathered again in her eyes. Her chest was heaving, as if she was struggling to take in a full breath.

"This is bullshit. You know that, right? People who love each other don't just decide one day that they're going to be *just friends* and then go on as if that's a perfectly normal thing to do. It's *not* a perfectly normal thing to do, Selene. It doesn't work that way."

Her eyes closed, causing the tears to fall. "I'm not saying it's going to be easy."

"Easy?" The calm exterior I was trying to maintain cracked, and my voice came out sounding angrier than I wanted it to.

"Please, Keir, don't be mad at me." She began sobbing, and it nearly killed me to see it, but she was nearly killing me as it was. "I just think it's for the best right now."

That's when my heart went completely blank. There was no mistaking the lie in her voice; it didn't even want to roll off her tongue. But it wasn't me she was trying to convince.

And staring at her in shock, a fresh realization hit like a blow to the stomach: "Did you ever imagine how it would be with us? I mean, when you thought about us as a couple?"

Selene looked at me, confused. No, she didn't have any idea what I meant.

Because she had never *actually* envisioned our future together. Sure, we talked about being a long-distance couple, and we talked about being in love. But what actually came next—the actual practice of all of that—was always an abstract thought for her. She'd even said it to me—she didn't want to think about her future. For her, the future held only heartbreak. So I had never truly figured into it, not in any real way that mattered.

In her mind, we had reached the edge of a cliff and the options were these: stop here and salvage the friendship or go over and lose everything we have.

"I did—imagine us," I told her, stepping closer so she had to tilt her head up to look at me. "I can't tell you how many times I've thought about our life together," I said, seeing it all so clearly in my mind, as I had a thousand times before. "The restaurant, the routines we'd have, the little insignificant moments that never felt insignificant to me."

Like standing at the hostess desk, going over the night's reservations when the front door opens and every head in the place turns to see this astoundingly beautiful woman walk in. And catching her eye and smiling, knowing she's there only for me. Knowing she's the one I think about all day long and the one I can't wait to go home to at night. She's the one I stay in bed with until noon on Sundays, the one I want to do all the most banal things with, like shopping for groceries and picking out plants and going to the paint store, where we'd probably end up arguing over some color. But she'd know I don't actually give a shit what color we choose; I just like it when she looks straight at me like there isn't another person in the world. I just like it when she looks at me.

Pressure threatened behind my eyes, and I had to close them to regain some control, to right myself again.

"There are a million things I've imagined. But you never did, did you? You never actually saw a future with me at all."

The silence that followed was suffocating. Finally she looked away, and her expression broke.

"I wanted to," she said quietly.

Staring down at her, those three simple words raked like rusty nails across my unprotected heart—hard words spoken by soft lips. I thought I was prepared for this but I wasn't. I didn't have a clue.

I opened my mouth to reply, but as it turned out, I had no *fucking* idea what to say. My love for her was not a voluntary emotion—not something I could just shut off at will. And at the moment, it felt like poison.

"So this is what you really want for us? *Friends?*" I said, ignoring the organ in my chest that twisted as I forced myself to ask it. There was no way to keep the bitterness from seeping into my voice now. I hated that I loved her so much I would tear my own heart out if that's what she wanted. I couldn't even stop myself from doing it.

"I just think . . . for now . . ."

"For now . . . *what?*" I demanded.

"Yes."

The word was barely audible, but she might as well have shouted it for the way I heard it in my head, like a glass house shattering. And quite frankly, any fight I had left in me dissipated when she said it.

What was I fighting for, anyway? To force her to see what she couldn't? To beg her to want what I wanted? To beg her to want me?

No, love isn't always voluntary, and sometimes you find yourself in it alone.

Grabbing my bag from her room, I walked out of the apartment. I was a tangle inside, hating to leave things like this—wanting more than anything to be close to her—but feeling for the first time since we met that she wasn't my solace. She had the power to hurt me like no one ever had before.

The sword I willingly wielded had now turned inward.

I had to build a fortress around myself, and I needed to find the will to keep her out.

Chapter 25

Selene

Twice every single day, the earth paints its skies in the most brilliant colors, and most of us fail to notice. We don't need to. Tomorrow it will happen all over again.

For most of us.

It was early November when my dad passed away and the world as I knew it came to an end. And it also didn't come to an end. I guess that's something you learn.

I watched him fight his cancer without complaint and with the same courage and spirit I'd seen in him my entire life. He never gave up, right up to the end—right up to the point when those feet that had walked for decades had no more miles left in them. In his final days, he drifted into a state of semiconsciousness, speaking words we couldn't understand, reaching for something—or someone—we couldn't see.

There were times when I felt the need to pull a blanket up around him, to put something of weight between him and the beckoning sky.

Heaven, it seemed, was too close to San Francisco.

But in the end, he had to go, and I had to let him. It was never my choice, anyway. And the sky, or whatever was beyond it, became that much more brilliant.

My dad wasn't a saint. It was tempting to think of him that way because he was larger than life to me. But he wasn't without his flaws, and I knew he wouldn't want to be remembered in any way that didn't ring true to who he was. Ultimately, I think we honor our parents by bringing the best of them forward and laying the rest down in forgiveness and understanding.

As for the hole his passing left in my life . . . well, there were no words for that.

Chapter 26

Selene

My father's service was a fitting, lovely, and brutal affair. I did my best to get through it, but every breath I took felt choked off, every movement robotic. I really just wanted to leave as fast as I could and be as far away as possible. The whole thing felt like a bizarre party where the guest of honor was stuck in traffic, and rather than wait, the event just went on without him. I wasn't sure if he would have liked it or if he would have been embarrassed by all the fuss.

And there wasn't a single second in which I didn't wish that Keir were there. But I'd made such a mess of everything; I had no right to ask that of him. Since he walked out of my apartment six weeks back, our calls and texts were seldom, and mostly limited to news of my dad and words of support. I couldn't blame him; there was no reason at all for him to want anything to do with me after the way things ended. It was so painfully ironic that in trying to protect some part of our relationship, I had inadvertently destroyed it—all of it.

And I wouldn't have thought that a heart in pieces could break any further than it already had. And yet mine did, every single day when I thought of him. Familiar things seemed to turn on me—things I'd been doing for years, places I went long before I knew him—now it all served as a painful reminder of us. Now I seemed to find him in everything. Maybe because I was seeking him out, maybe because that's just where he was, still present in everything I did. And every single day, I tried to convince myself to let him go and move on, like I pledged I would. But the silent words never came. When I closed my eyes, he was all I saw. Memories of him and of us. And then I was right back loving and missing him with an intensity that made every muscle in my body ache with an unanswered need—a long, hollow, lonely ache that nothing else could assuage. Occasionally the feeling within was so strong I could have been physically sick.

I imagined him so many times, just showing up unannounced at my apartment, or the office or the coffee shop on the corner that we always went to. I looked for him constantly in the faces I saw on the crowded streets of San Francisco. Like there was some hope that he wasn't in Seattle and that I'd just magically run into him somewhere. It was stupid and kind of heartbreaking, but that's what I always did. That's just how love is, I think. Logic takes a back seat to longing, and you convince yourself there's a possibility, just because you want it and need it so very much.

So when he walked in to my dad's service, without any warning, just feet away from where I stood, it felt like my imagination was taking pity on me.

I wouldn't have believed my eyes, except that I heard someone, maybe Danny, say his name and he turned. My vision quickly became blurry and unreliable. Only my heart could see him clearly, and it leaped into my throat as my lungs gave up their efforts to function normally and just shut down.

Seeing him standing there, actually standing there, hair nicely cut and clothes pressed and neat, I burst out laughing. It was a hideous, loud, and inappropriate reaction. But it was the most accessible outlet I had in that moment to vent an overwhelming flood of emotion.

Keir knew it. He took four quick strides to reach me, understanding instinctively what was to come.

One minute I was hysterical with laughter, the next with tears. It was more than just grief. It was relief maybe, too—though I was ashamed to admit it—and complete physical exhaustion.

And I had no idea where my blood had gone. Every drop had left my head, but none of it was supplying my legs. I felt them dissolve beneath me.

Keir wrapped both arms around me and lifted me firmly, carrying me outside to where he could ease us both to the ground. There against a wall, he held me tight as the feeble stitches holding my composure together came completely apart.

I have no idea how long we stayed like that—me curled up against his broad chest, tears spilling down my cheeks and soaking into the soft cotton of his shirt. He held me until the shivering stopped, and I could finally take a full breath.

"I can't believe you came," I whispered, sniffling hard.

"Of course I came."

His hands caressed my back gently, lovingly, as he murmured small and gentle things, saying my name over and over and over again. No one ever said my name like he did. He had a special way of saying it, all his own, like the word itself was laced with all his favorite things. I could have stayed like that forever, just listening to his voice and to the soft sounds of the birds in the trees nearby, just resting my head against his shoulder, grateful for the simple touch and human warmth.

Still, all time is borrowed.

And it always seems to require repayment at exactly the moment we most need an extension.

Like a slow dawning, I realized that his arms had come to rest lightly around me, no longer in the natural way of two people at ease with each other. And it occurred to me—belatedly, as so many things did these days—that this was a level of physical intimacy that went beyond what I could rightly ask.

"Is this okay for you?" I asked him, tracing a seam on his shirt with my fingertip, and caught in the familiar smell of him.

"Honestly, I don't know," he said quietly, and I felt, once again, the battle raging inside him between our friendship and whatever else was left of the feelings we'd shared.

"Just give me a minute more and I'll be okay."

It was a lie, of course. And he didn't bother trying to act like he believed me. But I truly had no desire to cause Keir any further heartbreak, just to distract me from my own. Though it ran contrary to every human reflex, I pushed back from his chest and arranged myself against the wall at his side. My entire body felt cold and empty.

"I'm just not ready for all this," I told him, wiping my eyes and gesturing to the room behind us where the service was still going on. "I thought I was prepared but . . ."

Keir took up a hand from my lap and encased it in his own. It was big and secure—like a clamp around mine. I knew it wasn't a romantic gesture; it was about giving me an anchor. And it was as instinctual to him as reaching to catch me if I fell. That's just who he was. His kindness ran deep. Too deep, sometimes.

"You're never really ready, Selene. You're just"—he shrugged, and there was a crease between his brows as his body released a long sigh—"as ready as you can be, I guess."

I knew he was right, of course. How does anyone prepare for love lost?

"You handled it better than I have."

"Not really. There were days early on after my pop died when I was so angry and sad. If I could have wished away all emotion, believe me, I would have because I was a wreck. You met me right in the middle of that." He caught my eyes, looking for understanding, and I nodded. "Some days you were the only thing that chased away the sadness. But it was enough. It was enough to remind me that I had to just let it all come, and then let it pass, because it will. Selene, you can't feel love without also feeling sorrow. I couldn't love you without allowing myself to miss my pop, which I do, every day. But that's also how I know I was loved by him. And I'll always be grateful to you for that."

"Keir—"

"You're going to be okay is what I'm trying to tell you. Just look around," he said, nodding his chin in the direction of the service. "You have people who will help you through all the hard parts of this, and then you'll be able to enjoy your successes and look forward to your life."

His eyes smiled when he said that, and then his mouth did, too, a little. And his hand was warm and firm around mine. I bit my lip so I wouldn't cry again, but it happened anyway. Sometimes it felt like I'd never be able to stop. He pulled me to his shoulder, turning me a little so that one hand rested softly on the back of my head. The position we were in made continuing to hold his other hand a little awkward, but he didn't let go, and I never, ever would.

"Are you okay? Have you been okay?" I said. As his friend, I wanted him to be okay.

"You mean about us?" He sighed, but the corners of his mouth bent in a way that let me know he wasn't upset that I'd asked. He cleared his throat, then raised his eyes, looking into mine with an honesty raw enough to make me want to look away. But I didn't. "No. Not at all."

"Me either. I miss you, and I hate that I don't know what's been happening in your life."

"There's not much to know. I'm just working a lot," he said shrugging. "And brooding. A fair amount of brooding, actually. So, yeah, I've been busy with that."

He was trying to make light—teasing, but also not.

"I didn't mean to end things between us, Keir. And I didn't say what I said because I didn't love you or want to be with you."

"I know." He looked away when he answered, his heart in his eyes.

"But I made everything worse. And I hurt you, which is something I never wanted to do."

"This really isn't the time, Selene," he said directly, and I knew I had touched a nerve.

He was right; it wasn't the time. But I didn't know if I'd ever have another. I couldn't stand the thought of letting him go and never asking. "I just need to know if you think we'll ever be able to talk or be in each other's lives again?"

He was quiet a long time, and then he shook his head softly. "I don't know. I guess we'll just have to"—he lifted one shoulder—"just have to figure it out."

A single, dry laugh escaped me, hearing him say the words that had been our downfall. None of it was funny, of course, but it was the first truly familiar thing that had occurred between us in weeks— we were experts at kicking the can down the road. As though something similar had occurred to him at almost exactly the same time, his wide, soft mouth curled into a little smile.

"Unfortunately, we sucked at doing that," I said dryly, and for a moment we were back in that easy place where words like *we* and *us* were possible again.

"We *really* sucked at doing that," he agreed, smiling a tiny bit more carelessly.

I loved his smile, with the creases that weren't quite dimples but were there on his cheeks because smiling was something he did often. And I loved his easy laughter, and the way he could always make me blush. And the way he held me, and the way he looked at me and listened to me, and the way we made love.

"We didn't suck at everything, though."

"No," he murmured thoughtfully in his way. "We were pretty great at a lot of things."

He met my eyes for a lingering moment. There were so many unsaid words in that look—so much yearning and regret, love and pain. The air between us went still. I could see his pulse beating fast in the hollow of his throat; my own blood was thundering in my ears. And then his eyes dropped down to my mouth, as if, behind those eyes, he was seeing everything I was seeing—so many perfect memories: the joy and the laughter, dancing at The Arthouse, my first hockey game, our first I love you, making love to him the first time—and every time. Sharing each other's thoughts and histories, and healing, and helping each other through hard things, as though the connection we had was more of a reconnection—so much older than the brief time we'd shared.

In that singular, beautiful moment amid all the heartbreak, I wanted to lean forward and kiss him—to go back in time. To do this all better. To erase the mistakes I'd made and to soothe every grain of hurt I had caused him. I can't even describe how much I wanted that. And if the look on his face and the way his breathing picked up was any indication, I thought he wanted it too.

But the tension of the moment snapped, revealing its cruelty: bringing us closer, only to remind us of just how far apart we actually were.

He looked away, and his face sobered, eyes unreadable. He dropped my hand lightly to run his fingers through his hair, but it didn't feel like the mindless gesture he was going for—it felt like he needed space—and my hand immediately felt icy again. It was impossible to get warm. I never realized how much he touched me until he held himself back from doing it freely.

"But I heard what you said before," he continued, "about trying to balance everything. And you're not wrong that it's probably easier to do that as friends. I just don't know how to have you in my life right now without breaking my own heart every time I see your face."

I might have cried, hearing that. But there were no more tears in me. The wound went too deep.

"Well, maybe we could just—"

"Selene," he said interrupting me gently but purposefully. He shifted his body, turning slightly so that we were now facing each other more directly, though all I felt was the distance between us, and it nearly gutted me.

"I came today because I love you, and I want to be here for you, and that will never change." His eyes went warm and soft, the way they did when he felt urgent about something. "You and I have been through something awful and extraordinary together. And I think the people you know in those times of your life are people you never forget. But right now, I'm not sure we're in the same place. And I think the time apart gives us a chance to get centered and be more thoughtful about what we want. And I guess I also need some time to figure out how to feel easy around you again because I don't want to lose our friendship either."

Nausea rolled through me. There was a part of me that wanted to argue with him—to tell him that we *were* in the same place and that I *did* know what I wanted. Keir was my Oxygen, my Galaxy, my Big Love. I knew that.

Our friendship was in itself a love story. It was *our* love story.

I knew I would never love anyone like that again. I wanted to tell him all those things. The words were right there on my tongue, but it didn't feel fair to him to say them just then.

Because the truth is, I'd been such a mess of wildly erratic and unpredictable emotions for weeks—and my cheeks, tear streaked and blotchy, only underscored this point. I could hardly pretend that I was suddenly something better than these broken pieces; I could hardly argue that I had my shit together enough to be a safe place for *his* heart to land right now. He was still tender from his own loss, and he was wise to be cautious of me. I couldn't fault him for that. I didn't honestly trust *myself* all that much.

So, though it felt like a stabbing wound in the pit of my stomach, I nodded and said nothing, gave no resistance to what he was telling me— at least none that he could see. Inside, I railed against the thought of letting him go, the idea that tomorrow I would look around my life and find that he was no longer there. Keir was everything to me.

But he was also better than me. Because even in his own heartache, he was *here*. For me. Being the friend he had pledged to be. Being the man I knew him to be. Being selfless and kind and generous.

And I needed to rise to his example.

No strings attached, and no hard feelings.

Maybe it was finally time to keep that promise. It felt long overdue. Still, I knew that letting him go would take something more than ordinary courage. Something that went beyond human instinct and I feared I did not have it. I hoped I could hold on to my conviction just long enough to let him walk away.

So we sat for a while in a heavy silence, alone with these thoughts. And there was a big part of me that wanted to close my eyes and let that silence swallow me whole.

A couple of times Keir seemed poised to say or ask something further but instead breathed in and let it go. I suppose I could have asked what it was; I don't think he would have told me. And maybe I didn't really want to know.

"We've been out here a while," he finally said. "Should we go back inside?"

"You go. I'm going to stay a bit longer."

He studied my face. "You sure?"

"Yeah. I'm sure."

"Okay."

He leaned forward and placed a soft kiss on the top of my head that nearly broke my heart with its simplicity. Then he pushed himself up to stand, lingering for a moment, head down, eyes on me, as if, again, there was something on his mind. In the end he held back and merely settled on *"See you inside,"* before turning for the door.

I watched him go with a burning intensity, as though in an effort to absorb every bit of a sight that I might not see again after today, to squirrel away whatever tiny things I could so that in the lean days ahead, those crumbs might provide some little bit of sustenance.

I watched him go until the image in my eyes was misted and smeared. Tears. I thought there were no more left, but it was like somebody opened the floodgates and ran away with the key. My heart felt far too small in my body, missing him, though he had just left—wanting him so badly that every limb hurt, like a physical pain. I hugged my knees to my chest to stem the hollowness inside.

I'd always thought the way our lives came together, both jarring and serendipitous, meant that the universe had something particular in mind for us. But was this it? This brief, beautiful, painful intersection? This crash that had left us both a little damaged?

Was *this* how it was meant to end between us? God, it all felt like such a waste. Everything did. Everything.

Cancer was such a waste.

And death was such a waste.

And anger was a waste.

Fear was a waste.

And tears. Tears, too, were wasted.

I missed my dad.

Letting my head fall back against the cold cement wall behind me, I looked up to the sky, where fingers of white clouds weaved their way through the cornflower-blue day. The breeze on my face felt like a soft caress, drying my tired eyes with a gentle hand. Birds called to each other in flight, communicating what? A summons? A warning?

There were so many things I would never understand about the universe. So many mysteries that could never be solved. It was the *why* of things that always got me.

What was this bigger picture I couldn't see? What was the reason for any of it?

I wondered if my dad could see it—now that he was somewhere beyond the sky? Did he have a better vantage point to a world I couldn't understand? Did he know why he had to go when I wasn't ready for him to go? Did he know what it was the universe had planned?

If he did, would he ever be able to tell me?

I closed my eyes again, as tears fell helplessly to the ground.

And silently I asked him.

Chapter 27

Keir

What followed Selene's father's service was two months of ineptness. Selene and I didn't know how to be in each other's lives, but we couldn't quite let go either—though I had the strong feeling she thought she would somehow be doing me a favor if she did.

Whether that was true or not was hard to say. She had my heart in her hands, and if she didn't want it, it wasn't like I could just take it back. She was the love of my life, for Christ's sake, my heart's feast or famine. All the time and distance in the world wouldn't change that.

So a lot of weeks went by, and though we wanted to, we had no idea how to bridge the divide.

For the most part, our friendship now felt like an overstarched shirt—far too stiff to be comfortable, and every day eating away at the longevity we might have hoped to achieve. We hadn't been *us* in a long time; it was hard to see a way back.

But it was the first Friday in February, and I was catering a charity event for three hundred people when something changed—though, I couldn't have said quite what it was.

My phone buzzed in my pocket with a text, and expecting Kelly,

I was surprised to see the message was from Selene.

For a second I just stared at the phone in my hand, while some form of reluctant excitement fought its way through the part of me that, over the last couple of months, had become protective against feelings like that.

But what really threw me was the text itself. A photo. I couldn't imagine how it fit into the context of where things stood with us.

The photo bordered on obscene—it really did—and she sent it to me just as my crew and I were getting ready to pull 150 pounds of rib eye and salt-packed sea bass off the fire. Which meant I would have that damned photo in my head for the next hour at least before I had another chance to look at it again privately.

Her timing was impeccable.

"What is it?" my event manager, Paul, asked, probably wondering why I was still staring at my phone like it might explode in my hand at any moment.

"Nothing," I told him, waving it off and slipping the device back into my pocket. He didn't believe me, but it's not like I was in any position to explain.

Still, through the entire food service, that photo was all I could think about. Not because of what it was so much, but more because I hadn't realized how much I had longed to see this side of Selene return—how much I had missed the old canons of our relationship, even if the aftereffects of that relationship had left my heart feeling like a pebble inside an empty soda can.

These days, we texted much more than we called, probably because it was easier on both of us, given how messed up everything had gotten toward the end. I was glad at least that our messages had progressed from being unnaturally careful to a little more familiar.

But now there was . . . this. Whatever this was.

That's what I couldn't quite figure out. Was she messing with me?

Or did she send it to me by accident? I'm not too proud to admit that I did a mental assessment of how likely it was that *Keir* was close enough on her contact list to *Kevin* to have resulted in a misfire to the wrong ex.

It may have been totally unjustified, but I couldn't stand that fucking guy.

And I couldn't stand the idea that she might tease him in the way she used to tease me. Just the thought of it made my skin crawl. After all, I still vividly remembered how she felt beneath me, her curves, the feeling of her knees pressed to my sides, her breath on my neck. And to think she might be having that with someone else. With *Kevin*.

No.

I could not go there. And for the next ninety minutes, I didn't.

But still, the question burned in my head. Enough so that as soon as I had a free moment to step away, I found a log to sit on down the beach and pulled my phone out again, examining the photo intensely as if it might suddenly break into a thorough explanation of itself and offer up its sender's current state of mind.

Spoiler alert: it didn't.

But why would she send me a photo of a *carrot?*

In fairness, this wasn't just any carrot: it was an Instagram photo of conjoined carrots that looked like a pair of legs and appeared pretty well endowed, as carrots go. There was no note, no nothing. Just carrot legs with an obscenely large carrot dick and an unfortunately placed root hanging from the tip that made it look like the carrot was urinating.

It didn't *feel* like an accident of recipients. It felt like she was messing with me.

It kind of felt like us.

The question was, Was I ready yet to have that playful side of

Selene start to mess with me again like this? Or would it just mess me up?

I'm not fussy, I remember telling her on that first afternoon when she'd teased me about my tendency to be overly discerning when it came to produce. And I could still see the look on her face—the one that said *no way* was she going to believe me. And, in fact, I knew I'd probably never hear the end of it. I kind of relished that idea. I was happy to be teased by her. I was happy just being with her. Even that first day.

I'd thought about that afternoon a lot, actually. About the innocence of it, the simplicity of our circumstance then compared to now. So much changed so quickly, and sometimes I felt bad about the fact that the very worst thing in her life had given me quite possibly the very best thing in mine. Maybe that's why it ultimately didn't work out for us: because for me, she was the beginning of a better chapter; and for her, my appearance in her life marked the start of a worse one.

Still, I missed her. Take everything else that happened—take the sorrow and the disappointment and the heartbreak—I still missed her. I was never able to separate our friendship from everything else we had—not like she could—but I guess I never really thought they were separate to begin with.

I guess I got that wrong.

And yet.

And yet here I was, trying to do that very thing. Trying to separate—trying to wall off one side of me so the other could figure out what the playbook was for being friends with the girl you're still crazy in love with; the one whose smile in your head still has the power to wreck you; the one who wasn't ready for your love and let you go, rather than just asking you for a little more time.

Was there actually a playbook for that?

And did it involve a *carrot?*

The most devious thing about her text was that she must have known there was no way for me to respond in defense of my position on unattractive produce in general, or this phallic-looking carrot in particular, without coming off sounding incredibly sexual, or at least very gay:

Yes, but I bet it tastes delicious!

Love to get my hands on that!

You won't care what it looks like when it's in your mouth!

Her sense of humor was evil.

I missed it.

After brushing some sand off the phone with my forearm, my thumb hovered over the Photos app for several pounding heartbeats. Then I opened it, quickly skipping over the many I had of the two of us, until I came to the one I was looking for: something I'd taken weeks ago because it reminded me of her, but never sent because it reminded me of us. It was an ad I knew would be equally goading to her sensibilities as the carrot was to mine—one I'd seen for a Chinese restaurant, all done in that horrible Asian font that she considered slightly racist and the ultimate in lazy graphic artistry. Like how could anyone possibly know that Hunan Gardens served Chinese food, unless advertised in wacky calligraphy and bamboo-like letters?

I knew she would hate it.

There were so many times over the last weeks when I'd had the urge to call her or reach out in some way, but held myself back because the feeling behind that impulse wasn't strictly governed by friendship. And even now, I didn't know if the response I wanted to send her would come off as flirtatious or out of line for where we were. But where was that line with her?

Where did the lover end and the friend begin?

The whole question left me even more confused.

This was insane. I had to stop this. If we tried to measure every word, we'd never get our friendship back. We'd never figure out how to do this, and I wanted to. It mattered to me. She mattered to me.

So, denying myself any further chance to second-guess, I typed a single line under the photo of the ad and hit send.

There. It was done. However she might interpret it.

Breathing in the smell of the sand and the saltwater and the distant fire, I stared out into the night, trying to imagine her reaction.

But whom was I kidding? I'd studied her so carefully over the months we were together that I could picture her like she was right here in front of me—the way her laugh would burst mightily from her throat, probably scaring off any nearby birds or rodents. And the way she would cover her mouth like that laugh wasn't one of the best things about her. The way she would crinkle her nose as she examined the picture more closely now, and the way her eyes would never stop dancing as she came up with new ways to retaliate.

No, I didn't need to see it. I remembered everything about her.

I wasn't angry with Selene; I knew she never meant to hurt me. And even knowing what I knew now, I didn't regret anything about being with her—not the time we shared, not my feelings for her, not even my total lack of caution. Toward the end I'm sure I sensed we were on a path to nowhere; I still ignored the signposts. After all, there are only so many opportunities in life to love someone. And because I loved her as I did, she had given me back the very best part of me. She had helped me to understand my priorities and the shape I now knew I wanted my life to take.

You can't really begrudge those lessons, no matter how painfully you come to learn them.

Setting the phone down on the log next to me, I stretched my legs out long and dug my bare feet into the cold sand. Away from the tents and the heat lamps, the winter air was a lonely companion. But the moon over the water was breathtaking, a shimmering pathway extending out farther than I could possibly see, to some distant place you needed a leap of faith to reach.

Somewhere out there was probably where our easy friendship lay. We'd get there eventually. And in the meantime, I'd allow myself to mourn that other piece of my heart that belonged only to her. No, I couldn't take it back simply because she didn't want it, but I was learning to live on half breaths, as I suppose my pop did after losing my mom.

My cell phone buzzed beside me, and even without looking, I knew it was Selene. If she could do this, I could do it too.

This time, she had outdone herself. This text was a photo of a gorgeous cut of filet mignon, criminally smothered in ketchup. *Ketchup.* Seriously, who does that to filet mignon?

No, she remembered about me too.

She knew I'd never be able to stand by and let that kind of pornography go unanswered on my phone, no matter *how* unsettled things were between us. I was grateful that in her own strange way, she was fighting for us the best way she knew how—she was reminding me that we spoke the same language, and when we got it right, it was poetry.

So later on, she received from me my entire menu printed in Curlz MT and, just for the fun of it, over the coming week, every meme I could possibly find that involved a fawn. There were dozens of them. And I shot them off randomly whenever I knew she was sitting in a meeting or working on a design.

Timing was everything.

Timing *was* actually everything. I had already seen the painful truth of how this applied to asking someone to change her life to be with you. And I hoped, at least, I was doing better with the memes than I had done before with that.

Chapter 28

Selene

Well played, Piggy.

That single text changed everything.

I stepped outside into the cool morning air, and the fog coming off the water wrapped itself around me in a reassuringly familiar way, clinging to my hair and lashes and resting lightly on my skin. In my hand, my cell phone lit up with a meme of a fawn.

Say it to my face, bro. I deer you.

It was just after eight o'clock on a Monday morning. His timing was perfect.

I touched his name in my list of favorite people, and it rang twice before he answered.

"Hey there, stranger," he said softly. God, I loved the sound of his voice.

"I think that's the worst one so far."

"Well, be patient," he said, and I knew he was smiling. "I'm just getting warmed up."

"It is early," I conceded. "Where am I catching you?"

"I'm at the office. I wanted to get in and get some stuff done before we open."

Just then a cab pulled up to the curb, and I got in, tossing my bag on the seat beside me and pulling my coat inside before shutting the door.

"Hold on a sec," I said to Keir.

"Here." I handed the cabdriver the address. "How long, do you think?"

"Twenty-five minutes."

"Okay. Faster would be even better." He ignored me.

"Where are you?" Keir asked me.

"On my way to a meeting. But I think you already knew that."

"A meeting? Really?" he asked devilishly in a way that caused a grin to burst across my face. "What time does it start?"

I pulled a lipstick from my purse and dug in deeper for a mirror. "I'm not telling you that."

"Why not?"

"Because you're a menace, and I have important things to do today."

He laughed, and when he did, I felt a tiny fragment of my heart slip back into its rightful position. I missed that sound. The texting we did—no matter how frequent now, no matter how many LOLs used—could never fill the gap left in my life by the absence of that low, smoky rumble. It was like warm chocolate cake and moussaka and fuzzy slippers and everything I loved all rolled into one.

"Well, it sounds like you're taking a cab, which means San Francisco is a little safer this morning."

"How so?"

"Because it's early. And we both know what an ogre you are in the morning, so you're probably running late. And I'm guessing you're still putting on makeup."

I looked at the lipstick in my hand, poised for application. "I hate you."

"You don't," he said, and I heard that beautiful sound again, rolling through my phone. "How was Sunday dinner with the family?"

"Good. Really good, actually. Well, not actually the dinner part. Mia brought her moussaka so . . ."

I didn't have to see him to know he was smiling. God, I missed his smile too. I missed everything.

"You sound good," he said, growing a little more serious. "I feel like we haven't actually talked in a long time."

"I know. I miss that," I told him honestly, and I wondered if he could hear in my voice what I was really saying. *I miss you. I love you. I was such a fool.* "But yeah," I said instead, "I'm feeling good. Work's going really well, and in terms of my dad, I mean, you know how it is. It hits me at weird times, but . . . it's better."

I could almost feel him nodding. "That'll probably happen for a while. It still happens to me, sometimes. Maybe it never goes away."

I leaned my forehead into the window beside me, just listening to the heavenly sound of his voice in my ear. A patch of condensation formed where my breath touched the glass. With my index finger, I drew a little heart in the mist.

"It's good to hear your voice," he said, reading my thoughts exactly. There was a quiet intimacy in his tone that sounded almost like a confession, and I closed my eyes and just listened. I wanted to let that tone wash through me the way an ocean wave washes over you on a sunny day, making you feel lucky to be in your own skin.

"It's good to hear yours too."

"How long can you talk?"

How long? That was always the question for us, wasn't it? Time had been our constant, relentless companion, putting gates and boundaries around everything we did together, even simple things, like talking on the phone. There was always a ticking clock in the background of our relationship, and I couldn't imagine anything more satisfying than smashing it against a wall.

"Maybe fifteen minutes," I told him.

I wasn't actually sure how long I'd been in the cab or where in the city I was, and had to force my eyes to focus on the world beyond the window, beyond my little, misty heart. Digesting the street signs we passed, I realized we were actually making pretty good time.

"Keir, I have so much I need to apologize for," I blurted, terrified of not getting another chance to say it.

"Sel, no," he insisted, and the familiarity in his voice made a shiver break out along my skin. "You don't."

"I do. I've thought so much about what you asked me that last night—about whether I ever imagined us—and I wish I would have answered you better."

He went silent, and I could hear his breathing, softly through the receiver, as if he'd dropped his head away from it. I could picture him pushing a hand through his hair like I'd seen him do so many times.

"And you were right," I continued. "I never let myself imagine us."

"Selene, you don't have to—"

"No, let me just say this," I said, looking at my watch, counting the minutes, hearing the ticking. "When we were together, all I ever prayed for was that time would stop. Because then it couldn't take my dad away. And it wouldn't be able to take you away either."

I knew by his silence that this hit him hard, though he was still listening closely. Keir always listened closely. To him, everything I said was important.

"I understand that," he finally answered.

"Still, I should have been more willing to actually talk about us and our plans. Because it wasn't fair not to. You tried so many times, and I wasn't receptive."

"But it also wasn't fair of me to ask you to consider moving up here, or even taking on the restaurant, when you were in the middle of dealing with something so disorienting."

"I don't blame you for that."

"I do. All the time." He let go of a heavy sigh that trailed a world of what-ifs in its wake. "It's just . . . I don't know how to explain it, Selene. I could see everything. I looked at you, and I could see everything I wanted for my life. It was all right there in front of me, all within reach."

"I know." That was one of the things I admired most about him—his quiet confidence in setting out to do something and always trusting in his ability to accomplish it.

"I told myself that we were on the same page because I wanted to believe that was true. I think I believed I could make it true. Because we were happy. Or, because I was happy."

"I was happy too, Keir."

"But I've been where you are. I know how grief messes with your head, how it fucks with your emotions. I should have known better than to push like I did."

"And I should have trusted you, and us, and everything I knew about who we are. I never should have thought I'd lose you just because we were busy or because we were apart."

An army of feelings threatened to unleash itself but I forced my gaze skyward, holding it back. And he was quiet, too, like he was struggling with the same big emotions.

"This is the place?"

The cabdriver's voice sliced abruptly into the heavy quiet between us, unwelcome like a siren in the night. He pulled up in front of a modest office building with a lone Audi sedan in the parking lot. It was still early; the place looked deserted.

"Yeah," I said, taking in the one-story structure and its well-kept surroundings. I leaned forward and handed the driver cash, and shuffled out of the car as best I could with the phone wedged against my ear.

"Keir," I said, standing alone in the gray, overcast morning. "I think I just thought that by making a proactive choice, I was somehow protecting myself from the prospect of one day losing you altogether. Looking back, I know that was misguided."

"Fuck," he said, breathing into the receiver and probably realizing that our fifteen minutes were nearly up. "I wish we'd had this conversation a long time ago. I regret that so much."

"I know. I regret it too." A chill set in under my coat, and I watched the cab's taillights disappear into the foggy morning, acknowledging to myself that I counted more than one regret, when it came to how I handled things with Keir. "That and the fact that I never actually got to ask you what you imagined for us when you thought of our life together."

He was quiet a long time after that, so long, in fact, that I shut my eyes tightly with the thought that I'd overstepped the boundaries of our first real conversation in weeks. I wondered if he could hear my heart pounding in my chest.

"Another time, maybe."

"Yeah," I said, and made my way toward the front entrance. "Of course."

It was quiet still, and the door to the office building was locked. I had to push the buzzer on the adjacent wall.

"Selene, it's not that I don't want to tell you. It's all just strange for me still."

I understood what he meant. I wished it weren't true, but I knew it was. "I know," I told him, and absently pushed the button again.

"And I'm just trying to figure out—" He paused midsentence, and it sounded like he had lowered the phone from his ear. But then he was back. "Can you hang on a sec? I'm sorry. This is terrible timing."

"What is?"

He was quiet for another beat. "Oh," he said, sounding a distracted. "Maybe it's nothing. I just thought I heard someone at the door." There was another long pause. "Yeah. Shit. There it is again."

"Do you have to go?"

"No, fuck it," he said, and I loved him a little more for that.

"But it's your company, Keir."

He sighed a long, frustrated growl of defeat, and I heard him push up from his desk. He was walking now. "How much time do you have before your meeting starts? Can I call you right back?"

"Yeah."

"I'm really sorry—I want to finish this conversation. Let me just get rid of whoever this is."

"Don't worry about it. There's time."

"Okay."

I hung up and slid the phone into my pocket.

Moments later, a figure began to appear through the opaque glass door. As soon as it did, my lungs sucked in one last, massive, fortifying breath of the cool Seattle morning air.

My heart was beating so fast I could hardly take another. It actually hurt in my chest. The very possibility of seeing him now was suddenly too real, too risky, not rehearsed enough.

For the love of god. I was not even a little ready for this.

And why was I surprising him, again? Why not just call and talk it out and make a plan to see each other?

A flood of panic washed over me—an energy of just wanting to literally throw up—and I had to tamp it down, breathing deeply.

Because. That was the answer I sought.

Because I could not accept the chance that he might say no. Because I remembered every press of his fingertips on my skin, every plea and sigh and sound of relief he made. Because his heart beckoned me to be near to where he was. Because the love I had for him couldn't be undone or unwritten by time or distance or mistakes or regret. Because we couldn't unlive what we'd lived through together.

Because I wasn't here to rehash the past. As far as I was concerned, we had finally said all that needed to be said of that.

Because it was time to make something new.

Because in the time we were together, we had been given the stars, and this is given only once.

As he drew closer with that long, familiar gait, the mere thought of his looming proximity made every nerve ending prick along the back of my neck and down my spine. My body hummed like a live wire, like it was coming to life again, vivid and raw, after a long, sad sleep. It was an energy born of excitement and fear, of hope and angst, of anticipation and apprehension and joy.

All those things. And love and friendship.

Which, as it turns out—in very good humans—really are exactly the same thing . . .

Chapter 29

Keir

My irritation was growing with every step, and I made no attempt to conceal it. Selene and I had made more progress in that fifteen-minute call than we had in months. Fifteen minutes more and who knew what might have happened. Whoever was ringing that goddamned bell had better be able to handle the less-than-optimal version of me they were about to encounter.

I could see the outline through the watery glass—a woman, maybe, shifting on her feet. With my phone still in hand and a hard look firmly in place, I turned the lock and pulled the door open.

And then I saw her face.

And I forgot everything I knew.

I forgot everything.

For the first several seconds we just stared at each other, neither of us making a move. And at some point, my mouth must have fallen open, because when I tried to speak, everything was thick and dry. It didn't help that my heart was beating fast and my throat was constricted—every muscle tight.

"Hey," Selene said, her eyes wide and intense, searching mine for some reaction. "Surprise." Her voice was tinny, and the inflection in the last word made it sound like more of a question.

I can't even say I knew what I felt at the sight of her on my doorstep—shock, certainly, and so many other things I couldn't possibly name.

"You're here?" That was the best I could do. I quickly glanced at the traitorous phone in my hand like it should have *told* me.

"Is that okay?"

I had no idea. "Why didn't you tell me you were coming? I would have picked you up, or . . ." I pulled a hand roughly through my hair. "Showered."

She laughed. It was nervous but genuine—and not soft—and fuck I'd missed that.

For a second she looked up at my hair, which must have been a total mess, judging by the way the smile stayed on her lips. Then her eyes were back on mine.

I can't explain how surreal it was to see her there. I was still reeling from our phone conversation, still trying to process all the things we'd said and how frustrating it was to be interrupted. The irritation hadn't fully left my body, and now my brain was dumping all sorts of new chemicals into the mix.

"Well, maybe I could come in?"

"Yeah, shit, of course," I said, remembering myself. Stepping to the side, I slipped my phone into my pocket and gestured her into the room, letting out a breath I guess I was holding. "I'm just surprised to see you. It's not bad," I quickly added. "It's just . . . come in."

I could see the relief register in her eyes. She let the bag on her shoulder slide down her arm and, moving past me, set it on the floor by the door.

I was so nervous all of a sudden. I wanted to hug her like normal people do in these situations, but I didn't really trust myself to do it right. My arms felt like they belonged to someone else's body, and I couldn't figure out what to do with them. I tried crossing them and then quickly uncrossed them, realizing that might look too defensive.

"Let me take your coat."

It was all I could manage not to stare; it was hard to believe she was *here*. She slipped out of her cream-colored raincoat, revealing jeans and a flowery blouse underneath. The first few buttons were open and I could see the tiny diamond solitaire she always wore, draping over one flawless collarbone. Her hair was long and unstyled, tucked loosely behind her ears.

She was honestly the most beautiful thing I'd ever seen.

When she turned and met my eyes, suddenly, it was there—that *something* we'd always had, that pull that made me want to rush forward, grab handfuls of her hair in my fists, and cover her mouth with mine.

And the way her light eyes became a sea of ink told me it wasn't just me. Call it chemistry or whatever you like, it wasn't just friendship, and it wasn't as simple as attraction. I felt my chest squeeze, and tried to control the impossible hope clawing up in my throat.

"I'm so nervous," she admitted. She handed me her coat, seemingly not even noticing what nerves were doing to my flopping appendages. "I almost vomited on your front step."

That was oddly comforting. "Do you need to use the restroom?"

"No," she said quickly, eyebrows shooting up her forehead. "God. No. I'm . . . I'm okay now."

She turned away from me quickly, flushed, and looked around the reception area. Still leaning on the open door, I allowed myself just one more second to take in her face in profile. It seemed almost impossible to me, but I think she was even lovelier than I remembered. I felt like a starving man, wolfing down every detail I could shove into my face.

"So this is your office?"

I closed the door behind her and clumsily hung her coat on the rack. Glancing around at the place, I tried to see it through her eyes. It wasn't fancy, but it was clean and bright: light-colored wood flooring with steel-gray walls and matching seating. Kelly had added some colorful pillows, and we framed three photos of our bonfires at night. I thought it was enough. We didn't get a lot of clients at the office. At the level we dealt with, I went to them most of the time.

"Yeah. It's a little sparse," I conceded, rubbing the back of my neck. "But it works."

She stepped closer to me now—close enough that I could see the subtle movement of her throat as she swallowed, and it was impossible not to remember how amazing it felt to press my tongue right there, to where her pulse now throbbed.

That *something* just beneath the surface of my composure grew hungrier and more insistent. I wanted her so much it made my skin ache.

"No, it's nice. I like it. I really do." She turned back to me again, licking her lips under the pressure of my attention.

I looked away; I couldn't do this.

Five minutes ago I thought she was in San Francisco, and I was trying to make myself be okay with the bits and pieces of our relationship that remained.

Now she was here, but I had no idea what had changed. And I was starting to realize I was insane for thinking I could handle this *just friends* thing. It was one thing when there was no chance I would see her; it was something else entirely when she was here, sharing the same space. My entire body burned with the need to take her hand and to pull her to me, to be close to her in a way that was no longer an option. The effort to hold back was excruciating.

"Can I get you coffee or water? Or I think we have orange juice."

"No, I'm good."

"You sure?"

We made some small conversation, which neither of us was the least bit interested in, and the whole time I felt like I couldn't catch my breath or even remember how to swallow. It was all so fucking normal, except that it wasn't normal at all.

I stuffed my hands into the pockets of my jeans and offered her a tour of the office, but she didn't seem to want that either.

"Maybe we could just sit for a minute?" she asked.

But neither of us sat right away. She went to one of the side tables where we kept the various awards we'd won and picked up one of the glass pieces. I noticed her hands were shaking. I wanted to hold them, to press them between my palms.

You are so beautiful, I wanted to say but didn't.

I love you more than you could possibly know, I also didn't say.

"Selene, why are you here?" I didn't expect it to come out quite as harsh as it did, and in the empty office space, my abrupt tone surrounded us. "I'm sorry, that sounded . . . not very nice. I'm just . . . I'm trying to understand."

She blanched, looking devastated. "I'm sorry. You're right. I shouldn't have just shown up like this."

"No . . ." I felt so messy inside. "That's not what I meant. I'm glad you're here. I want us to be able to be friends. It's just . . . seeing you—when you're here like this—honestly, I'm not sure I'm ready. I'm not sure I can feel nothing. I'm trying but . . ."

"Is that what you want?"

What I want? I didn't understand what she meant. None of this was what *I* wanted.

"Why would you ask me that?"

I sank down onto the arm of a chair and dropped my head into my hand. Running a business never exhausted me half as much as all this did.

The truth is, I loved her. I could tell myself whatever I wanted, and so could she, but the reality was, our friendship wasn't something we shared in addition to the love we felt. It was the basis of the love we felt. You couldn't pull the two apart; you couldn't isolate one from the other. They clawed like feral cats to be together.

And even more exhausting than that was the probability that it would *always* be this way. In the beginning, I told myself this was just a thing between us. But being away from her and then seeing her again, I realized that was wrong. It was *the* thing. And no matter how much time went by or how many other people came into my life, she was the one I would always compare to. She would be that unfair mark against which no one else could quite measure up. My first true love. My best friend.

I scrubbed my face with my hand, feeling defeated, and then looked up into the face that haunted me every night. It looked every bit as tormented as mine.

"I miss you," she said quietly.

"I miss you, too. So much, you have no idea. But it's so confusing to me."

"I know." Her voice fell away as she blinked down to her shoes.

But I needed to understand what was happening, how she'd gone from loving me so intimately to telling me she couldn't commit to us, to showing up on my doorstep without even a word of warning.

"I'm not sure you do, Selene. I think about you all the time. I want to call you *all* the time. I want to hear your voice, to listen to you breathing and feel your smile, even when I can't see it. But having you here makes me realize I can't keep my feelings out of this. I don't want to pretend we're just friends. I've been doing it because I want you that much, because it's better than having nothing at all. But I know myself. I'll always be hoping for something more, making myself miserable when it doesn't happen. And reading into things when I shouldn't be. Like that goddamned carrot. Why the hell did you send me that, anyway? What did it mean?"

Selene set down the glass piece with a shaking hand and moved close enough for me to pull her by her hips to stand between my legs like everything inside me was screaming to do. But I made no move to touch her, and her hands fumbled at her sides before falling still.

"The carrot was actually my second choice," she said softly. "I thought my first choice was too inappropriate."

That pulled a disbelieving laugh from my chest, and I glanced up at her wryly. "A urinating carrot with a giant dick was the more appropriate of your two choices?"

She nodded, and a tiny smile worked at her mouth.

"I can hardly wait to see your first choice."

She looked at me for a moment like she was actually considering it, and then she pulled her phone from her pocket. I was going to tell her I wasn't serious and not to bother, but she started doing something on it, and because she was busy, I got to give myself this one last chance to really look at her face. She was so pretty it was almost hard to describe. She had a softness that made her seem so real and genuine. She didn't wear a lot of makeup; she didn't need it. She was just open and unprotected in a way that made me feel like I wanted to wrap myself around her and guard that quality with my life. I didn't think I would ever get over that.

I was openly staring—I knew I was. But if she noticed, she didn't say anything. And it wasn't until my phone buzzed that I realized she'd finished sending whatever it was she was sending. Honestly, I could not have cared less what it was. I was happier just looking at her.

But when she met my eye, I could tell she was waiting for me to open it; reluctantly I did.

And expecting some picture of god knows what, all I saw was a text. Just a simple text. I read it. And then read it again. And again and again. All the while I could feel her eyes on me, waiting for me to react. I didn't know if she could see it, but the reaction inside my chest felt like Chernobyl.

"This was your first choice?"

She nodded. "But I was afraid you wouldn't respond. I thought you might just delete it. I wouldn't have blamed you, but that's why I went with the carrot."

Adrenaline shot into my veins, pumping through my every limb, filling my head with a wildness that made me feel a little unhinged.

I read the text again.

I love you, it said. *And if by some miracle your offer still stands, the answer is yes.*

"To everything," she added softly.

I looked up, studying her face, trying to understand what she was telling me.

"You were right. I hate being apart, but it doesn't change how I feel about you. And I *can* commit, Keir—I mean, I *am* committed to you. Already. I have been all along. I want to move up here when my project is done, and I want to be a part of your life and your work. If you still want me to. That's what I came here to tell you."

I was . . . stunned. Completely unprepared.

I'd imagined dozens of conversations with her over the months, but none of them went quite like this. And in none of them did I ever imagine Selene coming here to my office, asking me to want her.

Even more, it was the first time I'd heard her say anything about her future in a very long time, and I didn't even realize how much I needed her to take ownership of it again until she spoke. I was so proud of her and so happy to see her reclaiming her life that it made me want to collect her in my arms and hold her close like every fiber of my body was dying to do.

"I don't know what say."

"You could always say *yes*." She swallowed hard.

The temptation was massive, believe me. But our downfall had been putting off the conversations that were paramount to our relationship. I understood what she wanted from me, but we weren't there yet.

"I'm selling Blaze."

"What?" She stared at me in disbelief. "What do you mean?"

"That's why I was in early this morning—to review documents. I'm selling it to a group of employees. They built it, same as I did."

"But why, Keir?"

This was the question I had wrestled with incessantly since the bonfire in Half Moon Bay, and the decision I came to felt like the sanest one of my life. The answer, honestly, was that I felt like a different person trying to go back and live the same life. My priorities had changed, and I couldn't figure out a way to fit these new things I wanted into the life I had before.

"I'm grateful for the catering business because it gave me my start. And I'm really proud of what we built. But it's not my dream. The restaurant is. That's what I've always wanted to do."

"Okay." She didn't understand. "You can't do both?"

"I can," I went on carefully, because this was where it got tricky. This was where I messed everything up before. "But the thing I've learned is that I also want to have a life outside of work and to have something left of myself to give to another person at the end of the day. Because what good is having something you love if you have no one to share it with?"

"Mel was right," I continued. "It would be hard to have the catering and the restaurant and a personal life without being too busy to actually enjoy any of them. So I'm selling Blaze to the people who will love it like I've loved it."

In a sense, my relationship with Selene had explained my life to me like a patient, if not slightly patronizing, parent. *This* is what's important to you; *this* is what matters. It was good to realize its aftereffects were more than just pain or sorrow, but also clarity and wisdom and a stronger sense of myself.

"Keir, I'm really happy for you. And I can't wait to see you open the restaurant."

"Yeah," I agreed. "And thank you for that. But you should know one more thing. I didn't sign the contract."

For the longest moment, Selene just blinked at me, emotionless. "I don't understand. Are you saying you gave up the restaurant *too*?"

"No. I'm not saying that at all. I'm saying I gave up the building."

It's funny that, for a while, even in my head, the two were one in the same. But I found that every time I went by the building, every time I imagined what it would look like—what it would be like—all I could think about were the mistakes I'd made. I was ready for a clean slate. And the idea of having the time and space to rediscover myself made me feel really fucking happy.

"The restaurant is my dream. And I didn't want to open it in a place that had any baggage for me. When I open it, it's going to be one of the best days of my life. I don't want to look around and feel the weight of any past regrets."

"But you said it was perfect."

"It's just a building."

She nodded, but I could see there was something conflicted behind it.

"Why does that bother you?" I asked her.

"It doesn't . . . I don't think." But her brow furrowed like she was still making up her mind about that. "Maybe I'm just sad you didn't tell me about this. I feel like you've been making all these huge decisions, and I've missed everything."

"I planned to tell you, Selene. When I was ready. And when I thought you were ready to hear it. When you'd understand that these decisions were about *me,* and how I wanted my life to look, whether I was able to have you in it or not."

There was something blunt and uncompromising about the way that came out, but it was the truth, and I didn't want to sugarcoat it. I could see what those words did to her. Maybe it hit her that I'd been making plans for a life without her. Maybe it was just the shock of feeling left behind.

A little numbly, she sat down in the adjacent chair. Her mind seemed far-off and troubled. I could tell there was something she wanted to ask but maybe didn't because she wasn't sure she'd like the answer.

For several seconds, she was quiet. It was a meaningful quiet, and I made no attempt to fill it. When she finally looked up at me, it was with such vulnerability that everything inside me silently melted.

"Maybe when you're ready, I could come up here and help you look for a new place."

I thought about that—and about how much I would love to show her Seattle so she could see it the way I see it: Chihuly Garden and the market and the Space Needle. And Washington Park and Mount Rainier and the beaches, where I'd spent a significant part of my adult life. I loved the idea of playing tour guide, so I found myself nodding as I imagined her being in all those places with me. And still processing everything: Selene coming here today, telling me she wanted to make a life here with me, the way she looked at me when she admitted she loved me, the way I loved her still.

And us. And who we were and *where* we were and where our place was together. I was thinking about all that when I realized I hadn't answered.

And then I watched her face fall.

"What? Why do you look like that?"

"It's just . . . this not-quite-yes-and-not-quite-no thing you do sometimes. I never know what it means."

"I didn't realize I did that."

"Okay." She shrugged, lifting one shoulder, but she didn't look at me. She just picked at a spot on her jeans.

In that moment, looking at the girl I loved, I knew I'd chosen a path. It wasn't a revelation; it felt more like the next natural step for me in my life. And this one arrived with a certain sense of peace.

"I think in this case"—I ducked lower to catch her eye directly—"maybe it means that instead, I'll come down to San Francisco. And you can help me look."

Selene's eyes widened with all the implications of that, so much that she looked like a lemur in a floral shirt. I had to laugh, despite the seriousness of the moment.

She seemed to be making a full sweep of my face, searching for any misunderstanding. There wasn't one. After all, she was my friend, my lover. My choice.

"You would do that?"

I could no longer hold myself back. I reached out and stroked her cheek as the dormant half of my heart stirred to life again. She leaned into my palm with a bursting exhalation, and her skin was just as smooth as I remembered. I felt like I could take a full breath for the first time in months.

"I love you. I want to *be* with you. I want you to have your success and your family and your friends. I want us. I want you to be part of the restaurant, every day. Of course I would do that. I can't very well ask you to change your life for me if I'm not willing to do the same for you. Right?"

She was still too lemur-like to be able to answer, and her eyes shimmered with emotion.

"But in return," I added, "I need something too. Okay?"

"Okay," she nodded eagerly against my palm.

"I need you to talk to me and always be honest with me. And if you're scared or stressed or you need time, you just have to let me know. I'm not going anywhere. I love you, but I'm also trusting you not to hurt me."

"I understand."

"Okay, then," I said pushing to my feet and tugging her to me, chest to chest, her heart beating with mine. "What else is there?" She froze for a moment and then reacted with this tiny perfect sound of relief. Her arms came around me tightly, and she pressed her head to my sternum, like she was my missing piece.

For a few breaths, my entire world went still, and everything that mattered was right here in my hold.

Even my thoughts were quiet for the first time in months. I closed my eyes to savor it.

"I didn't realize we were negotiating." Her voice rose up between us, muffled against my shirt, and a laugh burst from my chest. But I still couldn't bring myself to let go of her. Instead, I nodded happily against her head. "Okay, smart-ass—let's negotiate."

"Well," she said, pushing back a little so I could see her face. Tears were there, but they weren't sad ones. "So here it is—" Her fingers came up to touch my cheek and my heart practically exploded inside me. How could one tiny organ hold even a fraction of the love I felt for her? I didn't think I'd ever be able to keep these feelings from seeping out from every corner of my body—my adoration, my pride, my desire, my complete and utter devotion. For me, she was *it*, and whom were we kidding: negotiate, my ass. I would give her anything she wanted.

"I'll go to Sharks games with you whenever you want," she told me, stroking the stubble on my jawline like she was fascinated by it.

"But when it comes to your own league, if I have to watch you so much as crack a tooth, I swear, Keir, I will personally knock the rest of them out myself."

My grin was so wide now I was probably showing off every tooth I had. "Done."

"And we need to talk about paisley."

"Paisley is a deal breaker," I told her, though I'm sure every inch of my face said otherwise.

"No paisley shirts," she agreed. "But if a paisley pillow should find its way into our place . . ."

"*Our* place?"

And there it was, that breathless, hopeful silence—a million words spoken inside it.

She was talking about an *us* that was still to come. A future *us* she hadn't been able to see before. But she was imagining it now, the way I'd imagined it so many times: Going to bed every night with my arms around her and the vanilla scent of her hair coloring my dreams. Waking up with her mouth on me and the smell of her on my body.

Just picturing it made me feel light-headed and slightly euphoric. The image became a massive blooming emotion that made my cheeks heat and my stomach curl with pleasure. I pulled her tightly to me again and dipped so that her mouth was just an inch from mine.

"Any objections?" she asked breathlessly.

I was lost in her. And in the idea of us finally making the life we wanted. Together.

I began to shake my head slowly, back and forth, leaning in closer and closer until finally my lips brushed with hers in a dozen featherlight kisses. I wanted to give her a hundred more.

A tiny sound of need and relief escaped her throat, and she moved her hand to the back of my neck, pulling my mouth more firmly to hers.

Time stopped.

Everything stopped except the taste of mouths and breath. The touch of a tongue. The slide of teeth. Goose-bumped skin, and fingernails down my abdomen, and the sound of me growling her name.

My fingers slid into her hair, both hands cupping her head, devouring her like I had so many times before. But this time it felt different. Even when we were at our best before, there was always some hesitation, some uncertainty that hung over us.

Now, she felt like mine.

She was mine. And more to the point, she had made me hers.

"You're here," I whispered to her lips, and then kissed her chin, her cheeks, each eye.

"In your text, you called me *Piggy*."

She looked half-drunk and so completely perfect, and I leaned my forehead into hers, smiling. "It was my Bat-Signal."

"The worst nickname ever."

"But it got you here so that makes it kind of awesome."

The smile that curved her mouth became my new favorite shape. It was the shape of my heart, my dreams, my future.

After everything we'd been through, there was just this time, this place, and this nascent trust in ourselves and in each other to move forward.

After all, we can't know what's to come, and we may never understand these lives we lead. Are we granted many of them, lined up nose to tail like horses on a trail ride? Or do they sit side by side, in parallel, as we make this decision or that, go this way or that? Hand back insurance cards and go on about our life, or knock on a door at precisely the right moment to be able to make a difference in someone else's?

Are there those who we know across time? With whom our connection is just a little deeper, a little longer, not quite so random as the evidence would suggest? Maybe time just washes through us and over us and between us in a constant, humbling ebb and flow.

It's possible, too, that there's just this one life, just this one chance to take it all in, and then to leave behind something greater than ourselves, something lasting.

In my own life, I'd spent so much energy fighting time, or trying to manage it. But maybe the better energy is spent on just living within its watery construct, on really looking at each other, on listening, on experiencing joy and giving it, on touching and being touched. On love and friendship—which really are one in the same. Because maybe love is the only thing that doesn't bow to time, the only thing not subject to its rules and its restrictions. Love never ends because it's told to, and it doesn't die when we die.

Love is timeless.

That's something I just know.

§§§

Bonus CHAPTER

Author's note: This holiday epilogue was written for the Aftereffects virtual book tour in December 2018. It was originally featured in a post for the Shared Links and Wisdom blog site. I thoroughly enjoyed writing it, and thought readers might like to have it as a fun glimpse into what comes next for Keir and Selene. As such, in December 2021, when I was refreshing everything for the publishing of Side Effects, the epilogue was added to Aftereffects as a bonus chapter. It is now part of the novel's permanent content.

Holiday Epilogue

Keir

"Okay, so what's the emergency?" Dan asked me, sliding into the booth on the opposite side and holding up a finger to signal the waitress. "Wait, did you order?"

Jamie shook his head. "Not yet, mate."

It was just barely six o'clock on a Thursday evening at The Rose & Crown and the happy hour crowd was already humming.

"What can I get for you?" she asked.

"Two Plinys," Dan said, gesturing between us. "Guinness for this guy," he added pointing to Jamie, "and . . . what?" he asked Marcus. "A Shirley Temple? Extra cherries?"

"You're a riot, grandpa," Marcus mumbled. "I'll have an IPA."

Dan leaned back with his arm draped across the booth and turned to me again. "All right. So what's got you stress-eating bar nuts? And by the way, I wouldn't do that," he cautioned, pointing at the cashew I'd just picked up. "Marcus licks his fingers and double-dips."

I tossed the cashew back onto the table, and on a gusty exhale: "I need your help. I still haven't figured out what I'm giving Selene for Christmas."

I could almost hear the screeching of brakes that ripped through the bar at my admission. Time stopped. Conversation went silent. Three pairs of eyebrows shot up and there was a subtle shifting of bodies around the table.

"You do know it's—" Dan turned his wrist and the screen on his watch lit up with the date. "December 13th?"

"I'm well aware." I leaned forward and dropped my head into my hands. Apparently, this situation *was* as bad as I imagined. "I've been running through all these ideas but nothing feels right. It's our first Christmas together, our first real gift-giving occasion. I can't blow this."

Like an act of divine holiday magic, our waitress returned with alcohol and lots of it, materializing through the crowd and setting our drinks down on coasters in front of each of us. As we descended into our glasses, there was a general consensus around the table that, yes, I was totally screwed if I blew this.

"Okay, here's the plan: You need a gift," Dan said to me. "We'll just do some research." He pulled out his phone and opened the Google app. "What. Women. Want," he mouthed, typing. "Here," he said pointing to his phone. "Good Housekeeping's thirty-seven best gift ideas for the woman in your life. Number one: face cream." He frowned. "Number two: a life planner." He looked up. "What the hell is a life planner?"

Marcus sat forward. "Isn't the correct answer to this problem always jewelry?"

"Are you both *mad?*" Jamie asked. "Keir cannot give his fiancée a generic gift on their first Christmas." Turning to me, he said, "Mate, you need to come up with something that demonstrates some thought. Some individuality."

A sinking feeling took hold in my gut. I knew he was right, of course, which is why I hadn't slept in a week and my brain was practically melting in my head. "What was the first gift you gave Mel?"

"Ah," he said, nodding. "I wrote her a love song and performed it for her in front of thirteen hundred people at The Fillmore."

My heart immediately bottomed out. I could only look at the bastard and blink.

"I suppose that's not much help," he added quickly and with an apologetic wince.

"Not much. What about you, Moore?" Dan looked up from his phone where he was still scrolling the list for something better than face cream.

"I surprised Sarah with a piano. And above it, I hung a portrait of her I'd taken on our first date. She says she thinks it was the exact moment we fell in love."

The grimace on Marcus's face matched my thoughts exactly. Groaning, I rubbed a palm over my mouth. My stomach felt twisty and gross. I was *so* screwed.

"The most amusing part of all this," Marcus said, "is that the women are probably sitting around right now, having this exact conversation. And what you just heard from these saps," he said nodding his chin at Dan and Jamie, "*that's* your measuring stick. So good luck."

"You are such a dick right now." I shook my head, knowing he was right.

"Did you expect any different?"

"I thought maybe your seven-year friendship with my bride-to-be would've been some use in this situation."

"Don't look at me for advice about women." He said it lightly, but his expression suggested there was something tighter beneath it— and nothing he would ever say to me. Marcus was an enigma.

Silence engulfed us again and I glanced around, feeling the weight of every Christmas wreath and blinking light and *Ho, Ho, Ho* resting heavily on my chest.

"Well . . . I did have one idea." I was hesitant to even mention it because for all I knew it was just as terrible as giving Selene face cream. "I was thinking I could take her to Vegas."

My eyes flickered to Dan, measuring his reaction. For several beats, he said nothing. Then slowly I watched his expression go from blank to wide-eyed as my meaning dawned. *"Elope?"*

I winced. "It's bad, right?"

Jamie laughed. "Depends how do you feel about castration at the hands of your future mother-in-law?"

"No castration required," I said holding up both palms. "We'd still do the whole wedding thing exactly as planned. I'm not talking about cancelling that. I'm talking about something private just for us. We wouldn't even have to tell anyone, if she didn't want to."

God, *was* this a terrible idea? I hadn't actually said it out loud until just now, and the response around the table was not reassuring.

Selene and I joked often about eloping because the wedding planning was reaching comedic levels of absurdity within her large Greek family. But in truth, I think I was only partly joking. Yes, a part of me was excited to proudly holler my love for her in front of a big crowd of everyone we knew. *Look! Look what I got!* But there was another part of me that only needed her, and that part of me was happy to whisper my commitment between us in this small, quiet space where only we existed, because that was the only place that really mattered.

"Being married to Selene is the only thing I want. Just to stand before her and pledge myself to her and promise her a life together with love and respect at its core. Anything else I'd give her wouldn't do justice to what she means to me."

I let go of a deep breath and lifted my glass, feeling mildly defeated and, honestly, not even caring if my crew gave me a mountain of shit for being so whipped. I deserved it. Truthfully, I relished the feeling that I'd finally been claimed.

But instead they were conspicuously silent for what felt like an eternity. Dan and Jamie exchanged a brief look. I had no idea what any of them were thinking.

"Damn, Stevens," Marcus finally said, shaking his head. "You certainly do know how to throw down when you want to."

I sniffed out a laugh. "So, is that a thumbs up or a thumbs down?"

Marcus shrugged. "She already said she'd marry you, so what the hell? I say do it."

Dan hummed thoughtfully, considering this. He was, himself, a newly wed. "I can't believe I'm saying this but I think I agree with Marcus. My wedding day was one of the best days of my life, and I wouldn't trade it for anything. But you do get pulled in so many directions. It would've been nice to have a moment to just let it all sink in and enjoy the significance of what we'd done. So yeah, I get it. I think Selene would, too."

"Seriously?"

"Seriously." He held my gaze and I felt a knot loosen in my chest.

"I agree. It's brilliant," Jamie added with a grin. "And if nothing else, you'll get a whole weekend away together—some great meals, a few shows. What do you have to lose?"

A surge of relief flooded my system and I couldn't fight the smile that burst across my face. I felt a little shaky and slightly euphoric at the thought that this crazy idea might not be so crazy after all—that my girl might hear me out and not think I was a total lunatic for wanting the future we envisioned together to start, well, . . . now.

"Thanks," I told them, and I couldn't make my cheeks go back to their normal shape. I thought they just might stay like this forever.

"Okay, then," Jamie said, "the only question remaining is, D'ye need a few witnesses?"

§§§

Acknowledgements

I'm sure it's true that if you spend enough time with a writer, you'll eventually show up in their work. When I look back on my own small body of work, I see reflections of so many people in my life, so many of their stories, and our stories. It's such a gratifying and wonderful thing to be able to capture moments in this way, and to be reminded of them as I look back on the things I've written. In Ripple Effects, one of my favorite scenes shows Danny and Sarah sitting in bed, each with a pair of binoculars, watching a spider spin a web on the wall across the room. The inspiration for that goofy little scene came from doing exactly that with my, then, eleven-year-old daughter. It was one of those parenting moments that seemed small and insignificant at the time, but continues to reveal its enormous gift as I look up from my life and realize that my daughter is now fifteen and no longer into bugs. She's still endlessly entertaining and amazing, but that little moment remains more precious to me than all the gold in the world.

Of all of my books, Aftereffects most baldly tells these stories. So my greatest and most heartfelt thanks goes to all of those whose presence in my life has given me a rich and beautiful palette from which to draw from and, more importantly, a rich and beautiful palette of relationships and experiences that feed my soul every single day.

I also want to extend my sincere gratitude to a new addition to my writing life, Paul Zablocki, copy editor extraordinaire. His knowledge of all things grammar, his enormous talent, his diplomacy, and his professionalism empowered me to make this book far stronger than it would have been without him—literally, from the title to the last word. The thing about writing, though, is that regardless of whether we as authors are acclaimed or amateur, we bleed our words just the same. It is an especially vulnerable art form. So I am equally grateful to Paul for always recognizing this—for his kindness, his humor, and his respect for the craft, however well or poorly I may have executed mine.

As always, I want to thank Joshua Bruce at X Book Cover Design for his eerily perceptive and beautiful cover, which just hints a the mystical in a way I didn't realize would be so fitting when we designed it two years ago. His talent is limitless.

I also want to thank Jason and Marina at Polgarus Studio for their expertise and meticulous care in formatting the entire Ripple Effects series. I wouldn't trust these years of work to anyone else.

Finally, Aftereffects is all about time—our most precious resource—and how we choose to spend the chunk we're given. So, from the bottom of my heart, I want to thank *you*, the reader, for bringing these characters into your heart and your home, and for choosing to spend your time getting to know their stories. And mine.

§§§

Side EFFECTS

L.J. GREENE

Who can you trust?

Ally Michels is fresh out of her MBA program at Cal and has landed her dream job at hot, up-and-coming video game developer, Jet Stream Studios, all thanks to her uncle, Jet's largest venture capital investor. She's feeling pretty good about her future until an inadvertent blurt in a company meeting brings down upon her the dangerous attention of Jet's co-founder and chief developer, Marcus Abby.

Beautiful, brilliant, and vicious, Marcus is every bit the arrogant, deceitful founder her uncle warned her about. But in the power-fueled world of venture capital investing, things aren't always what they seem. When Ally finds herself caught up in a play for corporate control, she must work with Marcus to save the company and an ideal she believes in, while navigating perilous family loyalties and fighting to hold onto her own integrity.

For Ally, there's just one rule: never, ever trust Marcus Abby. Because the one man she needs to stop a high-stakes plot is the one man who has every reason to want her gone.

SIDE EFFECTS is a standalone adult contemporary, twisty, underhanded, certainly unscrupulous . . . romance.

Chapter 1

The conference room door swung open and Julian Dannen swept in. He had all the insouciant confidence of a blond, shiny, twenty-seven-year-old CEO. Everything about him said energy. Said kickin' ass and taking names. Said the place to be was right here, right now, in this staff meeting, at this moment in time, because Jet Stream Studios, the hottest independent video game developer in the Silicon Valley, was getting ready to blow the doors off an entire industry.

I was the newest member of the team, and I was 100 percent convinced he was right.

"All right! Let's do this," Julian said with a vigorous clap that brought the room to attention. "I invited Marcus to join us. Has he come?"

Around the table, Julian's staff of twenty or so marketing, finance, and operations people glanced right and left, but all of us came up empty.

Marcus wasn't here.

Not that anyone thought we'd somehow overlooked him. Marcus Abby was like a wasp at a lovely picnic. His mere presence put everyone on edge. Even the mildest interactions were precarious. But he went with the territory; he was the twenty-five-year-old creative genius behind *Quest of Legends*, Jet's indie title. "A revolutionary,"

The Verge called him. Our chief developer. He was the guy whose fantastical imagination and wunderkind programming skills were matched only by his wanton unpleasantness. Granted, I was new here, but it seemed almost unfathomable to me that Marcus and Julian, whose bright presence was on an epic scale, could have founded this company together.

"Okay, well, let's get started anyway," Julian was saying. "I have some great news. The *New York Times* wants to do a story on us!"

Around the room, a buzz of excitement broke out in all directions. Jet was a small company—revered by die-hard gamers for having launched what many considered a near-perfect title on a shoestring budget—but small, nonetheless. And now, it was in the process of developing its first major expansion, this time with the generous backing of venture capital. An article like this could mean broad exposure and a major step forward in our success.

For me, it was just one more reason that my uncle Dave was the greatest of all uncles. Not only was he the smartest, savviest man I knew, but also, he recommended me to this dream job. He was on the board, and his venture capital firm was the lead outside investor in the company. As soon as I completed my MBA at Cal, he put me up for a position in financial planning.

My uncle's only word of caution was Marcus. For all Marcus's genius, my uncle wanted me to understand the personality that went along with it: *Difficult* is how he'd described him. And undisciplined—an arrogant founder used to operating unchecked, which, of course, the board could no longer allow him to do, given the amount of money now at stake.

I'd met plenty of people like that in academia—self-absorbed and self-serving, encouraged by flattery to overestimate their own worth.

I wasn't deterred by it. Anyone who knew me knew the best way to galvanize me to a challenge was to tell me I might not want to take it on. Besides, none of it really mattered. From day one, Marcus had ignored me completely. It would probably always be that way.

So it was of no consequence that the object of my thoughts strolled into the conference room just then, beautifully, as if on cue. He seemed sublimely unaware of the stir his presence caused. But that was a lie, of course. He knew he made people uncomfortable, and he seemed to enjoy it.

It wasn't that he was physically intimidating. He didn't look scary or gifted or strange—or like, *magical,* despite how *QL*'s devoted streamers invoked his name with almost panting ecstasy.

On a quick glance, you might even call him boyish. He was of average height, slender build, lightly muscled. He had a loose shock of dark, wavy hair that curled off his brow, and the most delicate facial features, with skin so smooth he looked almost angelic. But that was also an illusion.

There was fierceness in Marcus Abby, and it was all in the eyes. They had this quality that immediately drew your attention and held it—some combination, I thought, of brilliance and militant boredom. Beneath it lay a razor's edge. When those hazel eyes landed on you, the implicit challenge they posed was as irresistible as it was dangerous. *Go ahead,* they seemed to dare. *Try to impress me.*

If you had any sense of self-preservation, you just didn't.

Marcus chose a chair near the end of the table and settled in as though the place had been made for him. He adopted the posture he typically favored: a graceful sprawl with one leg straight out before him and one fine-boned wrist balanced elegantly on the armrest. Occupants of the chairs on either side of him casually rolled a few more inches away.

Clearly, the wasp could relax as he wished; the picnickers could not.

"When exactly are we talking about?" Jeanine from marketing asked.

"Well, that's the question. We have to figure out the timing. I'd like to pull in the development schedule a bit so we can do it sooner rather than later." Julian looked to Marcus for agreement.

"Pull in the development schedule," Marcus repeated levelly.

"It *would* really help," Jeanine said. There was a nervous burst of cheerfulness in her voice. It occurred to me that people were always reduced to sounding that way in front of him.

"It's not possible," he replied. His voice, of course, was as urbane as ever, and his face emotionless.

"Come on, Marcus," Julian shot back. "We're months away from launching the expansion. You're telling me we can't squeeze out even a few weeks so we can do this interview before they lose interest?"

"Do you understand what you're asking of my team?" Marcus said, directly. "We're in alpha. We're still finishing the codebase. We haven't nailed the artwork yet. It's at least eight months before we hit code release. That takes us to June, and even then, we'll still be debugging—"

"That takes us to *May*. And I think we can make it April."

"June is what we've talked about."

There was a shift in the air; everyone in the room seemed to notice. Julian was angry. It took me a minute to realize it because I'd never seen him that way—his normally smiling mouth was pressed into a thin line and his blue eyes had lost their usual sparkle. Marcus didn't seem particularly concerned by this, or anything.

"We've never talked about June," Julian insisted. "I don't think I've ever heard you say June."

"I've been saying June."

"Not to the board. We told the board May."

Julian was right. I knew it for certain because it was all laid out, right here in front of me in the form of a color-coded, highly detailed, impeccably formatted financial plan for the business. I'd been working on it for a month. It had VBA functions, and pivot tables and arrays that worked together like a highly trained unit of Navy SEALs. I knew every glorious number. I'm not bragging; I was just proud.

I had scenario plans for every possible contingency between now and the scheduled launch date. In May.

But Marcus and Julian were now in a silent standoff as though this date was somehow in question. There was no question. There was a correct answer here, and I had it.

And it was just at that moment—for some unknown reason, I'll never know why—Marcus's eyes shifted in my direction.

Go ahead. Try to impress me. The thought must have subconsciously taunted my brain. There was no other explanation for what came next.

"Julian's right," I blurted, pointing at my screen. "May is what we told the board. If we're saying June now . . ." I made a face at my spreadsheet. "That means the development schedule has slipped. A lot actually." I half laughed. This whole financial table was going to have to change. I got a little excited about that because the way it was set up, I could probably make the corrections with just a few keystrokes once I had the new date. "The budget will need to be adjusted, and we have to look at cash flow to make sure we have enough to last—"

It occurred to me suddenly that the room had become very quiet. I looked up. And around. Eyes were wide. Mouths hung open. Somewhere, birds probably fell from the sky. All faces were turned to me, but one seemed to have landed with a particularly sharp focus.

Maybe that's when I knew. Maybe that's when I realized I was swimming in very deep waters.

"Ally Michels, is it?" Marcus asked. Those were literally the first words he'd ever spoken to me. Ever. In fact, I couldn't recall a single moment over the last month that he had even looked in my direction. I was invisible. Just some nerdy finance girl from Indiana. Unimportant. "To what do we owe the pleasure, Ally? Oh, that's right," he said mildly as if he were suddenly remembering. "Nepotism."

Nepotism.

It took a moment for that to hit, for the implication of that lightly spoken word to make itself understood by everyone in the room, myself included. When it did, there was a short, *spectacular* silence.

The clock ticking on the wall was too loud. I went very still, and a sensation of sudden, prickling heat washed over my skin. It turned my face a humiliating shade of pink. I could practically hear the blood coursing through my body.

Breathing became hard.

"Marcus." Julian's intervention was swift. But it was too late; my world was already folding in on itself. Everyone was looking at me and I knew exactly what they saw, what he saw.

Nepotism meant only one thing to most people.

Privilege.

Not skill. Not top of my class in business school. Not a deep understanding of a multitude of forecasting models. Not, most certainly, the best candidate for the job.

Not here because my talent merited it. Here because of my uncle.

My pulse sped up, an almost panicked reaction. I felt suddenly naked in front of all of them. I didn't share my uncle's last name so it was unlikely that more than a few of my coworkers even knew there was a connection. And for all my qualifications, it shouldn't have mattered anyway. It didn't matter. Except that in that crushing moment, it felt like it mattered. A lot.

"I just meant—"

"What? What did you mean?"

Marcus's eyes were locked on mine with an unreadable expression. I now knew better than to be taken in by the pleasant tone. In the space of one crucial moment I had gone from being as habitually overlooked as a piece of furniture to openly despised. No one needed to tell me I was not going to enjoy the experience.

"I didn't mean to—"

"Question my work and that of my team in front of my employees? No, by all means continue."

He leaned back in his chair and his whole attention seemed to narrow as he waited, as if he were rearranging his understanding so that he could despise me with just a touch more precision.

There were a few shocked murmurs around the room; the atmosphere, already devouringly curious, became electric.

I willed myself to become invisible. Unsuccessful. Tried blinking him into a yellow minion. No. He was still himself. The polar opposite of a minion.

Brief visions of strangling him weren't helpful.

Blood was beating against the inside of my skin like even *it* was desperate to distance itself from me. Very carefully, I forced myself to do nothing. Give no reaction.

Julian's voice cut in. "The fact is, she's right, Marcus. We are behind schedule."

Marcus's intractable gaze transferred to Julian with a cool, intellectual lack of emotion. The distraction should have been a relief. But as I sat listening to the conversation unfold, I couldn't discard the memory of that look in Marcus's eyes, and it was hard to know whether Julian's intervention had just made my new situation better, or much, much worse.

"The schedule was never intended to be set in stone," Marcus said. "An open-world environment in the cloud like this is unprecedented. I can't predict exactly how long every stage is going to take."

"The board wants dates."

"Then you have to manage the board—that's your job. Or

perhaps Ally here can instruct you on how to do it. She seems to feel qualified to instruct me on mine."

My stomach dropped.

I dived so deep behind my laptop you couldn't dig me out with a backhoe. Any chance for eye contact was to be avoided at all costs. Behind the cover of my spreadsheet, I silently begged the universe to implode or swallow me up or leave me alone so I could hide or cry or eat my feelings with a box of Cheez-Its.

"And what do we tell the *New York Times*?" Julian asked.

"Same thing you tell the board. Tell them to wait."

§

I tried to control my breathing. The wide-eyed looks of my coworkers in the conference room had been looks of sympathetic outrage. I told myself that. That no one could think for a moment I'd been given preference for a job just because . . .

God, my head was pounding. I sat at my desk with my forehead resting in my hands, and no template for what to do next. There was a furious powerlessness in all of this. To have my friends here question my credentials, to have anyone think I was unworthy of the position I held, to have the one thing in my life that I was confident about suddenly brought into question—

"Cheer up, buttercup."

Standing in front of my desk with her big silver bag hooked over her arm was Lizzy, our controller, and the very best friend I had at Jet. Lizzy had the kind of smile that lit rooms, and at the end of a long day, her shoulder-length black hair, bright eyes, and amazing brown skin still looked freshly done up to perfection. I, by comparison, looked every bit the part of Pale, Mousy, Muddy-Eyed Girl Who'd Had a Very Trying Day. It was depressing.

"Don't look so down," she said. "Everyone thinks he's an asshole.

Except the development team, but they're probably just afraid they'd get fired for calling him Satan. Out loud, that is."

"I feel like people are looking at me differently."

Lizzy cringed. "They may be looking at the soup spot on your shirt."

"What?" Sure enough, there was a yellow stain on the curve of my breast that I'd apparently been flashing around for hours. Just my luck, I had a spinach smile to match.

"I just noticed it or I would have told you."

She would have. She was good like that. I let out a breath and rubbed a hand across my forehead, squeezing it briefly. "I wasn't trying to hide my relation to my uncle. I just never thought it mattered."

"No one cares about that. Half the people at Jet were hired because they worked with someone here before."

"I don't think that's the same thing."

"The only thing that matters is that you're doing a great job. Just look at your nerdy spreadsheet. It's brilliant." She gave me a reassuring smile.

"I undermined him, though, didn't I? In front of a lot of people. He was right about that."

"You were just doing your job. He didn't have to make it personal."

"But it's always personal, isn't it?"

"Come on, let's go get a drink," Lizzy said. "There's a place on Union Street where all the cocktails are named after anime characters. Don't try to tell me that doesn't appeal to you."

Of course it appealed to me. Who wouldn't want to belly up to the bar and call for a Panyo Panyo just to see what came back? Even if all I did with it was pretend to want it while it sweated profusely and shamed me for being a geek, as was proving to be my typical relationship with alcohol. And the men I dated, for that matter.

No, as much as it killed me, Panyo Panyo was going to have to wait. I heaved a heavy sigh. "I can't leave yet. I think there's something I have to do."

"Do it tomorrow."

"Tomorrow's too late."

Marcus was still here. His glass-walled office was within my eyeline, and from where I sat, I could see him in profile in front of the two large monitors that occupied most of the horizontal space of his desk. In the early evenings, he kept the overhead lights on low, so tonight he was bathed in a multi-colored glow of code that reflected off the glasses he wore when we worked at his computer.

He was kind of a beautiful sight, actually. If you ignored everything else, he looked like a young man deeply absorbed in a creative process, peaceful and solitary, completely in his head. I imagined that he took in the lines of code and saw something else entirely—epic battles and small mysteries, all playing out across a screen of letters and numbers and symbols. The light enveloped him like a warm cocoon.

If you didn't ignore everything else, you saw him for what he was: the kind of guy who probably spent his free time tormenting small children and relishing the petty tyrannies he could inflict on others.

Nonetheless, his wrong today didn't make mine right.

I knew what I needed to do. I knew what my uncle would do. And if he was always a big enough person to admit when he was at fault, it shouldn't trouble me to do the same. All my life, my uncle had been a set of ideals, a standard by which I could measure my own behavior. I was lucky for that. Today it guided me.

My heart beat roughly in my chest as I looked across the expanse of space to where Marcus quietly worked. Hope flared for a moment that I might be able to salvage some dignity in all of this, but it was quickly extinguished. No, it would not be dignified, but I was pretty sure it would be quick. Marcus had little use for me. That was something, at least.

I took a deep breath for courage, gathered all my good intentions about myself, and rose.

And then his phone rang.

He hit a button on his earpiece to answer the call. Deflated, I sank back down in my chair for another excruciating wait. I wanted to blame him for that, but of course I couldn't. Not fairly, at least.

"Marcus Abby," I heard him say crisply. There was a short pause before he sat forward and reached for the black elastic-bound notebook and pen he always carried. "Yes, thank you very much for the call back."

I knew he had the ability to be civil. Charming, even. Twice I'd seen him with distribution partners where he seemed to have remembered some manners. He'd talked intelligently about the business side of video game development, and if every now and then a little edge glimmered, it came across as wit—not cutting, but just enough to say, *You see? I may look young, but I deserve a seat at the table.* This conversation apparently called for that same kind of good behavior. I watched him become immediately absorbed.

But I felt the moment he realized he wasn't alone in the office. He turned his head and, unfortunately, I was looking in his direction when he did. The way he glanced at me, I felt almost guilty for it— which was ridiculous. He got up from his chair and shut the door. Decisively.

He loathed me. I didn't understand it. Never in my life had I inspired such animosity from anyone. It had to be a misunderstanding. There was no reason I shouldn't be able to change his opinion about me. He just needed to know me better. Surely I could prove I deserved this job. I would let him know how grateful I was for the opportunity and would let him see that I was worthy of the position. That I would work harder and longer hours, that I was in this for the long haul, not as a stepping-stone on my way to something bigger.

When his call ended, I stood up from my desk and for the second time this evening steeled my nerves to approach his door. I recognized in myself some internal hesitation that I disliked so much, even knowing it was rightfully attributed to his talent of turning your most harmless words against you. Asking to speak with him was exactly the sort of thing he would enjoy twisting to his own advantage. Instead of giving him the chance, I just knocked and pushed inside.

And was momentarily awestruck.

Although I'd never been invited in, Marcus's office was my favorite in the building. On one hand, you could call it minimalist. It had almost no items of a personal nature, save for a collection of framed early pencil sketches of the game that hung in a cluster above his desk. There was also a small bonsai tree in a shallow ceramic pot on the sideboard.

On the other hand, the space was a creative wonderland. Covering the expansive wall opposite his desk was a massive floor-to-ceiling mural of a dragon, a creature of both fantasy and nightmare. It was the central figure in the video game that was our life blood.

Poured from Marcus's imagination, the dragon seemed to come to life in relief on the wall. It was as terrible as it was majestic: a monstrous fire-breather with rows and rows of sharp teeth and spikes protruding like a thorny crown from its head. Its body was heavily muscled, with powerful shoulders and haunches, and a wingspan that stretched out across the wall in a stunning palette of glowing pastels and deep blues.

Standing this close, I could see that the scales and marks adorning its body appeared to be ancient symbols that continued all the way out to the tip of its mighty tail. Every detail was perfect and beautiful, patterns within patterns, the twisty creations of an inventive mind.

This breathtaking dragon dominated the space, dwarfing the conference table set up in front of it and stealing thunder from the wall of windows adjacent. I probably could have looked at the detail in it for hours.

But the swish of the glass door opening had Marcus lifting his head from where it had been bent to his hand, a familiar, enervated gesture. When he saw me, surprise changed to something else in his expression, something cold and immoveable.

"I just wanted to apologize," I said with no preamble. "I never meant to cause a problem for you. I was only trying to help."

For a drawn-out pause, he studied me, perhaps measuring my intent. And I studied him too. I studied the incongruity of lips that were such a youthful pink, the color of an innocent blush against his alabaster skin. They were nicely shaped, and you could almost imagine what they would look like if they curled up into something soft and forgiving.

But then the opposite happened. A clench of his jaw pulled them into a thin, hard line.

"Yes," he answered, "how lucky we are that we now have your help in keeping this highly complex, multiyear development schedule on track."

"No, I wasn't saying—"

"Why are you here?" His curt question left me a little bewildered.

In the cool of the evening office air, a warm flush shot over my neck and face. "I told you, I just wanted to apologize if I—"

"I mean why are you *here*?"

One second passed, then two, then three as I processed his meaning. A cold sweat now accompanied the flush, breaking out across my skin.

It occurred to me for the very first time that there was some significance in the fact that I never interviewed with Marcus. I met with Carol in human resources, and more than once with Steven, our head of finance, and Julian, of course. Julian had all functions, except the development team reporting to him. He had been my champion.

But as I took in the arrogant lines of Marcus's frame, the hard challenge in his eyes, I felt in myself a growing sense of outrage. I could surely set aside my pride for a man who could accept my apology with grace, or even cool indifference if that was all he could muster. But *this*? This sort of humiliation was not going to happen twice in one day. I didn't care if he was thirty feet tall and an actual wasp. It just wasn't.

I could feel my flush change in quality and bitterly regretted the impulse that had led me to want to apologize.

"I'm here because I'm good at what I do."

And yes, I could hear myself. I knew my tone was all wrong for this conversation—all wrong for this man, a founder, my superior. Still, I thought about the very public mortification of that earlier meeting. I thought about how he had unjustly reduced my qualifications to a single word in front of everyone I was working so hard to impress. I tried to think of my uncle, but the part of my brain that told me this was a time for humility was drowned out as my pride lashed its tail.

"Your company needs a financial plan. It doesn't matter how brilliant the expansion is if we run out of money before we're able to launch it. So whether you like it or not, I'm here to make the budget work and to apply some discipline to our spending."

"Discipline."

The corners of Marcus's mouth twisted up in some private amusement at my use of the word. It was hardly the smile I had envisioned, and the joke didn't reach those extraordinary eyes. He studied me for an excruciatingly silent beat. Though it was uncomfortable, I did not look away, showed no regret for my choice of phrasing, felt nothing but loathing. The all-knowing reptilian eye of the dragon passed its own harsh judgment as Marcus let the moment stretch out with no visible tempering of his expression.

Then, whatever dark humor he found in our conversation drained away.

"Stay away from my team. And stay away from me."

§§§

Ripple Effects
by L.J. Greene

Science teachers are supposed to be nerdy, combed-over and, quite frankly, a little dull. They're not supposed to be like *him*. And while he may be the ideal person to help 22-year-old Sarah Kyle nail her fellowship essay for Stanford's master's program, he may also be far more life changing than she bargained for.

Daniel Moore is certain he would never date a former student. No question. Still, he's not quite prepared for the schooling he's about to receive from that four-chambered muscle in his chest that is suddenly adapting to an entirely new mandate. Yep, evolution is a bitch!

Because life is only one part science; the rest is art. And life can turn on a dime; they both know that, all too well. In their own ways, they both live with the enduring effects—the ripple effects—of sudden loss. This powerful connection draws them together in the unspoken understanding of things that are just hard to explain. But will it ultimately prove to be the bond that unites them or the force that tears them apart?

RIPPLE EFFECTS is a standalone dual POV adult contemporary romance that contains no twenty-something-year-old billionaires, no private jets and no bedroom accouterment. It does contain the first reference to dinoflagellates in women's literature (full disclosure: this may not be true), an ardent love affair sparked by the misuse of a hyphen (that is true), and a heartfelt and generously humorous journey of self-discovery, forgiveness, and the restorative quality of love.

Sound Effects
by L.J. Greene

What is *your* passion?

When an uncharacteristically rash decision lands law school graduate Melody Grayson in San Francisco's dicey Tenderloin District, she comes face to face with a dangerously tempting man who embodies every mistake she swore she would never repeat. Passionate, sexy, and far more insightful than she'd care to admit, he causes her to question everything she thought she knew about her future. Now she'll have to decide where the bigger risk lies: in the prudent path she's been working tirelessly to pursue, or in the intriguing but uncertain one he's offering.

Up-and-coming, Irish-born musician Jamie Callahan is no stranger to chaos; he's lived a lifetime of it. But in the fall of 2004, when the music industry is on the verge of massive upheaval, the life he aspires to could come at a heavier price than he's prepared to pay. And while Melody may be the ideal person to help him navigate the gambles he must take, a relationship with her might be his biggest gamble yet.

SOUND EFFECTS is a standalone dual POV adult contemporary romance that captures the gloriously unpredictable nature of life, in which the path from who you are to who you're meant to become may not be a straight one. It may also have a few bumps. Sexy, humor-filled, and relatable, *Sound Effects* is a story about living passionately, staying true to yourself, and finding that one magic person who makes the journey of self-discovery an adventure worth taking.

About the Author

LJ Greene is a self-professed obsessive multi-tasker who writes really boring stuff by day and lets her inner romantic fly by night. This California native is married to the most amazing man and has two beautiful children, now old enough to read her books but not interested because of the *ew, gross* factor. She's an avid reader of all genres with an embarrassingly large ebook collection, and a penchant for reading the acknowledgements at the end of a novel. She's also a music lover with no apparent musical talent, a travel enthusiast, and a cheese connoisseur.

Come find me on Twitter: @authorljgreene, and online at www.ljgreenebooks.com.